T0301092

One Bad Apple

Also by Jo Jakeman

Sticks and Stones
Safe House
What His Wife Knew

ONE BAD APPLE

Jo Jakeman

CONSTABLE

CONSTABLE

First published in Great Britain in 2024 by Constable

1 3 5 7 9 10 8 6 4 2

Copyright © Jo Jakeman, 2024
Map by Liane Payne

The moral right of the author has been asserted.

A CIP catalogue record for this book
is available from the British Library.

ISBN: 978-1-40871-839-1 (hardcover)
ISBN: 978-1-40871-840-7 (trade paperback)

Typeset in ITC Stone Serif by Hewer Text UK Ltd, Edinburgh
Printed and bound in Great Britain by Clays Ltd, Elcograf S.p.A.

Papers used by Constable are from well-managed
forests and other responsible sources.

Constable
An imprint of
Little, Brown Book Group
Carmelite House
50 Victoria Embankment
London EC4Y 0DZ

An Hachette UK Company
www.hachette.co.uk

www.littlebrown.co.uk

For James, Alex and Danny

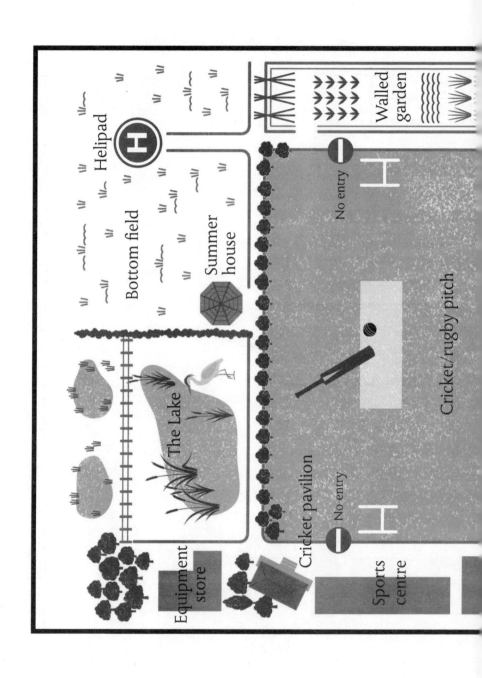

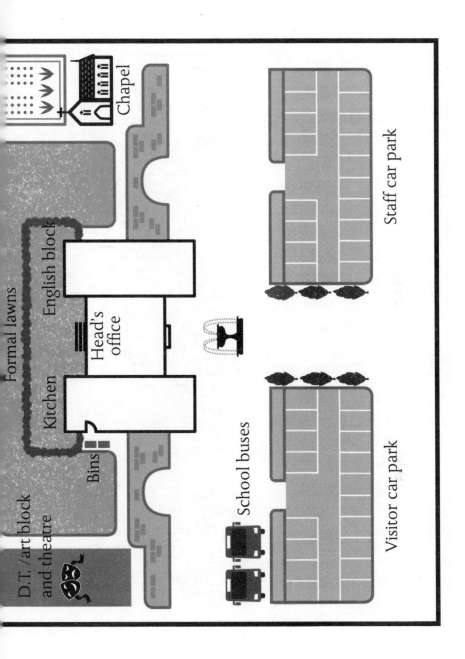

Chapel

Formal lawns

English block

Head's office

Kitchen

Bins

D.T./art block and theatre

School buses

Staff car park

Visitor car park

Welcome to Aberfal High.

'Non ducor, duco.'

Aberfal High is an eminent independent boys' school with a long tradition of providing academic excellence across the southwest of England. Though established in 1629, little remains of the original building commissioned by Charles I.

Consistently among the top performing independent schools in the country, Aberfal High continues to strive for unrivalled academic success, pastoral care and intellectual curiosity.

Aberfal High educates in the region of eight hundred pupils from eleven through to eighteen years old. Tradition is at the heart of our guiding principles. The school's founding ethos is that of strong moral values, always expecting the best of ourselves and never accepting failure.

Each year ten per cent of our pupils are offered places at Oxbridge, going on to excel in their chosen fields. Our results are unparalleled and the opportunities afforded to our pupils are boundless.

Bursaries are available to those pupils of limited means who show significant promise and commitment to the spirit of Aberfal High.

Prologue

Though they didn't know it yet, the boys of Aberfal High had just played their last cricket fixture of the season. The games teacher would reach out to other schools across the southwest, but none would be returning his calls after today.

This afternoon, spirits were high as the pupils tumbled out of the sports pavilion. Each shot re-enacted, each wicket re-lived. Parents milled around the car park laughing in the way that victors do, promising to bring picnic blankets and jugs of Pimm's next time.

'Come on then, Thomas. Let's get you home. Much homework?'

'Rupert, darling, where *is* your blazer?'

Kids limped and listed under the weight of sports kit, schoolbooks and last term's design and technology project. Still pink-cheeked with the elation of winning the match, they accepted kisses atop their sweat-dampened heads.

It was a stinging-hot Friday, a sure sign that summer was here. Mums dared to bare their salon-bronzed legs while dads removed ties, rolled up their sleeves and spoke about the games of their youth when, if they were to be believed, they single-handedly led their teams to victory. Many of them had left it a little bit later to start a family, some of them waiting for second wives before bringing progeny into the world. Their social lives revolved entirely around Aberfal High and the other parents. Schooldays had been *'the best years of their lives'* and they loved being back watching concerts and plays. Some of the fathers had attended Aberfal High themselves and swore there was nothing better for their sons than to follow in their brogue-clad footsteps.

The quiz, the fair and the summer ball were marked in diaries and babysitters booked weeks in advance. The theme of this year's ball was the roaring twenties and there wouldn't be a feathered headband nor pair of long gloves left in Cornwall by then. It was the gem in the school's social calendar but, this year, it was extra special; Jerry Newhall's twentieth year as headmaster. Some feared he was about to announce his retirement. What would they do without him?

They would have seen his Mercedes in the car park, but not paid much attention. He was often there as the shadows lengthened and silhouettes got absorbed by the night, because that was the kind of man he was. Dedicated.

People would recall how they'd seen him watching from his office window with someone at his shoulder. A woman maybe, or a man. Tall perhaps or, quite possibly, short. Dr Charles Yardley would swear he'd seen a slight woman wearing a pale blue dress. But Rose Entwistle would insist it was one of the sports teachers in a distinctive blue and red tracksuit. Who could say for certain? All the attention was on their precious boys, tearing the grammar school from Devon apart, one glorious wicket at a time.

As the match spun towards its final over, teachers joined parents on the freshly clipped lawn. Otis Blake was to be

4

commended for the way he kept the grounds. Everyone said so. There was quite a crowd by the end. Dads, mums and a handful of grandparents patting each other on the back as the sports scholars led the school to a comprehensive victory. How clever they were for producing the finest lads Aberfal High had ever seen. These boys would be paraded on open days to show prospective parents that you, too, could have a son like this, if only you could part with eight thousand pounds a term. Not that expensive compared to some. In fact, you could call it a bargain.

For less than a new car, your son could stay pimple free, excel at sports, drama and maths. And did we mention we have the best academic record in the whole of the south-west? With alumni of politicians, actors, barristers and doctors, you're not paying for an education; you're paying for a network.

And so, the parents bought the blazers and the hyperbole, because there was no doubt that they wanted the best for their children. Most of them could still afford to drive top-of-the-range cars and take five-star holidays. Those who spent every penny on the school fees were the exception. Limping into the car park in their Ford Fiestas, pulling up next to the shiny Audis and the BMWs. Always looking the slightest bit apologetic when replying, 'No, we'll probably spend this summer at home, what with Ade's work and everything'.

But, that afternoon, everyone was smiling as they called out to each other to enjoy the weekend. Teachers waved and made jokes about being 'free at last', though there would be no respite from marking those history papers.

Boys tussled and chased, as parents tried to herd them into cars and no one, no one at all, seemed to have the slightest clue that the headmaster, Jerry Newhall, was lying on the floor beside his walnut desk, eyes wide open, his last breath having left his body to the sound of a cricket ball being hit for six.

Chapter 1

Last July

'Here, put your hood up,' Asha said.

'I'm fine.'

'Cass, did I ask if you were fine? Hood. Now.'

Asha tugged at his coat, while Cass ducked and swerved, batting her away, as if her mothering was smothering.

They'd missed the bus and the next one was still twelve wet minutes away. Asha's van hated the wet Cornish summer almost as much as she did. This morning it had groaned, tutted and died. But she still needed to get out of the house, make the most of their new home and convince Cass how great life here could be. Convince herself.

The pounding rain was a harsh and unwelcome substitute for the sharp clear summer that Asha had envisaged when she'd moved them down here two weeks ago.

She looked around for somewhere they could shelter, but the shops were full of people pretending to browse shelves while keeping an eye on the rain that, according to the weather app, wasn't due until tomorrow.

'Let's walk some of the way,' she said.

'I'm hungry. Can we get something to eat?'

'Maybe.'

Asha had expected to be on her way home to their small, but fine for now, rental house. Fish-finger sandwiches for lunch. Instant hot chocolate. At a push, they could walk the four miles, but not in this weather, not with the rain already making Asha's trainers squelch and her jeans stick to her legs. Asha swapped her shopping bag from one hand to the other and put her arm around Cass's shoulder as they crossed the road. As she passed a newsagents, a flyer caught her eye. It was the same advert she'd seen on the large sign on the roundabout and at the Tesco Express where she'd worked every day this week stacking shelves from 6 a.m.

'Aberfal High open day and summer fair.'

Her eyebrow twitched as she read the word *summer*. This wasn't summer. Not even close. She lowered her head against the sudden gust of wind that snatched her hood, and trudged up the hill with nothing to say. When she'd told Cass about her plan to start afresh in Cornwall, she'd painted a picture of seashells in pockets, of sand in sandwiches and defending their chips from seagulls on harbour walls.

Asha was only aware of the woman in front of them fighting with her umbrella which was angled against the wind because she was slowing them down. As Asha stepped into the road to pass her, the woman clattered to the ground all angles and gasps and bitten-back words. Asha dropped her shopping bag and darted towards her. 'Hey. Are you okay?'

The umbrella skidded and spun like a spinning top just out of reach. The woman's face darkened with the effort of keeping in the growing balloon of profanity until it popped with a – 'Fuck. Bollocks. Shit. Ya bastard!'

'Here. Let's get you up.'

Asha directed Cass towards the umbrella and ushered the woman into a shop doorway to shelter from the rain. 'Small step up. That's it. You all right here?'

'It's an ice rink.'

'I know.'

The woman nodded at a piece of paper which was white against the darkened pavement. 'Slipped on that thing.'

'Are you hurt?' Asha asked.

'I'll have a bastard of a bruise tomorrow.' She rubbed her wet hand over puddle-soaked trousers.

'Yep, I'm afraid so. Do you need help to get you home? Can I call someone for you?'

'No. I'll wait here for the rain to pass though. Catch my breath. Thanks, love. You're an angel.'

'No problem. Here. Don't forget your umbrella. If you're sure you're okay . . .'

'I'm sure.'

Asha stepped back into the rain and, though she'd only been out of it for a minute, it felt colder. She bent to pick up the paper that the woman had slipped on.

Aberfal High open day and summer fair.
Pasties and Pimm's.
Gifts and good company.
FREE ENTRY.

'Let's get going, Cass. We don't want to miss another bus.'

Her son's eyes were on a black jeep that was easing past them. Asha wished she could find someone who looked at her the way Cass looked at cars.

'Cass. It's time to go, buddy.'

Dragging his attention back to her, he said, 'The eggs are broken.'

Asha sighed. 'Of course they are.'

She was standing in the rain in a coat that, it turned out, wasn't waterproof, with a perpetually hungry child and a bag of broken eggs. She took another look at the flyer in her hand and said, 'Hey, how do you fancy a Cornish pasty and a look at how the other half live?'

It was good to be out of the rain, though Asha's skin itched as it warmed. She wanted to pull off her damp jeans along with her skin, and drape them in front of a fire before putting them back on crisp and dry.

'Welcome to Aberfal High. Do go through. Can I take your coat?'

'No thanks.'

Beyond the double doors was a hall full of stalls, of jewellery, scarves and cakes. A woman stepped in front of Asha wearing a smile, a badge that gave her name as Pippa, and the air of someone who belonged here. 'Hello there, can I interest you in a glass of Pimm's?'

'How much is it?'

'It's complimentary.'

'In that case . . .' Asha took a glass from the wide table. Paused, then took a second one.

'And how about a drink for the young gentleman? We have juice, hot chocolate . . . tea?'

Cass looked to Asha for approval before saying, 'Hot chocolate, please.'

'Do help yourself to cream and marshmallows,' the woman said.

Turning back to Asha, she said, 'Plenty of stalls here today for you to peruse. And can I recommend the cheese stall? All locally produced and lots of free samples to try before you decide which ones you want for your cheeseboard.'

Asha had never knowingly shopped for a cheeseboard, but she nodded all the same. 'Thanks.'

'Would you like a tour of the school? It's easily arranged.'

'God, no, you're all right. We're just here for the fair.'

'Well, if you change your mind, ask for Pippa. That's me. You'll find plenty of pupils on hand if you do have any questions.'

Asha moved through the crowds, finishing one drink before starting the next and leaving her empties by the handmade soap display.

'Stick with me, Cass. We'll blag a load of free stuff then get out of here.' She held her hand up for a high five, but Cass's attention was on the other side of the hall.

'Is it okay if I . . .'

'Fine. But we're not staying long.'

Cass weaved through the crowds and was at the other side of the hall, looking at photos of cars before the squirty cream on his hot chocolate had begun to melt. The school's racing team would hold Cass's attention for as long as Asha needed it to.

From a foil platter, she took a chunk of golden saffron cake, wrapped it in a paper napkin and slid it into her bag. There were beautiful silk scarves, dainty jewellery, prints of local beauty spots and coastlines. It had been a while since

Asha had painted but, if the rain ever stopped, she might get out her sketchbook again. Maybe she'd sell her art at a fancy fair like this one.

Even as the rain drummed on the windows, Asha had to admit that it was a beautiful building. She felt cocooned in here and warm for the first time today. She wondered how many doors would open for Cass if he went to a school like this. And how many others would close.

Asha sampled cheeses, chutneys and chocolates. Pretended to consider buying but moved away as soon as she could. On to the next stalls for bread, wines to accompany fish, wines to accompany meat, special ones for dessert. She picked up a plastic cup of unctuous liquid and swallowed it in one. It set her teeth on edge. 'No. Not for me. Thanks though.'

A woman with long hair in one thick braid was standing on a stage pointing a camera in Asha's direction. Asha spun away before the shutter closed. She bent her head, pretended to consider the handprinted greetings cards and, when she looked up, the woman was taking shots of a group of students in matching grey blazers.

Click, click, click.

By the time Asha caught up with Cass, she was considering undoing the top button of her jeans. Her son was deep in discussion with another boy. Older. Taller. Handsome in a clean-cut way. They were leaning over the table watching something on an iPad.

'Hey,' she said.

'Mum, this is so cool, you need to see this,' said Cass. 'Every year they build a car and race it against other schools.

They haven't won in ten years, but they think next year might be their year.'

A large man was standing to one side, his arms folded. 'Your son is remarkably knowledgeable about engines,' he said.

'Yeah. He helped me rebuild our camper van. It's his passion.'

'Well, I do hope you'll consider sending him here. He would be quite the asset to our racing team.'

Asha was already shaking her head, trying not to laugh at the thought of Cass at a school like this.

'Sorry, should have introduced myself,' the man said. 'I'm Jerry Newhall, headmaster of Aberfal High.' He held out a hand which Asha ignored.

'Nice to meet you,' she said. 'Cass, we should get going.'

'Have you had the tour yet?' the headmaster asked.

'Thanks, but we're not in the market for a new school. We're . . . you know, here to get out of the rain. And eat some cheese.'

'I don't blame you,' he said. 'We've some wonderful stalls here today. Usually, we'd be out on the lawns but I'm afraid the weather had other ideas.' He stuffed his hands into his pockets.

'Which school is your son at now?'

'He's not. We only moved here a couple of weeks back. All being well, he'll start at Freemill Academy in September.'

Mr Newhall's eyes widened before he caught himself and smiled. 'Are you sure we can't get you to consider Aberfal? He's obviously a very bright lad and it'd be a shame to waste that on Freemill.'

'It's not the lack of brains that's the problem,' Asha said. 'More the lack of funds. Come on, Cass.' She put her hand on his back to guide him away, but he was deep in conversation. 'Cass.'

'They have a 3D printer,' he said.

'You know,' said Mr Newhall stepping closer, 'Aberfal High is keen to reach pupils from all backgrounds regardless of whether they have the funds. We have bursaries, grants, scholarships . . . I think you'll find that we can aid every budget.'

'Yeah, no. That's not going to help. I don't even have a budget for you to aid. Cassius, we need to go.'

She tried to move away from the table, but Mr Newhall was tracking every movement.

'I probably shouldn't say this, but our drive to attract pupils from diverse backgrounds hasn't got off to a great start so you'd be helping us out really.'

'Mr . . . Newhall, is it? Listen, I appreciate your enthusiasm. Honest, I do. Another day I might even be flattered. But treating me like a charity case is not the way to win me over.'

He lowered his eyes, cleared his throat. 'Certainly not. I didn't mean for you to—'

'Hey, I'm sure Aberfal High is a lovely place, but it isn't the school for us. Even if you offered us fifty per cent off the school fees, we still couldn't afford it.'

'Mum, this place is awesome. Do you know they work with Spaceport Cornwall and Virgin Orbit? And there's this pool and it's the deepest in the world and—'

'For the right student we'd give a scholarship of up to eighty per cent,' Mr Newhall said.

Asha sighed. 'You don't know when to let it go, do you?'

Mr Newhall scratched behind his ear and smiled. 'Of course,' he said. 'As you say, it might not be the school for your son. Some people can't hack the pace and we do have very high standards here at Aberfal High.'

Asha became aware that the rain had stopped. She glanced at the window and saw that the grounds were no longer blurred. They stretched further than she'd imagined. And was that a lake? It was a far cry from her school and her childhood. Nice, if you liked that sort of thing.

'Mum, d'you know that the cricket team went on tour to Barbados?'

'Hmm?' Through the window Asha saw the break in the clouds, a hint of blue. 'We really should get going, Cass.'

'It goes without saying,' said Mr Newhall, 'that Cassius would have to pass the entrance exams first and some children do find them rather challenging. So, if you don't think your son would be up to the task . . .'

'My son would have no problem passing your exams. The only issue he's ever had is boredom from not being stretched. In fact, not only would he rise to the challenge, but you'd be lucky to have him here.'

'Excellent,' said Mr Newhall. 'In that case, why don't I give you a tour of the school myself, while Myles takes Cassius to look at the workshop where we tinker with the cars? I'm sure we'd be grateful for his input.'

Over Mr Newhall's shoulder, Asha saw the perfect arch of a rainbow as the school choir began to sing a tune that she felt she should know.

'Fine,' she said folding her arms. 'But the answer will still be no.'

Chapter 2

Two weeks before the cricket match

It was the first day of the summer term and, though Asha was full of good intentions and wall charts, she was already late for her meeting with headmaster Jerry Newhall. It was Cass's third term of being an Aberfal High boy, but Asha still felt like she was one step behind everyone else. A minute too slow.

The dress that Asha had carefully laid out last night was now soaking in the sink, with half a bottle of stain remover and a hollow prayer presiding over the coffee stain. It was the universe's way of telling her to stop pretending to be someone else but, to be honest, she was more concerned about the waste of good coffee.

Asha slammed her van into a space reserved for blue badge holders and stumbled out of the door, her arm entangled in the seatbelt. She swore, leaned over the gearstick and plucked her bag from the footwell where it had fallen.

There were two sharp *beeps* behind her and Asha twisted her head to see Pippa Yardley leaning an elbow out of her car window. Her vehicle was low to the ground, sleek, dark grey. The kind of car that wouldn't smell of tatty trainers and blackened banana skins.

'Hello, darling! How were your Easter hols?'

Pippa was wife of the chair of governors, mother of two of Aberfal High's poster boys and one of the nicest people Asha knew. Which was a shame because Asha had intended to dislike her.

'Yeah, it was okay. Good, I guess. Can't chat. Late for a meeting with Mr Newhall.'

'Jerry? Oh dear, is everything okay?'

Asha pulled down her sleeve to cover the lighthouse tattoo on her forearm and tried to remember if she'd brushed her teeth this morning. 'Um. I hope so, but I'd better not keep him waiting any longer. So . . .'

'I've been meeting with Katy Lane about the summer fair. I can count on you to help at the open day on Saturday, can't I, darling?'

'I'm not sure what work I've got over the weekend. Can I let you know?'

'Absolutely. Chat later, sweetie.' Pippa wiggled her fingers and, with her chin up as if she had trouble seeing over the steering wheel, drove away. Pippa knew everyone at the school, was on first name terms with all the teachers thanks to having an older son who'd been at the school for years and she'd never had to run up the driveway with forgotten PE kit, textbooks or money for school trips. Pippa was the first person you asked if you wanted to know when the maths homework was due, or if next Thursday was non-uniform day. She was the one who arranged collections for teachers' birthdays, volunteered to run the cake stall and helped sew costumes for the school play. Everyone needed a Pippa in their life.

Darting for the school entrance, Asha didn't lock the van. She untwisted the strap of her dungarees, pressed the buzzer and waited for the click of the door-latch. Sixth formers sauntered by in crisp suits, heading through the archway that led to the chapel. They seemed too old and rangy to be in the same school as Asha's little boy. The way they held themselves; the way they spoke. They were entirely, unapologetically, comfortable in their own skin. They'd already found life's golden ticket.

The school prospectus could sum up its selling points with just one word. *More.*

More facilities, more top grades, more students going to the best universities, more money raised for charity, more sports cups, more maths awards, more music recitals. More, more and more.

At the clicking of the door, Asha pulled herself up a little straighter and corrected her pigeon toes. An apology was already forming on her lips as the deputy head, Miss Katy Lane, appeared.

'Ms Demetriou, we've been waiting for you.'

She said *Ms* as if she had a bee stuck behind her teeth. They shook hands and Asha noticed that Miss Lane wore an opal ring on her right hand. It looked old, a family heir-loom perhaps. Opals represented love and passion, but Miss Lane didn't strike Asha as capable of either.

'If you'd like to sign the register, I'll take you through to Mr Newhall.'

Asha fumbled with the pen and checked the clock twice before she wrote down the time and, by then, she'd forgotten the registration number of her van. The receptionist said it didn't matter and Asha covered her flustering with a grateful smile, mumbling words about not having had enough coffee.

'Shall we?'

Asha followed Miss Lane up the imposing, wide stairway adorned with navy carpet that was held in place by brass stair rods. When she'd been here for the open day everything has seemed so shiny and new but now she could see that the carpet was threadbare and the only thing holding the window frames together was the twenty coats of paint.

Outside Mr Newhall's office was an antechamber of sorts. Two chairs for those waiting for an audience with the great and powerful Newhall. On the opposite side of the room was a desk where Mr Newhall's assistant, Mandy, usually sat. She was absent now, the angle of her chair suggesting a hasty exit.

Miss Lane glared at the space where Mandy should have been and pushed her lips together until they lost their colour. She knocked on a heavy wooden door and pushed it open.

'Ms Demetriou here to see you, Mr Newhall. Shall I sit in on the meeting?'

Asha pulled at her sleeves again and heard Mr Newhall's muffled voice carry on the back of a sigh. 'No, no. Absolutely no need. Send her in.'

'Actually, Mr Newhall, I really do think that I . . .'

Asha could see Mr Newhall leaning against the wall by the window, as if the effort of holding himself up was too much. 'I'm sure you've got much better things to be getting on with, Miss Lane. Besides, Asha and I have a lot to discuss.'

Chapter 3

Two weeks before the cricket match

As with the other times she'd been in the headmaster's office, Asha marvelled at the high ceilings and the wood-panelled walls. It was the kind of room that always smelled of furniture polish. Stirring up memories of her grandparents' house. There was something other-worldly about Aberfal High, like she'd stepped back a century or two. Stern-faced oil paintings of previous headmasters chequered the walls, not a headmistress among them. Mr Newhall was yet to add his own portrait to the line of stern, pale faces, but it would be there soon if the rumours were true.

A sagging brown sofa faced an empty fireplace. A black rotary telephone sat on the blocky desk. No computer. No mobile phone charging in a wall socket. There was, however, blotting paper and a bottle of blue ink by the telephone. Asha wouldn't have been surprised to find Mr Newhall smoking a pipe and checking his pocket watch.

Asha looked around the room and saw that the one thing that was out of place was a silver strip of pills by the desk lamp. When Mr Newhall noticed her looking, he opened a drawer and slid them out of sight.

'Thank you for coming in today, Asha.' As if he'd been the one to request the meeting.

'I thought it would be better if we spoke face-to-face,' she said.

'Quite.'

Getting past Mandy, Newhall's combative PA, had been quite a challenge. In the end, Asha said she was coming into the school anyway and, unless Mandy wanted a scene, Mr Newhall had better be ready for her.

The door swung open and Mandy came rushing into the room carrying two coffees on a silver tray. Asha sat up a little straighter.

'Apologies,' Mandy said looking at Asha. 'I hadn't realised you'd turned up. I was beginning to think you'd changed your mind.' Her smile was tight. 'Will there be anything else, Mr Newhall?' She set the tray down on the broad desk and flicked her hair over her shoulder.

Newhall looked at the tray and, ignoring the coffees, reached for a biscuit. 'Ah, you always know how to satisfy a man, Mandy. Shut the door on your way out, would you? There's a good girl.'

The 'good girl' that Newhall was referring to was older than Asha's mum and had a look that could freeze a glass of water, but somehow Newhall got away with talking to her like that. As Mandy left the room she smiled at Newhall as if he was a naughty little scamp.

'Nice weather for the start of the term,' Newhall said.

Weather. The smallest of small talk, setting the foundations for weightier discourse that couldn't be avoided.

'Yes,' said Asha. 'Gorgeous, isn't it? I hope it stays like this for the cricket. This'll be the first cricket match Cassius has played in.'

'He's a very talented boy, young Cassius. An asset to all our sports teams.'

'I don't know where he gets it from,' Asha said. 'Neither me nor his dad were particularly sporty at school.'

She didn't know why she said that. Asha didn't know what Cass's dad was like at school. He'd only been in her life for a short time and never in his son's. Being a single parent was a challenge at times but being a single parent at Aberfal High . . . well, it was an anomaly. She always felt like she had to over-compensate and, though no one had asked her why there was no dad on the scene, she could see they were itching to know. For now, she was content to let them scratch. Not even Cass knew all the details. She chose to tell him that he was the result of a one-night stand rather than disclose the distasteful truth.

'I do love the sound of leather on willow.' Newhall stood and took a cricket bat from behind his desk. He mimed blocking a cricket ball. Asha could see writing on the face of the bat.

'The wife keeps telling me I should put this in a display case. But then I wouldn't be able to play with it, would I? Or,' he winked at Asha, 'use it to discipline the boys.'

Asha picked up her coffee and spilled a drop on the table. She used her sleeve to wipe it away.

'And what about you, Asha? Do you like a good spanking?'

'Do I *what*?'

'Or are you one of those parents who believe in rewards charts to keep children in line?'

Asha gripped her coffee as tightly as the set of her jaw. 'Yeah. I'm afraid I'm one of those woolly liberals who don't believe in violence against children.'

'I do miss playing cricket,' Newhall said.

He cradled the bat with all the love of a new father. 'Signed by every member of the Ashes-winning team of 2005. Paid a pretty penny in the auction at last year's summer ball. I do hope you're coming to the ball this year, Asha?'

'Pretty sure I'm busy that day.'

'More than fifty per cent of our annual fundraising money comes from that one night, you know. The ladies do a stellar job of organising it. You must come.'

'Not really my scene.'

'I don't believe I saw you at any of the hockey matches last term. Or rugby the term before.'

'Some of us have to work,' Asha said.

'Did you come to the Easter quiz night?'

'No, I didn't.'

'Come now, don't be shy.'

Newhall leaned the bat against the wall again and, without taking his eyes off it, sat down. The wooden chair creaked under his weight and he pulled his earlobe.

He turned to her and said, 'No sport for me now. Got a dicky hip. Plays up like the devil some days. Used to play squash every Sunday evening like clockwork but haven't been able to pick up a racket in four, maybe five months now. Anyway, where were we?' Newhall looked about his desk for inspiration.

'I'm here to talk about the bullying,' Asha said. 'Before Easter, you told me you were going to make some changes. But over the holidays there's been some online abuse. I know that it's not on school time but, if it affects the kids, the school should play a part in managing it. Don't you think?'

Mr Newhall frowned at Asha. Tilted his head. 'You're not here about this morning's altercation?'

'What altercation? What's happened?'

'Ah.'

'Mr Newhall, has something happened that I should know about?'

'So, Miss Lane didn't call you and ask you to come in this morning?'

'No, she didn't.'

'Right. Yes. Well.' He tugged his ear again. 'Since we last spoke, several measures have been put in place to safeguard the welfare of our students. We're a lot more stringent about peer-on-peer abuse. It's not always easy, as a parent, to see the full picture and it saddens me to say that Cassius . . . well, let's just say he gives as good as he gets.'

'In what way?' Asha asked.

'Well, it appears that young Cassius has a bit of a temper on him.'

'Nope. No, he doesn't.' Asha sat on the edge of her seat. 'Never. I have literally never known him lose his temper.'

Cass was the sweetest of boys. He was thoughtful, he was kind, he was passionate about things that meant a lot to him, but never violent. When spiders the size of small mammals scampered across the rug, Asha would beg Cass to kill them, squish them, leave their heads on spikes outside the back door to deter other eight-legged marauders, but Cass would scoop them up and speak in soft tones as he set them free outside the back door, politely asking them to stop scaring his mum.

'According to Miss Lane,' began Mr Newhall.

'Well, she's hardly his biggest fan, is she?'

'She tells me that Cassius and another boy were trying to knock spots off each other this morning.'

'Are you telling me that someone hit my son?'

'I'm telling you that it was Cassius who threw the first punch.'

'I beg your pardon?'

'It was during this morning's history lesson. Mr Higgs tells me that they were discussing genealogy when an argument got out of hand and it turned into a nasty brawl. As you can imagine, this isn't something we tolerate here at Aberfal High.'

Asha placed her drink on a leather coaster and took her time before responding.

'Right. So, let me get this straight,' she said. 'They fell out over a family tree. What was it? Is it the fact that our family can't be traced back to the Doomsday book?'

'I don't know the specifics but, no matter what started it, violence is never the answer.'

'I agree. But this ties in with the reason I asked for this meeting today. Cass has been bullied ever since he joined this school last September. Everyone keeps telling me that it's early days, that he's hardly had time to find his feet, but I've said repeatedly that if bullying isn't stamped out early it will escalate. And it sounds like today, it escalated. Just like I said it would, because the school – *your* school – is failing to address the problem.'

Mr Newhall said nothing.

'And . . .' Now that Asha had found her voice, she wasn't sure she could stop. 'I also heard that, when he spoke to you about one of the incidents before Easter, when the other boys hid his clothes when he was showering, you told him to "man up". Is that correct?'

Mr Newhall laughed through his closed mouth, so it sounded like he was humming. 'You see . . .' He linked his fingers and rested them on his stomach. 'Part of my job, Asha, is to encourage the boys to deal with their own problems without running to their mothers. In my day . . .'

'Let me stop you there,' she said holding up one finger. 'This is not about you. Or *your* day. This is about the welfare of the kids who attend this school – not only my son. Language like "man up" is outdated, offensive and unhelpful. I thought this was a progressive school, Mr Newhall. So instead of me pointing out where you've *failed* in your duty of care to my son, why don't we skip to the part where you tell me how you're going to make it right.'

There was the slightest crack in Mr Newhall's demeanour, the curl of his upper lip. He slumped back in his chair, his legs spreading.

'We have a zero-tolerance approach to bullying,' he said.

'It's not working.'

'We teach our boys to think of others,' he continued.

'Again,' Asha said. 'Not working.'

26

'We talk about bullying behaviour in assembly and we have policies on our website that—'

'I'm not asking you about policies. I'm asking you what practical measures you're putting in place.'

Mr Newhall sighed. 'Look. You say that Cassius is being bullied, but none of his teachers have noticed anything. When asked, he wouldn't or couldn't tell us which boys were responsible. What can we do? We only have your word for it that he's being bullied at all. A certain amount of robust behaviour is normal in a boys' school.'

Asha sat forwards again; her hands spread on the desk in front of her. 'Robust? Are you saying this is his fault for not being tough enough?'

'Your concern is for your son,' Newhall said. 'And I appreciate that. But my concern is for all our boys. Which is why I have no choice but to punish Cassius for today's behaviour. Usually, he'd get a Saturday morning detention but seeing as we have the open day this weekend, he'll be helping there instead. It's time that he contributed to the wider school. Perhaps you should consider doing the same.'

Year seven school mums' WhatsApp group.

Pippa Bennysmum: Happy back-to-school day my darlings xx

Rose Oliversmum: And parents all over the country heave a sigh of relief! Here's to an awesome summer term!!

Becky Rupertsmum: Is cricket club on 2day?

Clare Withoutani: Yes. Checked with Hinch. He says pick up at five thirty. How was everyone's Easter?

Becky Rupertsmum: Thanx. Hols good. Victim of the all-inclusive buffet. No clothes fit me anymore!! Should run later. (Spoiler: I won't)

Pippa Bennysmum: The boys and I stayed in a yurt in Wales. Thankful for the good weather but poor Charles had to stay home and work. Are we getting together soon? xx

Sarah Teddysmum: Never been to Wales. Never had all-inclusive hols either. Is that like a package holiday? We went to our villa in Tenerife. Glorious. Back to work today though ☹

Rose Oliversmum: I'd be up for a get-together, Pippa! Been too long. Anyone want to join me for paddle boarding and coffee at Gylly beach this morning?

Pam Geoffreysmum: Welcome back, all. Don't forget that the boys' environmental projects are due by Friday.

Pippa Bennysmum: Thank you Pam. Managed to get it done before we went away xx

Becky Rupertsmum: Shit. 4got about that. Looks like trip 2 Hobbycraft then!!

Rose Oliversmum: FFS Pam. What a way to ruin my day.

Chapter 4

Two weeks before the cricket match

Katy Lane shaded the screen of her phone against the sunlight's glare. She almost didn't answer the call but, once she'd seen that it was Charles, the chair of governors, she didn't have a choice.

She took a few steps away from the school building.

'Hello,' she said.

'Can't talk for long,' said Charles. 'Got a couple of minutes between patients.'

Dr Charles Yardley was using his important voice. Not that he had any other tone.

'It was you who phoned me,' Katy reminded him.

'How's Jerry?'

Katy was standing outside the school waiting for the groundskeeper so they could finalise plans for this weekend's open day. She looked to make sure he wasn't lurking nearby before answering. 'Useless,' she said. 'He's in with a parent now. God knows what he's saying. I wish he'd leave it to me.'

'I'll suggest it to him if you like. Tell him his time is better spent elsewhere and to let you take control of the outward-facing relationships.'

'You know he won't listen. But at least we only need to keep him from messing up for eleven more weeks.'

'Lord, is it that long?'

'I was thinking he could announce his retirement at the ball but start relinquishing some of the authority now. Then I can show the board that I'm up to the job so that when they go out to advert—'

'How many weeks is that?'

'The ball? Five.'

'It's doable I suppose. Okay. We can keep him in check until then. See you on Saturday?'

'I'll be here.'

She slid her phone back into the pocket of her cardigan muttering 'as usual' as Otis Blake marched across the lawn.

'Good morning, Mr Blake.'

'Miss Lane.'

'The open day,' Katy said. 'Anything I need to know? Any problems I should be aware of?'

'Depends what you mean by problems.'

Otis Blake bent over and pulled at weak green fronds of grass peeking between the paving slabs. He was wearing shorts today just as he did every single day of the year, even when frost hardened the ground and sharpened the air.

'We'll need to use the top lawn and the garden area. I'd like to keep the focus up this end of the grounds.' She nodded towards the lake. 'Shall we?'

Without waiting for an answer Katy headed down the path at the side of the walled garden.

'It's going to be a dry weekend,' Katy continued. 'So, I'd like to show off the grounds, Mr Blake. You do such a wonderful job that I truly think it's one of the selling points of Aberfal.'

Katy didn't look at him but, out of the corner of her eye, she thought she saw his shoulders straighten and his chest expand.

'We're having two gazebos on the top lawn and two by the walled garden,' she continued.

The school grew their own vegetables – or rather, Otis did with the help of an after-school club. It was both a blessing and a curse; whenever they suffered from a glut of courgettes, Chef lost the ability to cook anything but ratatouille. After sixteen years of vegetarianism, Katy was considering reaching for a sausage.

'One gazebo for drinks and three for food. One will be run by the sixth form boys raising money for charity by selling homemade cakes. Chef will be doing a hog-roast at one and we have an outside catering company providing pizza at the other. I'm sure I don't need to remind you how important this day is to us, Mr Blake. If we don't attract more pupils to the school, you won't have any grounds to keep.'

Katy looked down at the path where an ant was appraising her shoe. She lifted her foot then stepped down, hard. Scraped the sole of her shoe and continued walking. Otis Blake matched her step.

'We will end the tours by bringing people into the gardens and letting the parents and children mingle with staff and pupils. Peacock cries in the background. Butterflies on the flowers. Jazz music on the breeze. So, I ask you again, do you foresee any problems with this, Mr Blake? Because my job pretty much depends on this weekend being perfect.'

Otis Blake hitched up his shorts. 'We've got a cricket match against the grammar school in two weeks and you know what he's like about the grass.' Otis Blake looked towards the school.

'Mr Newhall understands that attracting new children to the school is our priority.'

And it was, but retaining them was proving to be just as tricky. Katy had heard that some parents were already looking at alternative provision for their precious boys. And once one person starts complaining, that little niggle you thought you could overlook suddenly becomes a huge problem and you start saying things like, 'Well, I wouldn't mind, but when you're paying this much money . . .'

It was a difficult subject to broach, but the truth was, no school was perfect, no matter how much money you paid for it. A lot of it was about perception, which was why most of Katy's day was spent managing parents instead of concentrating on her A-level English group. There was no denying it, Mr Newhall was running the school into the ground. He cared more about how the school looked, than how the boys felt. He cared more about exam results than whether the boys left Aberfal High as well-rounded individuals. Katy cared about results too but she knew that, unless they addressed some of the underlying problems in the school, they would lose some of their best students to their competitors. But, no, it wasn't about the competition and it wasn't about finances either. She believed with her whole heart that, when Aberfal was at its best, there wasn't a school in the southwest that came close.

'So,' Katy continued. 'Putting aside the worries about messing up the grass before the cricket match, everything is fine, yes? There's nothing I need to worry about?'

'Has Mr Newhall said anything else about plans for that bottom field?' Otis asked.

'Looks like he's going with a 4G pitch, but we still need to raise the funds. Anyway, back to the—'

'He said it could be a wildflower meadow.'

'And he told Mr Hinchwood that he could build a climbing wall, but you know what he's like. Says whatever he thinks will make people like him but, when it comes down to it, he'll do what he wants depending on today's mood.'

Katy patted the top button of her cardigan and cleared her throat. 'Which is exactly how it should be.'

She was normally so careful about saying anything negative about the headmaster, but it was getting increasingly difficult to keep a lid on her annoyance.

'Anyway,' Katy said. 'Back to the open day. I think certain areas, such as the summer house, the lake and the pavilion, should remain off limits.'

Otis smiled and said, 'I bet you do.'

Katy felt heat creeping up her neck and she wriggled her nose, causing her glasses to slip down her face. She pushed them back up with her index finger. A thin ringlet of the honeysuckle bobbed in front of her face and she stepped backwards.

'Mr Blake? Do you have something to say to me?' She lifted her chin, daring him. She thought they'd already dealt with this. She'd told him that he'd been mistaken. That what he was suggesting was simply absurd. Otis had said he saw her kissing someone she shouldn't. Katy said he needed glasses.

They were both right.

Otis Blake reached into his back pocket and pulled out orange-handled pruning shears. A smile twisted the corner of his mouth. 'You know me, Miss Lane. My lips are sealed.'

Katy flinched as he reached past her and snipped at a bright green tendril, letting it fall to the ground.

There was something all too familiar about Otis Blake. He was only a gardener, so how did that give him the right to strut about the place like one of the school's peacocks judging her for a small lapse in judgement. They stood in silence for a moment: he with a knowing smirk on his lips, she with so much she couldn't say.

'They look sharp,' she said, motioning to the secateurs.

'They have to be.'

She looked at him and he looked back. Still so much she couldn't say.

'Were you here the Friday before the Easter holidays?' she asked.

'Why d'you ask?'

'Nothing. Just wondered.'

'I'm always here,' he said.

'Yes,' Katy said. 'You are, aren't you?'

They were standing by the walled garden and Katy could feel the heat from the red bricks. From here they could see the lake through the trees. The water stretched out before them like a polished oval platter. It was the largest of the three lakes on the grounds and the only one that wasn't permanently out of bounds. 'Now, then,' Katy said. 'The lake.'

Katy and Otis stood side by side and considered the problem. It was beautiful, a selling point for sure, but it was a health and safety nightmare. There were rumours among the boys – and Katy hadn't been able to discount them – that several children had drowned in that lake over the last century. It was against school rules to put so much as a big toe in there now, but that didn't stop the seniors from jumping in there on the last day of exams each year. Even some of the parents, when merry on free bubbly at the summer ball, sometimes let high spirits get the better of them. It was expected, a blind eye turned, but it was never encouraged. If it was up to Katy – and one day, it would be – she'd have that lake filled in. She didn't care that Jerry Newhall had stocked it with trout so he and Charles Yardley could fish in it over the summer months.

'Signs,' Katy said. 'I think we should put signs across the paths saying *no entry*. What do you think?'

'I don't get paid to think,' Otis said.

Katy didn't know why he felt the need to be so infuriating. Something about him got under her skin and it wasn't only because he knew enough to destroy her reputation and her career.

'I want you to close off the paths to the lake and to the summer house.'

'Consider it done,' Otis said.

'Right.'

'Right.'

'And you'll be here on Saturday?' Katy asked.

Otis nodded. She didn't know why she'd bothered asking. He was always there. She knew very little about him, not whether he had a family, nor where he lived. All she knew was that he was everywhere she looked and always poking his nose into other people's business. When she was in charge of Aberfal High she'd make several staff changes – and Otis Blake would be the first to go. And if he caused any problems at the open day, it might be sooner than he thought.

WITNESS ONE

Dr Charles Yardley.
Chair of governors at Aberfal High School.
Father of Myles and Benny Yardley.
Husband of Pippa Yardley.

We're a family at Aberfal High and we've lost someone terribly dear to us. I do hope you'll tread carefully when conducting your investigations. It's going to take some time to recover from this. Jerry was, quite simply, the backbone of this school. I spoke to him moments before the cricket started about everything and nothing. The weather, the summer ball, and there was nothing out of the ordinary. He was in good spirits, cracking jokes. Sure, it was strange that he didn't come out to watch the match because he's a man who loves his cricket. Loved. Apologies. I still can't get my head around it.

Yes, when I thought about it later, I suppose I was surprised Jerry hadn't come out to watch the match because St Francis Grammar are our biggest rivals and they've always got the better of us. This year though, well, the year sevens were in with a real chance of beating them.

Jerry and me? Oh, we met at boarding school when we were eleven. We lost touch for a few years, as one does and then reconnected about five years ago when my elder son started at Aberfal High. We saw each other at the school of course, but more often when I became chair of governors two years ago. We've also played squash together pretty much every Sunday evening since then. I'm somewhat disoriented without him.

I'm not saying you're wrong, Detective Mullins, but are you certain that there's been foul play? Could it have been an accident? A fall? As you know, I'm a doctor and I wouldn't be surprised to find he'd had a heart attack. The stress of the job. His age. His weight. It does seem like the obvious cause. No, I'm not his GP, goodness that would never do, but I see this kind of thing all the time.

I'd invited Jerry to join my wife and I for a barbecue that evening, but he declined. Wasn't in the mood. I can't help but wonder whether this might have all turned out differently if I'd have insisted. He's had it tough of late. Number of pupils falling and we've been struggling to attract a more diverse student body. We're trying to dispel the misconception that this kind of education is only for toffs and trust-fund kids. He seemed to take it personally that we weren't attracting new boys, but it was more to do with the fact that every-one is feeling the pinch lately and we haven't adapted as quickly as some of the other schools in the area.

During the match – it would've been in our innings, so around three thirty I suppose – I looked up at Jerry's office window and I saw someone in there with him. If I'd known what was going to happen, well, I'd have taken more notice. I can't be sure, but I think they were wearing pale blue. The way the light hits that window in the afternoon means it's difficult to make anything out, it could have been the reflection of the sky, but I think . . . maybe I assumed it was his PA, Mandy? But honestly, I couldn't say for certain. Sorry.

Mandy is great. Truly. Of course, you'll find some people who'll tell you that she's not the easiest woman to get on with. Very difficult to get in to see Jerry if you don't have Mandy on your side. I find it most curious that Mandy didn't . . . well, she usually sees everything that goes on. She's completely trustworthy of course, so I'm not doubting her account of events. And if she says that no one got past her . . . Well, it's a mystery, isn't it? I mean, how did someone get in there and kill Jerry without anyone noticing? Preposterous. There were people everywhere. It was the best turnout we'd had for a match for quite some time and I just can't believe that no one saw anything untoward.

Your guess is as good as mine. You won't find a single person at Aberfal High with a bad word to say about Jerry. Not one. I'm sure when you get the post-mortem results back, you'll find that Jerry had a heart attack. If you could and I hope I'm not overstepping here, Detective Mullins, but can you keep this out of the press? I only ask because a school like Aberfal, well, we pride ourselves on our reputation and, well, a murdered headmaster is hardly a selling point.

Goodness, don't get me wrong. Finding out what happened to Jerry is the absolute priority here, but he'd be the first to tell you that reputation is everything.

Pippa Bennysmum: Who's free this Saturday? Helen-Louise is looking for vols for open day. I said we'd do the drinks tent. Should be a lovely day xx

Becky Rupertsmum: Count me in. In need of stiff drink. Already feeling back-2-school stress 😫

Pam Geoffreysmum: Rebecca! We're meant to be showing the school in its best light to the new parents. When you drink, the only thing you show is your underwear.

Pippa Bennysmum: Pam, shall I put you down for the first shift from 10-11? Xx

Becky Rupertsmum: Missing – Pam's sense of humour. If seen, please approach with caution.

Rose Oliversmum: Ollie wants to enter the school cake-off competition. He says the theme is Freedom. WTAF??!! How do you do a Victoria Sponge in the shape of FREEDOM???

Becky Rupertsmum: 😆 Perhaps U give him 'freedom' 2 bake it himself this year?

Rose Oliversmum: Not funny Becks. You have no sympathy for my nerves. Can you imagine the humiliation of presenting a cake that was ACTUALLY made by a child? Helen-Louise would explode!

Chapter 5

One week before the cricket match

Pippa Yardley stood in the school car park with her hands on her hips and a smile on her face. There was no doubt about it. No doubt at all. It was perfect weather for an open day. If she could put the events of the last twenty-four hours behind her Pippa could fool herself into believing she lived a charmed life.

She surveyed the sky. Light cloud was forecast from about two o'clock, gently guided overhead by the faintest of breezes. There would be no rain, no temperatures rising to skin-burning levels, instead it would be the kind of weather that would encourage people to stay awhile and make the most of the entertainment and refreshments. Yes, Pippa thought as she adjusted her name badge, it was a perfect day.

Charles was looking in the boot of the car for something he'd mislaid. His sighs of exasperation were getting louder, but Pippa didn't rush to help. Instead, she watched Myles and Benny walk towards the school. She was proud of her sons. They were clever, kind and handsome. Their faces were all over the school website. Myles was quite the musician and performer. He was the youngest pupil in Aberfal's history to get a grade eight in piano and his cello was coming along nicely, too. He was often the lead in the school plays, always winning the talent competitions. And they hadn't had to worry about him and girlfriends at all because he was too busy with his studies to concern himself with members of the opposite sex. Next year he'd be sitting his GCSEs and he'd been predicted nines across the board. There was no denying that she was a little biased, but who could blame her?

Pippa found it gauche to brag about her children's achievements so she kept it all to herself and whenever anyone mentioned their talents, she countered it with a 'well you should see the state of his room,' or a 'but, darling, he can't even boil an egg'.

Benny, her younger son, was the sports scholar and team captain for each sport he played at Aberfal. A little rougher around the edges than his brother, he'd inherited his charm from his father and the school adored him for it, especially the games teachers. He had a cheeky smile and quick wit that somehow made you smile instead of chastise. In a school where everyone knew his brother and were quick to compare, Benny was forging his own path and doing every-thing his own way. Benny and his father didn't see eye-to-eye, but he was still hugging Pippa, kissing her cheek and telling her she looked pretty, so she had no complaints.

Every time Charles raised his voice to Pippa or talked over her, she saw Benny's fists clench. He was a good boy. She didn't want either of her sons to find out about the mess their father had driven them into. And, more impor-tantly, Pippa had to get them out of that mess before it was too late.

44

Look at them. Just look at them! Four years age difference and, though Benny had been increasingly surly recently, they were laughing together as they disappeared through the archway.

'I need to catch Jerry before the circus starts,' said Charles.

'Hmm?'

The sight of Charles standing at her shoulder burst Pippa's dream of the perfect family. They were only as strong as their weakest member and, right now, that was Charles.

'I must talk to Jerry. School business.' He checked his watch.

'Could you wait a minute, darling? Now the boys are out of earshot, we should talk.'

'Not now.'

'Darling, we can't pretend that nothing happened.'

'Not now, Pippa.'

She smiled broadly so, if anyone was watching, they would assume this was a friendly conversation between loving husband and wife. In reality, there hadn't been many friendly conversations of late and it had been a long time since Pippa and Charles's relationship could be described as loving.

'Darling, someone threw paint over your car. We can't pretend that it didn't happen. Did you call the insurers?'

Pippa had wanted to call the police, but Charles said that low-level vandalism wasn't worth the paperwork.

'We'll talk about this later.'

'And what about the school fees? Are you going to explain why Jerry thinks we haven't paid?'

'I said,' hissed Charles, 'we'll talk about this later.' Charles gave her his *and that's the end of the matter* look, a look with which Pippa was far too familiar. She sighed. There was no point trying to talk when he was in one of his moods.

Charles used to call Pippa 'Wonder Woman'. He'd said the thing he loved most about her was the way she fought for what she believed in and how she fought for the rights of people without a voice. Funny that, because now she'd lost her own voice and there was no one around to advocate for her. Nowadays the nicest thing he ever called her was his *beautiful little fool* and that wasn't the compliment he thought it was.

She watched him walk away and wondered idly whether she'd be heartbroken if a meteorite dropped straight out of the sky and flattened him. Right now. She concluded that, though it would be a terrible shame, she wouldn't feel a thing.

Pippa put her hand to her throat. She'd been feeling rather under the weather recently. Sleep eluded her on an almost nightly basis and, more than once, she'd put orange juice in her tea and keys in the fridge. Silly things that the children laughed about and Charles shook his head over, but they didn't see how much it terrified her. As recently as twelve months ago she would never have made such mistakes. She used to remember everyone's birthdays without having to write them on the calendar. She used to know which day the binmen took the recycling and when the boys needed sports kit, but now she rarely knew which day of the week it was. Of course, this is how it started with her mother. First the little things but, within months, not remembering how to fasten a button and not being able to match names to faces. In the end it was a blessing when she passed.

Pippa reached into the car for the red cake tin then pulled herself up straight and glanced about her. The chair of the PTA, Helen-Louise, was talking with Miss Lane but they were pretending they hadn't seen how easily Charles had brushed her aside. Rearranging her silk scarf with one hand and gripping the cake tin to her stomach with the other, Pippa walked towards the archway that led to the lawns.

She checked her watch, pleased to see she was exactly on time. Nine a.m. as agreed. Every open day was important but this one especially so. An ice-cream van would be on the premises from eleven. It would park in the courtyard, where the jazz band would be playing, away from the heat of the hog-roast and the pizza oven. When Benny was at junior school, Pippa would organise the summer fair with pony rides and bouncy castles, but today was different. The Aberfal High open day and summer fair would show the parents the lives they could have if they enrolled their children here. It let them see the opportunity that awaited the entire family.

Waving to the teachers who were arriving ahead of her Pippa called, 'Perfect day for it!'

'Isn't it just?'

The first visitors wouldn't arrive for another hour yet. They would be taken on a tour of the school by the prefects and the head boy and a few hand-picked ambassadors. In the hall there would be a display of the boys' recent schoolwork, regular music recitals, a choir performance starring Myles and Benny and a cake competition judged by Mr Newhall himself. And then out through the hall and into the grounds, where more food and music would be waiting for the prospective parents and pupils. It was a simple offering really. Jewellery stalls, local produce, cookery demonstrations, visiting dignitaries and ex-pupils who'd gone on to walk the halls of Westminster or perform operations on minor royals.

Pippa was pleased to see that the gazebos were already up. The groundskeeper, Otis Blake, was directing people who were carrying tables and chairs. He looked up at her and nodded.

'Perfect day for it!' Pippa called.

She kept her smile wide as she walked through the open doors of the hall. No one must see that she was ready to break. No matter what Charles had told her about the school fees, she wouldn't let this be the last term that the Yardleys would spend at Aberfal High. She'd been part of this school for almost five years and had expected to be here for five more. She kidded herself that this school was vital to the boys' development but, the reality was, it meant more to her than it did to them. Aberfal was her anchor, her social life, her work. And she couldn't believe that Charles had risked everything. Or that Jerry Newhall had let him.

She was volunteering, as she did every year, because she wanted the school to do well. But today she wanted to show Jerry that the school wouldn't do nearly as well without her boys, nor without her input. If Jerry kept pushing them out, she'd simply have to push back harder.

Chapter 6

One week before the cricket match

Asha pulled the van up onto the kerb at the end of the school drive. Cass unfastened his seatbelt before they'd come to a standstill.

'Here?' she said.

'Yeah.'

'You don't want to be seen with me now. Is that it?'

'They need the car park for visitors.'

'You're embarrassed.'

'You're embarrassing.'

'Is it me, or the van?'

Cass shrugged. 'Got to go.'

'Wait!'

He paused with his hand on the door.

'You used to love this van,' Asha said.

'Used to.'

'Used to love me.'

'Still do,' he said. 'And don't fish. It demeans us both.'

He shook his head at her but, under his annoyance, Asha saw the twitch of a dimple. She leaned over and kissed the side of his head. God forbid she should touch his cheek. He'd be scrubbing his face for days.

Asha smiled. 'Demeans,' she repeated. 'You're so clever, you know.' She stroked his hair.

'Mum.'

'Fine. Off you go then,' she said. 'Do you have your water bottle?'

The shrugging of his shoulders didn't answer her question, but it was all she was going to get today.

'Call me when you want picking up, yeah? Look, I know this is the last thing you need today, but—'

Cass slammed the van door. He dragged his feet as if he was on the way to the guillotine rather than the school fair. Helping at school, as punishment for a fight that wasn't his fault, was peak humiliation for him. Asha had tried to make him see that it wasn't torture but an honour. He should be proud that Mr Newhall wanted him to show prospective pupils around Aberfal. She told him that it was a vote of confidence.

'Neither of us are stupid enough to believe that,' he'd said.

Asha's priority was Cass. Always Cass. He was the best of her. It broke her heart to sit him down after her meeting with Mr Newhall and tell him that, to avoid suspension, he had to write a letter of apology to Ryan.

Cass paused halfway up the driveway and turned. For a moment optimism overcame experience and Asha lifted her hand to wave, but Cass frowned and shooed her away.

Okay, she mouthed. *Jeez.*

Asha sighed as she bumped off the kerb and joined the slow-moving traffic. She'd have been the same if her mum had ever taken her to school. Cass, who'd always loved their mint green camper van, now wanted them to get a car like a normal family. Normal. The very idea made Asha's toes curl. She liked driving a van with blankets and beers in the back. She kidded herself that they could pack up their minimal lives at a moment's notice and drive wherever the mood took them. Cass called it the Getaway Van and it was true that it was always primed for her escape. But it had become apparent that this was the last thing that Cass wanted. And it was the last thing that Asha needed. Still, though, they were not getting a normal car. End of.

She glanced at the clock. There was enough time to do a couple of hours' work before Cass needed picking up. Even though the school had offered Asha an eighty per cent discount on school fees, she was struggling to put aside enough money each month. And no one had mentioned how expensive the uniform would be and the theatre trips. She'd picked up more shifts at Tesco, took every bit of graphic design work that came her way, and it was barely enough. But how could she turn down the opportunity for a son of hers to attend a school like this?

As she changed lanes, her ringtone filled the van. Glancing at the display she could see it was her mum. Her second glance was to check the clock again, a habit. It was early enough in the day that Asha could take a chance on Mum still being sober. She hadn't spoken to her in weeks as the contact between them was sporadic at best, but she didn't want anything more than that from her.

To Asha, Mum was two people – the person Asha wanted her to be and the person she truly was. It was Asha's own fault that she was forever disappointed.

51

'Hello?'

'Hi Kitten, it's me.'

The new music system and ability to take calls hands free was Asha's one concession to modernising the van.

'Hi Tessa. Y'okay?'

'Why can't you call me Mum?'

'Why can't you act like one?'

There were a few seconds of silence that caused Asha to look to the display and check they were still connected.

'So how are you?' Asha asked.

'Ed's lost his job again.'

Asha rolled her eyes. 'I thought you two had split up.'

Asha let the silence settle as she indicated and turned right at the roundabout. She imagined her mum's hand squeezing the phone.

'Are you busy? You sound busy,' Mum said.

'I'm driving. Just dropped Cass off at the school.'

'Do they do Saturday mornings there?'

'No. He's helping at the school open day. Well, it's a sort of detention for getting into a fight, but all he has to do is show people around the school so . . .'

'A fight?' Mum's laugh filled the van. 'The apple doesn't fall far, does it?'

Mum seemed to take the fact that Cass was at Aberfal High as a personal insult and Asha was fine with that.

'Thankfully,' Asha said, 'I'm proof that it does.'

'What was the fight about?' Mum asked.

'Turns out that our family isn't exactly an asset when you're researching your family tree for a school project.'

'What's that meant to mean?'

'You know what it means.'

'It's not my fault he doesn't have a dad, is it?' she said.

Every phone call with Mum was like navigating a minefield. So much to avoid, to sweep aside. Asha wondered why they kept putting each other through this torture.

'Heard anything from Georgie lately?' Asha asked, heading for safer ground.

'Spain.'

'Spain? What's he doing in Spain?'

'You'd know if you ever called. Shacked up with some . . . *woman* over there. Says he's running a bar, but I doubt it. Who in their right mind would pay him to run anything?'

From the passenger seat, Asha heard a *ping* that meant Cass had received a message on his mobile phone. It had to be a good sign that the other kids were messaging him. He hadn't yet found his tribe, but she'd told him to be patient. They'd been in Cornwall for twelve months. It had to happen soon.

'Well, at least he's out of your hair,' Asha said. 'And it's good that he's found someone.'

The brake lights in front of Asha lit up and she swore under her breath. She could see people getting out of their cars up ahead.

'I don't know what I did,' Mum said, 'to make my children go to the ends of the earth to avoid me.'

'Don't you?'

'Of course, it'll never last. It never does,' said Mum. 'Bet you a tenner he'll be home in a month.'

'He might surprise you this time.'

Cass's phone pinged again. He was popular this morning.

'Crap!' Asha said.

'What's that?'

'The phone. Cass has left his phone in the van, but he's meant to call me when he wants picking up. I'll have to drive back to the school to give it to him.'

'He'll manage.'

'What?'

'I said, "he'll manage". He'll never get anywhere in life if you do everything for him.'

'Yeah, that's pretty much your entire parenting technique, isn't it? Left us to feed ourselves, clothe ourselves, get ourselves to school on time.'

'And you're so perfect, are you? I seem to recall a certain shoplifting incident.'

'This again? *This?* It was a pack of biscuits for Georgie because *you'd* spent all our money on vodka, so don't you—'

There was a *click* and Mum had hung up. Asha rested her head on the steering wheel. She couldn't help but antagonise her mum. Perhaps she should try and bite her tongue more often but, whenever she did, she felt like she lost a bit of herself. She hated this unsettled feeling whenever they spoke. Perhaps Georgie had the right idea and if she hadn't promised Cass they would give it a go here, she would've booked flights to Spain by the end of the day.

Asha sat back in the seat. In her wing-mirror she could see a traffic jam behind her. No cars were coming in the opposite direction so the accident must have blocked both sides of the road. She pressed a button and the window jerked downwards. Behind her, someone honked their horn.

She picked up Cass's phone. As soon as the traffic started moving, she'd do a U-turn and drive back to the school. He'd said he didn't want her there today, but she'd been gifted a reason to check up on him and make sure he was okay. He'd panic when he realised that he didn't have his mobile. Worry he'd lost it. Yes, she was being caring, not overbearing.

The phone in her hand chimed again. This time a message from Ryan popped up. He was the boy that Cass had got into a fight with. She felt a twinge of guilt as she started reading the message, after all, she tried to give Cass his privacy as much as possible, but the words were right there on the screen in front of her.

Though the day was warm, Asha felt cold. She sat forwards, the seatbelt giving resistance. She read the message again. And again.

Later, when she was asked why she'd looked through Cass's messages she'd say that no sane person could have resisted unlocking their child's phone, especially if they'd seen what she'd seen flash up on his screen.

WITNESS TWO

Mandy Gulati.
Jerry Newhall's PA.

Murder, is it? You wouldn't be investigating his death if it was a stroke or something. God, you don't think it was me, do you? Is that why you asked to see me? I hope you're talking to everyone who was at school that afternoon, because if I find out that you're only talking to people of colour . . .

Yes, I'm defensive. Wouldn't you be? I was outside Mr Newhall's room all afternoon. Me. Literally sitting feet away from where Miss Lane found his body. Something happened in that room while I was sitting outside the door and you wouldn't be doing your job if you didn't question whether I saw or heard something. But I didn't.

The doors to the school are locked. You can't simply walk in off the street. And even if that wasn't the case, I was outside Mr Newhall's office most of the afternoon. I only left my desk once to get some water. Five minutes, tops. How would anyone get in and out of Mr Newhall's office, without me noticing and do . . . *that*?

You know, at the last school I worked at we had CCTV in the corridors, and in the playground, but I never thought we'd need it here. You wouldn't think something like this could happen at Aberfal High, would you? Goes to show.

Do you think I'm in any danger? What if they think I'm a witness and they come back to shut me up? I mean, I didn't see a thing, but they don't know that, do they? I don't understand how anyone could have got in there without me seeing. But then . . . oh, I don't know. That's your job to work out how it happened, not mine. My job was to protect him. Not from . . . *this*, but from, you know, people bothering him all day long. If I didn't manage his visitors, he'd never get a moment to himself. The teachers are always saying 'Is he in? I only need five minutes.' But I send them away. No one gets in without an appointment. Well, no one apart from Mr Yardley and Miss Lane. But he needs them. He relies on them. And they're both so busy and half the time they really do only have five minutes, so they make it count.

Mr Yardley was in with Mr Newhall before the cricket match started and then they came out of the office together. Mr Yardley looked unhappy and Mr Newhall was saying, 'It's not personal, Charles, but my hands are tied.'

I mean, I don't know for certain what they were talking about, but then Mr Newhall asked me to type up a letter to the Bursar about Mr and Mrs Yardley having trouble paying the summer term's school fees. It's not . . . well, let's say I was surprised. They don't look the type to have money troubles, you know?

The only other person who went into his office that afternoon was Mr Newhall's wife, Gemma. I didn't see her go in because that was when I went to get a drink but when she came out, she looked pissed off, sorry, I mean *annoyed*. After that, Mr Newhall emailed me and said he didn't want to be disturbed. He often does that. Would it be that hard for him to walk twenty paces to tell me himself?

Anyway. I'd been about to offer him a coffee when I saw the email. That usually means he's going to take a nap, so I left him alone. I think he hadn't been well. There'd been a lot of naps this year.

The games teacher, Mr Hinchwood, came to see him at about . . . goodness, not long after Gemma left. And when I told him that Mr Newhall was busy, he went away again, said he'd catch him at the end of the match.

I went home at four forty-five on the dot and . . . and . . . honest, if I'd have known . . . well, I feel terrible that I didn't even go to say goodbye. I wanted to get away quickly and, sometimes, he could chat for hours. I think he was lonely. It's a thankless task being head of a school like this. There's the pressure on him to get top results and the parents are all a bit too involved in their kids' lives, if you know what I mean. Lately he'd been shutting himself away more and more.

The school has a target for the number of new pupils they want for September and they were nowhere near it. That's why the open day was important to him and so, when it all went pear-shaped, he was none too happy. It was dreadful and he was in bits about how it would affect admissions.

The open day? I can't believe you haven't heard. Has no one said anything? Goodness me, it was an absolute disaster. I've never known anything like it.

Chapter 7

One week before the cricket match

Katy Lane stood outside the main doors of Aberfal High. Chin up, shoulders back. The grounds were glorious, the weather was glorious. It was a wonderful day and there was a fluttering of excitement in her belly. Days like today allowed her to see the school through the eyes of others. The amazement when they saw the theatre, the thrill as they saw the computer suite, the library and the prized display of signed first editions. Aberfal High really was the best and today would confirm it beyond any doubt.

Only the brightest pupils were on show today. The polite ones and the handsome ones, the ones who shined their shoes without needing to be told. None of the pupils would be rude on purpose, but some were still growing into themselves and were awkward in front of the parents. Confidence took you a long way at Aberfal.

Benny Yardley and Oliver Entwistle were positioned as parking marshals with yellow high-visibility jackets over their school blazers. Even though they were hot, not one layer of clothing would be removed. It was important that, from the moment people set foot on school grounds, they got the full Aberfal experience. This was the last open day before the summer break. The last chance to get parents to sign their children up for September's intake. The school was running at fifteen per cent under capacity and couldn't continue that way for much longer. Today could change all of that. And when it did, it would be thanks to Katy Lane.

Inside the front door, a handful of Aberfal's best were waiting to welcome the new families and give them a tour that would blow their minds. Most of today's visitors would be there out of curiosity but that was okay because, once they were inside the school, Aberfal had a good conversion rate. The boys were their product and their salesmen. Each one of them had been hand-picked because they were Aberfal High boys through and through. Katy had used the phrase so many times that she never stopped to wonder if that was a compliment.

Katy wanted to be the first face the visitors saw. Though Jerry Newhall was still headmaster, today was entirely down to her. This was her chance to shine and to show everyone that she could lead this school. The thought of getting her hands on Aberfal High and shaping it to her vision, made Katy's palms sweat and her heart beat that little bit faster. It wasn't as if Jerry was a bad headmaster, not really, but he was becoming a liability. Erratic. Argumentative. Forgetful. Lecherous.

Katy hadn't known that she wanted to become head of a boys' school, but then she'd been made deputy head and Jerry made no secret of the fact that he was grooming her to take over from him. She'd allowed herself to imagine sitting at that colossal desk of his. Already wondered how she would pose for her portrait. But then Jerry changed his mind and said that she wasn't the woman he thought she was. All because of a silly mistake. Though, technically, could it be called a mistake if she'd happily repeat it?

Jerry had decided to leave it late to announce his retirement – no one wanted the sharks to sense blood while the school was trying to attract new students. He seemed to think that his hand on the helm was a selling point. Katy didn't. However, this could play in her favour because, even if Jerry wouldn't support her application to take over from him, no one else could step into his shoes at such short notice.

Jerry Newhall treated Aberfal High like an old boys' club and tried to sand off the edges of anyone who dared to stick out. He saw bullying as an important part of education; experience that would prepare them for later life. He believed in leaving discipline up to the children themselves. 'Never did us any harm' and all that rubbish.

Lately, he'd overstepped a line and she'd seen a side to him that didn't fit with the persona he portrayed to others. And then there was the whole issue of those pills. He swore he didn't have a problem, but they both knew he was lying. Between her and Charles Yardley they'd kept Jerry sheltered, protected. And in turn they'd protected the students and the school. But enough was enough and now it was time to focus on her own future.

She truly cared for each one of these boys and was committed to providing them with the best education and the best pastoral care. For some of these children, school was the only stability they had in their lives and she would open the school around the clock if she could, to provide a safe place for them all.

After a slow start to the morning, more people were starting to arrive. As she watched a family get out of their car, she heard Hinch's voice shouting. 'Miss Lane!'

She put a finger to her lips to silence him.

'I swear to God . . .' he began.

'Mr Hinchwood, we are not on a rugby pitch. Please lower your voice.'

'I need you to have a word with Mr Newhall or, God help me, I'm going to swing for him.'

Katy Lane forced a smile and, through clenched teeth, said, 'Problem?'

'He's told Blake we can't have cricket on the bottom field this morning because we need to preserve the grass. What does he think we're going to do? Dig holes? We always have a sports exhibition. Always. I've got twenty lads ready to show the parents how we do things here at Aberfal, but at this rate all the parents will see is me hitting the . . . *twerp* around the head with a cricket stump.'

Katy Lane nodded, appreciating the fact that Hinch had used the word 'twerp' when something much stronger was on his tongue.

'Get set up, Mr Hinchwood, and I'll have a word with Mr Newhall. You leave him to me.'

She fixed her smile and turned back to greet the visitors. Hinch turned to face them too, sighing heavily.

With clenched teeth Katy said to Hinch, 'What are you waiting for? Go!'

He nodded and tramped away.

'Good morning,' Katy said to a young couple with their hands on the shoulders of a round-faced blond boy.

'Welcome to Aberfal High School for Boys. I'm Miss Lane and who do we have here?' She bent to get a closer look at the child.

'This is our son, Reuben.'

It was a perfectly cherubic name for a perfectly cherubic-looking child. If Katy's experience had taught her anything, those were the ones you had to watch out for.

'Nice to meet you, Reuben. Shall I get one of the students to show you and your family around? I bet Myles knows where Chef keeps the biscuits.'

This boy seemed too young to be setting foot inside the hallowed halls of Aberfal High. Katy preferred students to have a touch of maturity about them, a natural curiosity. Whenever she saw very young students – primary aged – she felt herself recoil. Katy had never been one for fluff or sparkle. She would never have survived as an infant-school teacher. The glue and glitter brigade were a different breed and hats off to them. The very idea of teaching young children made Katy touch the crucifix at her throat.

She beckoned Charles Yardley's broad-shouldered son over to continue the charm offensive. She could see a lot of his father in him. So handsome. So upright.

Myles was already talking, asking the parents whether they lived locally, as they slipped away without a backwards glance. The sun was strong, but Katy Lane wouldn't wear sunglasses. It was important the parents saw her eyes. Saw her integrity.

The effort of not squinting was making her eyes water and, though she couldn't focus on the figure marching up the driveway, Katy sensed a problem. She had a sixth sense for trouble. It was the first thing she'd learned at teaching college.

A figure, a lone woman, was walking fast, arms swinging by her sides, pebbles flicking up behind each step. When she saw Katy, she started waving. Katy moved towards her to keep the commotion contained and away from the school. She'd throw her body on that bomb if she had to.

She blinked hard. 'Ms Demetriou? Is everything okay?'

Asha put the back of one hand to her forehead. Her eyes were darting left and right, looking for someone.

'I've been reading Cass's WhatsApp messages,' she said, lifting the phone until it was in front of Katy's eyes.

'Well, strictly speaking, children shouldn't have WhatsApp until they're sixteen years—'

'Now's not the time, Miss Lane. I've tried to keep out of it and let the school handle this but . . . Is Ryan here? Are his parents? I'd like a word.'

'I . . .' Katy looked away, trying to remember who she'd seen this morning. 'No. Ryan isn't here, so unless his parents are helping out on one of the stalls . . . which I'm almost certain they're not, but you'd have to check with Helen-Louise.'

'Fine.'

Asha took two steps towards the noise of the fair and then stopped and turned back to Katy.

'Hold on, you're telling me that Cass got a detention for the fight, but Ryan didn't? I don't even . . . Christ, I don't have time for this right now.'

Asha set off towards the gazebos at a jog. Katy watched

her for a moment and then trotted after her as fast as she could go without breaking into an unladylike run. 'Ms Demetriou? Excuse me?'

She wasn't going to let Cass's mum cause a scene today of all days. Katy had been all for giving Cassius Demetriou a scholarship, even though he'd barely scraped through the entrance exams. What she hadn't expected was the combative nature of his mother. You'd have thought she would have been more grateful.

Katy heard Helen-Louise say, 'Asha, isn't it? We don't have you down to help this morning, but we're always grateful for an extra pair of—'

Asha cut Helen-Louise off and was speaking in low tones, but she stayed still long enough for Katy to catch up to her and hear Helen-Louise say, 'It's rare they volunteer to help. Of course, the father is terribly important.'

'Ms Demetriou,' began Katy. 'If we could just—'

'I don't care how important he is,' said Asha. 'He needs to deal with his son before I do.'

Katy touched Asha's arm but seeing the look on the other woman's face, she withdrew her hand. 'This sounds like a delicate school matter. Shall we discuss it inside?'

Asha looked at the phone in her hand. 'I want to talk to Mr Newhall.'

Katy glanced about her with a fixed smile on her face. 'The headmaster is rather busy today. Why don't you let me deal with your concerns and I can fill him in later?'

'No.' Asha looked determined. 'You, me and Mr Newhall. Now. And I want you to go and get Cassius.'

'But Cassius isn't here today. He—'

'I beg your pardon. What do you mean "he isn't here"? He'd better bloody well be here, Miss Lane, because I dropped him off myself an hour ago.'

Her eyes were ablaze with anger and Katy's voice faltered a little.

'But . . . My understanding is . . . I mean, didn't you email to say he couldn't come in today? A stomach bug, wasn't it?'

As Katy watched Asha's face went from an angry red, to unsteady yellow, then settle on white. Katy took a step backwards. She'd lost a student. She'd never lost a student before. There'd been no truants, no miscommunications. Katy Lane didn't make mistakes like this and especially not today of all days. She felt her face get hot and it had nothing to do with the sunshine.

'Perhaps Mandy passed on the wrong name,' she said. 'Maybe it was someone else. I'll need to check with her but . . .'

'But?'

'But I've not seen Cassius. I'm sure I haven't. He simply isn't here.'

A few people had stopped what they were doing and, though they kept their eyes on their shoes, Katy knew they were listening.

Asha put her hand over her mouth.

'Perhaps you should tell me what you wanted to talk to Mr Newhall about. Could the mystery of Cassius's whereabouts be related to that issue in any way?'

Asha bent forwards and for a moment, Katy thought the woman was about to throw up. 'Ms Demetriou?'

Asha took a deep breath. 'The reason I wanted to talk to Mr Newhall . . .' she straightened up again and looked at the phone in her hand. 'Is because the bullying has got worse. Significantly worse. Newhall said he'd do something, but he didn't. I'll tell you this now, Miss Lane, if something has happened to my son, I'll hold you and Mr Newhall personally responsible.'

Becky Rupertsmum: Remind me what time U want me at open day, Pippa. Did you say 12?

Clare Withoutani: I'm at the school now, Becky. Can't see Pippa anywhere. Just me and Pam. Doesn't look like we'll be run off our feet BUT I have just seen my arch-nemesis Tash Saunders. She has twins. You should have seen her face when I told her about Freddy. She asked, "just one child?" like popping out twins meant she had a super-vagina!!! Do you think I should have a word with Helen-Louise? See if we can start vetting prospective parents?

Pippa Bennysmum: Cassius is missing. @ Clarewithoutani Can you hold the fort? Xx

Clare Withoutani: What do you mean "missing"??!!

Becky Rupertsmum: U R joking! What happened?

Pippa Bennysmum: Pretty sure he's on school grounds. Asha dropped him off this morning, but he didn't turn up for duty. Keep this between us, obvs. Helping Asha look for him now. If you see him call me immediately xx

Pam Geoffreysmum: Anything we can do to help, Pippa?

Pippa Bennysmum: Just smile and pour the drinks, Pam. Will let you know when I have any news xx

Rose Oliversmum: Fuck that. If one of our boys is in trouble, I'm going to look for him. Who's with me?

Chapter 8

One week before the cricket match

'Try not to panic,' Pippa said. 'We've all played truant at some time in our lives.'

Asha paced around the desks. Pippa was always no more than three steps behind her and Katy Lane hovered in the doorway.

'It's more than that,' said Asha. 'He's not bunking off school, Pippa.'

'He might be sitting in the chapel right now trying to make sense of things.'

'He's not religious.'

'I used to say the same, but I can never walk past a church without going inside.'

'Yeah? Well, he's not like you. He's not like any of you. Right. I can't stand here and do nothing,' Asha said. 'This waiting is driving me insane.'

'Please,' said Katy Lane. 'Let me handle this. You don't know the grounds like we do. I've got staff checking the classrooms and the usual hiding places right now. They'll call me as soon as they find him.'

'Is Newhall on his way?' asked Asha.

'No.' Katy blinked several times. Swallowed hard. 'He's . . . busy.'

'Of course he is. Shows where his priorities lie, don't you think?' Asha turned to face Pippa. 'Do you ever look at the boys' phones?'

Pippa didn't answer immediately. There was the right answer and the *right* answer. Morally right would be to say 'Oh, no, that would be infringing on their privacy', but parentally right would be to say 'Damn right. Nothing happens in their lives without me knowing about it.'

It was a modern parental problem. How much do you respect your child's freedom while also making sure you're keeping them safe from bullies and predators?

'Well,' Pippa said, 'Myles is old enough to make his own decisions now and Benny isn't that interested in social media.'

'Is that yes, or no?'

Pippa cleared her throat. 'Sometimes.'

'You both need to see this.' Asha unlocked Cass's phone and handed it to Katy. Pippa moved to stand behind Katy so she could see the screen.

Asha couldn't watch. She went to the window and put both hands on the glass. She scanned the crowd for Aberfal High's grey blazer, her heart skipping a beat each time she saw one on a boy who wasn't hers.

All she'd ever wanted was to keep Cass safe. It was one of the reasons they'd moved to Cornwall. She thought life would be better here. Less danger, less chance of falling in with the wrong crowd. She'd wanted to give him the opposite of the upbringing she'd had but, as the saying goes, wherever you move to, you take yourself with you. She

71

heard Pippa gasp behind her and knew exactly which bit she'd read because the messages, the words, were etched in Asha's mind.

You're a waste of space.

If I were you, I'd kill myself.

Useless.

If you're going to do it, get on with it.

What are you waiting for, loser?

Asha turned to Katy expecting some explanation or denial, but Katy's mouth was hanging open. Pippa was shaking her head. 'I've known some of these boys since they were in nappies. I'm sure they don't mean—'

'This has been going on for months. They've been making fun of his hair, his accent, even his bloody avatar name on Fortnite. He can't do anything right. He got into a fight with Ryan on Monday – an actual fistfight – and I should've known this wouldn't go away. I've spoken to Mr Newhall about this three times.'

'We will sort this. I promise you,' said Katy. 'Finding Cassius is the only thing on my mind right now but, when we know he's safe, we'll address this. Trust me.' She handed the phone back to Asha. 'I'm going to check on progress. Stay here and I'll be back with any news.'

Katy left the room, closing the door behind her. Asha whimpered and pushed her thumb against her mouth, biting down on her flesh. 'This is torture. How can she expect me to sit here and do nothing?'

The door swung open and Asha's breath caught in her chest. Cass's name was on her lips, but it came out as a sigh when she saw it was only Charles Yardley. He took two long strides into the room, looked between Pippa and Asha, saying, 'Where's Miss Lane?'

'Have you found him?' Asha asked.

'What? No. I came to find out what was going on. What's this about a missing boy?'

Pippa said, 'Cassius was meant to be showing people around the school this morning, but he didn't turn up.'

Charles loosened his tie and said, 'All this fuss because a boy didn't turn up to school? This is the last thing I need today.'

'Charles, this is serious. We've been looking at Cass's phone. There have been messages between the boys and . . . well, there's reason for concern.'

Charles turned his reluctant attention to Asha. Shadows under his eyes suggested he hadn't slept well.

'Cassius, yes. I think I've met him.'

'I dropped him off at the end of the driveway,' Asha began. 'And then when I came back to give him his phone—'

'Technically he's not our responsibility until he's on the school grounds. Next time, you should see him to the door. Have you tried calling him?'

She shook Cass's phone in front of Charles's face. 'Weren't you listening? He doesn't have his phone with him, or I wouldn't have seen messages from boys at this school goading him into killing himself.'

Charles ran a hand through his hair and scratched his neck. 'It's imperative that we don't jump to conclusions here. Sometimes it's how boys speak to each other and if your son can't handle a bit of robust language . . .'

There was that word again. Robust. First Mr Newhall and now Charles Yardley, suggesting that all Cass needed to do was toughen up. Asha was inches from Charles's face.

'You know nothing about my son or how he speaks. Who are you anyway? Chair of the PT fucking A?'

'Chair of governors actually.'

'What the hell has this got to do with you? Where's Mr Newhall? Has anyone called the police yet?'

'I'm sure Mandy will have called them by now,' said Pippa.

Charles's narrowed eyes didn't leave Asha's face. 'No, she won't, because I told her not to. Last thing I need is the police turning up because a boy is playing truant. He seems to have inherited his lack of respect for authority from his mother.'

'Or,' Asha said, 'he just recognises a twat when he sees one.'

'I'm starting to question whether you're Aberfal High material,' he said. 'I'll be talking to Jerry Newhall about this.'

'Good,' Asha said. 'And while you're there, tell him that because he can't control his students, my son is in danger. Tell him . . .' she poked Charles's chest. 'Tell him, that if Cass is hurt in any way at all, I will be going straight to the press and he can kiss his precious school goodbye. Just as soon as he's finished kissing my arse.'

She felt, rather than saw, Charles's entire body tense and braced herself for a slap. At that moment the door opened and Mandy rushed in.

'Someone saw Cassius,' she said. 'He was heading towards the lake.'

Asha pushed Charles aside, ran from the room, through the corridor, through the hall, ignoring the alarmed looks of parents, knocking into people without stopping to apologise.

She was outside then and momentarily blinded by the sunshine, but she pushed on, losing her footing at the top of the stone steps and crashing down, her shoulder taking most of the impact. She hardly felt the pain, only the desperate need to get up and keep going.

The jazz band was playing. Helen-Louise called her name. But she ran. She sprinted past the walled garden towards the water, her pulse beating in her ears as the water came into sight. The call of a peacock sliced through the air as she thundered closer. Not enough air in her burning lungs to call out Cass's name. Every ounce of energy was keeping her legs pumping.

Ahead of her, Asha saw the slight figure of Katy Lane moving through the trees towards someone standing by the water's edge. Sweat stung Asha's eyes, blurring her vision and she slowed to suck in her breath. She shaded her eyes against the light reflected off the water as she came out of the tree line and came to a halt, taking in the scene in front of her. Looking, looking, *looking* for her son, not sure whether to go left or right. Water lilies, pads the size of umbrellas, stopped her from seeing anything in the lake.

'Cass!'

Katy Lane turned and Asha saw that it was Rose standing with her.

'Rose! Cass is missing, he . . .'

Asha saw that Rose had a blazer in her arms. 'Is that . . .?'

'I found this on the grass by the water,' she said. 'I don't know if it's Cass's but . . .'

'It's his.' Asha took the blazer, saw how the name label had come away at the corner. She stepped towards the water, dropping Cass's jacket on the ground. Everywhere, movement caught her attention, but it was only a heron taking flight, a fish flitting through the water, a leaf falling from the tree. She couldn't see Cass anywhere and yet she kept thinking she saw him everywhere. If she concentrated, wished and prayed, he would appear.

'Cass! Where are you?'

She stepped into the lake, hardly noticing the cold water tightening her skin. She began wading through the weeds. There was a sudden drop and the water was already at her neck, shocking the breath out of her. She wiped the hair from her face so she could see properly but taking another step, she went under the water. She tried to open her eyes, to look for Cass, but everything was green and murky beyond the bubbles. She came up for air. Gasping.

'Cass!'

She spat the water from her mouth and Rose's hands gripped Asha's shoulders, dragging her backwards.

'What the hell are you doing?' Rose said. 'Get out of there.'

'I must find him, Rose. If he's here . . .'

Katy let out a small yelp as a man came striding into view. 'Mr Blake,' she called. Her voice was shrill, full of fear. 'I told you. I told you to stop the boys from coming down here. Didn't I say that—'

'I found him,' said Otis.

Asha scrambled out of the water on all fours. 'What? Where? Is he okay?'

Otis scratched his chin. 'You need to come with me.'

WITNESS THREE

Gemma Newhall.
Headmaster Jerry Newhall's widow.

So, to be clear, Detective Mullins, you think someone murdered my husband, but you can't work out *how*. Can't work out *who*. And you have absolutely no idea *why*. You haven't a bloody clue and I'm sure I don't need to tell you that this is completely unacceptable.

What's your theory about how he died? What are we looking for? Good God, man, how difficult can it be? Shot? Stabbed? Strangled? Poisoned? You must have an idea. Katy Lane tells me there wasn't a mark on him, but I trust her about as far as I can throw her, so . . .

I don't know. Nothing in particular, I suppose, but she's a cold fish who gives nothing away and I can't trust someone who's that closed off. She's made no secret of the fact that she wants to be headmis-tress of Aberfal High one day, but Jerry wouldn't support her applica-tion and she was bloody livid. Lately she's been undermining him, trying to get the board and the other teachers to back her to . . . I don't know, stage some kind of coup I suppose.

When can we expect the results of the post-mortem? Come on, man, where's the urgency? There's a murderer on the loose. Of course, we're all hoping this is an isolated incident but if I'm about to get murdered in my bed, I wouldn't mind advance warning.

What are your theories about how someone managed to get in and out of Jerry's office when a hundred people were outside his window and Mandy was outside his door? The chimney? Air vent? Secret panels? Think, man. Think!

Well, yes, usually I'd agree with you that it's your job to ask the questions but, if I can refer you to my previous comment, you haven't a bloody clue.

Fine, yes, I was at the school on Friday. I was going away for a couple of nights and I came to tell Jerry that I'd left a curry in the Aga and to remind him of some jobs I wanted him to do. And, you know, this might surprise you, but I was going to miss the old goat while I was away. Not that it's any of your business, but we'd had a bit of a tiff that morning. He'd decided that he wasn't going to retire this year, after all. It's a full-time job being wife of a headmaster, you know, and I felt that I deserved more of a say in the decision. I didn't want to go away for the weekend with there being any bad feelings between us and I was still hoping to persuade him to change his mind.

He'd had a difficult couple of weeks, but he wasn't one to complain. Dropping numbers of pupils, escalating costs. He'd had a run-in with Hinch about the sports equipment and with Otis Blake about the grounds. Always thinking about themselves, not what's best for the school, see?

I tell you what *did* bother me on Friday . . . When I went to see Jerry, he was hiding in his office. There's no other way to put it. Usually, he'd be out watching the match, talking with the parents, supporting the boys. Made me quite cross if I'm honest. I told him 'You can't let them see they're getting to you. You made this school what it is today, now bloody well get out there.' He thought they blamed him for everything that was going wrong and he was start-ing to believe them. He dedicated his life to the school and look how they repaid him.

79

I told him that I'd wait outside until half past if he wanted to join me. Thought he might need the moral support. But he didn't come out and I never saw him again. I don't know if he didn't want to or if . . . I um . . . could I get a glass of water? Thanks. It hits me sometimes.

Can hardly believe that he's dead, you know? It's simply absurd that someone did it on purpose, or that he didn't fight back. He was a strong man. Past his prime, perhaps, but he wouldn't have sat there and let someone . . . hurt him.

Christ. What a bloody mess.

So, where was I? Yes, so I got the dog out of the car and went to watch a few overs, let Biffy stretch her legs before the drive to my sister's. There was a bit of a scene when she went off after the cricket ball. Still a pup, see. Not fully trained yet and Border collies can't resist a ball. Caused one hell of a commotion. Children, parents, all running after her and Biffy thinking it was the greatest game. Jerry would've found it hilarious.

God. I can't stand the thought that I'm not going to hear his laugh again. Jerry was a difficult man at times, Detective. Stubborn like you wouldn't believe. But he had the biggest heart of any man I've ever met. He laughed every single day. Me and him, well, we were a team. I wasn't meant to grow old without him.

I don't think . . . I mean . . . Look, it might be nothing, but a couple of the senior management team have been targeted over the last few weeks. Did Charles tell you that his car was vandalised the night before the open day? And Katy Lane had her tyres slashed on the Friday before the Easter hols. I told Jerry that if they wouldn't call the police, then he should. But he was worried how it would look if the police were sniffing around. My guess is it's all related.

Jerry's murder had to be something to do with the school because there wasn't anything else in his life. I bet that sounds pathetic to you, but the school was everything to him. Perhaps if Charles and Katy had been less bothered about how things looked, my husband would still be alive today.

Chapter 9

One week before the cricket match

'Where is he? For God's sake, tell me!' Asha was close to screaming at Otis. His face was impossible to read and so her frantic mind filled the gaps, gaping and stretching until she fell through the cracks.

'He's fine.'

'What?'

'He's fine. He's wet and embarrassed, but he's fine. You might want to get him checked out at the hospital to be on the safe side.'

Asha felt Rose's hand in hers and it was hard to tell who was clinging on to whom. She swallowed hard. 'I thought . . .'

'I bet you did.'

Otis Blake marched around the lake, ducking under tree branches and sweeping them aside. Asha staggered after him. Her clothes were wet, sticking to her fear-weakened legs. The adrenaline had left her washed out, barely able to hold herself up. 'Is he hurt?' she asked.

'You can ask him yourself.'

Rose and Katy were at Asha's shoulder, Rose saying, 'Should I call someone? Does he need an ambulance?'

Katy, though, was struggling to contain her anger. She threw questions like daggers at Otis Blake's back. 'Where were the signs that I asked you to put out? How many times do I have to tell you—'

'You're sure he's okay?' Asha asked.

'Ask him yourself,' said Otis again.

'But I'm asking *you*. Why won't you tell me?'

Otis stopped walking and spun around so that Asha almost collided with him. 'He's fine, thanks to me. But if I find him in that water again, I won't drag him out. Get a handle on your son and tell him to keep away from my lake. Or else.'

Asha stumbled backwards. She would have said something, to match his fury with her own, but she was too relieved that Cass was okay to care how anyone spoke to her.

'Why was he in the lake?' she asked.

Otis continued to glare at her. 'That's something you'll have to ask your son. I am not his teacher; I am not his therapist; and I am not his fucking lifeguard.'

'Mr Blake!' said Katy. 'I'll thank you to watch your language. If you'd done what I told you to do . . .'

Behind Otis, Asha could see a functional, patched up storage shed hidden from the school by a thick bank of trees. Asha hadn't seen it before, but why would she? Everything about Aberfal High School was about focusing on beauty while ignoring the beast. A wide wooden porch hung over the decking at the front of the shed. It looked more like a log cabin than somewhere you'd keep a lawn mower but there, on the step, was Cass. Asha could have collapsed with relief. Until that moment she hadn't let herself believe he was safe.

He looked so small. His shoulders were hunched and he was resting his head on his knees. He looked up, saw Asha and, as his face crumpled, he lowered his head again.

'Cass,' she whispered.

Asha looked at Rose and Katy. 'Do you mind if we have some privacy?'

'Sure,' said Rose. 'We'll head back up to the school.'

Katy tugged her cardigan closed. 'Yes, of course. But I'd like to talk to him about why he came down here when I expressly told the boys—'

'Not now, Miss Lane.'

'No. No, of course not. I'm just saying, well, I'm relieved that he's okay, but it could have been far worse than this. Would you ask him to come and see me first thing on Monday morning? I meant what I said earlier. I *will* sort this.'

'Thank you.'

'Call me if you need anything, yeah?' said Rose.

Asha nodded. 'Would you let Pippa know that Cass is okay? I was in a bit of a state when I ran out of there.'

Rose nodded and retreated through the trees. The sound of music and laughter threaded its way through the leaves. Katy followed but kept looking over her shoulder at the lake as if it held something sinister below its surface.

At last Asha turned to face Cass. Part of her wanted to run to him, scoop him up in her arms, hold him tight, but there was a reticence that hadn't been there before. Now that the initial relief had waned, she was left with the question of why he'd gone into that water in the first place. And she didn't like the answer she was leaning towards.

'Hey,' she said, taking a few steps in his direction.

'Hey.' He lifted his head but didn't meet her eye. He picked at the hem of an oversized borrowed T-shirt, worrying a stray piece of thread.

'Hey,' she said again as she sat down.

Why, when there were so many words running through her head, couldn't she think of a single thing to say? Though it was a warm day, there were goosebumps on Cass's arm. His hair was already beginning to dry in that curl that he hated and she loved.

'So . . .' she began.

Over Cass's head, Asha saw Otis Blake leaning against the door frame with his thumbs in his pockets.

'I was worried,' Asha said to Cass.

'Yeah. Sorry.'

'Jesus, Cass!' Asha threw her arms around his shoulders and pulled him to her chest. His foot came off the ground and he toppled into her. When he tried to pull away, Asha held him tight. 'Not so fast.'

He gave way to her arms and shuddered against her.

'Are you going to tell me what happened?' Asha asked.

Cass lifted his head and looked over his shoulder at Otis. Otis Blake rubbed his chin, nodded, as if to himself and said, 'I saw him come down to the lake a while back. Miss Lane was clear she didn't want anyone here, but your lad seemed troubled and I didn't see how he was doing any harm, so I got on with setting out tables and chairs on the lawn. Doing what needed to be done. And when I came back . . .' Otis stopped speaking and looked at Cass again as if hoping he would take over, but Cass appeared to be getting smaller by the minute.

'Yes?' prompted Asha.

'I must've heard something. So, I went to the lake and I saw him in the water.'

Asha tensed. She wanted to hear it all, even though she knew she wouldn't like what Otis was going to say.

'Just tell me.'

Otis shrugged. 'He was in the water, flapping his arms about like an idiot. He was never in any real danger. I dragged him out, brought him back here and that's pretty much all there is to it.'

But Asha knew it wasn't the end of the story. It was the smallest part of the story. A story of fear, of bullying, of a boy losing his way.

'Cass?' She pushed his shoulders away so that she could look into his face. Still, he kept his eyes down. 'I saw the messages on your phone from Ryan. I have to ask, were you trying to hurt yourself?'

Cass shook his head. 'No. It wasn't that.'

Asha exhaled and relaxed as he leaned against her once more. 'You know I love you, right? But you're going to have to start talking before I really lose my shit.'

Cass tightened his arms around her. She'd not noticed how tall he'd become until he had to stoop to lie his head on her chest. Asha could have stayed like that all day.

Otis brought Asha a coffee and some dry clothes. Her wet mobile phone was in a plastic bag surrounded by grains of rice. Cass's was lost somewhere between school and the lake.

Asha and Cass sat side-by-side on the steps, close enough for their thighs to touch but so much keeping them apart. The music from the open day came to them on a soft breeze from time to time. Occasional laughter. The smell of food.

'It was a dare,' Cass said.

'Who dared you to get in the lake? Who was it?'

'It wasn't about getting in the lake. I was meant to swim across to the other side.'

'Godsake, Cass. Do you have any idea how scared I was?'

'I took my blazer and trousers off first.'

'Like I care about your uniform, you idiot.'

'You're always saying how expensive it is.'

'If I've ever given you the impression that the uniform is worth more than you are . . . I haven't, have I? Because, if I have—'

'They say there are bodies in the lake,' Cass said.

Asha looked towards the water. So serene and picturesque. Right up until the moment she thought she'd lost her son in there.

'They grab your ankles,' he continued. 'I didn't believe Benny Yardley when he said it, because it's stupid, but when I was in there, I swear something touched my leg.'

Asha looked at Otis, who was crouched a few feet away staring at the water.

'Yep,' he said. 'Chock full of ghosts.'

Cass said, 'I did feel something grab me. Honest.'

Asha sighed. 'If you say so. But I still don't understand why you got in the lake in the first place, Cass.'

'I told you. They dared me to swim across it to prove how brave I was, or something. I'd pretty much do anything to get them to leave me alone.'

Asha kissed the top of his head. His hair was damp and somehow still smelled of his shampoo.

'Are you cross with me?' Cass asked.

'Yes,' Asha said, but then she shook her head and groaned. 'No, I'm not. Christ, Cass.'

Cass was usually so sensible. It wasn't like him to feel the need to prove himself to anyone.

'You're lucky Mr Blake spotted you. Why do you care what these idiots think about you anyway? Say the word and we'll leave this school today. We'll home-school, we'll travel. We'll run away and join the circus. I'm begging you, babe, say the word and we'll leave this place.'

Cass picked a long strand of grass near his foot and started ripping it to pieces. 'I don't want to move again.'

'Uncle Georgie's in Spain. How about we go visit him?'

'Can't we stay somewhere long enough for me to make friends?'

'These aren't the kind of friends I want you to make.'

'Then why send me here in the first place?'

Asha took her time responding. 'Okay,' she said. 'Okay. You want to stay here, that's fine, but . . .' She held up one finger. 'First. You do anything like this again and we're gone. Okay?' Cass nodded.

Asha held up a second finger. 'Second. There must be better ways to make friends. Arrange to meet at the beach, the park, invite them round for pizza. Shit, I'd be happier if you stole alcohol and got pissed in the park.'

She took a deep breath, looked at her two raised fingers, losing her train of thought for a minute.

'And three,' she said. 'I'm going to see Mr Newhall right now to tell him he has to do something about this bullying or, if he doesn't watch it, it'll be *him* floating face down in that bloody lake.'

Cass almost smiled. She could see it in the twitch of his cheek.

Otis got to his feet so suddenly that both Asha and Cass looked to him. 'I need to go,' he said. 'You'll see yourself back to the school, yes? Good. Right then.'

Asha watched him stride away towards the trees at the back of the lake, away from the noise of the school. She opened her mouth to call after him, to say 'thank you' but he'd already disappeared and all she could hear were his feet on dry twigs in the shadow of the woods.

'Is he okay? Asha asked. 'He seems a bit . . . odd.' She instinctively disliked the man. It was one of her less appealing character traits that she was quick to judge. Perhaps she should've felt warmth towards the man who'd saved her son's life, but it wasn't that easy.

'Mum?'

'Uh-huh?'

'Please don't say anything to Mr Newhall. Not yet.'

'I can't sit by and do nothing, Cass. Miss Lane saw that you'd been in the lake and I don't want her thinking you fancied a dip. You shouldn't get into trouble for this when it was Ryan's fault for goading you into it.'

'You'll make it worse. Besides, it's my fault for laughing at them for being scared of the lake. I should've swum yesterday at first break but then when I didn't, they started saying that I was a pathetic wimp, so I decided to do it this morning to get them off my back. But now they'll never leave me alone, will they?'

'You leave that to me,' said Asha with a smile.

Rose Oliversmum: GOOD NEWS, ladies. Cass is fine. Asha says he decided to swim across the lake! Honestly, these boys will be the death of us. In hall now waiting for cake judging. Wish me luck!

Becky Rupertsmum: Thank GOD!

Sarah Teddysmum: What a relief!! Glad he's okay. I told Teddy that Cass had swum the lake and he cheered. I didn't know this, but that lake is part of Aberfal history. The seniors jump in at the end of term. If they survive (!) it means they've passed their exams. If they get sucked under it means they've failed!!

Pam Geoffreysmum: What a load of rubbish. Glad Cass is ok. For once I agree with Rose – these kids will be the end of us.

Clare Withoutani: That's great news Rose. So glad he's safe. On way to hall myself now. See you in there.

Becky Rupertsmum: I'm holding fort at drinks tent. Hurry back unless U want me 2 drink all the profits.

91

Sarah Teddysmum: Apparently kids have drowned in that lake in the past. Did anyone else know about that? Should we petition to have a fence put up to keep the children out?

Pam Geoffreysmum: I'd feel safer if the lake wasn't there at all.

Clare Withoutani: OMFG!!!!!!!!!!!!!!! You will never guess what is happening in the Great Hall!

Sarah Teddysmum: WHAT??

Pam Geoffreysmum: Clare?

Becky Rupertsmum: Spill the beans!!!!!!!!!!!!!!!!

Sarah Teddysmum: WILL SOMEONE TELL US WHAT'S HAPPENING!!!!!

Chapter 10

One week before the cricket match

There was a steady stream of parents coming through the school. Most with children, but a few without. Pippa smiled, waved and pointed them in the direction of the drinks tent.

'Do stick around. The choir will be performing the songs they won the regional finals with.'

She'd come into the Great Hall to take a break from the sunshine and the smiling, but it was no cooler in here. The whole length of the hall under the windows was dedicated to the boys' environmental projects and Pippa had to lean on the table in front of it to stop herself from swaying with fatigue. She put one hand to her temple and closed her eyes for the count of five. She wondered whether the school had a sick bay where she could go and lie down with a wet paper towel on her forehead.

Though she'd hoped there'd be a perfectly good reason for Cass's disappearance, she had to admit that she'd feared the worst. That's what she did nowadays. Hoped for the best and planned for the worst. When Rose had called to tell her that Cass was fine, she'd burst into tears. Not a ladylike dampening of the eyes, either. No, she'd sobbed until her throat was raw and the tears had dropped from her chin

93

and then she'd reapplied her smile and gone back to greeting and shepherding. 'Pimm's, anyone?'

She loved Aberfal High. Couldn't bear to think what would happen if she couldn't find a way to keep Myles and Benny at the school, but Charles's reaction to the missing boy had scared her. Was Asha right? Did he and Jerry care more about the school's reputation than the boys themselves? Reputation was everything to Charles. Which was why it was incomprehensible that he would ever let them get into a situation where they couldn't pay the school fees. There was no way she would consider sending the boys to Freemill Academy.

Pippa focused on the projects in front of her. She couldn't see Benny's anywhere though she'd put a lot of – no, sorry, *he'd* put a lot of time into that project. It would be a shame and a surprise if the school weren't displaying it. Perhaps the Yardleys were already falling from grace and this was the beginning of the end for them.

There was an experiment showing soil erosion. The cut-open water bottles ranged from bare soil to a fully planted garden and the containers underneath showed the amount of soil washed away when the same amount of liquid was poured into each one. The next project was a time-lapse film showing what would happen if the Lego world kept getting hotter. As the film went on, Batman figures were left melting and disfigured.

There was a painting by Cassius Demetriou showing the effect of deforestation. The boy was a talented artist, obviously taking after his mother. Pippa felt responsible for Asha and Cass if she was honest. Could she have done something

94

to stop this morning's incident? The stunt at the lake was concerning and she wouldn't sit by and ignore the bullying. She'd call Asha later and come up with a plan to tackle the issues head on.

'No bloody way did Ethan Carmichael do that on his own.' Pippa jumped at the voice in her ear.

She turned to see Rose standing with her arms folded and an eyebrow raised. 'Let's call it what it is – a competition for the parents. Let us fight to the death but leave the kids out of it.'

'Shhhhhh! You mustn't say that!' Pippa took hold of Rose's arm. 'How's Cass?'

'Wet.'

'And Asha?'

'Scared to death. She thought, for a moment there, well . . . I'm sure you can imagine what she thought.'

'We need to talk to the boys,' Pippa said. 'I don't like the way they speak to each other, Rose.'

'Agreed. If I find out that Ollie has had anything to do with this, I'll bloody kill him.'

The two women stood shoulder to shoulder looking at the projects but not seeing them.

'Which one is Oliver's?' asked Pippa.

'Not here. It was a drawing of the world crying. That's honestly the limit of his creativity. I don't think any of these projects were done entirely by the kids. Do you?'

Pippa smiled because Rose was probably right. Each time Benny had a project to do, she vowed to leave him alone to do it. Charles said the children would never learn if she kept helping. But then Benny would get frustrated and upset and of course she was going to lend a hand. What kind of parent would she be if she left him in tears at the kitchen table? And it wasn't like she did it all. They worked on it together, with Pippa simply tidying the end results.

'But' – Rose leaned closer to Pippa and whispered – 'the cake is entirely my own work. I couldn't risk poisoning our beloved headmaster.'

She gestured over her shoulder to the cake display. It wouldn't be long until they would be judged by the headmaster and then be transported to one of the gazebos where they'd be sold by the slice.

'It was almost a disaster,' Rose said. 'My chocolate dome cracked and I had to do a second batch. Made it thicker second time around, but when I burst the balloon that we were using for the mould—'

'A chocolate dome?' asked Pippa.

'Yes, well the theme is *freedom*, isn't it? We did a white chocolate egg and inside it is a lemon-frosted chick. You know, freedom from the shell and all that.'

'Oh goodness, that makes our cake look rather unimaginative.'

'Why? What did you do?'

'A banana cake made with parsnips like they used to do under rationing in World War Two. We were going for a "freedom from the tyranny of war" feeling.'

'Nice.'

'Thank you.'

'Bet it tastes like shit though.'

Pippa glanced to the doorway as Helen-Louise breezed into the room. Keeping her voice low, Rose said, 'No wonder it got colder in here.'

Something about Helen-Louise made Pippa's scalp prickle. She made Pippa feel ashamed of herself. People like her made *all* mothers feel ashamed because she managed to pop out perfect children at the same time as having a pedicure, running a business and a marathon and never ever breaking into a sweat. Talking of which . . . Pippa picked up a school prospectus and used it as a fan.

'Ladies!' The booming voice of Jerry Newhall echoed around the hall and everyone quietened for a moment. Pippa didn't look at him, just scanned the faces around the hall. Half of the women smiled and preened, Helen-Louise most of all, and the other half pretended they hadn't even noticed him. Pippa caught sight of Jerry's wife, Gemma. She was always in the background at these events. The headmaster's wife was neither preening nor ignoring. She was holding a stack of paper cups and watching her husband as if he was a puzzle she was yet to solve.

Gemma and Jerry Newhall were a peculiar couple. In all the years Pippa had known them she'd never seen them touch fingers, never mind hold hands. A peck on the cheek would be unthinkable. They appeared to have the kind of relationship that required much mockery and no kindness. As their husbands were such good friends, Pippa and Gemma used to spend a lot of time together – barbecues, dinner parties, weekends away, holidays – but they no longer spoke.

'Morning, Mr Newhall,' said Rose. 'I'm going to inspect the competition. I don't suppose you're open to bribes?'

'Always, Rose. Always.'

Rose smiled and moved towards the cakes, leaving Jerry Newhall standing with Pippa.

'Looking ravishing today, Pippa.'

Pippa tilted her head but didn't look him in the eye. 'Did Charles catch you? The boy is safe and well, which is such a relief.'

'Which boy's that?'

'Cassius Demetriou. I thought you knew. We lost him for a while this morning. Quite the panic. We had to get a search party together.'

'Oh, yes. Of course. Good stuff.'

'Don't you care, Jerry?' There was something wrong with Jerry's eyes. Too dark and glassy.

He sighed. 'I've given up caring, Pippa. Never seems to get me anywhere.'

'Are you okay?

'Yes and no. Gemma's on my back about retiring, Katy Lane's after my job and the other teachers treat me like I'm a doddery old fool. It's astounding how easily respect turns to pity if you don't nurture it.'

'I'm sure I don't wish to add to your woes, but can I get a moment in private, Jerry?'

'Sounds interesting,' he said.

'It's about the school fees. We could go somewhere quieter?'

'Let's not,' he said. 'It's such a lovely day. Why don't you leave that kind of talk to the grown-ups?'

'Jerry, I hardly think that—'

Helen-Louise touched Jerry Newhall's arm. 'Sorry to interrupt, Mr Newhall, but we're ready when you are.'

'Smashing. On my way.'

Helen-Louise smoothed her hair as she went back to the judging table. A small crowd was beginning to gather.

'Actually,' Jerry said, 'I was hoping to bump into you, Pippa, because I've got you a little gift.' Jerry smiled as if he had a secret.

'I'd rather we spoke about the money issue if that's okay with you, Jerry dear.'

'Now, now. Don't be like that.'

It was difficult to believe that he and Charles were the same age. Though both were older than Pippa by almost a decade, Charles still looked youthful whereas Jerry's hair was almost white and disappearing in wedges at his temples. Though his hairline was receding, his waist was going in the opposite direction. He'd been handsome in his youth, mostly because of his lust for life and his ability to command attention in any room.

Pippa didn't resist when he lifted her hand so that her palm was facing upwards and hovered his clenched fist above hers. And then, slowly, he gave her an AA battery.

Pippa squinted as if she hadn't quite got the joke yet.

'What's this?'

'Wait for it.'

He kept his hand underneath hers. It was too hot. Damp.

And then, from his trouser pocket, Jerry produced a white and blue sachet of salt. The type you get from the canteen. He placed it on top of the battery and leaned in so Pippa could smell his heavy cologne, though it did little to mask the musky scent of sweat beneath.

'A salt and battery. Get it? Assault and—'

'Yes, yes. I get it. It's not funny, Jerry.'

He put his free hand on her waist, laughing too loudly, making people look in their direction. Pippa looked across the room and caught Gemma's eye. The other woman shook her head and turned away.

Pippa didn't know what she'd done to encourage this kind of behaviour from Jerry. Perhaps it was because of his friendship with Charles. Though that didn't seem to count for much anymore. Of course, he might be alluding to what happened between Gemma and Charles at that villa. It was the reason Gemma wouldn't speak to Pippa anymore. Or was it the reason Pippa wouldn't talk to Gemma? Either way, it amounted to the same thing.

Pippa felt her face grow hot as if she'd been the one to cross the line. Jerry winked and turned away. Arms wide, he approached Helen-Louise and the table with the cakes on it.

Pippa had grown up surrounded by men like Jerry. Like Charles. They were the ones who made the rules, who set the boundaries and she'd always had to fight to be heard, to push back against their unreasonable behaviour. But lately, she'd been too tired to push. She may as well have lain down on the floor and let them wipe their feet on her.

She heard Jerry's voice, strong, unabashed. 'What delights do we have here?'

He should have taken more of an interest in Cassius going missing. For a man who'd once said he'd put his life on the line for this school, he barely acknowledged that the school was going under. And now there was this problem with Charles and the money. She could just imagine how Jerry would be lording it over him. It was a cash-flow problem, or so Charles had said, but Jerry wasn't willing to give them extra time to pay the fees. After all they'd done for this school, it was unfathomable that Jerry could be so cruel.

Jerry said something that had the mums giggling and Pippa felt herself stiffen. It could have been the lack of sleep, or Charles's vandalised car that they couldn't afford to get fixed. It could have been the animosity that was radiating from Gemma from across the room, but today Pippa had a fizzing in her veins and a desire to smash something, hit something, throw something. It was an itch under her skin that couldn't be scratched.

Pippa saw how Jerry placed his hand on the base of Rose's back. She saw how Rose took a step to her right so that he had to drop his hand. She noticed how Rose, normally so outspoken, kept her lip buttoned. Pippa let Jerry speak to her that way, because he was Charles's friend and she knew he was harmless enough. She told herself that she didn't make a fuss because this was the best school in the south-west and Jerry was partly responsible for that. But what reason did Rose have for putting up with Jerry's behaviour? And why did Jerry think he had the right? That's what annoyed Pippa the most. What gave him the right? Besides, what was the worst he could do if she stood up to him? Suspend the children? Let him try. Thanks to him, they already had one foot out of the door.

She placed the battery and the salt on the edge of the table displaying the boys' projects and wiped her hands on her trousers. Pippa could hear Jerry's voice as she walked towards him, talking about Gemma's cooking.

'I'm not saying it was inedible,' he said. 'But even the dog refused to lick the plates.'

Pippa considered him for a minute. Why would he say something like that, even it was true? He was nothing but stories. Words stacked on top of words until you couldn't see which ones were true anymore.

'If it wasn't for Chef's cooking, I'd waste away,' he said, patting his stomach.

The women laughed.

Pippa was close enough to see flakes of dry skin on the shoulders of Jerry's jacket. She could have reached out and touched him.

'If I ever die unexpectedly, mark my words, it'll be food poisoning from the wife.'

Pippa saw Jerry caress Rose's elbow and Rose move to cross her arms. Jerry dropped his hand and his fingers stroked Rose's hip instead. There were so many little things that annoyed Pippa. She should report his behaviour, but to whom? The chair of governors was her husband and Jerry's best friend. Or at least, he used to be. And what would she say anyway? If she went above Charles's head, she'd only be branded a tattletale, but to stand by and say nothing was worse.

'How many cakes are there?' Jerry was asking.

'Thirteen,' said Helen-Louise. 'Unlucky for some.'

'Unlucky for my waistline.'

Laughter.

The other cakes looked far more appealing than Benny's faux banana cake, but he'd stayed up late to bake it and had put a lot of thought into it. Anger roiled in Pippa's stomach. She was annoyed that the school lined up the hoops and one-by-one the parents jumped through them. Did they have any idea how much effort it took to be on top of laundry and the homework and the extra projects and the cakes? And why did everything have to be a competition? And why didn't Jerry care what happened this morning with Cassius?

And then something happened.

It was subtle at first and then it became a force that Pippa couldn't control. For a moment she felt like she was having an out-of-body experience. It was a beautiful sensation, like she was weightless and nothing mattered anymore. She was light-headed yet she could see everything clearly. She moved towards the table, thinking she'd steady herself, wait for the episode to pass. But then she was watching a woman who looked remarkably like her, but a little thicker around the waist. The woman reached for the closest cake. It was Rose's perfect white chocolate dome. So delicate. So smooth and exquisite.

The same woman waited for Jerry Newhall to turn to face her. She pulled herself up straight and grew until she seemed taller than Jerry. And then Pippa was back in her own body again and the cake was already leaving her hand.

Jerry's eyes went from flat and emotionless to wide and alarmed. Rose's hand flew to her mouth in shock and Helen-Louise let out a strangled cry. Jerry turned his face just in time and the cake hit his jaw and shoulder, exploding like white chocolate fireworks.

And it was every bit as satisfying as Pippa had expected it to be. Especially when she saw Gemma Newhall laugh.

Chapter 11

Later that day

As the open day drew to a close, Jerry, Katy and Charles sat in the stifling office trying to unpack the day's events. Katy watched Jerry loosen his tie and unbutton the top of his shirt to reveal a wiry thatch of grey chest hair. He took a glass of water offered to him by Charles and sat back in his chair.

'I've had the mother in my office a couple of times,' said Jerry. 'Quite a firecracker. She wants me to do something about the bully, but she doesn't know who's bullying him. She's going to take him out of the school unless we make this bullying go away. I know it's only one boy, but we can hardly afford to lose pupils.'

'Looking at the messages,' said Katy, 'Ms Demetriou has a point. The language they're using and the way they talk to each other . . . I do think we have a duty of care, Jerry.'

'But we don't know for certain that this little episode down by the lake is anything to do with the bullying?' he asked.

'Not for certain,' said Katy. 'But . . .'

'I wonder if it was something to do with Otis Blake,' said Charles. 'I tried talking to him about it and he got quite aggressive. I don't know why you keep him around, Jerry. There's something not quite right about him. Mark my words, it's a matter of time before there's a complaint about that man.'

'I shouldn't have heard about this debacle from your wife though, Charles.'

'I thought you had enough on your plate, Jerry. No harm, no foul.'

Charles poured a glass of water for himself and offered the jug to Katy, who shook her head. She watched Jerry take two pills out of his desk drawer and swallow them.

'And don't get me started on your wife and that bloody cake. What the hell was that all about?'

Charles was already shaking his head. 'I have my suspicions, but I've not had a chance to catch up with her so . . .'

'One minute we were laughing and joking and then . . . Wham! A cake in the kisser.'

'I can't apologise enough, Jerry. If I could, I'd wash my hands of her.'

'If only it were that easy,' said Jerry. 'Wives have a habit of tightening their grip towards the end.'

Katy shifted uncomfortably in her seat. Charles let his head fall backwards and he closed his eyes. When he yawned, he didn't cover his mouth.

'We can only guess how much harm she did to the admissions,' said Jerry. 'I've got to tell you it's not looking good, Charles. If we don't attract more boys to the school . . .'

'Or girls,' said Katy. 'We still have the option to go co-ed.'

Jerry nodded but there was no enthusiasm for it. 'Though that'll cost us money upfront for separate bathrooms and changing rooms and whatever else girls need. We don't even know that there's a market for it. One of our selling points is that this is one of the last single-sex schools in the southwest.'

'That hardly means a thing if we have to close,' said Katy.

Jerry sighed. 'Fine. Let's talk damage limitation.'

'Sorry?'

'Damage limitation. We need to decide how to handle today. How do we explain why Pippa threw a cake at me?'

'Prank for charity,' said Charles before Katy had a chance to respond. 'Miss Lane already gave a little speech to say the highest bidder got to choose which teacher got hit with the cake. Money to the Nairobi fundraiser bla, bla. Kids chose their favourite teacher, which was you. Isn't Mr Newhall a good sport. Et cetera. Et cetera.'

'Which kid?'

'We didn't say. If asked, let's say it was Myles.'

'Was it? Good lad.'

Charles opened his mouth to say something and then shook his head and looked away.

'And the missing boy?' Jerry asked.

'I'd made it clear,' said Katy, 'that no one should go down to the lake. I'd told Otis Blake to keep an eye on it and to put up signs. While we needn't shoulder any blame, this might be the time for us to consider closing off the lake. This custom the seniors have of jumping into it, well, we've been lucky so far, but if anything were to happen . . .'

Jerry blew out his lips. 'You'll need to get a bit tougher if you're going to survive at a boys' school.' He smacked the open palm of his hand down on the desk and swivelled his seat to face Katy.

'And you,' said Katy, 'are going to need to get a bit softer if you don't want to lose all our best students.'

Charles was smirking but, seeing Katy's face, he stopped.

'I suppose,' Charles said, 'we could put a couple of signs up warning of danger. Cover our backs in case anything like this happens again. You know, legally.'

'This isn't about covering our backs,' said Katy.

Jerry hunched over the desk. 'I suppose it couldn't hurt. See if the lovely ladies of the committee can put it on their list of things to fundraise for, would you? I'll be buggered if I'm paying for it out of school coffers. There's nothing but a couple of coins rattling around in there now.'

Charles nodded and Katy grunted in frustration.

'So that's the end of it, yes?' Jerry asked.

Katy cleared her throat. 'Not exactly.'

Jerry groaned. 'What now?'

'The bullying, Jerry. We need to do something. Whatever happened down at the lake, his mother was panicking because she thought the bullying had driven him to do something extreme.'

'Yes. I can see that, I suppose. I don't want numbers to go down any more but maybe he's just not worth persevering with.'

'Of course he is!' snapped Katy. 'Every one of these boys deserves every opportunity available to them. We can't exclude children who don't fit your blueprint, or who bring the average exam scores down. How many times do I have to tell you that individuals like Cassius are not the problem.

You turning a blind eye to the systemic bullying in this school has brought us to where we are today.'

It was the first time she'd raised her voice to Jerry and she took several deep breaths until she felt herself gaining control of her emotions again.

'Sorry. It's just . . . it's not the first time we've had this conversation. If we don't act soon then we could be dealing with something far more serious than a boy going missing for an hour or two.'

'The thing is,' Charles said with a smile meant to diffuse the tension, 'every school has a certain amount of bullying. I'm not saying it's acceptable, I'm saying it's not the end of the world. We'll do what we can to help the lad out but, more than that, we can't afford to turn people away anymore, can we? One of the reasons we were so keen to have the boy at the school was to show that this school is welcoming of everyone.'

'As long as they can pay,' grumbled Jerry.

'Perhaps if you had a more flexible payment plan . . .' said Charles.

'Change the record, Charles. You know there's nothing I can do about that now.'

Katy sighed. Soon this would be her problem, not Jerry's. She was going to make the school co-ed and didn't think she'd have a problem getting it past the governors. However, until Jerry announced he was stepping down, she couldn't broach the subject with them. And if they didn't act soon, she wouldn't have a school to take over and instead, she'd be looking for a new job this summer.

'God, Jerry, it's stuffy in here. Can't we open a window?' asked Charles, standing up.

'No, you can't. Or more accurately, you can't close it once you've got it open. These bloody windows might look nice, but they're impossible.'

'Another one for the fundraising committee?' Charles asked.

Katy was looking forward to a glass of wine when she got home. A large one. She'd managed to contain the fallout from Pippa's assault on Jerry and managed a student's disappearance so that few people had any idea what was going on. If she expected any gratitude for what she'd done she'd be waiting a long time.

'Before we move off-topic again,' she said. 'Cassius isn't the only boy being bullied in the school, but it seems worse in his year group than any of the others. We should see this as an opportunity to put an end to the bullying at Aberfal High through an entire-school approach. The safeguarding of the children in our care—'

'Oh Lord,' said Jerry, looking at Charles. 'She's off again.'

Charles said, 'I don't know, Jerry, maybe she has a point. It can't hurt to be a bit savvier about these things.'

'What this does,' continued Katy, 'is bring into sharp focus the issue of cyber bullying. It's something that we didn't have to deal with when we were their age. They need to understand the repercussions of what they do online and how to handle it.'

Jerry stood up. 'I thought I was running a boys' school, not a tea party.'

He adjusted the belt of his trousers and walked over to the window. 'I wouldn't be the man I am today without a bit of toughening up. Bullying is a part of life.'

Katy clenched her hands until her knuckles turned white. She wondered whether she could give herself an embolism with the pressure of the fury coursing through her veins right now.

'Now, Jerry,' said Charles, 'I seem to remember you were on the other end of the bullying from me and from where I stood it wasn't such a pleasant experience. You know I'm a firm believer in not mollycoddling them, but this . . . this . . . what do you call it? Cyber bullying? Well, they need to know that there'll be repercussions of that too. Everything leaving a footprint and all that.'

Jerry put his hands in his pockets and grunted.

Charles caught Katy's eye, pointed to the cricket bat then mimed hitting Jerry with it. Katy put her hands together and mouthed, 'Please!'

'Fine,' said Jerry, spinning around and turning to point a finger at Katy. 'You've landed yourself the role of anti-bullying co-ordinator. For now, we'll send out an email to the parents, update the website and you can lead an anti-bullying assembly on Monday. I hope you didn't have any plans for the weekend, Katy.'

'I did, but . . .'

'Hot date, was it?'

'Something like that.'

'My wife's off to her sister's next week and I can't wait for the peace and bloody quiet. Sometimes I wake up in the middle of the night and she's just there, standing over me. I swear to God she's going to smother me in my sleep.'

'Well,' Katy said, standing up. 'If she ever needs a hand holding down the pillow . . .'

Jerry snorted as he laughed. He was the only man she knew who seemed to relish being insulted.

Charles was slightly behind Jerry and was rubbing the back of his neck, like the weight of the world was bearing down on him. Katy felt sorry for him. Being chair of governors was a thankless task and one she wouldn't blame him for walking away from, but Jerry had some sort of hold over him.

'You know,' Katy said, 'I don't mind working on anti-bullying measures. I don't mind giving up my weekends to do whatever I can to help this school, but . . .' Katy hesitated, took a deep breath. 'Seeing as you're so close to retirement, Jerry, it might be beneficial if you start relinquishing some of the responsibility for the running of the school. I was thinking that I could—'

'Good God, woman! I will not have a failing school as my legacy. No. At least another year before I could consider leaving.'

'But you said—'

'Forget what I said. The only way you're getting me out of this school is feet first.'

Clare Withoutani: I heard from Helen-Louise that numbers of kids joining the senior school is way down on last year. If they don't get more, they're going to start making staff redundancies. I'm telling you ladies, we are not getting our money's worth.

Sarah Teddysmum: I'm happy the numbers are down. Smaller classes are better for our boys. Pippa might have done us a favour by throwing that cake and put some people off. (PS Love you, P. I hope you're okay?) #TeamPippa

Pam Geoffreysmum: Not condoning what she did, but there had to be a good reason why Pippa threw that cake at him.

Rose Oliversmum: I don't care what the reason was. I'm still waiting for my apology. #TeamRose

Becky Rupertsmum: I think it's gr8 what she did. I bet she's not the first person 2 want 2 throw something at that sleaze just first 1 who had balls 2 do it #TeamPippa 👏👏🙌

Rose Oliversmum: Doesn't anyone care about my cake? 🎂 @PippaBennysmum are you reading this? I'M STILL WAITING FOR MY APOLOGY.

Pippa Bennysmum: Rose darling, I apologised at the time. I can't keep going over this with you. I was having a bad day. I did something stupid. Take this as yet another apology. And whenever you want to apologise to me for not asking whether I was okay, I'll be waiting. #TeamIDontHaveTimeForThisShit

Pippa Bennysmum left

Sarah Teddysmum: She left the group??!! Rose, do something. Get her back!

Becky Rupertsmum: Now she's gone . . . I wonder if this has something 2 do with Charles. I heard from Mandy that Mr N and Charles had a HUGE row last week. Charles stormed out of the room and called Mr N the 'c' word. (And I don't mean Conservative.)

Clare Withoutani: What is going on with her? Not wanting to jump to conclusions here BUT Charles argues with Jerry and then Pippa throws cake in his face. So it's something to do with the three of them. I don't want to say it out loud, but do you think Pippa and Mr N could be . . . you know!!!!!

Pam Geoffreysmum: What ARE you talking about?

Rose Oliversmum: 😖 😭

Becky Rupertsmum: Been rumours 4 a while that Mr N is having an affair. Pippa has been at this school 4 longer than the rest of us. It doesn't take a genius 2 work it out.

Pam Geoffreysmum: And you, Becky, are no genius.

WITNESS FOUR

Rose Entwistle.
Mother of Oliver.

I know you're not allowed to say much so . . . how about I say what I've heard and you nod when I'm getting warm? We could help you out. We mums. You'd be amazed at what we notice. You might call it gossip, but I call it investigative journalism. You don't raise boys without being able to spot a lie at fifteen paces.

Yes, Detective Mullins, I was there all afternoon on the day Jerry died. Had to head off sharpish after the match though. Cello lesson. There's always something, isn't there? Do you have kids? Well, you know what it's like then. I hardly have a moment to myself. Ollie has been picked for the county and, as soon as I've finished here, I've got to drive him to cricket practice. What I wouldn't do for a free weekend.

Anyway, back to Jerry. I know who did it and, let me tell you something else, I'm not scared of him. You should hear the way he talks to the boys. Would it hurt him to nurture them a bit more? It's the mocking that I don't get. Since when did humiliation spur someone on to run faster or throw further? It's only my opinion, but he shouldn't be allowed to teach children. I wouldn't let him train a dog. And guess what? He kept disappearing during the match. You don't need me to spell it out for you.

What? Oh, right. I should've said, I'm taking about the games teacher, Mr Hinchwood, but everyone calls him Hinch. He was stressed about the cricket match, everyone could see it and he took it out on the boys. I think . . . I mean, I can't swear to it because I wasn't paying that much attention, but I saw someone in the window of Mr Newhall's office and it was at a time when Hinch had gone AWOL, so yeah, I'm pretty sure it was him. Pretty sure that I saw the blue and red of the school colours, you know? So that could have been Hinch's tracksuit, right?

So, here's the thing: when the match ended, I expected him to be there, congratulating the boys, talking to the teachers from the other school, you know. The usual. But he was nowhere to be seen. And the boys couldn't get into the changing rooms because Hinch had the key, so we had to wait a good ten minutes before he appeared again. He looked shifty, didn't explain why he was late, didn't even say sorry.

I feel like I'm doing your job for you here. The least you could do is say 'thank you'.

Chapter 12

The day of the cricket match

Pippa was running behind schedule. She didn't like to use the word *late*. Delayed, yes, but never late. She slowed the car, searching for a parking space.

When had life got so busy? She missed the days when they used to have Mary come clean for them. And she'd iron too. The woman had been a Godsend until her daughter invited her to spend Christmas with her in Australia. Mary jumped at the chance and never came back.

It was around the same time that Pippa had left her job and then it seemed like such an extravagance to have a housekeeper. After all, Pippa was home all day now and their income had dropped considerably overnight. Her days consisted of driving the boys to and from school and running endless errands.

Today she'd spent most of the morning preparing for this evening's barbecue. Charles was going to invite Jerry and Pippa was going to apologise. Again. She was trying so very hard to make it up to her husband and, when he asked her to pick up his shirts from the dry cleaners she'd said, 'Of course. No problem.'

But it *had* been a problem because a quick dash into the dry cleaners turned into twenty minutes of huffing and sighing as they had trouble locating Charles's shirts. There'd been more shirts than usual because Pippa had taken to wearing them loose over a vest. Her own clothes were pinching lately and she couldn't afford new ones. She was going for a more casual look nowadays anyway. One that covered up the under-arm sweat marks and the line of perspiration running down her back. She used to love hot weather and now she found herself praying for autumn's turn on the seasonal wheel. She wondered how Mary coped with the heat in Australia.

She spotted a space and hit the brakes. Reversing, she listened to the sensors telling her how close she was to the SUV next to her. She felt a sudden and rare pang of jealousy looking at the black beast in the next parking bay. She wasn't interested in cars usually, but she was pining for a time when she and Charles used to replace their cars every year, go on holidays, have a housekeeper. Life hadn't been perfect by any means, but it had felt so much easier then. She knew, with a certainty that didn't please her, that she would never experience that level of financial comfort again. Charles was even talking about selling his car and becoming a one-car family. Goodness knows how they'd manage. It had been hard enough being down to one car for a week while Charles had his resprayed.

She had to admit that she hadn't looked at the bank statements recently so hadn't noticed their savings dwindling to nothing. Pippa had deleted the app off her phone so she wouldn't be reminded that she wasn't bringing in a salary anymore. But even so, she still couldn't understand why they couldn't afford the school fees. And why weren't they sitting down and coming up with a plan? Couldn't they re-mortgage? Sell something?

She'd planned to have it out with Charles on Tuesday evening. It was the one night when they were always home. Charles was already furious with her and she couldn't see how she could make it any worse by talking about money. Waiting for the boys to go to bed had been a mistake because, when she went to find him in his study, Charles was arguing with someone on the phone. Pippa could hear every word, but she felt like she was listening from the bottom of a deep well. He wasn't talking, he was *hissing*. Someone was threatening to report him to the General Medical Council.

Being a doctor meant the world to Charles. A cliché, perhaps, but true. He'd wanted to follow in his father's footsteps since he was six years old. He was proud of his job and his status. He was one of a dying breed of family doctors where he treated the same patients his father had done and had seen babies grow up to have babies of their own.

She'd almost asked him about the phone call and the GMC, but then she'd have to admit to listening to his conversation and things between them were bad enough.

Pippa got out of the car and swept her damp fringe away from her forehead, buying herself a precious minute before she had to greet everyone with smiles and gaiety. She took a sip from the flask she'd brought with her. Her homemade blackcurrant cordial was a little too tart, if she was being honest, but the satisfaction she gained from drinking it came from the fact she'd made it with her own hands with berries from her own garden.

Pippa had offered to run a stall selling refreshments at the cricket match, but Katy Lane thought drinks should be offered for free in case it suggested to the visiting school that Aberfal High needed money. Desperation wasn't a good look when trying to attract new families to the school and that was top of the agenda for this year.

Now though, as she felt the sun pinching her face, Pippa wished she'd been more insistent if only so she could have stood under a shaded gazebo. Had it ever been this hot in May before? Surely this was climate change in action. Somewhere there was a polar ice cap cracking and depositing great big chunks into the water, all while Pippa stood and sweated into her borrowed shirt and an old denim skirt that was from a maternity range from when she was pregnant with Benny.

Yes, she stood by her suggestion, a drinks stall would have been profitable today. But Katy Lane, who always had smiles for everyone else, shut down all of Pippa's ideas as soon as they left her mouth. As far as Katy Lane was concerned, the only thing worth selling was the school itself. Everything was an opportunity to promote the benefits of a Aberfal High education. Thanks to Charles being chair of governors, Pippa was all too aware of the issues facing the school. Dwindling numbers of students, teachers retiring at a rate of knots – it wasn't sustainable. There was something rotten at Aberfal High and, as everyone knew, one bad apple spoils the barrel. Though, and Pippa thought this for the first time standing outside the school, how could you expect anything to flourish if the tree was poisoned from the start?

Pippa heard the *thwack* of bat on ball and resultant cheers from the spectators. She couldn't put it off any longer. She'd found herself wishing for an excuse to miss the match because she knew that everyone was still talking about the cake incident. She didn't blame them but if she could hide away for ever, she would.

As she passed the art block and the theatre, she spotted the games teacher, Hinch, standing behind the cricket pavilion with his hands in his hair as if he'd tear it out if he could. She raised her hand to wave, but he glared at her and walked away, his hair sticking up in tufts.

Her step faltered. Did everyone hate her for throwing that cake? Did they blame her for ruining Aberfal's chances of attracting new pupils? She almost got back in the car and pretended she'd been waylaid. Though, now that she could see the cricket match in front of her, she knew she couldn't let Benny down.

She squinted but couldn't quite tell whether Aberfal High were batting or bowling. It made no sense to have both sides playing in cream. At least when they were playing rugby, she knew which side was Aberfal because of the red and blue stripes of the school colours.

As she got closer, she saw Charles and waved to him. He turned away. Mustn't have seen her. She paused for a moment before launching herself into the sunshine. She fanned herself with her hand, but it was useless, there was no relief from the heat, especially not the fire that was building inside her. She felt like she was losing her mind and without her mind – the part of her that she'd always been most proud of – who was she? She wasn't this person who dithered and flapped. She never used to forget or misplace, or even make mistakes – not that she was perfect, far from it, but she had always been precise. And now she lost her keys as often as she lost her temper. She touched her temple where that headache had started up again. She tried not to think the worst, but this pain was sharp, regular and always in the same place. She imagined a tumour the size of a golf ball eating away at her brain.

'Pippa!'

She looked up and saw Asha beckoning her. Asha was standing with Rose who fluttered her hand in Pippa's direction and then said something to Asha who laughed.

Pippa had spoken to Rose twice since the cake fiasco, but things were still awkward between them. The quickest way for things to get back to normal was to act like it already was. She still hadn't re-joined the WhatsApp group and wouldn't ask to be added either. She hadn't sunk so low that she would grovel. Pippa hadn't fallen out with a friend since her school days. Yes, she argued with her husband, but they didn't row. And, of course, she'd had a difference of opinion with Jerry but, instead of words, she'd used cake.

'Hello ladies,' said Pippa as she reached them. 'What have I missed?'

'Benny took a wicket,' Asha said. 'It was amazing.'

'Charles must have been pleased.'

Rose didn't look at her as she said, 'Charles wasn't here. Luckily, we were here to cheer Benny on.'

'But Charles said . . .' Pippa looked over at Charles. There he was, not even watching the cricket. Deep in conversation with one of the parents from the visiting school.

Rose cupped her hands around her mouth and shouted, 'Good fielding, Aberfal! Keep it up!'

Pippa knew that Charles loved the boys, so it wasn't indifference that led him to be late. It was whatever was going on between him and Jerry. She should do something, try to straighten it all out. After all, her run-in with Jerry at the open day wouldn't have helped the situation at all. A better wife might have cut Charles some slack. He was stressed about money and scared about being reported to the GMC. It was a lot for anyone to carry on their shoulders. What he didn't realise was it wasn't his problem. It was theirs.

It wasn't even like he'd been a terrible husband. It was the indifference Pippa couldn't stand. She didn't expect romantic weekends and bouquets of flowers, but it wouldn't hurt him to ask her how her day had been, just once. He was a busy man. The provider. She wished it wasn't like that, but she hadn't felt able to carry on working. She was only forty-eight, too young to be feeling like she'd reached retirement age. Her company didn't try to keep her once they'd noticed the mistakes she'd been making. With hollow assertions of how they'd take her back in a flash if she changed her mind, they put her in the lift with a bouquet of flowers in the crook of her arm and a bottle of champagne in her hand. And that was it – the end of her career.

Pippa cried all the way home.

She told herself that she should spend more time with the children while she could. But the truth was, she'd had no choice in the matter. Even with all this time on her hands, she hadn't noticed extra hours in the day. She was constantly tired, low and even unloading the dishwasher seemed a chore too far. There was a certain assumption from Aberfal High that she'd be able to do more voluntary work now. She'd said *yes*, because she'd never learned to say *no*, but she dreaded each event and every meeting. All she wanted to do was sleep and throw things and sleep some more. Now she realised that it wasn't work that had been draining her energy, it was her family. She envied working mothers. Instead of less time, they seemed to have more.

All the time that Charles had been giving to Jerry and the school had seemed so noble at first, but she was wondering now if there was more to it. The phone calls, the meetings, the desire to keep Jerry sweet. And then there was the conversation she'd overheard on Tuesday night. The one where Charles had hissed and spat like a cornered cat.

'Do it,' he'd said. 'Do it. Report me to the GMC if you must. I've told you I'm not doing it anymore and, if this ever comes out, well . . . I'm not the only one with a lot to lose. I swear to God, I'll take you down with me. You'll regret pushing me on this, Jerry.'

Chapter 13

The day of the cricket match

As a rule, Asha didn't attend the school sports matches. She was usually working, or searching for work, or catching up on sleep that work had stopped her from getting. Even without work, she wouldn't have rushed to be here on a sunny Friday afternoon. She'd wanted to teach herself to surf but was yet to find an afternoon where the conditions were right for heading to the north coast of Cornwall. This afternoon would have been perfect, but there were more pressing things on her mind than catching a wave or two.

If it wasn't for Cass she wouldn't be here. She liked the other mums but never knew what to say to those outside her immediate circle of friends. And even with Rose and Pippa, it was difficult at times. There wasn't any common ground, there weren't many shared experiences. There was nothing to talk to them about apart from the school and the children and those topics would only last ten minutes, at best, so what was she meant to talk about for the rest of the afternoon? She certainly wasn't going to talk about herself. She dodged any questions she didn't feel comfortable answering.

'Where have you moved from, Asha?'

'Up country.'

'Much family?'

'None.'

'And your partner, what does he do for a living?'

'Jeez, is that the time?'

Asha hadn't come to the cricket match for the small talk and the social interaction, that was for certain. She'd come to watch Cass, not the cricket. She'd come to study his teammates, not the opposition. And if she saw a hint of the bullying, well, she wouldn't hold back.

Cass had insisted that there hadn't been any bullying this week, but Asha didn't believe him. A week ago he'd put his life in danger to get these boys off his back. And that's the real reason why she was here. It was one of the few times she'd get to see how he interacted with the other children. His smile and his insistence that he'd had another good day at school seemed forced and he was spending more time with his headphones on, pretending he couldn't hear her speak.

Though Miss Lane hadn't given him a detention, Cass had been ordered to spend each Tuesday after school with Otis Blake in the gardening club, learning how to tend to the lakes instead of swim in them. He already spent every Monday at cricket club, every Wednesday working on the school's racing car and Asha was beginning to feel like Aberfal High was taking more of her son than she was willing to share. She didn't mind the punishment – after all, he'd broken a school rule which had been set for his safety – but she didn't understand why the boys who'd driven him to it hadn't been dragged in front of Mr Newhall and

126

expelled. Those parents paid the school fees in full, so Asha assumed that their kids were worth more to the school than Cass was. It was hard to decide who she was angriest with – Mr Newhall, the parents or those children.

But now, as she stood at the side of the cricket pitch, Asha found it hard to believe that Cass wasn't as happy as the rest of the boys. Looking at them on the pitch in their cricket whites there was no telling whose parents were dentists, whose drove a Bentley, whose parents had PhDs and whose left school at sixteen. They might go home to differing levels of comfort at night and varying levels of support from their parents, but today they were equal. A bunch of kids doing their best.

There was determination on Cass's handsome face as he bent with his hands on his knees, eyes tracking the red cricket ball. So kind and smart and funny. Why would anyone pick on him? He should be the most popular boy in the school. She knew Cass didn't want to move schools again but if she couldn't fix their problems, what choice did she have?

Pippa and Rose were chatting by her side. Though the two of them said they'd made up, the conversation between them was overly bright. They talked about dresses for the ball ('dusky pink with black sequins') and about that new fish restaurant in Falmouth ('do try the scallops'). They talked about the weather ('aren't we lucky?') and the temperature of the sea right now ('definitely warming up'), but they didn't talk about the cake or why each of them was so angry.

A woman who Asha recognised, but couldn't immediately recall, was striding towards them. Pippa muttered something under her breath and looked at the ground.

'Gemma!' exclaimed Rose. 'What a lovely surprise.'

'How are we getting on?' Gemma nodded towards the cricket pitch and everyone turned back to the boys.

'Good,' said Rose. 'Have you met Asha?'

Asha and Gemma nodded at each other. 'Hi.'

'No,' said Gemma. 'We've not met.'

'Asha,' said Rose. 'This is Gemma Newhall. Mr Newhall's better half.'

'Nice to meet you,' Asha said.

'I don't usually see you at these things,' Rose said.

'Here to say goodbye to Jerry,' she said. 'He'll only complain if I don't. Got a few days away with my sister.'

'Anywhere nice?'

'Bath. It'll be good to spend time with my nieces and nephews. And nicer to have some time away from the old grump.' She nodded towards the headmaster's window. 'I thought he'd be out here. Anyone seen him?'

'Nope,' said Rose. 'I guess he's busy.'

'In that case I'll have to go and sniff him out. I want to get on the road before it gets too busy.'

As Gemma walked away Asha noticed that Pippa seemed to uncoil.

Rose lowered her voice to say, 'Have you ever met a woman who dislikes her husband as much as Gemma Newhall does?'

'It's just their way,' said Pippa.

'If you say so.'

'What's that meant to mean?'

'Nothing,' said Rose. 'I'm agreeing that some relationships aren't what they look like from the outside.'

'Well, if anyone should know . . .' said Pippa.

Asha stepped between them.

'Whoa. Okay then, let's sort this out.'

'Sort what out?' Rose asked.

'There's still tension from the open day. You two need to kiss and make up.'

'We have. We—'

'No. I mean it. I need you to get along because I don't want to walk on eggshells around you.'

Rose and Pippa exchanged glances, but Asha could tell neither of them wanted to make the first move.

'Okay,' Asha said. 'First off, Rose, you're still upset about the cake, right?'

Rose pouted. 'I'd spent a long time on that cake and all I got was a "sorry".'

Pippa started to speak but Asha silenced her. 'Hold on a minute.' She looked at Rose. 'But you can accept that there isn't much else she can do except apologise, right? There's no point in Pippa baking you a cake, is there? And she can't rewind time.'

Rose folded her arms.

'And can you see,' continued Asha, 'how Pippa was hurt by you being more worried about your cake than about her?'

Rose let her arms drop to her sides and looked at Pippa. 'She's right. I'm sorry, sweetie, I should have asked.'

'Which brings me to you,' Asha said turning to Pippa. 'You've apologised and you think there's not much more you can do.'

Pippa shrugged.

'But there is one thing,' said Asha.

Pippa and Rose were both watching her. Identical confused looks on their faces. Polite applause rippled around the field as a ball bumped over the ground to score the visiting team a four.

'See, the thing is, Pippa. No one wants to make much of it. We're assuming you're a bit embarrassed by it. And partly, we're a bit scared, because it's, like, completely out of character. So, why don't you explain what Mr Newhall did to make you react like that and then everyone can stop tiptoeing around you.'

Pippa put her hand to the back of her neck. 'Um . . .' She was struggling to know what to say or, at least, where to start. 'The thing is . . .' Pippa sighed.

'You can tell us anything, you know,' Rose said.

'It's hard to unpick.'

'Try,' said Asha.

'It's been building for a while and when Jerry made this, this . . . stupid joke at the open day I snapped. And I saw him pawing at you, Rose. I'm fed up with holding my tongue all the time. And I'm fed up always being the moral compass. Sometimes I want to scream and shout and swear, you know? I couldn't stand it anymore. I've asked Charles to do something to stop Jerry, but he won't do anything because . . .' Pippa stopped for breath. Swallowed hard.

'Because he and Jerry go way back?' Rose suggested.

Pippa shook her head. 'No. I mean, yes, they do go way back but . . .' Pippa folded her arms and lowered her head. 'This has to stay between us,' she said. 'I don't want the boys to find out, but, you see, Jerry has Charles over a barrel.

Money's a bit tight. We haven't paid this term's school fees and there's a possibility . . . I mean . . . the boys could be kicked out of school at the end of this term.'

Rose gasped.

Aberfal High without the Yardleys, well, it didn't seem possible.

'They won't,' said Asha. 'They can at least do a payment plan. They've been great with me. There's no way they'll let Myles and Benny go.'

'After all you do for this school?' agreed Rose. 'Christ alive, if you left, we'd never win a sports match or a public speaking competition again. Not to mention that the social calendar would be all kinds of terrible.'

Rose put her arm around Pippa's shoulder. 'Sorry, Pip. I didn't stop to think what strain you must be under. But, trust me, the school would be stupid to let you go. I'm not sure cake throwing was the way to remind them of how irreplaceable you are but, hey, it got Newhall's attention.'

'You won't say anything, will you?' said Pippa. 'I'm so embarrassed. And now, of course, things are more strained between Jerry and Charles because I've made everything worse. I must find some way to make things better and to make Charles forgive me, to . . . to . . . find a way to sort our finances out and—'

'Not being funny,' said Rose, 'but why can't you afford it? Charles's job pays well and you must have *something* put aside for a rainy day?'

Pippa shook her head. 'I honestly don't know. Because, on paper, you're right. I mean, it's tight since I gave up work but, you know, still affordable. The thing is . . .' She took a sip from her drinks bottle. 'When I tried to talk to Charles about it properly, we got into a huge row and I never asked him where the money had gone because . . .'

She looked across the field to where Charles was standing. Someone had said something funny and he'd thrown his head back to laugh.

'Because what?' asked Rose.

Pippa shook her head and turned to her with a tight smile.

'Because it was at that precise moment that he told me he wanted a divorce.'

Chapter 14

The day of the cricket match

Katy was the only person in the staff room and, when the door slammed shut, she jumped up and banged her hip on the desk. No need to be afraid. There must be a window open somewhere, letting in a much longed-for breeze. But as she glanced at the door, she thought she saw a shadow beneath it. Feet blocking the light and then gone.

Ever since her tyres had been slashed, she'd felt someone was watching her. She told herself that it was a simple case of paranoia. Irrational and persistent and almost certainly not real.

Almost.

And she might have believed it too if it hadn't been for the emails. Warning her. Threatening her. There'd been fourteen so far and she hadn't responded to any of them. She hadn't even read the last five. Wouldn't give them the satisfaction. They thought they were so clever with their untraceable email accounts and their vague suggestions that they knew everything about her and telling her that it was a matter of time until they told everyone else her dirty secrets. Katy had an idea who was sending the emails. The question was, what should she do about it?

Katy straightened her dress and rooted around in her bag for lip balm. The swift change from soft warm days to harsh blistering sun had cracked her lips. A thin dark line split her bottom lip where she'd bled. She dragged her finger around the balm, rubbed it into her lips. She wouldn't hide away because someone was too scared to make threats to her face.

At first, she'd planned to confront them, but then decided on a different tactic. If she didn't rise to it, they'd get bored and go away. And even if they did know something and even if they *did* tell the world, well, she'd deny it. Because no one would ever expect her to break any rules. She wasn't the type.

She pushed her lips together feeling the tackiness of the balm catching, threw the pot back in her bag and rolled her head until her neck cracked. Katy picked up the book that she needed for her next lesson. She must have angered the gods of education, otherwise why else would she have been teaching English on a Friday afternoon? She strode to the door but stopped with an outstretched hand, wondering whether someone would be waiting for her on the other side.

She yanked it open and saw nothing but an empty corridor. Heard nothing except the drone of Dr Grant, the physics teacher, through the open doorway of the classroom down the hallway. There was nothing to be afraid of. She closed the door behind her, careful not to make a sound and moved down the corridor in the direction of D3.

She paused by a window to look at the cream figures of the year seven cricketers. Red-and-blue peaked caps. Smart. No sign of Jerry Newhall though. She was inordinately fond of these boys even if the feeling wasn't always reciprocated.

Katy liked to think of herself as a good person. She gave money every month to Dogs Trust. She ran marathons for charity. She sent book tokens to her nieces and nephews for their birthdays. But she wasn't without guilt.

It was quite the dilemma. To get what she wanted, Katy would have to hurt people. Did that mean she shouldn't go after her dreams? Would a man even stop to consider potential casualties, or would they assume it would be all right in the end and push through without a second thought? She had to decide which was the most important thing to her. Her career? Or love?

Love. Such a ridiculous notion. Those who had it were smug about it and eventually indifferent to it, even scornful. Those who longed for it, made it their goal, an answer to their prayers. But it wasn't a prize, it was a commitment. Katy Lane had the trophy, but did she want to keep it for life, or pass it on to the next woman.

She'd fought her feelings for a long time. He had too. Neither of them had done anything like this before. It was societally wrong yet emotionally inevitable. The fact that he was already married was the only drawback. Though it might not look like it to an outsider, Katy had more sense of self-worth than anyone she knew. She hadn't told her friends about him because one of them would be bound to say she deserved better and then she'd be at least one friend down. She didn't see herself as second best, quite the opposite. Given everything that he had to lose, the fact that he'd chosen her showed her value.

Of course, she could be fooling herself and when her heart inevitably broke, she wouldn't be able to seek comfort from friends, wouldn't be able to take time to mourn the end of a relationship that had meant so much to her, because everyone would judge and scold and tell her she couldn't cry over a relationship that she was never entitled to have.

But. And it was a big 'but'. This affair could ruin her chances of becoming head of Aberfal High. She couldn't change the fact that she was younger than the previous headmasters. Though that problem would lessen with the natural passing of time, there was no changing the fact that she was a woman. When people imagined someone in that role, they imagined . . . well, they didn't imagine someone who looked like Katy. And if they thought she was prone to swooning at the feet of the first man who showed her a little bit of attention she would never gain their respect. Love, or career. It was time to choose.

Katy had five minutes to gather herself before the next lesson started. It was a small class, only eight of them and they were discussing *The Great Gatsby*. It was one of her favourite novels and one of her favourite classes, but sometimes she wondered whether she identified with Nick Carraway too much. Always on the outside of a world, barred to her by breeding and money, and yet she was inexplicably drawn to it. Chasing a dream that she could never have.

There was a hum in the air today – of excitement, of joy – and she tried to harness that. The first-year students were the lucky ones who got to play in sports matches on Friday afternoons, so it felt like school finished early for those chosen for the team. She felt sorry for the children who weren't as sporty. They watched, cheered on their class-mates but only towards the end of the match when the battle was almost done. Katy had been an average student when it came to sport. She neither knew how it felt to be picked first nor last. Katy was one of those people who bumped along in the middle lane of life. Neither excelling nor failing. Neither flying nor falling. But it was time for that to change. She wanted more.

The double doors swung open and Mandy came rushing through. She was always dashing and never in the direction she should be going.

'Is there a problem, Mandy?'

'Problem? No. I was heading to the, um ... I've got a headache. I was looking for some pills or something.'

'What's that in your hand?'

'What?'

'Your hand.'

They both looked to Mandy's left hand which, very obvi-ously, held a packet of tablets.

'What I meant to say was, I was going to get a bottle of water from the canteen so I could take the tablets.' She hit her forehead with the heel of her hand and laughed. Anyone could see that Mandy was hiding something.

'Well, be quick. And then don't leave your desk again this afternoon. I don't want to have to talk to you about this again.'

Mandy hurried along the corridor with her head down. Her feet hit the carpet hard. She used to be such a good PA and seemed to know what Mr Newhall needed before he did. But recently she'd barely been at her desk. This week something had changed. She was secretive. Looked scared all the time. Katy had threatened her with a written warning if she left her desk again for no good reason. How difficult was it to sit in a chair all day? Jerry needed a gate keeper, or the parents would never leave him alone for one second. Who knew what he'd say or do when left to his own devices?

The bell chimed and, within a split second, doors opened and footsteps were all around her. Katy was about to go up the stairs towards the English room when she stopped and grabbed the banister with one hand.

'Sorry, miss.' A year nine almost collided with her but Katy was looking past him. Gemma Newhall was marching down the corridor. She was talking into a mobile phone but the noise from the students stopped any of the words from reaching Katy's ears. Her free arm swung by her side and the students scattered to the walls as she stormed on by. She looked angry, but then, didn't she always?

Katy started after her. After all, Mandy wasn't there to stop Gemma from barging in. But then, even if Mandy had been at her desk, there'd be no stopping the headmaster's wife. Katy hesitated, not knowing whether to follow or go to class.

'I told you,' Gemma barked into the phone. 'I'm sorting it. I'm on my way to see him now. And this time I'm not backing down.'

Chapter 15

The day of the cricket match

Asha caught Cass's eye and gave him a double thumbs up. She had no idea if the boys were winning or losing but Cass was smiling so that had to be a good sign.

The first two Aberfal boys were already at the crease, but the bowler from the visiting school had an erratic style and the batsmen couldn't get on the end of a ball.

'What does that mean when he puts his arm out like that?' Asha asked Rose.

'It means it's wide. We get an extra run for that. Come on, Ryan!'

'Which one's Ryan? The one batting now?'

'Uh-huh.'

Asha had been hoping to see him. She'd wanted to speak to his parents, but Cass had begged her to stay out of it. He was certain that her intervention would only make things worse at a time when things had started to get better for him. Ryan was smaller than she'd expected him to be. Not that she condoned violence, but Cass could easily take him. How was it that some kids seemed to rise to the top and be able to command others? What set them apart? In Ryan's case it only appeared to be arrogance, unless he had some hidden power that Asha wasn't aware of.

'Where's Pippa?' Asha asked.

'Gone to the loo. I told her she should go and have it out with Newhall, point out how unreasonable it was for him to kick the boys out. Or, if not him, then at least confront Charles about it. If Mick kept that kind of stuff from me, I'd kill him.'

'Do you have any ideas where the money's gone? Does Charles gamble? Have a drug problem?'

'Charles Yardley?' Rose said, as if to check they were talking about the same person. 'He's a GP.'

'And?'

'He doesn't even drink. This is probably some huge misunderstanding and there's a delay in getting his money out because of, oh, I don't know, his shares tanking, or something.'

Rose started clapping as the next ball was hit. 'Seen Hinch anywhere?' she said.

'Yeah, he's . . .' Asha looked around, but the games teacher had disappeared. 'Actually, no. I don't know where's he got to.'

'Ollie has a cello lesson tonight, so Hinch needs to put him in to bat early. I already told him that, but Ollie doesn't even have his pads on. I'm going to head to the pavilion and see if he's helping himself to cake.'

There were more parents at the match than Asha had expected. And there appeared to be a decent level of support from the visiting school too. This is how it should be, she thought. It meant a lot to the kids that their parents

140

saw their catches and their game-winning shots. It mattered to them that they were the priority for one afternoon. But, realistically, how many parents could afford that kind of flexibility, let alone afford to travel to other schools to watch the away matches? There was a desire by most parents to be there for their children, but how many of them could?

When Asha and Cass first looked around the school, Mr Newhall had told her that Aberfal High would become the focus of her social life. Asha had smiled but doubted it very much. In fact, the very idea had horrified her. Yet, today she was here, feeling part of something bigger than herself, feeling privileged to be able to watch Cass with a smile on his face.

Asha noticed a woman standing apart from the other parents. At first, Asha assumed that she was with the other school, but she wasn't talking to any of those parents, either. The behaviour that caught Asha's eye was when she put her head in her hands as Ryan narrowly avoided being caught out. And now that Asha was watching, she saw that Ryan kept looking in that direction, too.

Keeping her eye on the match, Asha approached the attractive woman. She had a hard face. Beautiful. More of a wicked witch than a fairy princess.

Asha looked up as Ryan hit the ball for four and it bumped along the ground coming to a stop by a group of vocal parents, who shouted. 'Great shot, Ryan. Keep it up.'

She was standing by the woman now and said, 'Is Ryan your son?'

'Yes.'

Asha wasn't good at small talk. Pippa would have known what to say. Talking about children was usually safe ground. 'I'm Cass's mum,' she said. 'Asha.'

'Right.'

There was no spark of recognition. It was as if she'd never heard of Cass whereas Ryan was mentioned all the time. Ryan did *this*. Ryan said *that*. As soon as Cass got in the door, he had a tale about how Ryan wouldn't let him play football at lunchtime, or how Ryan stole his water bottle and left it on the roof of the science block. Or how Ryan told him that he was trash.

'Ryan's a very good cricketer,' said Asha. 'That was a lovely shot.'

For a moment, the other woman stayed silent. When she did speak it was in a low, almost inaudible voice. 'He should have hit a six.'

All around them people erupted into applause and Asha looked up to see the two boys leaving the crease and bumping fists with Cassius and one other boy.

'Oh,' said Asha. 'Do they only play for a certain number of overs then, instead of waiting to be bowled out?'

The other woman frowned at Asha as if she was criminally stupid. With Ryan's innings over, his eyes were searching for his mother, but she turned and walked away leaving both Ryan and Asha wondering what they'd done to disappoint her. For the first time, Asha didn't see Ryan as the monster making her son's life hell. She saw him as a little boy, desperate for approval.

Asha looked up at the headmaster's window as something caught her eye. Movement behind the glass. Two people, one of whom was Newhall, though she couldn't make out who was with him.

Bullies. Everywhere she looked. But the difference between Ryan and Mr Newhall was that Ryan was too young to know better. Mr Newhall didn't have that excuse.

Chapter 16

The evening after the cricket match

Pippa stood in her garden as the sun set on a day that would change the trajectory of the lives of everyone at Aberfal. The smell of charred meat and smoke clung to her clothes. Charles would usually be the one standing at the barbecue, blinking against the heat, but today he'd jumped straight in the shower when he got home, then shut himself away in his study. It had fallen to Pippa to stand over the dinner, making sure no one got food poisoning and that the sausages were the right side of charred.

When she finally sat down in the shade, she realised how much her ankle was hurting. It was swollen, but almost certainly not broken. She really should watch where she was going. All she'd been trying to do was get a word with Charles at the cricket match, but somehow had only succeeded in throwing herself at him and spilling her drink all over the place.

Pippa was so exhausted that all she wanted to do was lie on the ground and sleep for a week. Benny sat on one side of her, while Myles sat opposite. Charles was as far away from her as he could be while still sitting at the same table, but he may as well have been elsewhere.

Pippa was looking at the tableau, like she was one step removed from it all, wondering how many family meals they had left. Though Charles had said he wanted a divorce, he hadn't given a timescale. She'd half-expected him to move out already, but he was still here, which meant, deep down, he must still care for her. No one in their right mind would want to ruin what they had. Couldn't he see how lucky they were?

'And then did you see me bowl him out?' Benny asked.

'What was that, darling? Sorry, I was miles away.'

'I said, "Did you see me get that boy's wicket?". Smashed it.'

'Yes,' Pippa lied. 'I'm surprised you didn't hear me screaming for joy. Myles darling, don't eat all the halloumi.'

Benny thought they were having a barbecue to celebrate his victorious cricket match, but it had been planned days in advance to ease them into the weekend, to celebrate summer and to remind Charles that their family was too important to give up on.

'Shame Jerry couldn't make it,' Pippa said.

'Hmm?' Charles looked up from his phone.

'Jerry. Shame he couldn't come over tonight. Did you talk to him?'

'Of course I did,' he snapped. Charles wiped his hand over his face. 'Sorry. I, um. Yes, I spoke to him before the match started.'

'So why couldn't he?'

'Why couldn't he what?'

'Come. Tonight. Charles, are you okay? You don't seem yourself.'

'I've got a lot on my mind.'

Benny reached for another sausage, but Pippa passed him the salad. He waited for a second or two before taking it. He was a typical growing boy. It wasn't that he didn't like, or eat, vegetables but he would have a completely carnivorous diet if left to his own devices.

'Can I get you anything else, Charles? There are still some halloumi kebabs. If I were you, I'd take one before Myles eats them all.'

'Not so hungry,' he said.

'Too much cricket tea, I bet,' Pippa said, trying to keep the mood light.

'Did you tell Jerry how sorry I was?' she asked.

'Water under the bridge,' said Charles.

'I saw Gemma today at the match. She came and stood right next to me and didn't say a word. She's made it clear she wants nothing to do with me and I'm happy to follow her wishes. She was looking for Jerry. Odd that he didn't come out to watch the cricket.'

'I expect he was busy.'

'I expect so. Was he in with Hinch, do you know? He disappeared during the match and was nowhere to be seen when it ended. I heard from Rose that Jerry threatened him with the sack if he didn't start winning more sports fixtures. Hardly his fault though. He'd be able to sue the school for unfair dismissal, wouldn't he?'

Charles cleared his throat. 'Is this a conversation we should be having in front of the boys?'

'Sorry. I thought ...' But she didn't know what she thought. All she knew was that her once certain future was lost. That she'd made a mess of everything. That the man

146

she loved didn't love her back. The worst five words in the English language had to be 'I don't love you anymore'.

Pippa sliced her chicken breast into bite-sized pieces, then cut them in half again, for something to do. Benny and Myles were talking with their mouths full. Laughing about Dr Grant throwing a bin at Matty Morrison for being a 'blithering idiot'. Dr Grant had an unorthodox style of teaching and, though Pippa had spoken to Jerry Newhall about it when Myles had first started at Aberfal, his results were among the best in the school. And Jerry was right. The boys loved him and his old-fashioned ways.

'Charles, do you need a drink?' Pippa asked. 'I've still got some of that cordial if you want?'

Charles shook his head. 'Talking of which,' he said. 'My shirt is in the boot of the car. See if you can get the stains out, will you? That blackcurrant cordial went everywhere.'

Pippa looked at him. Just looked at him.

'Of course,' she said. 'I'd forgotten about that. I'll get on it tomorrow.' She hardly had the energy to pick up her knife and fork and her ankle was still throbbing. It had been a trying day.

Charles sighed. 'I'd rather you did it today before it stains. After all, it was your fault. Is that too much to ask?'

'Actually, Charles, yes. Yes, it is.' Three heads turned to face her, conversations stopping. 'I'm sure you've noticed the washing machine. It's the big white thing in the utility room. There are stain removers under the sink if you're that bothered. I'm going to get myself another drink.'

She pushed herself up from the table as Charles's phone began to ring. He watched the display but didn't answer it.

'Why's Miss Lane calling?' Myles asked, glancing over.

Charles shrugged and declined the call. 'School business, no doubt. But I've earned the weekend off.'

As Pippa hobbled into the kitchen, she heard Charles's phone chime to indicate that Katy Lane had left a voice message. Pippa knew he wouldn't be able to resist listening to it. He was one of those people who could never ignore anything. Especially if it was something to do with the school.

Pippa opened the fridge. She'd bought a box of wine from the supermarket rather than a bottle. This served a dual purpose. Firstly, it was a lot cheaper and, secondly, boxes of wine took away the opportunity for judgement. No one would be able to tell her, pointedly, that she'd had the best part of a bottle now. It was anyone's guess how much she'd had to drink.

As she closed the fridge door and turned, she saw Charles's frame blocking the door. His arms were hanging by his side. He looked so pale in that moment. So vulnerable. Sick.

'Well?' Pippa said.

'That was Katy Lane.'

The look on Charles's face was enough to make Pippa steady herself against the wall. 'What did she want?'

'She wanted to, um, let me know that,' he took a deep breath. 'Jerry Newhall is dead.'

Clare Withoutani: OMFG have you heard about Newhall?!!!

Becky Rupertsmum: Helen-Louise just texted. Can't believe it.

Asha: Not heard anything. What's happened?

Pam Geoffreysmum: What's he done this time? They're going co-ed, aren't they? I knew this would happen. I said to Bruce the other day that we're off as soon as they make it co-ed.

Clare Withoutani: Can't believe it, Becky. I'm in shock.

Pam Geoffreysmum: Are we going co-ed?

Becky Rupertsmum: No, Pam. Newhall died.

Pam Geoffreysmum: Not funny, Rebecca.

Clare Withoutani: No joke, Pam. They found him dead in his office last night.

Asha: Christ! How did he die?

Sarah Teddysmum: Noooooo! That's terrible. I can't believe it.

Clare Withoutani: I heard he was due to retire next year due to heart probs? I'm guessing that's what killed him? HL didn't know for sure.

Pam Geoffreysmum: Oh GOD. Seriously??!! Can't believe it. So sad. He'll be such a loss to the school. The boys will be devastated. Will the school be offering grief counselling?

Rose Oliversmum: Anyone know what pages they're meant to do for chemistry? Ollie's homework diary says 'do questions 1-4' but no page numbers!

Rose Oliversmum: Shit. Sorry. Just read the thread. That's terrible. Fuck.

Pam Geoffreysmum: That poor man. And to think he died all alone. What about his wife? That poor woman. Didn't have kids though, did he?

Clare Withoutani: Nope. I always thought it was odd that someone who didn't want kids would become a teacher.

Becky Rupertsmum: Prob did want kids B4 he became a teacher and they put him off. LOL.

Becky Rupertsmum: Not that any of this is funny. Obvs. Trying to lighten the mood.

Chapter 17

Six days after Jerry's death

Thursday afternoon and, though it was a little early for school pick-up, there was already quite the crowd primed for gossip and intrigue. Parents bartering for titbits. Asha took her place in the shade of the tree where she could see everything while remaining hidden. There was a police car in the car park and it couldn't have stuck out any more if it had had its siren blaring.

On a normal day, the parents would wait in their cars for the boys to come out while they checked emails and made calls to let people know that they were still working, still relevant. But, today, the need to talk to other parents was greater. They wanted to know that there was nothing to worry about, that their boys weren't in any danger, despite the police being there. Despite them losing a man who had been a constant in their lives.

'Have you heard?' they asked in hushed voices. 'They're saying it was murder.' And they gave their opinions – for what they were worth – that the rival school were responsible. A games teacher from St Francis's sneaking in and strangling poor, poor Jerry with a school tie. Never underestimate a bad loser they said.

And while they were at it, they'd never trusted Jerry's wife either. She was at the match on Friday and she *never* came to the school matches. Was it true that he'd been having an affair with one of the school mums? And someone had heard Hinch threaten to hit Mr Newhall at the open day and wouldn't be surprised if he'd been suspended by now.

The boys were old enough to find their own way home but very few of them lived within walking distance. It helped the parents as much as it helped the boys because, for a little bit longer, they could pretend they were indispensable. It was difficult to make friends with other parents as your children got older. You no longer had to stay around at parties, nor sit next to other parents at the nativity play, or act as an intermediary for play dates.

Asha listened as people passed gossip from one ear to another. *Poisoned*, they said. *Suffocated*. The police still hadn't confirmed how Newhall had died and so guesses became baseless rumour. Ignorance became bliss. Mr Newhall became a plastic piece in a game of Cluedo. The headmaster, in the study, with the candlestick.

The gossip was all around the school, but no one could trace it back to its source. There'd been nothing in the local news, nothing official from the deputy head, nor the chair of governors and yet everyone was saying that the best headmaster in the school's celebrated history was murdered in his office while the rest of them cheered their sons to victory.

Everyone who'd been at the cricket match last Friday afternoon had to give a statement about what they remembered, no matter how small or insignificant it seemed, but Asha had cancelled her appointment twice now. Childcare issues, she'd said. Work. But she couldn't put it off any longer, not if what they were saying was true.

Murder. Asha almost laughed at the absurdity of it. Wanted to say, 'Well, I've heard everything now.'

Here, of all places.

Him, of all people.

The other parents spoke about Jerry as if they'd seen him walking on water before turning it into a fine merlot. Asha glanced towards the school to see if any boys were coming out yet and caught two women watching her. They covered their mouths, lowered their eyes, but they couldn't have made it any more obvious that she was the subject of their conversation. Ahead of her, Rose and Becky were talking to Helen-Louise. They were looking far too happy to be discussing the death of a man who, according to all sources, was the pride of the school. Had they stopped to consider what this meant? The only thing on Asha's mind now was that someone at this school – possibly someone she knew – was a killer. This was when the outsiders would get noticed. People like her, who didn't dress the same as everyone else. People like Gemma Newhall who didn't live for the school like her husband had.

Strange how one event can change everything. The turrets and the stone archways which had previously looked like Hogwarts now looked more like Amityville. The ivy that crawled around the first-floor windows without blocking out the light now looked like it was choking the bricks.

The main building, the oldest part of the school, was symmetrical but, over the years, state of the art science labs and gyms were added giving a Frankenstein's monster feel. The school motto above the main door had faded to a memory, but Asha knew it well from the stitching on Cass's blazer.

Non ducor, duco.

I am not led, I lead.

This school prided itself on excellence. It was almost impossible to fathom that there could be a murder. Here. Unless it was an exceptional murder. A perfect murder. Worthy of Marple or Poirot. Because if Aberfal High was going to do something, it was going to be the best at it. Asha imagined Mr Newhall's death as a footnote in the prospectus. The best murder in the southwest.

The doors opened and the first two boys came out. Bags slung over shoulders; hands pushed into pockets. The parents started edging forwards so that their children would see them when they emerged into the sunlight, but these two were heading towards the waiting school buses.

Asha thought she heard the man in front of her say the words *'tattoos'* and *'scholarship'* and *'Well, I wouldn't be surprised'*.

Asha cleared her throat, but when he looked at her, he didn't seem at all embarrassed. He gave a tight smile and turned away. Asha knew that she didn't fit in with the other parents, though she tried not to care. It only bothered her when she thought that Cass was being bullied because she didn't fit the mould of an Aberfal High mother.

Becky broke off from the huddle of mothers to collect her son, Rupert.

'Good day?' she asked him.

He bent his head to say something to the boy next to him who laughed and ran off. Rupert took chase.

Becky spotted Asha and sighed. 'You'd think they'd be worn out by now, wouldn't you?'

'We were the same at that age.'

'True.'

'I don't suppose you've heard anything else about Newhall, have you?' Asha asked.

'Well, now you mention it, Helen-Louise did have some interesting information,' she said with a hint of glee to her voice. 'But you know how I hate to spread rumours.'

'Of course. No. I only wondered if—'

'So, according to Helen-Louise,' Becky looked over her shoulder and leaned in closer to Asha. 'It was definitely murder. The school have pulled some strings to keep it out of the news. Don't want it to affect admissions. Anyway, they still haven't said exactly how he died, or what the murder weapon is. My guess is that they're holding back that information so they can trip up the killer in an interview. But it happened sometime between three thirty and four thirty. So, basically, while we were outside his office window and Mandy was outside his office door. It's quite the mystery.'

'Christ. Mandy's got to be the prime suspect, then. Unless she can prove she had an alibi.'

'Well, that's where it gets interesting. Mandy says she didn't leave her desk all afternoon. According to

155

Helen-Louise – and this is *entre nous* – the murderer got in and out through the office window.'

Asha looked up to the first-floor windows on this side of the school.

'But it's, what, twenty feet off the ground? I mean, you'd assume Mandy was lying about being at her desk all afternoon before you'd suspect Spiderman of climbing up the walls.'

'I know! But when they found poor Jerry, the window was wide open and the bushes underneath were all crushed and broken down. They found traces of blood in the rhododendrons.'

'I don't think . . . I mean, wouldn't we have seen someone climbing out of the window?'

'What about when we were distracted chasing down Gemma's dog? I'll leave it to you to draw your own conclusions, but I will say that it's strange that she'd turned up to school and creates the mother of all alibis while someone murders her husband. Anyway, I'm only repeating what Helen-Louise told me.'

More boys were coming out of the school and parents were peeling off to go with them. There was still no sign of Cass.

Asha shook her head. 'It would have to be someone quite agile to get in and out of that window though. That's if Gemma was plotting with someone else.'

'What, like the absent games teacher?'

'Maybe. But I think the person with easy access to Newhall is the obvious suspect.'

'You mean Mandy?' Becky asked.

'Who else?'

'She's tiny. How could she strangle Jerry?'

'Is that what they're saying? That he was strangled?'

'It's one of the rumours. But, anyway, you're missing the obvious suspect.' Becky raised her eyebrows and looked pointedly at Asha as if willing her to catch up.

Asha shook her head again.

'The Cake Incident,' Becky said.

It was all anyone had to say. The Cake Incident had become an event in its own right.

'You don't think—'

'She wasn't there when the dog slipped its collar. And look,' said Becky peering down the driveway. 'Here she is now.'

Asha turned to see Pippa leaning on a walking stick.

'With that limp,' continued Becky. 'From "twisting her ankle" at the cricket match.'

'That's the most ridiculous thing you've ever said,' Asha countered. 'You can't believe that Pippa had anything to do with it.'

'Well, I don't believe she twisted that ankle by stepping in a hole on the lawns. There are no holes. Otis Blake would never allow it. You can say what you like about that man, but he knows how to look after the school grounds. Like you say, it would take someone strong and sporty to get out of that window *without* an injury. I think she misjudged that drop from Jerry's office. All I know is that Jerry and Gemma used to holiday with Charles and Pippa but there was a huge falling out. Maybe the falling out wasn't with Gemma, just her husband. Perhaps the two of them remained tight and plotted this together.'

Asha shrugged. 'They didn't seem friendly at the cricket match.'

'And if they were in cahoots, that's exactly what they'd want you to think.'

Chapter 18

A week after Jerry's death

Katy saw the email as soon as she logged on to her laptop at first break, but she'd waited for a time when she could study it without distractions. She'd broken her own rule about ignoring them and was now back to scanning for clues. For a spelling mistake. Any mistake. The first thing she noticed was a change in tone. This one was more menacing.

Her lunchbox lay open, sandwiches untouched. Cream cheese and roasted vegetables going to waste, but her stomach was too full of fear and self-loathing. The other staff ate with the children in the canteen, but Katy needed a parcel of time when she didn't have to talk to other people, smile or deal with their problems. She still wasn't used to sitting at Jerry's desk, in Jerry's chair, in the place where Jerry had died. But it was symbolic and Katy had to show everyone that she was in control and that she wasn't afraid of ghosts.

She peered again at her computer screen. The email address was a jumble of letters and numbers with no pattern and no meaning. She kept looking at it, though, as if it was a riddle she could solve. She wouldn't engage. Mustn't engage. But she leaned in closer to the computer screen as if she could see all the way to the fingers of the sender. No 'Hello', no 'Kind regards'. Straight to the point.

ADMIT WHAT YOU'VE DONE BEFORE THE BALL OR YOU WILL PAY.

So, that was new. The addition of a time frame made this more worrying. Maybe they did have a plan after all. It was sent at eight minutes past nine. She wondered whether the time was significant. Thinking back to this morning, she'd been sitting on the stage and looking out into the crowd and there'd been a full hall. Teachers at the end of the rows. No one absent.

'What to do. What to do,' Katy muttered.

She tapped her fingernails on the walnut desk. *Tap tap tap.*

She couldn't sit here and do nothing, but she was clean out of options. She could ask Mrs Townsend, the IT teacher, to investigate the email address. There were ways to track these things, weren't there? But Mrs Townsend might ask questions that Katy didn't want to answer and, of course, there was a chance that she could be wrong. Another possibility was that this email was from Otis Blake, seeing as he was the one who'd caught her in the summer house. But why would he wait until now and why would he care? It didn't affect him personally.

Was it a parent trying to scare her? Because the emails might not even be about the kiss. It was no secret that they didn't think she was up to the job and they were annoyed that the school had closed for three days. She'd taken the decision to open the school as usual from the Thursday after the murder. The decision had been down to the governors. If it was up to her, she'd have stayed closed for a week at least. Preferably until the police had caught Jerry's killer.

Even on that first Monday after Jerry's death, Katy had received twenty-three emails of concern from parents. Not concern for Jerry Newhall's wife nor his friends and colleagues, but concern for the number of days of education that would be lost if the school stayed closed for longer than was necessary. That was the problem with a private school. The parents thought that, by paying fees, they deserved a greater say in how it was run. Technically, they were paying your wages and treated you as such. Forget about the children being bullies – where did they learn this behaviour from?

'Will we get a refund?' they asked.

'Does the school understand we have to go to work to pay these extortionate fees?'

'It's impossible to organise childcare at such late notice,' they chided.

And, while they were at it, *'Any idea who'll be taking over from Mr Newhall? I do hope it won't disrupt the boys' education.'*

Of course, the parents opened and closed their emails with condolences and declarations of shock and dismay, but what it boiled down to was . . . were they getting value for their hard-earned money? Katy understood where they were coming from. It was a lot of money to pay for something that, if you stopped to think about it, was offered for free all over the country. None of the parents wanted to look like fools. And none of them wanted their friends' kids, who went to the local comprehensive, to get better grades than *Junior*.

161

Katy rubbed her forehead; she knew she was being unfair. The supportive parents far outweighed the awkward ones. She'd had several messages of encouragement and offers of assistance. There was a group of parents who'd already volunteered to organise fundraising to commemorate Mr Newhall's life in some way. There had been talk of cancelling the summer ball, but Katy had decided that it would do them all good to have something positive to focus on. A distraction. It had only been a week, but people were starting to ask why the police hadn't arrested anyone.

The door swung open and Mandy appeared. 'Do you need anything, Miss Lane? Only, I thought I could grab lunch?'

Katy tried to give off an air of nonchalance. 'Yes. Of course. But, before you do, could I have a word?'

'Is there a problem?' Mandy asked.

'No.'

'Good.'

Mandy stepped into the room, letting the door close behind her.

'Well . . .'

'Oh.'

'Mr Newhall,' Katy said. 'That day that he . . . you know.' Mandy visibly tensed up. 'What about it?'

'Do you know why Mr Newhall opened the windows?'

'Must've got hot,' Mandy said.

'Yes. It does get the sunshine in the afternoon, doesn't it? Still, I remember him telling me that those windows were impossible to close again.'

Someone had managed to get them closed now, though, and they rattled in their frames with every gust of wind.

There was silence for a moment while Katy thought it through.

'Maybe it wasn't Mr Newhall who opened them,' Mandy said. 'The killer wouldn't have known, or cared, that they're a problem.'

'True. But it doesn't sit right with me. I feel like I'm missing something.'

'For what it's worth,' said Mandy, 'I think it was probably Gemma. It's usually the spouse in these cases, isn't it? My husband would've killed me if I hadn't left him when I did.' She wiped her eyes with the back of her hand, even though there were no tears. 'Sorry. But it's all so—'

'I know,' Katy said. She didn't know if she was meant to comfort the other woman. They didn't have the kind of relationship where hugs were exchanged, but she felt compelled to do something. Katy was getting up from her chair when Mandy shook her head and coughed.

'Anyway. My best guess is, whoever it was, slipped in when I was away from my desk and left through the window when I was back. It's the only thing that makes sense.'

Katy walked over to the window. 'Do you think so? None of it makes any sense to me.' From here, the drop didn't look far. She thought she could make it without serious injury.

When she'd thought about becoming head of Aberfal High, Katy hadn't expected to be trying to solve a murder in her first week, nor trying to get to the bottom of who was threatening her. She wondered if the two things were linked. Had Jerry received emails, too? Had they asked him to come clean about his addiction problem? Had they killed him because he refused to do what they asked? Katy put her fingers to her lips. Would they kill her if she didn't reveal her darkest secrets by the ball?

'Okay, Mandy. Thank you. You can go.' She heard the door open, but when it didn't close again Katy turned around. Mandy was standing there with a look of intense concentration on her face.

'Now I'm thinking about it,' said Mandy, 'if I was Gemma, I wouldn't have killed him here where there were all these witnesses. They live on a farm, right? I'd have made sure he fell into farm machinery, or put poison in his porridge, somewhere where there was just the two of us.'

'Perhaps she was so angry she didn't care who caught her.'

'It's not about being caught, it's so that there's no one about to call an ambulance or save him. Anyway, I'll grab some lunch now. Want anything?'

'Um. No. Thanks.'

Katy shook her head and rubbed her eyes behind her glasses. She went back to her laptop and looked again at the email. She considered responding to ask them what she should be admitting to. There were so many things she was guilty of and she seemed to add to the list every day. Maybe what had started as emails about her little indiscretion had morphed into something more. If they were watching her, then they might've seen what she'd done after the cricket match. Was that why the emails had intensified?

Katy could have sworn that no one knew what she'd done on the day that Jerry died. She'd been alone, only her car and Newhall's in the car park, and she'd been so careful. Everyone else had left for the day.

The police had combed the grounds for evidence, for a murder weapon, or anything that could lead them to the killer. They'd found traces of Jerry's blood on the trampled bushes below his office and assumed that the killer had made their getaway through the open window. While they waited for the results of the post-mortem the police could only guess. But then the gossip started about how Jerry died and how the murderer was someone at the school. And Katy couldn't tell the police what she knew. Not without implicating herself. Because Katy knew exactly how Jerry had died.

Because Katy had been the one to dispose of the murder weapon.

The only problem was, it wasn't where she'd left it.

Clare Withoutani: I heard that the police still haven't found the murder weapon but my friend's husband is a journo and says they're checking the cleaners' equipment for blood in case they hit him with it?!

Rose Oliversmum: I heard the killer jumped out of the window. We would've noticed someone running across the cricket pitch, dragging a Henry Hoover behind them!!

Becky Rupertsmum: Rumour among the kids is that Mr N met his untimely end at the hands of one of the ghosts that live in the lake. A boy who drowned is wandering the halls looking for vengeance!! 👻

Rose Oliversmum: What do they teach them at this school? Ollie told me the ghost theory too!

Clare Withoutani: I suppose the next step is to search the lake. Wonder how many dead bodies they'll find?

Asha: Sorry to change the subject but I don't suppose anyone has seen Cass's cricket bat? It didn't come home after the match on Friday. What with one thing and another I didn't notice. It's not named but it's . . . bat shaped? I think it's Kookaburra. Green on the top. So far this year we've lost three socks, two ties, a pair of brand-new trainers and a coat. What's he doing with them?

Rose Oliversmum: Tell me about it. We lost a hockey stick and now we've 'misplaced' his cricket whites, but I don't think we'll be playing cricket again this season. The very thought of watching cricket again gives me PTSD.

Sarah Teddysmum: Sorry, Asha. Checked and we've only got Teddy's here. I'm sure it will turn up.

Pam Geoffreysmum: Have you looked in lost property?

Rose Oliversmum: FFS Pam. What would we do without you pointing out the bloody obvious all the time? Who fancies meeting up at mine on Saturday night for drinkies?

Pam Geoffreysmum: Need I remind you that a man has died. I hardly think a party is appropriate.

Rose Oliversmum: No offence, Pam, but wind your neck in. I can't think of a better reason to get shit-faced. We've all been through hell this past week.

Pam Geoffreysmum left

Rose Oliversmum: Another one bites the dust.

Chapter 19

The day of the cricket match

Growing up, Asha didn't have a pet. No dogs, no cats, not even a gerbil. She would never have asked her mum for anything like that. Cass did though. All the time. He wanted a puppy with floppy ears and a tongue that didn't quite fit in its mouth. But Asha knew two things. Firstly, pets became family. But better. They were loyal. Ever present. A love like that would break her when the pet got sick or died.

Secondly, she knew that they couldn't move at a moment's notice if they were waiting for a wandering cat to come home. They couldn't board the next plane if there was a dog to consider. Cass saw a dog as a best friend in the making, something that would add a fun dimension to their family. Asha only saw obligation.

Gemma's dog, Biffy, well, there was no point in denying that she was cute. Especially as she tore across the cricket pitch with a ball in her mouth followed closely by Gemma shouting, 'Come back here, you little bugger!'

The children laughed as the parents patted their knees. 'Here, Biffy.' Making half-hearted lunges as she passed by. Otis marched onto the pitch grumbling, 'If that beast pees on my lawn . . .' And Rose stepped behind Asha as Biffy barrelled towards them. 'Keep that thing away from me.'

Asha lowered herself onto the grass, accepting wet-nosed introductions and fervent tail-wags as Biffy stepped all over her, dropping the cricket ball into Asha's lap. She slipped her fingers under Biffy's collar, but the pup was in no rush to move on now she'd found such lickable ears.

'Hey there, Biffy,' Asha said. 'Aren't you gorgeous?'

'She's a right royal pain in my backside,' said Gemma Newhall between gasps as she caught up to them. She was holding half a lead in her hand. 'Look at this! Chewed right through it.'

Asha rubbed Biffy's ears as Gemma knotted the lead through the collar.

'You're hurt,' Asha said pointing at Gemma's hand.

Gemma wiped the blood off her thumb. 'It's nothing.'

'Have you cut yourself?'

'Biffy's teething. Likes to have a good old chew. That's all.'

Asha got to her feet. Biffy, still trying to get to Asha's ears, reached up on her hind legs.

'Down, Biffy. Down!'

'It's okay,' said Asha. 'I don't mind.'

'Well, I do. She needs discipline.' Gemma yanked on the lead and Biffy dropped down and circled. 'Well, now that we've embarrassed ourselves, it's time we were off.'

Gemma said her goodbyes and dragged Biffy away while the boys got back in position for the next innings. No one was sure of the score but there was a general feeling that it was all going Aberfal's way.

Asha heard someone behind her and turned to see Charles Yardley standing there.

'Hi. Where did you spring up from?'

'I've been here a while.'

'Have you?'

Asha hadn't spoken to Charles since their run-in at the open day. Her past was never far from the surface and she'd always had a sharp tongue in times of extreme stress or vulnerability. She wasn't above saying sorry – not viewing it as the come-down that some people did – but she wasn't as apologetic as she could be. She still didn't think the school had acted quickly enough when they realised that Cass was missing. And she was certain that the school hadn't acted quickly enough when she'd brought the bullying to their attention. And, as a representative of this school and a father, Charles Yardley should have done more.

There was a cheer as one of the boys got a bat to the cricket ball. It fell short of the boundary and a slight boy from St Francis's gave chase as it bumped across the ground. Charles moved with it, slipping around the perimeter away from Asha.

'Four!' called Rose as she started waving her arm from side to side in front of her like some well-practised dance. Asha clapped and smiled. Even offered up a lacklustre 'Yay!'

As the cheers died down and companionable chatter started up again, Asha stepped towards Charles. He bent his head over his sleeve and rubbed at a mark on his cuff. She wondered whether she should say something. She could explain how scared she'd been that day, though scared hardly seemed the right word for it now. Terrified. Petrified. Even those words didn't seem strong enough to convey the sickening feeling of dread and panic that had made her breath shallow and her pulse quicken. Even now, she felt a thudding in her chest when she thought about that lake.

'Charles, there you are!' Pippa came rushing towards him, drink in hand, and Asha's opportunity to speak to Charles disappeared.

As she got closer, Pippa stumbled. Her ankle twisted beneath her and she tripped.

'Watch it!' Charles said catching her and pushing her upright. He pulled at his shirt where Pippa's drink had spilled.

Pippa looked at the ground behind her, then said, 'Sorry, did I get you?' She winced as she tried to put the weight on her ankle.

Charles looked down at his shirt. 'What *is* that? Is it blackcurrant?'

'I've done my ankle.'

'Lord, that'll stain.'

'I need to talk to you, Charles. Can we go somewhere?'

'You're a liability at times.'

Asha watched. Couldn't look away if she tried.

'Charles!' Pippa said. 'Have you been drinking? You smell like a—'

'This isn't the time.'

'It never is.'

Charles grabbed Pippa's wrist with lightning speed and they stared at each other. 'This. Isn't. The time.'

Asha walked over before the situation could escalate. 'Hey. Great game, isn't it? Am I right in thinking we're winning, Charles? I can't quite follow the scoring system, but the boys seem to be happy. But then, who wouldn't be smiling on a day like today?'

Charles turned to her and dropped Pippa's arm. He'd already composed himself and had the beginning of a smile on his face.

'Yes, we are doing rather well. Hinch will be delighted if we can pull this off. Cassius is having a great match, isn't he?'

Pippa's smile wasn't as convincing. 'Benny would love to beat St Francis's. They gave them quite the beating in last term's hockey. Do you remember, Charles?'

Rose came up behind Asha and threaded an arm through hers. 'What are we talking about?'

Pippa hadn't taken her eyes off Charles. She was swaying like tall grass in a faint breeze.

'Just saying what a great game this is,' said Asha.

'Yes,' said Charles. 'Great game. Unfortunately, my wife has decided to cover me in her drink. Would you excuse me while I go and get cleaned up?'

He began to walk away but Pippa called after him. 'Charles!'

'What?'

'I, um,' she stammered. 'There are clean shirts in the boot of my car. Here.' She threw him a set of keys from the front pocket of her handbag. He walked away without thanking her.

Awkwardness remained in the spot where Charles had been standing and Asha struggled to find something to say. Rose, however, had no such difficulties.

'Christ alive, Pippa. I don't know how you haven't slapped him by now. First there's the whole money thing and then there's the way he talks to you. He should be grovelling at your feet instead of asking for a divorce.'

Pippa looked at the floor. 'I'm sure he doesn't mean it.'

Asha and Rose looked at each other. It was hard to know when to push and when to accept it was none of your business.

'Asha,' Pippa said, 'I've been meaning to ask if Cass is okay. You know, with the bullying and whatnot. I'm so sorry I haven't checked before, but this week . . . well, you know how it is.'

'That's okay,' Asha said. 'Katy Lane is the new anti-bullying ambassador so I've got to talk to her about the whole situation. Actually' – she stood up on tiptoes to look over the heads of the parents by the pavilion – 'I've been looking for her. I don't suppose you know where she is, do you?'

Pippa shook her head. 'She has a class on Friday afternoon, but she'll be out as soon as the bell goes. Do you need her desperately?'

Asha tucked her hair behind one ear and folded her arms. 'It can wait.'

'Do you mind if I lean on you, darling? I seem to have sprained my ankle.'

A soft, coordinated moan came from the parents and, as Asha looked towards the batters, Benny had his head down and the wicket keeper had his head – and his hands – up. The cricket stumps were tilted at odd angles. Pippa grimaced. 'He won't like that. He's so much like his father. Hates it when things don't go his way.'

They stood and watched the rest of the match, applauding at the right moments, cheering at balls bouncing across the ground. More teachers were outside now, scenting victory in the air. Triumph by association was intoxicating. The Aberfal boys were getting louder and, as though there was a finite amount of noise to go around, St Francis's school got quieter.

And then, in what seemed like an instant, hands were being shaken and backs patted and Rose dashed off to get Ollie to his cello lesson.

'Good game,' the boys said.

'Well played.'

It was a glimpse of the young men they were becoming. Asha watched Cass as he patted shoulders, nodded respectfully. Every time she wondered if this was the right school for him, she saw how he was developing and couldn't imagine sending him anywhere else.

'Shall I get us a cup of tea?' asked Pippa. 'The boys will be a while yet getting their kit together.'

Cass caught Asha's eye and waved. It was the biggest smile she'd seen on his face in weeks. 'Yes,' she said. 'That'd be great.'

The boys were all crowding into the thatched pavilion for sandwiches and cake while the parents chatted, congratulating each other on their children's performances as if they'd played a part in the victory.

'Has anyone seen Hinch?' Rose asked, stepping between Asha and Pippa and throwing her arms over both women's shoulders. 'The changing rooms are still locked and we need to dash.'

'Nope,' Asha said. 'Everyone seems to have disappeared. I haven't seen Newhall, or Katy Lane either.'

'Or Charles,' said Pippa.

'Sounds like there's a party somewhere that we're not invited to,' laughed Rose. 'I bet they're all in Newhall's office drinking G&T while we're out here drinking weak tea in paper cups.'

Asha could imagine them looking down on the rest of them.

'Oh, hello,' said Rose. 'Look who's here.'

Asha was turning her head as Rose said, 'Don't look.'

'Look. Don't look. Make up your mind.'

'He's been hanging around all afternoon,' said Pippa. 'I know Miss Lane wants him gone but I've always found him to be quite lovely to look at.'

Otis Blake was wearing shorts but no top. He looked more like an athlete than a gardener. There was the hint of paler skin above the waistband of his shorts, but his torso was smooth and brown.

'Katy Lane will flip her lid,' Rose said. 'She keeps telling him to keep his clothes on, but she'll get no support from me on that one. Christ alive, look at him! He can tend to my borders any day of the week.'

Asha shook her head. 'Rose! Don't!'

'Every time I look at his shirtless back, I get a twinge in my nether regions.'

Asha put her hand over her eyes, but Rose wasn't finished.

'A minge twinge.'

'Please stop,' Asha groaned.

'A fanny flutter.'

'You're the worst,' Asha said.

Pippa started walking backwards, away from them. 'Sorry, darlings, I'd better go and see what's keeping Charles,' she said. 'Have a lovely weekend.'

She was limping and grimaced as she walked. She motioned to Benny who was sitting in the shade of a tree with his teammates, but hardly changed course.

'Oops. Do you think I offended her?' asked Rose.

'I'm pretty sure she's used to you by now. But she's obviously got a lot going on. This thing with Charles and the money . . .'

'I know. But great leverage for her.'

'Come again?'

'When Mick messes up there's always a piece of jewellery in it for me, or a holiday. Pippa could milk this for anything she wants.'

'I doubt it. He wants a divorce so he's hardly going to try and make it up to her.'

'Exactly. And if he wants anything more than the clothes he's standing in he'd better start treating her like a queen. He doesn't have a leg to stand on.'

They both watched Pippa as she paused with a hand on the pavilion wall and waited for Benny to catch up. She was looking up at Mr Newhall's office.

Asha glanced at the window too but, though she squinted, she couldn't make out what had caught Pippa's eye. She thought she saw someone moving around, but the sun glinted off the glass and made it difficult for her to see exactly who was there. By the time she looked where Pippa had been standing, she was gone and, when Asha turned back, so was the figure at the window. But now, the window was wide open.

WITNESS FIVE

Pippa Yardley.
Wife of Charles.
Mother of Myles and Benny Yardley.

Right. Yes. The cricket had already started when I got to the school, so I suppose it would be about twenty past two or thereabouts. I was delayed at the dry cleaners picking up my husband's shirts, but you don't need to know that, do you? My husband, Charles, was already at Aberfal. He'd gone straight from the surgery. He's a GP but he doesn't work Friday afternoons. Perks of being a partner, I suppose.

He was talking to some of the parents from the visiting school on the other side of the pitch for most of the afternoon and I was with Rose and Asha. That's Rose Entwistle and Asha Demetriou. Do you need me to spell that for you? Right. Okay.

We chatted and watched the boys. Nothing noteworthy until Jerry's wife, Gemma, turned up as we started our innings. We talked for about five minutes. Ten? And then she went to go and say good-bye to Jerry. She came out maybe fifteen minutes later and, well . . . Sorry, what was the question again?

Right. No, I didn't notice anything strange. The only time I was away from the cricket was when I popped to the bathroom. I don't recall talking to anyone on the way. Wait. No, I did. The grounds-man. Otis Blake. He was half working and half watching the match from behind the pavilion. We talked about the big tom cat that seems to live in the grounds. It had been making a mess of his borders. He was pruning the rhododendron bushes. Or at least pretending to.

179

I can tell, by the way that you're looking at me, that you already know about my little altercation with Jerry at the school open day. Yes, I threw a cake at him. I overreacted a teensy little bit but there wasn't any bad blood between us, or anything. Jerry gave as good as he got. He'd just played a joke on me, actually. Right before I . . . Look, if you'd have been there, you'd have seen that there was no malice. I hardly even remember the incident. I was distracted. A lot on my mind.

The day started off with us discovering that Charles's car had been vandalised. And given that money is a little tight since I gave up work, well it's the last thing we needed. But more than that, the person who did it was outside our home. My house is my sanctuary. My safe place. It unsettled me but Charles brushed it off, said he had an idea who it was. A disgruntled patient or something. But I didn't like the fact that they knew where we lived. I was already on edge by the time we got to the school and then Cassius went missing. It's a parent's worst nightmare, isn't it? But Jerry didn't seem worried. He shrugged it off like it was nothing. Cracking jokes like he didn't have a care in the world.

Look, obviously, this looks bad. One week I'm throwing cakes at him and the next, he's dead. But what would I gain from killing him?

And, yes, we're late paying the school fees but, before you jump to conclusions, it's hardly something Charles or I would lose our heads over. We hadn't considered how much we relied on my income. At least, *I* hadn't. I knew that we would have to cut back on spends and that we wouldn't be able to take the kind of holidays we'd been used to but . . . Okay, if I'm honest, I thought Jerry should have been a bit more understanding because Charles gives his time for free as chair of governors, I help organise events and fundraisers and my children . . . at the risk of sounding like I'm boasting, my children make that school look good. Did Jerry think he'd get that many admissions if it wasn't for my boys?

But what would be the point of having it out with Jerry? The person I needed to talk to was my husband. It wasn't Jerry's fault, it was Charles's. After all, it was Charles who'd failed to pay the school fees. And, if I'm honest with you, Detective, I still don't understand why.

Chapter 20

Eleven days after Jerry's death

The supermarket was cold and far too dark and it took a moment for Pippa to realise she was still wearing her sunglasses. And once she'd remembered her glasses, she'd forgotten what she'd come into the shop for. She hung onto her trolley like it was the only thing keeping her upright. She gripped it until her knuckles went white and her hands began to shake.

A voice behind her said, 'Excuse me. Can I reach past?'

Pippa jumped. 'Sorry. Yes. Just let me . . .' She picked up a pack of Pink Lady apples that she didn't want and pushed her trolley forwards. Nowadays she was always apologising. She was the kind of person who would apologise if someone walked into her. She said *sorry* to inanimate objects like bollards, or chairs, but never had she had so much to feel sorry about. Jerry was dead. The school fees hadn't been paid. And Charles wanted a divorce. It was a sorry situation.

There was no way to put a good spin on it; Pippa's life would never be the same again. She worried about what she would do for money. How could she get a job when even the smallest exertion left her breathless and the slightest setback left her in tears or gripped by fury.

Katy Lane had agreed a payment plan for them to pay off this term's fees over several months, but it didn't change anything in the long run. Charles would only commit to one more year of schooling. Once Myles had taken his GCSEs, they'd be done with Aberfal High. It wouldn't be the same without Jerry anyway.

Charles reasoned that the divorce would cost them money, even if it was amicable and, because he wasn't a callous man, he would continue to pay for the mortgage as well as getting himself a little place somewhere nearby. He wasn't made of money. There was no way he could afford two lots of school fees on top of two mortgages. Surely, she could see that.

She felt as if she hadn't slept a wink last night, though she must have done because the alarm had woken her from a nightmare. It was hard getting used to sleeping alone in the king-sized bed now that Charles slept on the sofa in his study. In the small hours of the not-quite morning, Pippa went over her interview with the police. She kept thinking of things she should have told them and things that she should have perhaps omitted. When she thought of the day that Jerry died, it merged with other similar days, other times when she'd been in that room and other days when she'd been angry with him. The more she tried to remember, the more she seemed to forget.

Pippa had spoken to the police knowing that she must leave them with nowhere to go. No suspicions. No questions. If she covered up the fact that she and Charles were having money problems, they'd soon find out and get suspicious. Money. It's the kind of thing people kill for. If she'd pretended that there hadn't been the Cake Throwing Incident at the open day, they would hear it from someone else and decide she was a liar as well as prone to unprovoked attacks.

One minute she was talking to the police about the murder of a man who used to be her friend, and the next she was standing in the fruit and veg aisle of Tesco with a trolley stuffed with bags-for-life and a head empty of why she was even here.

Pippa had picked up the nearest vegetable and leaned on her trolley. She stared at the ... *thing* in her hand and searched her memory bank for its name. For the life of her, she couldn't remember what it was. It was shiny. Beautiful in its own way, even if its stalk was a little spiky. Would you say that was purple or black? She wanted to call it an egg, but she knew it wasn't an egg. It was too big to be an egg, too long, entirely the wrong colour. What on earth was wrong with her? Was this how it started with her mother? Words for everyday items hiding in the fog. She'd been meaning to have an eye test. With any luck that would help with the migraines and inanimate objects would stop blurring like they'd just rushed into view as a photograph was being taken.

But if it wasn't her eyes ... What if it was dementia or a brain tumour? And why couldn't she remember the name of this thing in her hand? She looked about her and tried to recall the names of the other produce.

Courgette. Red onions. Butternut squash. Round white thing with green leaves. Oh, come on. Nice under a cheese sauce ...

'Cauliflower!'

Her voice was a fraction too loud and it caused other shoppers to swerve her aisle. When had she turned into the crazy lady who stands in the supermarket and shouts the names of vegetables?

Pippa rotated her wrist and heard it crack. Everything ached. Her head, her back and she still had no idea what she'd come to the shop for. This strange-shaped vegetable in her hand must hold the key. She tried pushing the trolley, but the back wheels spun. She looked down and saw that the wheel was caught on a split tomato. Juice was spreading over the grubby floor.

'Pippa?'

She jumped and almost dropped the aubergine in her hand.

'Aubergine! That's what it's called,' Pippa said. Asha was peering at her behind a curtain of dark hair. 'Sorry, darling, miles away.'

'Is everything okay?' Asha asked.

Pippa thought Asha must be able to see written all over her face that nothing was okay.

'Yes, fine. I'm doing a spot of shopping. You know how much boys eat. I'm always in the supermarket or the kitchen.'

She took a while to notice what Asha was wearing. That she had a name badge.

'Oh goodness. Do you work here?'

'I managed to pick up some extra shifts. And before you say anything, yes, I'm still doing the graphic design. Just I don't have much work on at the moment so . . .'

Pippa knew she was staring. She'd never met anyone who worked at a supermarket before. Why hadn't Asha told her? Had Asha thought she'd judge her? But then she noticed how Asha was looking at her. She wasn't embarrassed. She was staring at Pippa with a look that wasn't quite humour, not anger. It was more like a sad curiosity. There'd been a time when people would look at her with respect, with awe and now they looked at her like she was the wrong side of the crazy tracks.

'Listen,' Asha said.

What a strange thing to say. Pippa was always listening. She listened, she watched, she saw more of what was going on than anyone knew.

'Are you sure everything's okay?' Asha asked. 'We haven't spoken properly since the cricket match. Do you fancy grabbing a coffee or something? I finish in twenty minutes.'

Pippa's mouth was dry. At the end of the aisle, she could see bottles of wine on special offer. She was thirsty enough that she could drink straight from the bottle. A nice, chilled white. She remembered a time when she used to be horrified at the thought of a screw-top bottle, but nowadays she would sigh in exasperation if she'd purchased a bottle with a cork. She'd have to rummage in the drawer for the cork-screw and then battle to ease the cork out, which all ate into valuable drinking time.

'Pippa? Did you hear what I said?'

Pippa's skin was itching behind her shoulder blade. She tried to reach around to get to the site of the irritation, but her fingers could only glance her bra-strap. She was starting to get hot again. Even though it was cool in the shop, she could feel the heat building beneath her skin.

'Pippa?'

This was why she always wore darker clothes nowadays – less likely to show the sweat. And it was why she'd taken to wearing Charles's cotton shirts, so that she could wear them open over a vest top, roll sleeves up or down, depending on the heat of the furnace in her bones.

To her embarrassment her eyes started filling with water. She couldn't be sure if it was the exhaustion that seemed to have crawled into her bones or the fact that someone was taking the time to ask how she was.

Or maybe it was the realisation that there was something important that she needed to tell the police.

Asha was looking at her like she was expecting more from her.

'Pip?'

'I don't know!'

And it was true, she didn't. She didn't know what the question was, didn't know what she was doing half the time and didn't know how she was going to get herself out of this mess. 'Sorry,' began Pippa. 'I'm so sorry, darling. I shouldn't be here. I've got to be at the, um, gosh, I'd completely lost track of the time. But why don't we catch up another time, yeah? Will I see you at the school, later? Don't suppose you're going to the PTA meeting, are you?'

'Wait, Pippa.' Asha held on to the side of Pippa's trolley.

Pippa grabbed her handbag and put her hands up in the air as she backed away. 'Please Asha, don't. Not today. I can't bring myself to talk about anything right now. I'm so confused.'

'Confused about what? I don't understand.' Asha was edging closer.

'Jerry. The school. Charles. I've made such a mess of everything, but I can't talk about it now. I need to go to the police.'

Asha's eyes widened. 'Do you remember something about Jerry's murder?'

'Yes. Sort of. See, Charles told the police that he'd seen someone wearing pale blue in the window with Jerry and the police are bound to look through the photos to see what we were all wearing that day. And they'll see that I was wearing pale blue. I don't know if he really saw me or if he's trying to drop me in it. It's no secret that he'd like to get rid of me. I have to tell the police that I went to see Jerry that afternoon, because if they find out I lied . . .'

'You were in Jerry's office?'

'Mandy was behind the cricket pavilion with Hinch, so I knew that there'd be no one there to stop me if I went to see Jerry about the school fees.'

'I thought she was at her desk all afternoon.'

'She lied.'

'You mean that anyone could have—'

'Yes. But it wasn't anyone, was it? I went to see him and it's obvious what the police will think. And then there was Charles and . . . he's not been entirely honest either. Look, I must go.'

'What do you mean, "And then there was Charles"? What has Charles got to do with it?'

'God, I don't know what to think anymore. Don't listen to me. I shouldn't be talking about this. Forgive me. I really do have to go. I'll see you later, darling.'

She left Asha holding on to the trolley and her questions. Pippa kept her eyes down as she rushed out the way she came, ignoring the pain in her ankle that came and went. Two women were chatting at the exit. Pippa huffed as she stepped around them, hoping to make her displeasure known with the set of her face. There was someone collecting for charity by the doors and she avoided making eye contact with them. She could hardly look after herself, never mind contribute to the welfare of birds, or cats, or whatever they were collecting for today.

As Pippa broke into the sunshine, she squinted. The day was bleached of colour. The pavement was sand, the sky, the cars, all the colour of old bones. Nothing was the same anymore.

Pausing by the crossing, she couldn't remember where she'd left the car. She glanced up and down the road and then remembered she'd parked it up the hill, in one of the loading bays outside the old bank, so that she'd have extra room to open the car door. Room. That big room, the high ceilings. And Jerry. Poor Jerry.

Pippa heard Asha behind her, calling her name, but she was already searching in her bag for her keys, stepping into the road to put some distance between herself and all the uncomfortable questions. She needed time to put her thoughts in order before she went to the police.

Pippa didn't even hear the squeal of the brakes.

She didn't notice the car bearing down on her.

It was the open mouth and wide eyes of a woman on the opposite side of the road that made Pippa pause mid-stride. And then there was a car. And the impact. But, curiously, no pain.

Then she was weightless again like that time she hit Jerry with the cake. Though, this time, she really was flying. And the sky was so blue. Look at that. Not a cloud in the sky.

But then she felt herself falling and the car was still moving and the tyres were screeching on the tarmac and Pippa realised that this wasn't good. Not good at all.

Her last thought, before everything went black, was for the person driving the car. Poor thing. They mustn't feel bad about it. It was probably her fault.

It usually was.

Chapter 21

Eleven days after Jerry's death

'Pippa, can you hear me?'

'She stepped out in front of my car.'

'Pippa, it's me, Asha. An ambulance is on its way.'

'She didn't even look.' The blue Toyota had come to a halt beyond where Pippa lay with its engine still running. Its windscreen a spiderweb of cracks. Tyre lines on the road evidence that he'd tried to stop. 'I swear.'

The driver with his grey hair, grey clothes, grey skin, stood next to them, his grey shadow falling over Pippa's body. His hands were in his hair, shaking his head at the nightmare he couldn't wake from.

'I thought she'd seen me, but she kept going.'

A teenage boy, all limbs and angles, was on the ground holding Pippa's head still. 'Like this?' he asked.

'Yes,' Asha said, desperately trying to remember what she'd learned at the first aid class she'd taken years earlier. 'Be sure she doesn't move. There might be a spinal injury.'

Asha heard sirens in the distance cutting through the murmurs of the growing crowd. She could have cried with relief. She didn't know what she was doing. Needed help.

'The ambulance is almost here. I can hear them, Pippa. Hold on. You're going to be all right.'

She put her head on Pippa's chest. The weak heartbeat that had been there a moment ago was gone. She watched her chest for a rise and a fall, thought she'd seen something, but no.

'No, Pippa. No. Don't you fucking dare.'

'Is she going to be okay?' The shadow moved, came back again.

Asha felt Pippa's neck for a pulse but couldn't be sure she was doing it right. She didn't want to press too hard, or in the wrong place.

'Christ.'

She picked up Pippa's wrist and put her fingers over slack veins. Pushing. Probing. Seeking a sign.

'Please, Pippa. Stay with me. You have to stay with me.'

The sirens were still faint, didn't seem to be getting any closer. Roadworks. Traffic backed up.

Asha shuffled forwards on her knees.

'Keep her head stable, yeah?'

The boy nodded.

Asha placed the heel of her hand on Pippa's chest. Her other hand on top.

'I don't know if I can do this,' she said to herself.

'You can,' said the boy.

She looked up at the crowd who'd gathered to gawp. No one rushed forwards to help her. Asha was on her own.

Deep breath.

'You will not die on me, Pippa Yardley. I won't let you.'

Chapter 22

The day of Pippa's accident

It was the best turnout they'd had for a PTA meeting in the five years that Katy Lane had been at Aberfal High. Extra seats were brought in by Otis Blake. Katy looked at her watch then at Charles Yardley who was striding towards her. 'Where's Pippa?' she asked.

'Not answering her phone. This is typical of her,' he said, keeping his voice low and talking out of one side of his mouth. 'Not turning up to get the boys from school. Not at the meeting where she's meant to be presenting. She's making a point about how lost I'll be without her when we divorce.' He caught Helen-Louise watching and closed his mouth.

'Don't worry. I'll handle it,' Katy said. She walked towards the front of the hall with Helen-Louise at her shoulder. Pippa should have been giving an update on the ball, filling people in, getting them excited. Balls and concerts were usually Pippa's arena, but Katy didn't mind taking this one. 'If you could take your seats, please, ladies and gents.'

Chair-legs scraped over the floor, handbags were put under seats, phones were placed on silent. This was what they'd all been waiting for.

Katy put her hand on her stomach as if to calm the squirming. She wasn't worried about chairing the meeting, but she couldn't help but scan the faces of those assembled, wondering if any of them were behind the emails, or if any of them were behind Jerry's death. Her prime suspect wasn't here this evening but there were more people here than usual. She thought she read something on the faces of one or two of them. An animosity that didn't used to be there. But then she remembered that this was the first time a murder had been on the agenda.

When Katy had envisaged running the school, it wasn't like this. She'd expected to be triumphant but could hardly show her pleasure at a time like this. Newhall was meant to hand her the baton, give her his blessing – the Newhall seal of approval to win over the doubters. Or, at the very least, Katy should have been coming to this as a saviour, leading the school through this difficult time. She wanted them to look upon her as a hero, but they still didn't take her seriously.

She'd taken too long to speak and Helen-Louise jumped into the space that Katy's thoughts had left.

'Thank you all for coming,' Helen-Louise said, stepping closer to Katy so their elbows were almost touching. 'It has been the most traumatic two weeks in the history of Aberfal High. And no one has been more affected than I have, over Mr Newhall's passing.'

Katy raised a single eyebrow. That was debatable. She looked at her intertwined fingers so that she wouldn't catch anyone's eye. Charles Yardley took a seat at the end of the third row.

'I know you all share my sorrow at the sudden loss of such a well-loved pillar of our community and bedrock of our school,' Helen-Louise continued. 'I am sure we all agree that our priority now is the welfare of the children. They cannot bear any more setbacks.'

She paused as heads nodded in solemn agreement. 'As you know,' she said, 'Miss Lane will be *acting* headteacher until the end of the school year. We've instructed a recruitment consultancy to find us a new headmaster worthy of this school and our children.'

Katy lifted her head and tried to smile. They weren't even considering that she might be head permanently and she hadn't missed Helen-Louise's not-so-subtle emphasis on the word 'acting'. Helen-Louise. Even the fact that she had a double-barrelled first name, annoyed Katy. Didn't she ever get tired of saying her own name?

'Now,' Helen-Louise said. 'Miss Lane? You wanted to say a few words?'

'Thank you, yes.'

Katy took a couple of steps forwards and looked up and down the rows of parents. She had their undivided attention and she wasn't going to let it go to waste.

'Firstly, this isn't an ordinary PTA meeting. I wanted to use this as an opportunity to address any concerns you might have. The main subject is the situation surrounding the nature of Mr Newhall's death.' She paused for a moment and the room was silent. Everyone waited. Leaned forwards in their seats.

'It doesn't suit any of us to speculate at this time. There's an ongoing police investigation, as you know, but I can confirm . . .' She looked around the room. Front row to back row and back again in a figure of eight. 'Our worst nightmare has been confirmed. Mr Newhall's death is being investigated as a murder and the police assure me that they are getting close to making an arrest.' They'd done no such thing, but she needed everyone to believe that it was all in hand.

'And I'd like to reiterate,' she continued, 'that there is no danger to our children. The police say this was an attack of a personal nature. This atrocity was carried out by someone known to Mr Newhall. Someone who had a personal issue with him. This will come as a shock to those of us who cannot believe that anyone would hurt a kind man like him. I would ask you, at this time, to take every opportunity to tell other parents and your children that this was a one-off incident and that Aberfal High will not let the actions of one depraved individual keep us from our course. I hope I don't come across as callous when I say that I see this as a time for the school to double-down our actions, to make Aberfal the best it can be, to support our students through the upcoming exams and to make Mr Newhall proud.'

When she paused for breath, there was a smattering of polite applause. Glances passed from parent to parent like a sinister game of pass the parcel. When the music stopped, you'd found your killer.

Rose Entwistle put her hand in the air and Katy pretended not to have seen her. Everyone knew that questions were left until the end of a meeting. Typical of Rose to be so impatient. Katy opened her mouth, ready to broach the subject of the summer ball.

'Rose, yes,' said Helen-Louise. 'You had a question?'

Katy snapped her mouth shut and folded her arms.

'Is it true,' Rose asked, 'that the murderer climbed up the wall and in through Mr Newhall's window? And they're looking for someone sporty?' She looked at Hinch who was standing at the side of the hall with his arms folded.

Helen-Louise looked flustered, so Katy took a deep breath.

'We're trying to keep an open mind at this point but, yes, that's one possibility that the police are considering.'

Rose's eyes kept slipping towards Hinch.

Another parent raised his hand. He looked familiar but Katy couldn't remember his name. The woman next to him she recognised as being the mother of a year ten student. Katy's mind spun through the students' names like a rolodex. She took a guess that the man and woman were together.

'Mr Malek. You had a question?'

'We're all devastated about Mr Newhall's passing.'

Katy nodded. She could sense that there was a 'but' on its way.

'But this has come at a time when our children are about to take their exams and, not wanting to be insensitive, but when my son does his GCSEs what are you going to do if his grades aren't as good as the ones he was predicted?'

'I assure you, Mr Malek, that we are doing our best not to let it affect any of our students adversely but, obviously, they can't help but be shocked by an event of this nature happening at a place where they should feel nothing but security and love. Knowing how hard our students work for these exams I have no doubt that they will all rise to the occasion. In the very unlikely event that a student fails to reach what we expect of him we will review our practices. We've already been talking to the boys who are sitting exams this year and everything is in hand.'

She could see that Mr Malek was about to ask more questions and that what he'd said had struck a chord with some of the other parents. Some moved in their seats and a hand shot up from the front row.

'Pam. Yes, you had a question?'

'Yes. Hello, Miss Lane. Can I say, on behalf of all the parents and pupils, we appreciate how well you've kept the school going while ensuring the minimum disruption for the children.'

Behind her, Rose rolled her eyes and laughed. Pam frowned.

Katy inclined her head. 'Thank you.'

'One thing though . . . This will undoubtedly have an impact on attracting new students to the school—'

'I don't see why there should be any undue—'

'—and given that schools older than ours have had to close recently because of the dropping numbers of students accessing private education. Can you give us any assurances that this will not happen to Aberfal High?'

'Well, I—'

'Because we'd appreciate enough notice to find alternative places for our boys.'

'I'm not going to let that happen, Pam.' Katy looked around the hall again. 'I love this school and all the boys in it. We will continue to do what Aberfal High does best for many years to come yet. And on that note . . .'

The door at the back of the room banged open and Mandy came running into the room. Paused a moment, scanned the hall and then darted towards Charles Yardley.

Katy tutted as she saw that she was losing their attention now. Typical. Mandy never stayed where you asked her to.

'One final thing from me,' Katy said.

Mandy bent down next to Charles, hand cupped between her mouth and his ear.

'The summer ball. Now, I know some of you have expressed concern that we are still going ahead with it,' she said.

Charles Yardley stood up and strode from the room with Mandy on his heels.

Katy faltered. If there was a problem, she should've been informed, not Charles.

'However, it gives me great pleasure to confirm that the summer ball will be going ahead in memory of Mr Newhall. As before, the theme is the roaring twenties. The only thing that has changed is the fact that we are no longer fundrais- ing for the new 4G sports pitch, we are fundraising in Jerry Newhall's memory. This is not to say that the proceeds won't be spent on the 4G, but the focus is more a memorial for Jerry. A celebration of his life.'

Arms folded but heads nodded. They were going to make the best of it because that's what Aberfal High did. Mutterings turned into chatter as they turned to each other to discuss the merits of the news.

Helen-Louise lowered her head to Katy and said in a whisper, 'I hope you know what you're doing.'

'We need a distraction, something to raise everyone's spirits. Let's get everyone talking about something else other than murder, shall we? We'd lose the deposits on the fairground rides and the catering anyway. This way we'll be making money instead of losing it.'

What Katy didn't say was, this was the perfect opportunity to show everyone how great the school could be under her leadership. Given time, no one would remember Jerry Newhall, never mind gossip about who killed him.

WITNESS SIX

Katy Lane.
Acting Head.

Okay, well, as I've already said, I was about to go home. I can't quite remember the time, but it wasn't much past six. There were only two cars in the staff car park – mine and Jerry's. That wasn't unusual because he was spending more and more time at the school. He was always there before me and stayed long after I'd gone home. I got the impression that he was having marital problems. But that day, I'd heard he was going to the Yardleys for a barbecue, so I assumed he'd already left.

I almost drove off but, at the last minute, I thought I'd go and check. I don't know why. I suppose I felt guilty that he was still working. There was no one else in the building that I could see, apart from the cleaners. There was a chance, I suppose, that Otis Blake – the gardener – was still hanging around outside. He never seems to leave.

Anyway, I walked straight into Jerry's office and, well, I didn't see him at first. But then I noticed him on the floor. I thought he'd collapsed or something. I called his name and then I sort of pushed his shoulder, you know, shook him and then I noticed his eyes were open and I must have crouched there for a few seconds without moving. I think I knew he was already dead, but I hoped that he was only unconscious, so I ran outside to Mandy's desk and called the ambulance.

I don't know why I didn't use his phone. Or my mobile. Actually . . . Okay, let me level with you. I panicked. I ran from the room because I couldn't look at him. I called from Mandy's desk because I thought I'd throw up if I looked at him for one more second. And then I went downstairs to wait for the ambulance coming up the driveway so I could let them in. Maybe I should have checked for a pulse or something, but I couldn't bear to be in the same room as him. I didn't get the chance to notice if anything was out of place. Or if there were any signs of a struggle. I didn't notice if anything was missing. At that stage I thought he'd fallen. There were two things that struck me at the time. One was that there was a bottle of brandy and two glasses on Jerry's desk and the other was that the window was wide open. He never opened that window. Even when it got hot in there, he kept it closed.

It felt like I waited hours for the ambulance and police to arrive, but I'm told it was only nine minutes. It was the longest nine minutes of my life. I've hardly slept since. I didn't realise how much I relied on Jerry and how much he meant to me.

I've already had emails from parents saying they'll be sending their children elsewhere come September. Partly it's because of the loss of the, um, the leadership that Mr Newhall gave us. But mostly it's because they don't feel safe. Would you send your child to a school where there'd been a murder? Even I don't want to come into work anymore.

I just can't think . . . I mean, why would anyone . . . Goodness, I just don't know who'd do something like that. As far as I can tell, Jerry's wife, Gemma, was the last person to see him alive. I saw her that afternoon. She was talking to someone on the telephone and said something about how, this time, she wasn't going to back down. I have no idea what that was about, but she certainly wasn't happy.

The car? Oh, you've heard about that, have you? It was probably nothing. I had two flat tyres, which was a first for me. It was the

Friday before the Easter holidays and I only had one spare in the boot, so I called the AA. The guy said that the tyres had been deliberately slashed but, well, that was only his opinion, doesn't mean that . . . I mean, yes, I was worried and I've been a bit more diligent about locking the doors, but the more I thought about it the more I thought I'd banged the tyre against the pavement when I turned a corner or something. It's preposterous to think that someone would purposely . . . I mean, what would be the point? Who'd have anything against me?

Chapter 23

The day of Pippa's accident

Asha pulled up outside the school as the last of the parents were leaving the PTA meeting. Excitement vibrated in the air as if Newhall's murder had been staged for their amusement. Laughter and smiles were set alight by the setting sun.

She slid lower in her seat. Every Tuesday Cass went to gardening club, which was a good job seeing as she would never have made it in time to pick him up otherwise. Not today.

She took out her phone – her hands shaking – and sent him a text.

I'm here x

Usually, Cass would be waiting out front, checking his phone, kicking pebbles on the driveway. She checked the time. Twenty-two minutes late. She drummed her fingers on her steering wheel.

'Damn it, Cass.'

She needed to be away from here. Far away. She wanted to scoop Cass up and drive and drive and drive. She wanted to drink until she couldn't remember the way that Pippa's skin had felt under her fingers. The weight of her hand as she lifted it to check for a pulse.

'Christ's sake, Cass. Where are you?'

She closed her eyes. Opened them. Needed something to do. Something to occupy her mind.

Asha grabbed her phone again, pressed a couple of buttons.

In two rings, 'Kitten?'

'Hey, Mum.'

'Twice in a month. I'm honoured. If it's money you're after, you've come to the wrong place. And did you just call me Mum instead of Tessa? What's got into you?'

'Don't. A friend of mine had an accident outside the shop where I work. I had to do CPR on her until the ambulance got there.'

'She alive?'

'Think so.'

'You think so?'

'She was breathing when they put her in the ambulance, but she wasn't conscious.'

'You didn't go to the hospital with her?'

'Didn't think it was my place. Besides, I had to pick up Cass from school.'

'Some friend you are.'

Asha bit her tongue. She didn't say that, unlike her mother, she put her child first. She didn't tell her that she'd had enough of hospitals to last a lifetime. That the nights she'd sat by her mum's bed wondering if she was ever going to wake up had scarred her beyond recognition. The bandaged wrists. The vomiting. The wondering whether she had enough money for the bus so she could get back home in time to send Georgie to school. The fear that someone would take them away. The fear that they wouldn't.

'I've got shingles,' Tessa said. 'Doctor says stress.' Her voice trailed off, dragging a line of s's like ducklings behind her.

Asha rubbed her forehead. 'Is that why you're slurring your words?'

'You'd drink too if you had my life.'

Asha's mum had been on her mind for the entire drive to Aberfal High. If it hadn't been for her, Asha would never have signed up for that class, wouldn't have been able to save Pippa's life. No child should feel responsible for a parent's life but, for now at least, Asha was grateful.

'What did ya say?' Tessa asked.

'I didn't say anything,' replied Asha.

'Wasn't talking to you. Ed's here. Wants his tea.'

Asha held the phone away from her mouth for a moment and took a deep breath.

'Okay then. You go see to Ed. I've got to get Cass anyway.'

'Okay.'

'Love you.'

'Eh? And I thought I was the one who'd been drinking.'

Asha slid out of the van. Barely had the strength to close the door behind her. She took the path through the archway by the chapel and ignored the voices in the car park.

Part of Asha wanted to tell everyone what had happened to Pippa. That, one minute they were talking and, the next, Pippa was unconscious on the ground. But the other part of her wanted to keep quiet while she processed it. If she hadn't seen Pippa, hadn't questioned her about what she remembered about the day Newhall died, she wouldn't have run into the path of that car.

Asha couldn't help but glance at the bushes under Mr Newhall's window. There was no sign of crushed branches now. The police had finished searching the grounds and now the children were free to wander the gardens as usual. They were being pressured from all sides. Pressured by Gemma Newhall to find Jerry's killer and pressured by Charles Yardley to let the school carry on as normal with minimal interruption. Both things were not possible simultaneously. Their search of the lakes had been perfunctory at best.

There was the smell of woodsmoke in the air as Asha headed in the direction of the lake, cutting across the field. She could hear laughter as she approached. There was nothing nicer than hearing Cass laugh but she wasn't sure how she felt about him spending time with Otis Blake. It should have been enough for her that the school trusted him to spend time with the boys in gardening club. But no one else would be as thorough, or as suspicious as she was.

She pushed through the trees and Otis stood up to greet her. 'You're here.'

'Sorry I'm late.'

Cass was sitting on a tree stump next to a fire. Looked at her but didn't get up.

'PTA meeting?' Otis asked.

'No, there was this . . . thing at work.'

She opened her arms wide to Cass. 'Here now. No excuses. Mumma needs a hug.'

Cass stood up and approached her as he would a wild animal.

'Come on,' she said. 'Bring it in.'

He leaned into her but without much enthusiasm.

'Arms,' Asha ordered.

As he offered his reluctant hug, Asha squeezed him. Breathed him in. Marvelled at the fact that he was hers. She felt the moment he gave in and squeezed her back and she came closer to crying than she had all afternoon.

Cass pulled away and pointed to the fire. 'I lit it.'

'Great,' Asha said.

'And I don't mean with a lighter. Otis taught me how to light it with kindling and flint. And now we're going to cook fish on it. Aren't we, Otis?'

'Cass, you should call him Mr Blake.'

'It's okay,' said Otis. 'I'm not his teacher.'

Asha wasn't at all comforted. She preferred the distance that a title gave him. 'We need to get home.'

'Well, I won't be going anywhere while there's a fire lit,' Otis said. 'So, if you wanted to stay for a bit, we're cooking the trout we caught earlier.'

Asha considered Otis's offer and Cass's eager face. And she was so tired, it wouldn't hurt to sit down for a minute or two.

'We can't stay long.'

She lowered herself down onto a red chequered blanket and found that every muscle in her body ached. The door to the shed was ajar and she could see a rail of clothes and wondered whether Otis was living there. She forced herself to look away. Something didn't sit right with her about Otis, but she couldn't tell whether she had something to worry about or whether it was her natural distrustful nature that was uncoiling in her stomach.

Cass and Otis were busying themselves with preparing food. Asha hardly had the energy to talk, never mind help. She watched the lake turn to liquid gold and tried to keep her mind empty. Unless she concentrated, her brain would throw unwanted images and memories her way.

Otis handed her a beer. 'Food's almost ready,' he said.

'I'm not hungry.'

'You will be.'

Cass was standing by the edge of the lake throwing stones.

'There was an accident,' she said to Otis. She put the bottle to her lips. 'Pippa Yardley. She was knocked down by a car.' Asha took a sip of her beer.

'Is she okay?'

'I don't know. I had to . . . the ambulance took for ever and when they took her away . . . I don't even know who to call to find out how she is. I don't have her husband's number and I don't know if the hospital would tell me anything. For all I know she could be . . .' Another swig of beer. 'I don't know why I'm telling you this.'

'It sounds scary.'

'Yeah.'

She covered her eyes. Wouldn't cry in front of a man she hardly knew. 'Sorry.'

'It's okay. She's your friend. Must've been terrible.'

Asha nodded. 'Yeah.'

'I hope she's all right.'

'Thanks.' She turned her head away as the tears came. Asha wiped her eyes, but the tears on her cheeks were replaced by others quicker than she could brush them away.

Cass flung himself down next to her on the blanket and nudged her thigh with his elbow. She didn't turn to face him but reached out her hand. He took it and squeezed. They sat like that in silence while Asha composed herself. When she looked back, Otis was standing over the fire pit.

'Do you want me to message Benny to see if there's any news? I could get his dad's number if you like?'

Asha cleared her throat. 'Please.'

Otis handed them their plates. Alongside the fish were salad leaves and sliced, fried potatoes. She noticed he'd filleted her fish but left Cass's whole. She was both thankful and offended at the same time.

'Wow,' she said. 'This is something else. I was planning on putting a pizza in the oven.'

Despite her assertions that she wasn't hungry, she cleared her plate. Shadows lengthened and insects started nipping at her bare arms. But there was no response to Cass's message to Benny.

'That was gorgeous. Can I wash the dishes or something?'

Otis smiled. 'Nah, I leave the plates out for the foxes to lick clean.'

Asha was too tired to know whether he was joking. 'Come on then, Cass. Let's get going.'

As he dashed off to get his things, Asha said, 'Thanks for this. For, you know, letting Cass help you out. And for saving his life with the whole swimming in the lake thing. We should get you a superhero cape or something.'

'That would please Miss Lane. She keeps telling me to wear more clothes.'

'I wouldn't listen to her,' said Asha.

'You think I should wear less clothes?'

'Stop flattering yourself. That is not what I said.'

Otis smiled and it transformed his face.

'Miss Lane has a lot on her plate right now,' Asha said. 'She won't be thinking about what you're wearing.'

They both fell quiet as they thought about exactly what she did have on her plate. She was now headmistress of a school where her predecessor had been murdered. An ongoing police inquiry, dwindling student numbers and demanding parents.

Otis said, 'I guess you're right. But she won't get any sympathy from me. She never should have—'

'I'm ready,' said Cass.

'Never should have what?' Asha asked Otis.

'Nothing.'

Asha watched him, but his eyes wouldn't meet hers. Eventually she said to Cass, 'Let's go and get some homework done.'

'Nothing due until Monday,' Cass said.

'Okay.'

'I don't even need good grades for what I want to do when I leave school,' Cass said with a shrug.

'Yeah? And what's that?'

'I'm going to be a gardener like Otis.'

'Over my dead body. You can aim higher than that, Cass.'

Cass's eyes widened and slid to Otis before Asha could realise her mistake. 'Sorry, Otis, no offence meant, it's just . . .'

'Sure. I get it.'

'No, that's not what I meant.'

Otis shook his head. 'And I said "I get it". You think that gardening is demeaning.'

'No, that's not what I said. I see gardening as more of a hobby and don't want Cass to narrow his options. The whole point of his education is to make more doors open to him. I want the best for him and I won't let you make me feel bad about that.'

'If you're feeling bad, then that's on you, not me.'

'Good. C'mon, Cass.'

Asha took a few steps away then turned and came back at Otis, a finger wagging in his face.

'D'you know what? No. I'm not having this. Don't you dare suggest that I look down on anybody for doing whatever they can do to get by.'

'Never said a word.'

'I've worked every minimum wage job you can think of. I'm trying to show Cass that following your heart and taking risks pays off. But my heart doesn't pay the bills, so I still stack shelves every morning and most afternoons and I scrimp and save and account for every single penny that goes in and out of my bank account.'

Otis folded his arms but said nothing.

'And I lose sleep over whether I can put away enough money for the school fees each month. And I feel like the world's worst mother every time Cass mentions when one of his classmates gets a new iPhone, or where they're going on holiday this summer. And he never asks for a thing. Never. And that's even worse than him pestering me for a new bike because I know that he's aware of how little money we have. He's a kid who tells me, every Christmas, "It's okay, Mum, I don't need anything this year" and it kills me.'

Asha looked at Cass and the anger drained out of her. 'So, yeah,' she said. 'Yeah, I want better for him. I thought this school would give him the opportunities I never had – and it does – but it comes at a price. My friends and family think I've sold out, like I'm a class traitor or something for sending my son to this school. But the other parents look down on me because I don't belong here. I don't have a flashy car and a rich husband. I can't get it right. And if it was up to me, I'd be in my van and heading along the coast, but Cass wants to have a home for more than twelve months at a time, even though I'm suffocating.'

Tears sprang to her eyes and she wiped them away. 'Sorry. I don't know what's wrong with me today.'

Cass put his arms around her. Asha tried to laugh, but it came out as a sob. 'When did you get so bloody tall?' She rested her forehead on his shoulder.

'You know they're just kids, right?' said Cass. 'It's not their fault their parents have money. And a lot of them, they don't have as much as you think they do. They go without a lot of stuff so that their parents can afford the school fees. The other parents, they're not so different to us.'

'Oh, that's bloody wonderful, that is. How come you're the mature, sensible one?'

'If you hate it here, we'll leave,' said Cass. 'But this is my fifth school, Mum, and you've never made friends with the parents at any of them, so it can't all be about the money. I'm trying hard to fit in here. Maybe you should try it too.'

'Hold on a minute,' she began, but the rest of her words faded as she heard Cass's phone buzz. 'Is that . . .?'

Cass looked at his phone. 'It's Benny Yardley.'

Rose Oliversmum: The ball is on!! Thought they'd cancel. I'd better check if Mick can still fit in his tux.

Clare Withoutani: Is it still Roaring 20s theme?

Rose Oliversmum: YES. Tassels and sequins should cover these rolls of flab. Need tummy control pants.

Asha: Sorry to tell you this but Pippa's been in an accident.

Becky Rupertsmum: WTAF? What happened?

Asha: Just got off phone with Charles. She's okay but in hospital. Stable for the moment. In an induced coma while they wait for the swelling on her brain to go down.

Rose Oliversmum: What kind of accident?

Asha: Hit by a car while crossing the road. Nothing broken but head hit windscreen.

Sarah Teddysmum: Oh my God. That's awful. Poor Pippa. She will be ok, won't she?

Asha: Don't know. Charles said Pippa put in coma for own good. If they put her in, they can get her out. Right?

Rose Oliversmum: That has really shocked me. Don't know what to say.

Clare Withoutani: I feel terrible. Is there anything we can do?

Becky Rupertsmum: I hope she wakes up soon. For one thing, I have QUESTIONS. I mean, who was driving the car that hit her? Was it on purpose?

Asha: Spoke to her before it happened. She said she remembered something about the day JN died and needed to speak to the police.

Becky Rupertsmum: SHIT!! Any idea what about?

Asha: 🤷

Rose Oliversmum: OK. Bear with . . . What if Hinch was driving the car?

Asha: Wasn't Hinch.

Rose Oliversmum: Pippa knows that Hinch has something to do with the murder and he was trying to silence her.

Sarah Teddysmum: Erm . . . That's a bit of a leap!!!

Asha: Wasn't Hinch.

Rose Oliversmum: The man is a menace. Disappeared during the cricket match and I heard that he was about to get sacked unless he started winning some sports matches. AND he's known for having a temper. I heard his wife left him because he hit her.

Asha: Seriously. Wasn't Hinch. I saw the man who was driving the car. Not Hinch.

Becky Rupertsmum: Hinch's wife died of cancer, Rose!! Besides, I think Katy Lane had something 2 do with the murder. No one is buying that shit about her being the last person at school and 'happening' to find the body, are they?? She's had her eye on his job 4 ever. She thought JN was going 2 retire this year but I heard that he said that he'd decided 2 stay on. I bet she snapped.

Clare Withoutani: My money's on JN's wife. Remember when there was that rumour that Newhall was having an affair? No smoke without fire I say!!

Rose Oliversmum: My money's still on Hinch.

Becky Rupertsmum: Katy Lane.

Clare Withoutani: Gemma Newhall.

Rose Oliversmum: What about you, Asha?

Asha: Don't feel comfortable speculating. Am going to the hospital in the morning to see if I can find out any more about Pippa. Will let you know any news.

Asha: Also . . .

Asha: My money's on Charles Yardley.

Chapter 24

The day after Pippa's accident

Asha stood in the doorway with a bouquet of thick stemmed sunflowers in one hand. It was cool in the hospital but not cold. There was the faint smell of canteen cooking. She couldn't explain why, but it smelled soft. Mash. Mush. Sloppy food that could be spooned into the mouths of frail and fading people. There was a nurse by Pippa's bed. Shorter than Asha but she looked like she'd easily beat her in an arm wrestle.

'No flowers allowed.'

'Oh.'

'Were you the lady who called earlier?'

'No. Wasn't me.'

'Could hardly hear her over her dog barking. Shall I put those at the desk? You can pick them up on your way out.'

Bringing flowers for a woman in a coma wasn't her best idea anyway. It was like putting offerings on a grave. They didn't mean anything to the intended recipient. It only showed the world what a good friend, or relation, you were. But, for Asha, it was something to do with her hands, something to hide behind. She still hadn't looked at the bed. Still hadn't seen Pippa. Acclimatising, she told herself. Like taking tentative steps into a cold sea and waiting for her toes to go numb before going any further.

Asha said, 'Her husband told me she was doing well and that everything was fine, but . . .'

'Looks worse than it is. The bruising and the swelling will go down in time. You'll see.'

The nurse took the flowers from Asha and disappeared on soft-soled shoes. Asha looked out of the corner of her eye. Focused first on the white blanket. The curve of Pippa's legs. Her slender hands, one with a cannula taped to a vein. Asha approached the bed, placing each foot carefully, as if fearing creaky floorboards. It was difficult to get her head around the fact that her friend was in a coma. And that she was in a coma on purpose. Asha angled her body so that she could concentrate on Pippa's face and not the machines that whirred and clicked around her. If they were keeping her alive, then all it would take was for Asha to trip and pull out a wire and it would be game over. Shouldn't there be a guard making sure Pippa was still breathing? Security, linking arms. Keeping her safe from the world.

Asha stood by the edge of the bed, feeling like she was intruding, silently pleading with Pippa to wake up. Though they were friends, they didn't know each other well enough to watch each other sleep. This was too intrusive. She wanted to leave.

Now she was here, she didn't know what to do. She wasn't helping Pippa, only hoping, in some small way, to help herself. She wanted Pippa to open her eyes and say, 'By the way, darling, it wasn't your fault that I ran out of the supermarket and into the path of a car. Oh and by the way, Asha, let me tell you exactly who killed Jerry.'

She'd read that people in comas could hear what was going on around them, but Asha had been in too many one-sided conversations in her life to voluntarily enter another. And so she stood and stared, wondering whether this could be the moment that Pippa would open her eyes.

When Asha had admitted that she suspected Charles was responsible for Jerry Newhall's death it was the first time she'd let the words out of her head. Money problems and marriage problems would have been enough to increase his stress levels. Asha couldn't stop thinking about Pippa saying, 'And then there was Charles' before she ran out of the store.

Charles had the motive and he had the opportunity. He was absent around the time that Jerry died, reappeared in a new shirt and no one would ever question him if they saw him heading into the school building. He had a long history with Jerry and yet friendship meant nothing when it came to money. If Mandy had lied about sitting outside the office all afternoon, then Charles didn't need to climb out of the window. Asha put her hand to her forehead as if expecting to feel the heat from cogs whirling inside her brain trying to make sense of it all. If no one jumped out of Jerry's office, then why were the bushes trampled outside the window? Why did the police find traces of blood?

The police still hadn't found the murder weapon and that would make it difficult to link Charles to Newhall's death. If the police had failed to find it, there was no reason why Asha would fare any better. If only Pippa would wake up and help, she could change everything. Asha shouldn't have told the other mums that she suspected Charles. If he was the murderer, how far would he go to keep his secrets? How difficult was it to make sure that a woman in a coma never woke up? The best way to keep Pippa safe was to ensure that she wasn't the only one who knew who the killer was.

She cleared her throat. 'Hi. Pippa. It's me. Asha. How are you?' She shook her head and looked up at the ceiling. She was speaking like she was on the telephone to an elderly grandparent.

'Never done this before,' she said. 'I suppose I could tell you anything. I bet people will talk and talk to you because you can't talk back. You should get temporary priest status so that you can't divulge any secrets that you hear.'

Asha looked over her shoulder to check that she was alone.

'Listen. If I did this . . . if it was my fault that you . . . you know. Please wake up. Wake up for me, Pippa. Please.'

Asha turned at the sound of footsteps in the corridor and saw Charles stride into the room.

'Ah,' he said. 'You're early.'

'Hi. How are you?'

Charles had told her she could visit any time from twelve thirty and so she'd come at twelve.

'Fine. You?'

'Good, thanks. Any idea when they'll try and wake her up?' Asha asked.

'Best not to rush these things,' he said.

'How are the kids?'

222

'Fine.'

There'd been many times in Asha's life when she'd stood by hospital beds, or on the neighbour's doorstep as ambulances drove away and wondered whether her mother would ever come home again. She knew that Myles and Benny would be far from fine. Though she hated the life her mother provided for them, she'd been terrified at the thought of losing her.

As Charles picked up the chart at the end of Pippa's bed, Asha watched him. His hair had been trimmed since the cricket match; his nails were buffed. He was clean shaven, not a nick or a missed inch of stubble. This wasn't a man who'd spent a sleepless night worrying about his wife. He was going about his normal day but with the added irritant of having to visit Pippa in hospital to keep up appearances.

'They tell me,' said Charles, 'that you saved her life.'

'I only did what I could until the ambulance got there.'

'Where did you learn CPR?'

Asha wanted to tell him to mind his own business but, instead, she said, 'I did a course a few years back. Hoped I'd never have to use it.'

'I wish you hadn't had to use it either, but I'm grateful you did. I'd hate to think what would have happened if . . .'

'Let's not go there.'

They stood in silence watching Pippa's chest rise and fall.

'And,' Charles added, 'I hear that you're designing our menus and what-have-you for the school ball?'

'That's right.'

'Get your invoice in quickly. You want that paying before the school breaks up for summer.'

'Will do.'

She glanced towards the clock and wondered how long she should stay. Charles being helpful put her on edge.

'You're a doctor,' Asha said, changing the subject. 'You know far more than I do about any of this' – she waved her arm over Pippa's bed – 'stuff. How will this affect her in the long term?'

Charles put his hands in his pockets and swayed on to his toes then back on to his heels.

'Prognosis is good,' he said. 'She has every chance of a full recovery. There's no brain injury that we can see, though she'll have to take it easy to begin with. Her memory might be impaired. I wouldn't be surprised if she doesn't remember a thing about the accident.'

Asha looked at the bruised face of her friend. She hoped that wasn't the case because she needed Pippa back – memories and all.

'She suffered significant swelling to the brain,' Charles continued. 'It's standard procedure to induce a coma to give the body time to heal. To take the strain off. In Pippa's case, once the swelling has abated, the body will . . . ah . . . reboot if you like.'

It made sense when he put it like that, but it suited Charles to have his wife stay in a coma or, failing that, for people to believe her memory to be sketchy.

'Look, I'm sorry to ask,' Charles said. 'But I didn't have the chance to ask many questions on the telephone. What happened?'

'I'm not sure. I didn't see the accident just . . . just the aftermath. According to the guy who was driving, she crossed the road without looking. The car should have slowed for the crossing but . . .'

'You don't think she stepped in front of that car on purpose?'

'No. Why would she?'

'She's been preoccupied lately. Unhappy. I couldn't help but think—'

'No. She was fine. I bumped into her when she was shopping and we talked a while and then she went to get in her car.'

'Why did she leave so suddenly?'

Asha turned from him. 'Suddenly?'

'You said you'd bumped into her when she was shopping.'

'So?'

'She didn't buy anything. There were no bags with her. No transaction on the card either. Why would she go into a shop without buying anything? Was she there to see you, or did something happen to make her leave abruptly?'

'Neither. We chatted for a couple of minutes and then she remembered she had to be somewhere else.'

'Where?'

'I think it was the PTA meeting. You'll have to ask her when she wakes up.'

Charles was studying Pippa as if he was trying to see into her mind.

Charles stepped closer to the bed, sat on the edge and sighed. 'She's not been herself lately,' he said. 'Flying off the handle, forgetting conversations we've had. The children fear her. And there was that terrible business at work.'

'What business?'

'What? Oh, forget I said anything. It was never proven and, in the end, they let her resign rather than make a fuss about it.' He sighed. 'But it does makes one wonder what she's capable of, doesn't it?'

Asha looked at Pippa, too. If she could hear what was being said, what would she make of it all? Her husband, the man who should be protecting her against the world, was sowing seeds of doubt about Pippa's mental state. Dropping a trail of breadcrumbs hoping that it would lead Asha to suspect Pippa instead of Charles.

'This must be terrible for you, Charles. I can only imagine how worried you must be and coming so soon after the death of a close friend, too. I don't know how you're hold-ing it together.'

Charles lowered his head. 'I'm coping. I know that Pippa is in the best place and she'll get through this, but the same can't be said for Jerry, can it? We were close. Like brothers. It's taking some getting used to.'

'Pippa said that you played squash with him every week.'

'Like clockwork.'

'But Mr Newhall told me that he had a bad hip and hadn't played squash in months. Isn't that strange?'

Charles didn't flinch, only let a lazy smile curl the edges of his mouth. 'Isn't it just?'

WITNESS SEVEN

Helen-Louise.
Mother of Marco.
Chair of the Parent Teacher Association.

Things like this don't happen at Aberfal High, John. I can call you
John, can't I? How do I put this? We're not *those* sorts of people. Of
course, and bear in mind I *know* how this makes me sound but, I
must be honest with you, John. We sometimes let in boys from
non-traditional backgrounds if you know what I mean. Families who
can't afford the fees. I'm not saying that the lack of money makes
them prone to violence. It's not the money per se. Some of my
friends are poor. I've shopped at Aldi, John. What I'm saying, you see,
is that money breeds jealousy. We're not doing any favours letting in
children from low-income families. How do you think they feel when
they can't afford the skiing trips? When they're embarrassed to invite
friends around to their house? When they're wearing second-hand
uniform? Oh, we like to think that we're doing them a kindness, but
who wants help like that? All I can say is a few years back you'd never
have seen a tattoo at the school gates of Aberfal High and now look.

On the day that Jerry met his untimely end I was in the cricket
pavilion overseeing the production of the cricket tea. We are rather
well-known for our provisions, you see. Some schools hand out
sweaty cheese rolls in clingfilm and a bag of crisps, but we like to go
the extra mile for our boys and their parents. It was my initiative, but
I don't like to take all the credit.

I didn't see Jerry in person, but I know that he had a visit from his
wife that afternoon. I only mention it because it's rare for her to

come to sports matches. I'm sure there's no truth in the rumour that there was something going on between Jerry and Katy Lane, but one wonders whether Gemma had heard the rumour, too.

And I tell you who else stuck out like a sore thumb, John. The new parent, Asha somebody. Goodness knows how you pronounce that surname. I always feel embarrassed by these names, don't you? Like they're trying to trip us up. Anyway, the only time I've seen her at a school event was when she came to complain about something. She's never volunteered to help with anything and she never came to her son's hockey matches last term. I know this for a fact because I've never missed any of Marco's matches or recitals. So why would she choose this day, above all others, to take an interest in her son's sports match? Well, that's what I'd be asking her anyway.

The person who worried me the most was . . . well that is, sorry, what I mean is . . . goodness, listen to me falling over my words. I'm not a tongue-tied person, John. But after everything he's done for the school . . . You see, before the match ended, I noticed that we didn't have enough milk and I headed into the school to the kitchen. There's a fire escape at the back of the school, it leads from the science block and comes over the roof of the canteen and into the place where the big bins are. Most of the time those doors are open, so I thought I'd slip in through there. And that's when I saw Charles Yardley. He was sitting on the steps with his head in his hands. He looked wretched.

But that isn't all. You see . . . Goodness, I can't believe I'm saying this, but he had something on his shirt. And it looked a lot like blood.

Chapter 25

Three days after Pippa's accident

Katy sat in her car, in the car park overlooking Pendennis Point. The sea glittered like a million stars were submerged in it. A brace of paddle-boarders approached Castle Beach and, at this distance, they looked like a pod of dolphins easing through the water. The car windows were open and the soft breeze lifted her hair from her neck. It was a perfect evening, yet Katy had never felt so unsettled.

'You know I love you,' Katy said, keeping her eyes on the sea rather than the man in her passenger seat. 'But I think, for my sake and yours, we need to ... God, this is more difficult than I'd expected. This has to end. I'm so sorry, Charles.'

Charles sighed and said, 'You're right.'

Katy turned in her seat to face him and leaned back against the door. She'd expected more of a fight. 'That's it?' she asked. 'No begging?'

He took her hand. 'You know I don't *want* this to end, but you deserve more than I can give you. Things are complicated. With Jerry and then with Pippa's accident ... well, you know how it is. I should have left her months ago but how can I move out now? For a start, who'd look after the boys? I don't know how long it will take for her to recover. We could be looking at months. I love you too much to ask you to wait.'

How had he done that? How had he made it sound like he was breaking up with her when she was the one who instigated it? Katy watched his thumb make circles over the back of her hand. Even after a year together, his touch made her tingle all over.

'Maybe we can put a pin in it and try again when everything has died down?' he said.

'I don't know how to put a pin in feelings, Charles.'

He hung his head. 'No. I know. It was a stupid thing to say. I am going to leave her. You know I've already told her that it's over. But I can't do it yet. A year down the line if I'm single and you're single . . .'

Katy nodded but, now she was faced with it ending, she felt such an intense longing for him that her hand began to shake and she pulled away from him. It was just her luck to fall for a man when he wasn't hers to fall for. She used to be so careful with her heart.

Katy looked back at the expanse of water in front of them. She'd always been set against relationships with married men. In fact, she'd judged – and misjudged – women who embarked on affairs. At first, Charles was someone she worked with from time to time. Then he became a sounding board, a mentor of sorts, someone she could rely on. A friend. She couldn't quite pinpoint when that had begun to change, perhaps because she hadn't wanted to admit to it, but she became aware of when he was in the building, as if there was an extra spark of energy in the air.

His hands were so soft, his eyes so deep and then, without meaning to, they were confiding in each other, having meetings just the two of them. Sharing their dislike for Jerry's methods. Kissing.

'But,' she said, 'do you think that Pippa stepped in front of the car on purpose so that you'd stick around? I mean, you told her you wanted a divorce and then a couple of weeks later she's in hospital and you being a doctor, well you're in your sweet spot, aren't you? Caring for her. Making her whole again.'

'I've got to say the thought did cross my mind.' Charles shook his head. 'She's not been well and there's been this thing with Jerry and . . . can we not talk about her? I want to make the most of every moment I have left with you.'

It had been one of their early rules. When they were together, they weren't to talk about the real world, because if they did, the guilt would overwhelm them both.

How was it possible that she was losing out to an unconscious woman? Even from her hospital bed Pippa Yardley was controlling everything.

They sat in silence as a car pulled up next to them and two people got out to admire the view. Katy didn't think they'd bump into anyone they knew, but she still had to be careful. No snogging in the car like teenagers. Charles had suggested meeting at the flat, but Katy felt the walls closing in on her and stood a better chance of resisting his charms in public. She looked down at her bare hands. 'Oh, by the way, I think I left my ring at the flat.'

'You'll have to go and get it yourself; I won't be able to get away for a while. Now Jerry's dead I can't pretend I'm

231

playing squash every week. Speaking of Jerry, Gemma's asked me to do a reading at the funeral.'

'I thought she hated you.'

'Why do you think she's asking me to do the reading? That woman delights in torturing me.'

'You're not going to do it, are you?'

'How can I say no?'

'Your wife's in a coma. Gemma will understand.'

'Of course. Because she's known for her understanding nature, is she? I wouldn't give her the satisfaction.'

Katy would be at the funeral, wrestling her grief and her guilt. When Jerry was alive, she couldn't wait to see the back of him but, now he was gone, she felt sick. He should've retired to the golf courses of Spain, not died alone on the floor of his office. Had he been scared? Had he known what was going to happen to him? She kept imagining what his last moments would have been like.

Katy put her hands on the steering wheel to have somewhere to put them so she wouldn't be tempted to touch Charles again. 'Someone knows about us.'

'What do you mean?'

She hadn't wanted to tell Charles about the emails, but there was nothing left to lose.

'I've been getting emails telling me to admit what I've done. It must be about us, right? I can't see what else—'

'What? When?'

'They started before Easter. The first one came the day someone slashed my tyres.'

'Slashed? You said you'd driven over a nail.'

'The recovery guy said it was deliberate. There were several holes.'

'Why didn't you tell me?'

Katy sighed. 'Honestly? Because it was the start of that week we had together at the flat. I thought, if I told you, you'd panic and call the whole thing off. Everything was so perfect and I didn't want anything to ruin that.'

'That's not your call. You should have told me.'

While Pippa and the kids had been in a yurt in Wales, Katy and Charles had been living a blissful, beautiful lie. They used to meet at Katy's house until Charles bumped into her neighbour who was a patient of his. Too many house calls would have been suspicious.

'At first, I'd thought it was Otis Blake, seeing as he caught us in the summer house. And he's always wandering around with those garden shears . . .'

'Maybe it was Jerry? He knew that I was telling Pippa I was still going to play squash on a Sunday and, well, maybe he wasn't as stupid as I thought.'

'It can't be Jerry because I've had another email since he died.'

'What do the emails say?'

'That I must come clean before the ball, or else.'

'Come clean about what? And why the ball?'

'I'm assuming they want me to confess to our relationship or be humiliated at the event of the season but, if there isn't a relationship to come clean about, maybe the problem will go away.'

Katy hadn't told Charles about the other secret that she needed to come clean about. The fact that she'd hidden the murder weapon. Disposed of evidence. She'd thought, only for a split second, that Charles might have been responsible, that she was somehow protecting him, keeping him safe. Love making an idiot of her. She was certain that when he mimed swinging the bat at Jerry's head, at the open day, he was joking. She didn't know what she'd been thinking.

Katy and Charles met every Sunday evening without fail while Pippa thought Charles was playing squash. Jerry had been happy to cover for him but what Charles hadn't understood was that he'd so readily agreed because he saw an opportunity to take advantage. It wasn't long before Jerry started requesting *special* prescriptions. 'Come on now, Chaz, wouldn't want to be letting it slip to Pippa that I didn't see you last Sunday. It only costs you a bit of paper and ink.' And, from there, it wasn't far to, 'You wouldn't want me to expose your little scam, would you? I'm sure the GMC would be most interested.'

'What are you doing about them?' Charles asked.

'The emails? Nothing. Until now I've ignored them and hoped they'd go away.'

'You should have told me.' His phone began to ring. He frowned at the display and rejected the call. 'Bearing in mind the emails and the slashed tyres,' he said, 'there's something I should tell you.'

'God, you've not been getting emails too, have you? I wonder whether Jerry had them as well. You don't think they're coming for us next, do you?'

'No. It's nothing like that.' Charles frowned and tilted his head. 'Are you . . . are you okay?'

'You mean, apart from discovering Jerry's dead body, being sent threatening emails and ending a relationship with the man I love? Yeah, just peachy. Why do you ask?' Katy leaned her elbow out the open car window and turned her head so that Charles couldn't see how close she was to breaking. 'Anyway, what was it you were going to tell me?'

'The night before the open day, my car was vandalised.'

'I know. You told me.'

'Yes. Yes, I did. But I didn't tell you that "liar" was painted across the windscreen in green paint.'

'Oh, shit. So . . .' Katy thought about the emails. They hadn't expressly called her a liar but that was implied by their insistence that she should come clean. 'You think that this is related to the emails I've been getting?'

'It could be. I should also tell you that I recognised the shade of paint.'

'If you tell me Farrow and Ball have a colour called "infidelity" . . .' Katy said with a shake of her head.

'No,' said Charles. 'As far as I can remember, it's called Whirlybird. The point is, it's the same shade that we used to paint the kitchen.'

Katy gasped, though it was hardly a surprise. 'So, it's Pippa then? She knows about us. Oh God. This can't be happening.' She folded her arms around herself and leaned forwards as if winded.

'I would have sworn she didn't have a clue. We've been so careful. Maybe she tried too many times to get hold of me while she was in Wales? Maybe she put two and two together. When she wakes up, we'll need to convince her that she's got the wrong end of the stick.'

235

Charles rubbed his jaw. 'If Pippa and I remain amicable I should be able to talk her into selling the house. If not, she'll get a lawyer who swings it so that she and the children get to stay there and I get the privilege of paying for it. At least with her in a coma we have time to come up with a plan.'

It made sense that Pippa would be behind it. And who could blame her? The question remained, how had she found out? Had Otis Blake told her? Jerry? The only times they'd ever been spotted in public they'd had genuine reasons to be together.

'Wait,' said Katy. 'It can't be her.'

'Why not?'

'Well, the paint on your car might be her, but she can't be behind the emails because I got another one this morning. So, unless she's emailing from her coma . . .'

'Oh.'

Charles turned in his seat so quickly that the car swayed. 'No. This is good.'

'Is it? I'd be happier if I knew who was behind it all. If not Pippa, then who? Not Jerry because he's dead. Otis? Who else could know about us?'

'Gemma,' said Charles.

He tapped his fingers on the dashboard. 'She could have thought there's something between you and Jerry and I knew about it? I know there have been rumours for a while now that Jerry was playing away from home.'

'Don't be ridiculous. Me and Jerry?'

'Bear with me. Jerry won't have told her about the pills. There's some sneaking around. Something he's keeping from her. She knows it's something to do with me. Maybe I'm covering for him. There are rumours about the two of you and then you and Jerry fall out over something. The end of an affair perhaps?'

Katy shook her head. 'It's a bit far-fetched.'

'Do you have a better theory?'

She sighed. 'Unfortunately not. I suppose, if Gemma did think that there was something going on between me and Jerry, that would explain why she was going to confront Jerry on the day he died. I heard her saying on the phone that she wasn't going to back down this time. I'd thought that she was the most likely suspect until I found out that Jerry had sent an email to Mandy after Gemma left.'

'Did he, though?' said Charles. 'Or did Gemma send it while she was still in there? And then cause a commotion with her dog so that she would have an alibi. Everyone saw her then, didn't they? Not five minutes after Jerry was apparently sending emails.'

Charles's phone started ringing again and he took it out of his jacket pocket. 'Sorry. I need to take this.'

He got out of the car and slammed the door too hard behind him. Katy winced. She watched him walk towards the sea, his phone to his ear. She watched his mouth move but couldn't tell what he was saying. He looked at his watch and shook his head.

Could Jerry's grieving widow be responsible for all of this? For the emails? The vandalism? The murder? It didn't sit right with Katy but, as Charles had said, they didn't have a better theory and Charles had that huge falling out with Gemma a few months back. If it was true, though . . . If Jerry had been murdered because his wife suspected he was having an affair with Katy, then Jerry's blood was on her hands. The misunderstanding would only have arisen due to her and Charles sneaking around behind everyone's back. And if Gemma was angry enough to kill Jerry, then what would she do to the woman she thought he was having an affair with?

Chapter 26

Three days after Pippa's accident

Hello?

Though her voice was clear, Pippa knew she hadn't spoken out loud. The muscles in her face were slack. It must have been that voice inside her head. Natter, natter, natter. Never shutting up. It had something to tell her, but she refused to listen.

Go away, she thought. *Shush!*

She was in bed, but this wasn't her memory foam mattress, nor her pillows. She never slept on her back because it made her snore and that would never do. She wanted to turn over on to her side but got confused when she tried to put her body in motion. The base of her spine throbbed, sharp pulsing pain shooting down her legs.

'Pain,' she said. But this time it strayed outside her head and blew out her dry lips.

She nodded, or at least she thought she did. Yes, pain. But with the nodding came more pain. It was in her neck and around her neck. It was deep in her throat and up into the back of her mouth. Her ears. Her shoulders. She wouldn't try that again. If she could roll onto her side, she could go back to sleep.

'Hello, Pippa? Can you hear me?' The man who was speaking sounded short. His voice was right next to her ear.

She thought of her husband, Charles. He was tall. But this voice wasn't his because Charles had a voice like a chocolate truffle, whereas this one was like a badly tuned radio hissing and crackling. Pippa wanted to put her hands over her ears, but when she tried to lift her arms, they were too heavy. *Leave me to sleep*, the voice in her head said. How embarrassing to be sleeping in someone else's bed. She'd been found out, like Goldilocks.

'Pippa?'

This time it was a woman's voice. Momma bear. Papa bear. Were they Charles's friends? Where was he anyway? Charles would know what to do.

'Charles,' she said.

Or tried to.

The sound was there in the back of her throat, but she was struggling to put any oomph into it. Goodness. What on earth was wrong with her today?

'Her signs are good. Breathing on her own.'

Someone tune that Goddamn radio or switch it off.

God damn. She didn't think she'd ever said that before in her life. It made her want to giggle. A small sound escaped her mouth, like a hiccup.

'She's trying to speak,' said a woman's voice. Motherly. Not in a pat-your-head and play hide-and-seek way, but in that no-nonsense way. *I will not stand for any of your nonsense, Philippa. Go to your room, Philippa. You wait until your father gets home.*

'Should we call her husband?' the man said.

He shouldn't have left her alone with these strangers. Where were the children?

Momma bear said, 'We already have. Told him that we were going to attempt to bring her out of her coma, but he said he had other business to attend to.'

Poor Charles. Always busy. If it wasn't the surgery, it was the school. It was too much for him. One of these days something was going to have to give. Jerry asked too much of him.

Jerry.

She got hot every time she thought about her outburst at the open day. It was so unlike her. Charles had been furious. He said it was the last thing they needed. They needed to keep Jerry sweet, seeing as there was no way they could pay the school fees this term. She had tried to explain to Charles that Jerry owed her an apology, but Charles had told her to get a grip.

There was something else she had to remember about Jerry. A bad thing. That's what the voice wanted to tell her, but she didn't know how far she could trust the voice. Charles would know.

Just you wait, Jerry, until your father gets home.

Pain. New pain. Pain in her heart now at the thought of Jerry. Poor Jerry.

Pippa tried to open her eyes, but her eyelashes were in the way and she could hardly see a thing. Through the half-open slits, Pippa saw a woman shaking her head. So much like Mother. She never did think that Charles was good enough. She always said that good looks and money were nice, but they wouldn't make Pippa happy. For many years

Pippa thought she'd proved her mother wrong, but she should have known better. Mother knows best.

At the time, Mother had been in the minority. Everyone else who met Charles adored him. He had a story to fit every occasion and he was polite to a fault. He was the type of man to open your car door, to carve the roast and give his coat to you on a chilly day. It was surprising that Mother didn't fall for his charms.

His patients loved him, his friends loved him, the boys, the school. Everyone thought that Charles was one of the best. He and Jerry, as thick as thieves. Jerry and Charles. Such firm and fast friends. But not anymore because, oh, it was coming back to her now. If she could clench her eyes against the sight of something, could she clench that part of her brain that made her remember? She tried, but she didn't know which muscles to use to stop the onslaught.

Bad dream, she told herself. *It's a bad dream.*

But she knew it wasn't. Hearts didn't hurt this much when you were dreaming.

So, it was true then? Jerry was dead.

This news, which she had been holding in a glass jar close to her chest, dropped and shattered across the floor. Shards of sharp memories. Pointed questions which would make you bleed if you heard the answers.

Jerry Newhall was dead. The police wanted answers, but she only had the wrong ones. But now she realised she'd been asking the wrong questions. For one thing, the money. How could they have spent all their savings? She wasn't rash with her spending, didn't have expensive tastes. And there was the thing that felt like an itch at the back of her brain. The squash match. She wasn't sure why she hadn't questioned it at the time. Charles went out on Sunday night, as usual, to play squash. But his squash partner had been dead since Friday. Well, wasn't that a turn up for the books?

Oh, Charles, you are a naughty boy.

Charles and Jerry. Best friends, but not really. They'd all gone on holiday together once – not the kids because they'd gone to her mother's – but Jerry and Gemma, Charles and Pippa. That Greek Island. Such a lovely villa. A pool. All those tavernas in walking distance and lots of retsina to be drunk. But when Charles had too much alcohol he got into bad situations and that holiday was one of them. He said he hadn't touched Gemma, but her black eye the next day suggested otherwise. High jinks, he said. Jerry laughed it off and Pippa played the peacekeeper. One of those things, she'd told Gemma. Wrong place at the wrong time and Charles was always so expressive with his hands. Gemma said he hit her on purpose; Charles said he didn't. With no one else there when it happened, it came down to choosing a side. Pippa chose the wrong one.

Sober Charles was mortified. Handy that he could blame the alcohol rather than himself. He promised to never drink again and he'd been true to his word. Pippa wondered whether the alcohol made him violent or if it only removed the barriers that kept him from expressing his true nature. Either way, it hadn't happened again. His apology was accepted by Gemma, Pippa's wasn't.

Pippa could hear people moving around the room now. Several pairs of feet and soft-soled shoes. She felt their anticipation. Her senses were keener now. She could smell something sharp, medicinal. Could feel her tongue sticking to the roof of her mouth.

As the world came back into focus, she heard the woman's voice again. 'Welcome back, Pippa, love.'

Chapter 27

Eight days before the summer ball

Asha struggled to think of anything she detested more than shopping for clothes and yet, somehow, Rose had talked her into helping her find the perfect shoes. She stroked the silky materials, felt the weight of the full skirts and let them drop again. The hangers swung like see-saws at the park.

'Not those,' Rose said. 'Not twenties enough. You want to get something shorter, with fringes and sequins.'

'Wrong,' said Asha. 'I don't want anything. I'm not going to the ball.'

'Poor Cinders. Ready for a coffee?'

Asha nodded and followed Rose out of the shop, calling, 'Thank you', to the woman behind the counter.

'Do come. It'll be such fun. I tell you what, when you come to mine tomorrow night, you're welcome to look in my wardrobe and see if I have anything that'll suit you. I think we're about the same size?'

'That's sweet of you to say, but we obviously aren't. Besides, I don't want to go. For a start, the tickets are the cost of a week's shopping and I hate small food on large plates. I'm more of a chips-on-the-beach kind of girl.'

Rose smiled and tossed her hair over her shoulder. 'You do make me laugh.' Rose came to an abrupt halt and pointed up a side alley. 'Oh, this is new. Shall we?'

'Fine by me,' Asha said. 'Have you heard anything else about Pippa? I'm pretty sure that Charles hates me, so I doubt he'll call with any news.'

'It's not personal. He's not the only one who hates you.' She pushed open the cafe door. 'Joking. Look! There's a darling little courtyard out back.'

Rose picked up her pace to make sure she got to the only remaining table before anyone else. As she dropped her bags on the floor and sank down onto the painted wooden chair she said, 'You know, if I was Pippa, I wouldn't bother waking up. This whole thing is an absolute disaster from a PR point of view and everyone's talking about how she must have had something to do with Jerry's murder.'

'Are they? You are literally the only person I've heard say that.'

'Two tragedies in the space of a fortnight. Coincidence? I think not.'

'Can it be called a tragedy if Pippa's going to be all right?'

Rose checked her phone, turned off the ringer and placed it face down on the table. 'She's gone downhill since I've known her. A couple of years ago, you couldn't move around here without seeing Pippa's touch. The events, the balls, the fairs . . . she was all over it. She only gave up work around Christmas time, but she's lost her spark since then. The cake; this thing with the money. I mean, I'm not being rude but how does a person let themselves get in that situation? All she needs to do is sell her car and there's a term's school fees right there.'

Asha picked up a menu and pretended to be engrossed in the different kinds of coffee this place offered. Locally roasted beans. De-caff. Half-caff.

'I suppose,' Asha said. 'But unless the car is paid off it isn't an asset.'

'An asset?'

'If the car was bought on a credit card, or through a lease agreement, then selling it wouldn't help much, would it?'

'Leased?'

Rose looked confused for a moment. 'Funny story,' she said. 'I tried to get a credit card once, before we went on holiday to . . . I forget where it was now, but anyway, the bank turned me down. I've never had any debt. Never borrowed a penny so, would you believe it, I had a bad credit rating because there was no record of me ever being able to pay back money I'd borrowed.'

Asha attempted to smile as the waitress reached their table. She too had been turned down for a credit card, but for different reasons. 'Hi. Can I get a strawberry milkshake, please?'

'What are you? Ten years old?' asked Rose. 'I'll have a hot chocolate with marshmallows and cream. Thank you.'

The waitress hurried away and Asha pointed at Rose. 'Don't you judge me for my milkshake. You've ordered the same thing, except it's hot.'

Rose curled her hair around her fingers. 'I look sophisticated with a hot chocolate, but immature with a milkshake. You can get away with it because you're . . . quirky.'

From anyone other than Rose, Asha might have taken that as an insult.

'This is nice,' said Rose. 'And a stroke of luck that you don't work on Fridays.'

'I do work on Fridays, but I've already finished for the day.'

'Really?'

'Worked until midnight last night on the menus for the school ball and I've been stacking shelves at Tesco since 5 a.m.'

'Wait. What? I don't even know where to start with that.'

'I have two jobs. One in graphic design, one in Tesco.'

'I didn't realise things had got that bad,' Rose said.

Asha laughed. 'Bad? This is as good as my finances have ever been.'

Rose looked confused.

'I was working in Tesco when I saw Pippa. I was there moments after she was knocked down.'

'See? This is the reason I get my shopping delivered.'

'So you don't get knocked down by a car?'

'Any number of terrible things can happen.'

'Listen, about Pippa. She said something before she ran out of the shop and I don't know whether I should tell someone. It's not like she said anything definitive but . . .'

'Well, you should certainly start by telling me.'

Asha moved her chair closer to the table. 'I don't know . . . It's not like I—'

'Oh my God! Just tell me!'

'Okay. Okay. She told me that she knew something about what happened to Mr Newhall and that Mandy lied about not leaving her desk that afternoon. She said that she spotted Otis Blake hanging around and there was something about Charles, but she wouldn't say what.' Asha decided not to tell Rose that Pippa had admitted to going to see Jerry. That was a confidence that needed keeping.

'How? When did she see Mandy? I thought Pippa was with us the whole time, wasn't she?'

'She went to the toilet at one point, remember? She was gone for a while. I mean, should I tell the police about Pippa seeing Mandy? There's a killer walking around the school and we're standing by and doing nothing.'

Rose shook her head. 'If I were you, I'd keep out of it. And that's *me* saying that. If Pippa does know something about Jerry's death . . .' She stared into space, her eyes darting about as if she were trying to solve a puzzle.

'You won't tell anyone what I've said, will you?' Asha asked. 'I don't think Pippa would want anyone to know.'

'No, of course not. People who know too much about this murder tend to get mown down while crossing the road.'

They sat in silence for a while, Asha looking over her shoulder hoping that the waitress would come back with their drinks soon.

A cat appeared and wound its way around Asha's ankles. She put her hand down to stroke it and it sauntered away in that way that cats do, showing you up for being stupid enough to fall for their charms.

'You're right,' Rose said. 'There is definitely something odd about that family nowadays.'

'When did I say they were odd?'

'Charles and Pippa used to be a strong unit. I'd be astounded if they go through with getting a divorce. I think

249

that this accident could make Charles realise how much Pippa means to him. But the kids must have picked up on the tension. No matter how much you're convinced you're keeping it all in, there's always some leakage. Which explains all the problems they're having with Benny.'

'What problems?'

'Far be it from me to spread rumours but . . .'

'Don't give me that rubbish.'

The waitress appeared and placed their drinks on the table. After she'd left, Asha said, 'Go on.'

Rose shook her head. 'Ollie has had quite a bit of trouble with Benny recently. I would go and talk to Katy Lane about it but, with everything the Yardleys have on their plates . . .'

'What kind of trouble?'

'Silly things. Breaking his ruler, taking his water bottle, not letting him play with them at lunchtime. It's been building up all year. They've been friends since they were six, but Ollie says he hates him now. I'd offered to take Benny after school, you know, while Pippa's in hospital. Feed him at our house, help with the homework and what have you, but Ol says he'd leave home if Benny sets foot in our house.'

'He feels quite strongly about it then?'

'It's his *"go to"*,' Rose said, flapping her hands. 'He's run away a total of four times now. Never further than the allotments behind our house. He had this idea that he could catch and eat rabbits or something. Honestly, that boy and his dramatic outbursts.'

As Rose rolled her eyes, Asha thought she knew exactly where Ollie got his dramatic streak from.

'Are you sure it's Benny though?' Asha asked. 'Most of Cass's problems seem to be coming from Ryan.'

'Oh, it's definitely Benny. What's the problem with Ryan?'

'Well at the open day, Cass was in that lake because Ryan dared him to swim it.'

'Oh, I see. No, I doubt Ryan is the ringleader. He strikes me as a foot-soldier sort.'

Asha took a sip of her milkshake and got a dab of cream on the end of her nose. She wiped it off with the back of her hand.

'It was Ryan who was behind the messages on Cass's phone. If it wasn't for Otis Blake . . .'

'I'm not saying you're wrong, but . . . actually, that's exactly what I'm saying. Trust me, Ryan's the least of your problems but, before we get to that, let's talk about you and Otis Blake.'

'Let's not.'

'You brought him up.'

'Didn't.'

'You are into men, aren't you? Because the way that you dress . . .'

'The way I dress is fine.'

'What is it, men or women?'

'Both. Or neither. I've not had a relationship in a while.'

'Well, that's rather modern of you.'

'Not really.'

'Word of advice though. If I were you, I'd make your mind up.'

'That's not how—'

251

'I was asking Mick what he knew about Otis, by the way and he says he's some sort of weirdo genius.'

'Genius?' asked Asha.

'Yeah, the guy is some sort of brainiac, had a successful career making shedloads of money in finance or computers or something else mind-numbingly dull. And then he retired at the grand old age of forty and chose to dedicate his life to rebuilding the school grounds into the glory of its heyday, or something. I don't know.'

Rose stuck her finger in the cream on top of her hot chocolate and picked out a marshmallow. She took her time eating it and licking her fingers and then eventually her eyes met Asha's. 'There's something I've been thinking about telling you.'

'Okay. Now I'm worried. It's not like you to think before you speak.'

'See, Ryan *really* isn't your problem. Benny is. This week, Benny had Ollie play a prank on one of the other boys. He got him to move this kid's chair as he was about to sit down. Obviously, Ollie shouldn't have done it, I'm not laying all the blame on Benny here. The kid fell, banged his head. The thing is, Benny filmed the whole thing to put it on YouTube. Ollie only told me because he thought I'd see it and ground him for life. Though why he thinks I spend my time on YouTube . . .'

Asha felt her pulse in her temples and she put her fingers to her hair line to calm herself. 'Which kid?'

Rose had the decency to look away.

'Christ! Was it Cass? All this time I've been blaming Ryan but . . . God, I'm so sick of this. How many times can I tell

252

Cass to rise above the bullying? I'm tempted to tell him to hit back.'

'It wouldn't do any good,' said Rose. 'You don't want to cross Benny. You don't want to cross anyone in that family.' Rose took a sip of her hot chocolate. 'Just ask Jerry.'

Chapter 28

One week before the summer ball

Katy Lane paused at the end of Rose's winding driveway. This was a bad idea. She wasn't in the right frame of mind for drinks with the year seven mums. She wasn't in the right frame of mind for drinks with anyone.

She'd only said yes because the novelty of being asked was intoxicating. She'd seen it as a sign they'd finally accepted her as head of Aberfal High, but now she wasn't so sure. Perhaps it meant the opposite and they didn't respect her enough to keep her at arm's length. That feeling in the pit of her stomach was one of being invited to a party by the cool kids. And not belonging.

All afternoon she'd been hatching plans to get out of it. A fast-moving migraine? A broken wrist? She found herself wishing for some terrible illness to befall her so that she had no choice but to send her apologies. Katy wouldn't be lying if she said she was exhausted, because, the truth was, she'd never felt so drained of all energy in her life. It had been a tiring couple of weeks. For most people, an evening drink in the sunshine would be just what was needed but, for Katy, it was an extension of the work she'd been doing all week. Not the drinking – that was new – but the effort of keeping people happy, getting them on side, looking out for signs they were trying to bring her down.

She wondered which lies the rumour mill was grinding to make half-truths. Katy would be careful not to ask many questions. But these women – with a certain amount of alcohol and this much stress to shake off – would only need to be put on the right track and then Katy could sit back and listen.

The best thing about coming to Rose's house was that it was close enough to where she lived that it would save her the cost of a taxi but, as Katy looked at the front of Rose's house, she was amazed that this house could even exist within walking distance from her terrace. How could they manage to live in different worlds and yet still be almost neighbours?

She walked up to the door and, before she could press the doorbell, it swung open and Rose greeted Katy like she was an old friend who she hadn't seen in years. She hugged Katy and kissed her cheek.

The house was in complete silence. 'Am I early?' Katy asked.

'No. Right on time. You are the first though. Come on in. Let's sit in the garden until it gets cold. Make the most of the good weather. It's meant to turn next week, isn't it?'

Katy gave Rose the chilled bottle of white and two tubes of Pringles she'd bought from the shop on the walk over.

'Come through.'

She followed Rose through to the garden. It sloped to a stream that bisected the spongey lawn from an orchard where small misshapen apples glowed in the late evening sun. There was a pagoda at one side with tangled tendrils growing over it, presenting pale purple flowers. A terracotta chimenea was already primed and ready to be lit. Cream-cushioned seats and benches formed three sides of a square and lilac-coloured blankets were draped over seats. On the low wooden table were bowls of crisps and olives.

Katy could smell the Citronella candles that burned in large glass hurricane lamps at intervals around the seating area. Gardens like this were the reason Katy never invited anyone to her home. She was fond of her little courtyard, which always seemed to be drenched in sunshine, but there was only room for a table, two chairs and a rusty barbecue. As much as she loved it, she felt ashamed that she hadn't managed to amass the kind of money that the parents at the school had. She worked as hard as any of them, perhaps even harder, and she was proud of the work she did, but the mums she was meeting tonight – as nice as they were – were in a different league.

The truth was, she didn't drive a flash car, she didn't have expensive diamond rings on her fingers, she didn't have a maxed-out pension and couldn't afford to join their exclusive gym. Maybe she was wrong, maybe none of the mums cared – perhaps it was her own insecurities that made her sensitive. Comparing oneself to others rarely worked out well. But right now, she was wondering who she'd have to kill to get a garden like this.

'What can I get you?' Rose asked.

'Anything cold,' Katy said without taking her eyes off the view. 'Your garden is spectacular.'

'Thank you. It is, isn't it? We're so lucky to live here. The garden is a lot of hard work, but I love it. No matter the weather I'm out here most days pruning, or digging over, or mulching. Don't get me started, I could bore you for hours about the properties of the soil here.'

'I never knew you were such a keen gardener.'

'Keen isn't the word. I'm obsessive.' She held out one hand for inspection. 'Never can quite get the dirt out from under my nails though.'

If you'd have blindfolded Katy and asked her about Rose's hands, she would have told you they were smooth and tanned, with nails painted in whichever colour was hot right now. She was taken aback by her own assumptions. So often you see what you expect to see and no more.

'Take a seat and I'll be back in a sec.'

Katy sat so she could see the entire garden. She wanted to walk down to the stream, to kick off her shoes and wade in it. If she had a garden like this she would never go inside. Breakfast on the patio. Lunch on a blanket under the apple trees. Dinner in the pagoda. There was the faint sound of the running water as it skipped over the stones carrying twigs and leaves aloft to a faraway destination. In the distance, there was the sound of geese honking as they arrowed towards home.

Katy closed her eyes and imagined for a moment that she lived here, that her husband and child were inside the house lighting candles on a birthday cake. The boy would be blond, the man would be ... Her eyes sprang open. She turned her head from side to side, hearing a crunching sound in her stiff neck. That was never going to happen. She and Charles could never have the life she dreamed of.

A doorbell rang from deep inside the house and then, moments later, several voices babbling over one another. They got louder until they spilled into the garden and then they seemed to go up by an octave.

'Katy!' exclaimed Clare. 'I am so glad you're here. Oh my God, look at you! You look wonderful. Have you lost weight?'

Asha stumbled behind Clare. 'Hey! What a lovely evening.' And then, over her shoulder, said, 'Oh my God, Rose. Your garden is . . . I mean, it is a garden, isn't it? I've not walked into a National Trust property by mistake?'

'Where's Mick tonight?' asked Clare.

'London. Coming home on the sleeper train,' said Rose. 'We've got the house to ourselves.'

There were air kisses and hugs which didn't get past a loose hold on each other's shoulders and then they all settled down with a glass of wine. The doorbell rang again and this time Clare jumped up. 'I'll get it. I need the loo anyway.'

As Clare skipped inside, Rose turned to Katy. 'How are you, Katy? What a mad couple of weeks, huh? I bet you can't believe it, can you? What can you tell us about Mr Newhall's death? We know that it's not as straightforward as we first thought. Not a heart attack, obviously. And then there's this whole issue of Pippa throwing herself in front of a car which must be related somehow.'

'What?' Katy said.

'She didn't throw herself in front of a car,' said Asha, glaring at Rose. Asha shifted in her seat to turn to Katy. 'Ignore her. She must've been drinking before we got here.'

Rose wrinkled her nose. 'Details, details. I'm saying that it could be the sign of a guilty conscience. At the very least she must have had something on her mind to walk out in front of a car. Mark my words. She knows more than she's letting on.'

'Or,' Asha said, 'you're still annoyed that she ruined your precious cake – which, by the way, you should never have baked – and you've let that cloud your judgement.'

Rose's demeanour shifted, a crossing of her legs, a lift of her chin. Her smile was anything but friendly. 'You think me that petty?'

Asha shrugged. 'I'm saying that we should be supporting Pippa. She's lying in a coma. It'd be nice if she still had some friends when she wakes up.'

'You haven't heard?' said Katy, stopping the argument before it could escalate.

'What?'

'Pippa's out of the coma.'

This time, all the women turned to look at her.

'She's awake?' asked Asha.

'Really?' said Rose.

At that moment Clare came out of the house, trailed by Sarah and Becky who were carrying two bottles of Prosecco each. 'Who's awake?' Clare called.

'Pippa,' replied Rose.

'Oh my God!'

The women cheered and hugged each other. Katy smiled and hoped that was enough to convince them she was as pleased as they were.

'How?' said Asha. 'What happened?'

'I only know what Charles told me. Well, he told the school, not me specifically. They brought her out of a coma yesterday. Still in hospital but hoping to bring her home next week. I'm assuming that she's okay if they're talking about bringing her home so soon.'

'And can she remember the accident?' Asha asked.

'I've no idea.'

The women clinked glasses again. Katy noticed that Asha didn't take a drink this time. She was looking into the distance. Deep in thought.

Katy had hoped that Pippa would stay in hospital a lot longer. Surely it was rash to let her out so soon. But Charles, being Charles, had argued that she would be safe with him.

'Wow,' said Rose. 'This is turning into quite the celebration. It's so nice to see everyone. Thank you all for coming.'

'No. Thank *you*,' said Becky. 'This is what we needed after such a terrible couple of weeks. I mean, this term has been the worst, right? Speaking of which, we should also raise a glass to Jerry, don't you think?'

Together they held their glasses aloft and said, 'To Jerry.' But Katy was a fraction too late and her voice too quiet.

'And,' said Becky. 'To our new headmistress.'

'Cheers!'

'I don't know why you'd want the job,' said Rose. 'Especially given what happened to the last head of the school.'

'He wasn't killed because of the position he held,' Katy said.

'For your sake let's hope. So why do you think he was murdered? You must have a theory?' Rose said.

'I'm as clueless as everyone else,' she said.

'So,' said Becky. 'Have we all been questioned by the police then?'

'All of us who were at the cricket, I suppose,' said Rose looking around at everyone.

'What I don't understand,' said Asha, 'is how none of us noticed anything happening. Or why Mr Newhall didn't call for help? Someone would have heard a struggle, wouldn't they?'

'Especially,' said Rose, 'if he was strangled with a school tie. It would have taken a bit of time to, well . . . for him to, you know . . .'

Katy put her glass down too hard and everyone jumped. All eyes were on her now and she felt like she had to say something. 'He wasn't strangled with a school tie,' she said.

'Oh,' said Rose. 'What have you heard? Have they done the post-mortem then? I wonder why the school hasn't made an announcement. There's been nothing in the news but then no one cares about the headmaster of a school like ours, do they?'

Katy looked at each face. Every one of them eager to know something that only she could tell them. 'I . . . I shouldn't say.'

'Oh, come on,' said Rose. 'We won't say anything.'

The rest of the women shook their heads and offered up solemn oaths of silence.

'Well,' said Katy. 'Okay, but this has to stay between us,' she said.

They all nodded.

'It wasn't a tie. He was hit around the side of the head. Something solid, like a piece of wood.' She cleared her throat. 'Or a bat.'

The women were silent for a minute as their minds caught up with what they were hearing. And then Rose said, 'Asha sweetie, didn't you say that Cassius had misplaced his cricket bat?'

Becky Rupertsmum: Dying. Did I leave my shoes at your house Rose?

Clare Withoutani: Lovely evening. Thank you for being a great host Rose. So nice to see everyone. Sides hurt this morning from all the laughing xx

Becky Rupertsmum: Sriously. Am dead. RIP me. Ru burst into bedroom at 6 to tell me about his dream. FFS??!! Russ won't bring coffee. What's point of husband if he no bring coffee. I hate you all. U R not my friends. Why U let me drink so much. Sriously. U R dead to me.

Rose Oliversmum: Lovely to see you all. Feeling a little under the weather this morning.

Clare Withoutani: I feel remarkably clear-headed.

Becky Rupertsmum: In that case U R still drunk!

Sarah Teddysmum: I can't remember the last time I drank so much. All the talk of JN and Pippa sent me over the edge.

Rose Oliversmum: I know! I can't get over what Katy said about JN being hit with a bat.

Becky Rupertsmum: RIGHT??!! I keep thinking the same thing. Makes U wonder if U really know people. We probs KNOW the person who did it??? Not likely someone sneaked in off the street and killed him for no good reason. Don't think that Pippa would be capable of hitting someone with a bat so that rules her out though, yeah?

Rose Oliversmum: Dunno. She was handy with a cake!

Sarah Teddysmum: Not funny, Rose.

Rose Oliversmum: BTW Ollie says we should all be ashamed of ourselves. He looked out of window at midnight and saw Becky weeing in the garden!!

Becky Rupertsmum: OMG the SHAME!!! Sorry Ol!

Clare Withoutani: 🙄 Oh, ladies. Let's do this again soon x

Becky Rupertsmum: Anyone heard from Asha? ASHA ARE U ALIVE??

Asha: Just about.

Rose Oliversmum: Where did we land on ball tickets? Is everyone going?

Sarah Teddysmum: Actually, why not. Sign me up!

Becky Rupertsmum: My idea of hell. But fine if I have 2. Do U think Pippa will B going? I don't suppose she'll B well enough by then.

Rose Oliversmum: Would you go if you knew everyone would be gossiping about you behind your back? It's obvious that Pippa knows something about Jerry's murder. The whole thing is dodgy.

Becky Rupertsmum: Rose!!!! U can't really think that??!!

Rose Oliversmum: The more I think about it, the more I think that she and Jerry were having an affair. Did I tell you that Charles asked Pippa for a divorce?

Asha: Pippa asked you to keep that quiet.

Rose Oliversmum: It all sounds a bit suss to me. I think she killed him to cover up the affair then threw herself in front of car because she couldn't live with the guilt.

Asha: The reason it sounds 'suss' is because it's a load of bollocks. If Charles wants a divorce it's because he's a dickhead. Pippa walked out in front of a car because she wasn't looking where she was going. Sometimes, Rose, you can be such a fuckwit.

**Asha was removed from the group
by Rose Oliversmum**

Becky Rupertsmum: Christ, Rose. At this rate
there'll be no one left in this group.

WITNESS EIGHT

Henry Hinchwood (Known as Hinch).
Head of Games.

Yeah, Jerry Newhall and I argued a fair bit, but I wouldn't read much into that if I were you. We didn't see eye to eye. Different approaches. He was all about the big wins. He wanted to see goals, wickets, tries. I wanted to develop the boys' love of sport. Get them enjoying it, teamwork, discipline. But he could never see the big picture. That was Jerry through and through. No patience. He wanted to retire on a high. Wanted the school to be the best at everything, with a full trophy cabinet so he could leave some impressive legacy behind. 'Course, he'll be remembered now, won't he? But not in the way he wanted.

His wife will be able to tell you more than me, but he had some big plans for retirement. Spain, it was. They had a house there. Or maybe they were buying one, I don't know. You're barking up the wrong tree if you think one of the teachers could have done this to him because all we had to do was bide our time and wait for him to retire.

Let me address the elephant in the room. It's true I wasn't there at the end of the cricket match, but it wasn't anything to do with Jerry Newhall. I can promise you that. But there is something you should know. It's about Jerry's PA, Mandeep. Yeah, well you know her as Mandy because that's what Jerry called her. He denied that he was racist, but he preferred her name to be anglicised, so make of that what you will. I always thought he was a bit of a dick to be honest. No point pretending otherwise. But back to Mandeep. Well I'm going to be in the doghouse for telling you this; she's a private person but I've never seen any reason to hide anything. See, she wasn't at her desk all afternoon even though she said she was. And the reason I know she was away from her desk was because she was with me. We've been seeing each other for a while, but in secret like. She had this violent ex-husband and she thought she saw him at the school open day. Really shook her up and I've been looking out for her and persuading her not to leave Cornwall. She was going to hand in her resignation the day that Jerry died. I didn't want to let her out of my sight. Don't want her to leave.

Anyway, she waited behind the pavilion, but I knew she was there. I signalled to her and then we met in the staff room about five minutes later. I think she must have been away from her desk for about twenty minutes in total. A lot can happen in twenty minutes.

Katy Lane . . . she's a funny one. She told Mandeep that if she was away from her desk again, she'd sack her, so Mandeep . . . well, she didn't want to get in trouble. Mandeep, see, her conscience got the better of her and she went to Katy Lane and told her that she was away from her desk more than she'd let on. Even though she knew she could get in trouble. That's the kind of woman she is. And, get this, Katy Lane told Mandeep that, if she wanted to keep her job, she'd better stick with the original story that she was only away from her desk for five minutes and the only person who saw Jerry in that time was his wife, Gemma.

I don't know what Miss Lane has told you, but it seems to me like she wants you to believe it was Jerry's wife that killed him. You've got to wonder about her motives, haven't you?

Chapter 29

Six days before the ball

Sunday mornings could be one of two things. They could be languid hours filled with coffee and the papers. A stack of pancakes. Fruit juice. Classic FM playing in a sunny kitchen. Or they could be sharp hours filled with preparation for the week ahead. Laundry. Ironing. Last minute homework. The feeling that a small window of freedom was coming to an end and next week was already stealing the hours away.

'Think, Cass! Where did you leave it?'

'Mum, I think you're struggling to understand the concept of *lost*. If I knew where I'd left my cricket bat, it wouldn't be lost, would it?'

'Now isn't the time for you to be a smart-arse, Cassius.'

Asha had dragged everything out of the back of the van and found several water bottles, a pair of trainers that no longer fitted Cass and a pile of Christmas cards she'd forgotten to post last year.

'It's okay. I can borrow one of the school bats.'

'That's not the point,' said Asha. 'Have you any idea how much money all this equipment costs? The kit, the trips, the books. Every pen you lose, every school tie that needs

269

replacing, every pair of socks. Money doesn't grow on . . .'
Asha put her hands over her eyes. 'Urgh! I give up.'

'It's trees,' Cass said.

'I beg your pardon?'

'The phrase is "money doesn't grow on trees".'

'I know what the bloody phrase is! I'm asking you to pay more attention to things. To look after your belongings. I'm not replacing your school coat, so you'd better hope the weather stays good for the rest of the term. We need to find that bat now!'

'I don't have a match this week, do I?'

'No, Cass, you don't have a match. But that's not why I want to find it.'

'I had it with me when I went into the pavilion but then it was gone by the time I'd got changed. Maybe someone took it home by accident. It's not that big a big deal.'

Asha began to place all the rubbish in a carrier bag. Crisp packets, skinny apple cores, sweet wrappers. 'I'm sure you're right. It'll turn up eventually.' She had to hope that it didn't turn up with Mr Newhall's DNA all over it.

It was a warm morning filled with the droning of a lawn mower. Bubbles floated over the fence that separated Asha's driveway from the child-filled house next door. They shimmered pink and blue before hitting the ground and popping. Asha envied them their ability to disappear without a trace.

The way that Rose had looked at her on Saturday night made Asha want to simultaneously hide under a rock, while also slapping Rose's face. She should have known better than to embarrass Rose by bringing up the cake incident again, but it was wrong of the other woman to repeat things that Pippa had told them in confidence.

Now Asha had to decide about going to the police and telling them that Cass's bat was missing. Her gut instinct told her to keep it to herself for now and pretend she hadn't heard how Mr Newhall had died. She didn't want the police to take one look at her and make the link between the missing bat and the argument they'd had before his death. She felt uneasy about the whole situation. She came to Cornwall to escape drama, not to become a part of it.

While she'd checked the cupboard under the stairs, the minefield of Cass's bedroom and the inside of the van, Cass had replaced the windscreen wipers of the van and checked the tyre pressure. It was naive to think that a Cornish summer meant there wouldn't be rain and plenty of it.

'Here,' she said to Cass. 'Grab a sponge.'

They worked side by side washing the dust off the van, stopping every now and again to use a thumb nail to dislodge the desiccated body of a bug from the bumper, or the solidified offering of seagull shit.

She was still feeling the after-effects of a night at Rose's house. She hadn't drunk as much as the others, but it was more than she was used to. She should have trusted her first instinct to take her own beers to the party but, instead, she'd spent the evening drinking bubbly wine and eating salty crisps, neither of which agreed with her. After that initial conversation no one had mentioned the cricket bat, but Asha had felt the echo of it all evening until she'd made her excuses and gone home early.

271

This morning she felt desperate. Perhaps it was the hangover bringing her low, or the argument she'd had with Rose over WhatsApp. Every small task seemed impossible; every decision fraught with danger.

'You missed a bit,' she said.

Cass stood back, saw what she was pointing at and then crouched down to clean the mud off the door.

'Why did you have me check the tyres?' he asked.

'Thought we might go over to Porthcurno this afternoon.'

'It'll be rammed today.'

'Maybe.'

Cass flicked the hair out of his eyes. He needed a haircut. She'd already received a warning from school for letting Cass's hair grow long enough to touch his collar.

'Talk to me about Benny,' she said.

'Why?'

'I heard that he's the bully, not Ryan.'

'I never said it was Ryan.'

'How bad is it, Cass?'

He shrugged. 'It's okay.'

'Truth,' she said.

He dipped his sponge into the bucket and squeezed out brown water before scrubbing away at the wing mirror. 'He's given up doing anything to me because I don't react to it, but now he's picking on the people who sit next to me or talk to me at break.'

'Have you told Miss Lane?'

'Told you, I'm not reacting to it.'

'So that's a "no" then?'

'That's a no. But it is a lot better than it used to be.'

'You can't let him get away with it, Cass.'

'I'm not.'

Out of the two of them Cass was the more level-headed. If she'd managed to ignore things that upset her, she might have been a lot more content with her life. This sweet new start had gone sour too quickly.

'Cass, can I ask you something?'

Cass shrugged.

'You won't get into trouble or anything. I want you to be honest, okay?'

He shrugged again.

'You and me. We've always been close, right?'

Shrug.

Asha finished wiping the hub caps and got to her feet, arching her back against the ache. 'But since we've been in Cornwall I feel like, maybe, we're drifting apart. You used to tell me everything that went on with you. I need to know, Cass, is there anything you want to tell me? Anything at all. I get the feeling that there's something going on. You don't need to protect me, you know. And I won't be cross, won't try and help, won't wade in. Unless you want me to.'

'Promise?'

'Promise.'

Cass dipped his sponge into the bucket again, squeezed it and went around to the front of the van. Asha followed. 'Cass?'

'There is something.'

'Okay.' Asha waited. Wouldn't rush him.

'A couple of months ago I got Instagram.'

Asha nodded. 'Okay. Well, the fact that you've kept that from me means that you already know how I feel about it so there's no point me creating a fuss. But fine. I'd like to talk to you about keeping your account private but ... okay. See? Not losing my temper. Anything else?'

Cass didn't meet her eye. He scrubbed hard at the headlights.

'Cass, is there something else?'

'I got a message.'

'Right.'

'From this guy called Mark.'

'Oh Christ. Did he send you something inappropri—'

'He says he's my dad.'

Asha felt the ground tilt beneath her feet and she reached out to steady herself on the side of the van. She'd worried about this day coming but had covered her tracks so well that she never truly believed it would. It was one of the reasons she never went home. She never wanted to bump into him or anyone who knew him. That part of her life was over, it wasn't meant to follow her here.

'He said Gran told him about me. Until she said something he had no idea I existed.'

Asha put her free hand to her mouth. Her fingers were cold. Too much to take in. Too much to unpack. Mark was on to them and her mum was to blame. She owed Cass an explanation but couldn't speak.

'He says he started looking for me last year,' Cass continued. 'Is that why we moved? Is that why we're always moving?'

This was too much to take in and her usually busy mind had stalled. He'd had no way of knowing about Cass. She'd been so careful. Would he even recognise her after twelve years? They had no mutual friends. People who'd known them as a couple had been dropped from Asha's life before the pregnancy had started to show. The only people who knew the truth were her mum and her brother. Even Cass's birth certificate said *Father unknown*. Cass was hers and hers alone.

'Mum?'

'Sorry, Cass, but the man is lying. Tessa must have . . . I don't know, been drunk, or confused, or making things up as she goes along. God knows why she'd say something like that. I mean, I almost feel sorry for the poor guy being told something so obviously false.'

'You're saying that he's not my dad?'

'Nope. Sorry. You're going to get all sorts of nut-jobs approaching you on these social media sites. It's best you delete Instagram, don't you think? We'll talk about it again when you're older.'

Asha looked into Cass's eyes. No sign of Mark behind those brown eyes. It was almost possible to believe that no one else's DNA was involved. She and Cass looked similar, had the same sense of humour, liked the same foods, the same games. He was the part of her that had been missing.

It was difficult to read Cass's face. There was confusion in the knitted brow, but disappointment on his protruding bottom lip. But one thing was clear – he didn't know whether to believe her.

'So . . .' he began.

'So nothing. Have you spoken to your grandmother recently? She hasn't said anything to you about this man, has she?'

Cass shook his head. He and Asha's mum didn't have the kind of relationship that involved swapping messages and calls. Asha was to blame or, depending on how you looked at it, to thank. Though her mum offered on many occasions, Asha had never let her babysit. Though her mum had begged, Asha had refused to stay the night at her house in the room that had never felt like hers. Visits were few and far between and she never left Cass on his own there. A few times, Tessa had said that she'd like to see more of Cass but then there'd be a new boyfriend on the scene and her focus would be elsewhere. Though she'd never been in contention for the title of world's greatest mum, telling Mark about Cass was lower than Asha thought she could stoop.

Mark had been a regular visitor to the house when they'd been dating but Tessa had never thought much of him. So why had she chosen to tell him the only thing that Asha would have killed to keep secret?

'This man – Mark – wants to send me something for all the birthdays he's missed. Said I could have a new iPhone if I sent him our address.'

'You didn't, did you?' Asha rushed at Cass now, grabbed his upper arm. Knew she was squeezing too hard, but the fear was overwhelming. 'Cass? Tell me you didn't!'

'I didn't.'

'Does he know we're in Cornwall? Are there photos on your Instagram feed showing where we live?'

'No. Nothing like that.'

Asha let go of him and put her hands over her face. 'Good,' she muttered. 'Good.'

Cass pushed past Asha and threw his sponge into the bucket so that foamy water sloshed over the side. 'Why aren't I allowed anyone else in my life?'

'What d'you mean?'

'You're so full of crap.'

'Cassius!'

'You lied to me! You told me that I didn't have a dad. You've never let me get to know Gran and Uncle George. You never let me stay anywhere long enough to make friends. You want to keep me all to yourself because you've got no one else and you thought you could grow a person and make them love you. Well, that's not how love works, is it? You're selfish. Selfish!'

'Cass!'

'And now you're going to make us leave again, aren't you?'

'Cass.'

'You said we could stay,' he said.

Asha took a deep breath and felt every ounce of strength leave her body. 'And you,' she said, 'said we could go.'

Cass stood tall so he towered over her. 'Looks like we both say things that we don't mean.'

Chapter 30

Four days before the ball

The smell still clung to Pippa even though she'd had a bath last night and spent twenty minutes in the shower this morning. She'd used the Coco Chanel body lotion that the kids had bought her last Christmas, but she could still smell the hospital on her.

She kept looking at the calendar on the kitchen wall to remind herself that it was Tuesday. Strange that the days had kept ticking over without her knowing it. A whole week since she'd had the accident.

The house was too quiet. She'd expected Charles to take time off work, but he'd told her that she'd only be sleeping anyway, and they needed the money. How could she forget? Pippa bent over the back of the kitchen chair as another wave of nausea hit her. She was still groggy from whatever concoction of drugs they'd filled her with. Or perhaps it was the brain injury. She'd been told it would take time to recover. That she shouldn't push it. Charles had made her promise to stay in bed but seeing as Charles had broken a few promises in his time, she felt no compunction to stick to hers. She took a glass of wine for breakfast to smudge the lines while she decided what to do next, but it sat like acid in her stomach, so she made coffee instead. There was a chalk board in the kitchen where she would usually write her shopping list, but today it had names and words on it. Things she felt she would forget if she didn't write them down. But now she stood and looked at the board she wasn't sure it made any sense.

Asha supermarket. Remember???

Charles and Jerry. Squash. Sunday. Tablets!

Cake.

Window.

Mandy cricket. Hinch climbing.

Dog on loose – Gemma.

She opened the kitchen door, slipped her feet into a battered pair of Birkenstocks and went outside to sniff the air. A change was on its way, she could feel the brittleness in the morning. Pippa took a slow walk to the bottom of the garden where she could see the sea between the pointed roofs in the valley. She liked to check the ocean was still there every morning. It was a daft little ritual. There was a better view from their bedroom window and it was one of the reasons they'd bought this house a decade ago. They'd always meant to build a balcony to take their morning coffee. It would never happen now. She considered crying, but then realised she was all out of tears.

She would miss the house. How ghastly it was to be one of those couples. She wondered how long they'd be able to keep it from the children. They were bright boys and certainly knew more than Pippa wanted them to know. Benny and Charles had never been close but, recently, Benny had been openly combative. She knew she could count on him to be loyal to her but wasn't so sure about Myles. If they drew up battle lines, whose side would he be on?

It was hard to recall it now, but there was a time when she and Charles used to have such a strong relationship. They matched each other in intellect and ambition. They wanted the same things from life; were both passionate about helping people, about making the world a better place for the children they were going to have. She hadn't changed but somewhere along the line she'd lost focus. And now, instead of having dreams, she had To-Do lists. Instead of a vision board she had an ironing board. Instead of a future, a past.

And she couldn't complain, because her life had been wonderful up until the point that it wasn't. Her childhood had been happy, her parents loving. Her work had been fulfilling and her children affectionate. But before she'd even hit the half a century mark, she felt like it was coming to an end. She'd had a scare, a wake-up call and she wasn't going to waste another day being someone's second choice.

Plenty of couples rebuilt their relationships after the spark had been lost. But this morning had brought a new awareness – she didn't want to save their relationship. She wanted to save the house and save herself the embarrassment, but she didn't want to spend the rest of her life with Charles. One of the positive outcomes from the accident – and yes, there were positives to be had – was that she'd had an MRI scan that confirmed there was no tumour and that lovely doctor, the one who reminded her of Mother, said it was unlikely to be dementia either. The probable cause for her feeling like this was a lot simpler.

She shuffled back to the house. Her body was stiff, as if she'd been using all her muscles instead of using none. In the hospital they'd had Pippa sitting up. Lying down. Raising her arms and gripping their hands.

Watch my finger. And again.

She'd looked up and down and side to side until her eyeballs ached and the doctors were satisfied.

Brain injuries are tricky blighters, better to be safe than sorry.

But on balance they'd let her go home to her own bed. There appeared to be no lasting damage from the accident, but her short-term memory was sketchy at best. She felt like the word she wanted was always just out of reach, but this was to be expected, they said. Everyone said she'd been lucky, though she felt anything but. A few bruises but nothing broken. It was her head that had taken all the impact and they were strong things, skulls.

Stronger than hearts at least.

She'd been convinced she was dying. Or worse, losing her mind. And now she knew that she wasn't, that her symptoms were something far more common, then she was no longer at liberty to throw her future away. The doctor said, 'Your age and your symptoms? Sounds like the peri-menopause to me. Get yourself to your GP. I tell you, HRT changed my life.'

She could have laughed. Something so simple, blighting her life, making her feel like she didn't know herself anymore.

Back in the house there was a message on her phone from Charles, 'checking in' and reminding her that he'd be picking the boys up from school tonight seeing as Pippa wasn't allowed to drive.

The children had been so pleased to have her home that Benny hadn't left her side and had even tried to stay off school so he could be with her. Her surly teen had been replaced with a sweet boy who needed his mummy. She wondered whether it was wrong to be quite so pleased about that. Given that Charles wasn't comfortable in the kitchen, and she was in no fit state to cook, Myles had taken over the kitchen duties. It turned out he had quite the knack for cooking. Last night's meal was a simple chilli con carne with a not-so-simple homemade lemon cheesecake. He said he'd try something more adventurous at the weekend. Pippa was concerned by how much her waistline would be expanding over the next few weeks, but she liked the idea of good food more than she liked the idea of fitting into her favourite dress. It was all a matter of priorities.

Pippa started wandering through the house, seeing each room afresh. She loved this house but not the way it was decorated. Charles had chosen the kitchen cabinets. It was Charles who'd insisted on leather sofas that stuck to your skin in the summer and were too cold in winter. It was a man's house.

Charles's study looked much the same as the rest of the house. Bookshelves, leather furniture, fringed lamps, oil paintings. He didn't need a study. He never worked from home because he needed the patients, or at least their records, in front of him. What did he do when he came in here at night?

As far as Charles was concerned, she was still feeling weak and sleepy from her accident. As far as Charles was concerned, Pippa would do anything to save their marriage. As far as Charles was concerned, she hadn't remembered that he went out on the Sunday after Jerry died to 'play squash'.

Five weeks ago, Pippa had realised that Charles always came home from squash smelling freshly showered, yet she never saw his sports kit in the laundry. That's when she'd first started getting suspicious. She'd resisted the urge to follow him, but only just and so she still didn't know who he was seeing on a Sunday evening. She'd thought, or rather, she'd *hoped* that Charles was being honest about meeting with Jerry and only lying about exercising. She'd thought he was covering up the fact that he was drinking again and she might have forgotten all about it if Charles hadn't continued with the charade of going out to play squash with Jerry two days after his death and if someone hadn't painted the word LIAR on Charles's car.

Pippa was a lot of things, but she wasn't stupid and Charles was going to regret treating her as if she was. She sat in the big leather chair at Charles's desk, cajoling her mind into thinking straight. Her mind was a little foggy. Pippa had struggled to remember the names of simple things when she'd first woken up. It had taken several attempts for her to remember the word for television.

The picture box.

The rectangle with the faces in.

But, in some ways, she'd never seen anything so clearly.

'Where did you go on Sunday night – and who were you with?' she said aloud.

Looking back over their marriage, Pippa couldn't have done any more than she had. She had brought up their children to be amazing, considerate and interesting young men. She'd run the house, paid the bills, tended the garden and the community. She'd done all of this while thriving in a particularly fulfilling career. What more did Charles want?

Charles's study was one of the nicer rooms in the house. It seemed to be bathed in sunlight all day long and there was never any suggestion that it would be anything other than his personal space. She opened the drawers one by one, careful not to miss a thing. Nothing was locked because he suffered from the malady of arrogance. He didn't have to hide anything from her because she'd always been too blind to see what was in front of her face. She'd hoped for a bundle of love letters tied with red ribbon with a clear name and address, but it wasn't going to be that easy. No cards declaring love. No trinkets she didn't recognise.

Pippa sat back in the chair and looked at Charles's desk. It was surprisingly untidy for such an organised man. There was an empty teacup, biscuit crumbs and a pen without a lid. There was a pristine copy of *Cornwall Life* on his desk waiting for a quiet moment. His diary was open to last week, but the pages were largely blank.

She wondered about his secret life. Wondered about the graffiti on his car. Wondered why she hadn't questioned him more at the time. But so much had happened since then that it had slipped her already slippery mind. Pippa's mouth was dry, so she stood up to go and get herself a glass of water. From this angle she could see the corner of a folder beneath the magazine. She slid it out and saw that it was a sleek cardboard folder with the name Miller Countrywide Estate Agents on it. If Charles was already looking at putting the house on the market, he could think again. She wasn't quite ready for that.

She frowned at the typed letter inside. Had to read and re-read it to make sense of it. It was a rental agreement for a property in Truro. An apartment that he'd taken on six months ago and paid twelve months rent in advance for. Charles had told her that their savings had diminished thanks to the drop in their joint income. But she could see exactly where they'd gone now. A secret flat. Was he paying for an apartment for his mistress?

'You idiot.'

She took a piece of paper and wrote down the address. Every promise they'd made to each other, every vow. It counted for nothing because Charles wasn't the man she thought he was.

Chapter 31

Three days before the ball

As they waited by the drinks hut, Asha said, 'I'm glad you called.'

Pippa had hardly said more than a dozen words since Asha had picked her up. Though she was smiling, her eyes were vacant.

'I wanted to come and see you as soon as they let you out of hospital,' said Asha. 'But Charles said that you wouldn't be up to visitors this week.'

'Did he?'

'Two cappuccinos?' a woman called out.

'Thanks,' said Asha, taking both drinks and handing one to Pippa. Do you want to walk by the river?'

For the first time in weeks there were clouds in the sky, though it felt no cooler and no less bright. Asha was already regretting wearing a jacket.

'Did you get the flowers I sent?' Asha asked.

'Yes, I did. Sorry, I should have said something. They're nice.'

Pippa's words, like her clothes, were plain and simple. Her shirt was almost the colour of her skin, a cream vest underneath. Stone coloured linen trousers. On Asha, the clothes would have washed her out but on Pippa they looked chic and classy.

Asha would have said that Pippa wasn't acting like herself, but she was no longer sure who the real Pippa Yardley was. It all came down to perspective. Knowledge. Not so long ago, Pippa had been the perfect mum, the perfect friend. And now she was the woman who'd hit Jerry Newhall with a cake, run out from a shop while Asha was asking her about a murder and was the mother of the boy who was bullying Cassius. Pippa hadn't changed, but everything Asha knew about her had.

The park was busy. Cars were bumper to bumper along the roadside for free parking. The tennis courts were full, but the table-tennis tables empty. Young children peddled around and around on trikes while tired parents sipped their caffeine, struggling to remember when they'd last had a good night's sleep.

Asha hadn't been here before, but Pippa had insisted that this was where she wanted to come. Not the beach, not a coastal path, but a park in the city. It spread out alongside Truro River, though the tide was out, leaving the estuary thickly mudded. Boats listed while they waited for the tide to return and lift them aloft. On wooden posts, gulls called to each other, hopping down into the silt to peck for delicacies. Asha loved the rivers and creeks around Cornwall almost as much as she loved the coast, but she was working most weekends and hadn't had the time to explore as much as she would have liked.

Truro Cathedral glowed caramel above the city. Asha was about to ask Pippa if she'd ever been to a service there, but the fixed look on the other woman's face stopped her. There was something cold in her eyes, like the thoughts behind them shouldn't be shared. Though it wasn't a surprise that Pippa's mind was elsewhere, the intensity of her focus on the apartment block on the other side of the estuary made Asha bite the rim of her coffee cup. They were expensive-looking flats. All of them had balconies perfect for an evening G&T and they represented a different world to the one Asha lived in – one that screamed of young child-free professionals, of money, of class – but surely it didn't warrant the look of hatred on Pippa's face.

'How are you feeling?' Asha asked.

'You've already asked me that,' Pippa said. 'Twice. I think it's *your* memory we need to worry about, not mine.' Her smile took the sting out her words. 'Don't worry. I'm fine.'

'I don't want to be a fuss-ass, but maybe it's too soon for you to be out and about? This time last week you were in a coma.'

'Medically induced,' said Pippa. 'It's not like I've been lying in bed for eighteen months wasting away. Darling, I am a grown woman and, if I hadn't felt up to a trip out of the house, I wouldn't have called you.'

Asha nodded, but there was something different about Pippa today. She carried herself differently, a slight limp slowing her down. Her makeup didn't quite cover the bruise around her eye. Her voice was softer and yet there was a quiet confidence about her.

They walked side by side without saying a word, listening to the call of the gulls, the peal of the bells. The silence felt loaded and Asha was compelled to disrupt it. 'You know the day of your accident? Listen, was that me? Did I cause that? One minute I was asking you to go for a coffee with me and the next minute you were saying that you remembered something about Newhall's death and were running out of the shop. If I did something that made you . . .'

Pippa looked at Asha and, for a moment, she looked more like her old self. 'Oh, goodness, Asha. Is that what you've been thinking? Oh, bless you, my darling. It wasn't because of anything you said or did.'

Pippa looked up to the sky where patches of blue peeked between the clouds. 'I don't remember a great deal about the accident itself, but I do remember standing in the middle of the shop and feeling completely overwhelmed and not knowing what to do next. It was ridiculous that I was choosing fruit and veg when Jerry was lying dead some-where. Preposterous that we were all going on about our days, sending our children to a school where there'd been an actual murder. How is it possible that we can take that in our stride and leave it to the police to sort out? We made it someone else's problem and moved on. If we aren't in any danger, why should we care?'

'But we do care,' Asha said. 'At least, you and I do. And I think that the others do, but they're scared. It's natural to put some distance between yourself and something terrible. No one likes to dwell on things like that.'

'Do you think I like to dwell on it?'

'That's not what I'm saying.'

'I should be more traumatised by the accident than I am. Everyone tells me I've been lucky, but all I know is one minute I was shopping and the next I was waking up in hospital with a headache. But at least I got to wake up. Jerry never did.'

'And did you talk to the police about what you'd remembered? You know, about Jerry?'

Pippa took the lid off her coffee and blew on the foamy liquid. 'Not yet.'

'But you are going to tell them what you know?'

'The thing is, darling, I don't remember what I was going to tell them.'

Pippa blew on her coffee again and a cloud of froth escaped over the side of the cup. 'But I do wonder if I should tell them that Jerry was blackmailing Charles.'

Asha had been about to take a sip of her coffee but, instead, it spilled down her chin and she jumped backwards before it reached her clothes. She held the coffee away from her body while it dripped to the ground. 'Blackmailing?'

Pippa took a tissue out of her pocket and handed it to Asha.

'Thanks.'

'I only know what Charles told me and I doubt he's telling me the whole story. He says that Jerry was an addict. That Jerry had him prescribe painkillers a while back and liked them a bit too much. I think there might have been more than painkillers, but you know Charles. Jerry must have something over him because it's not like Charles to break the rules.'

'I saw tablets on Newhall's desk,' Asha said. 'And when he saw me looking, he hid them in his drawer, so he obviously didn't want me knowing about them. But why would Charles keep prescribing medication if he knew Newhall had a problem with it? They were friends. Why didn't he try and help?'

'Well, at some point, Charles must have realised it was getting out of hand because he told Jerry that there wouldn't be any more prescriptions. It was about that time when Jerry threatened to report him to the General Medical Council.'

'And that's a bad thing, I assume?'

'He'd lose his job, never work in medicine again. Then there was this whole thing about us not being able to get our hands on the money for the school fees. Charles told Jerry he'd get him more pills if Jerry let us pay late, but he wouldn't budge. He wanted the pills *and* the money.'

Asha balled up the tissue and threw it into the bin. 'Jerry dying might not have changed anything about the late payment, but it's taken away the threat of Charles being exposed to the GMC.'

'Exactly. Jerry wouldn't have been able to drop Charles in it without exposing himself. He would never have gone through with it. He was never a real threat.'

'I'm sure you're right, but what if there was something else? What if Jerry knew something else that could cause Charles problems?'

Pippa raised an eyebrow. 'You have a theory, darling?'

Asha pointed towards a bench. 'Do you mind if we sit?'

They both sat down. Straight backs, knees together.

'So,' began Asha. 'Mr Newhall told me he had a bad hip, which explains the painkillers.'

'I suppose.'

'He also said that because of his hip, he hadn't played squash in months.'

'Right.'

'But Charles told me they were still playing every week.'

'Ah.'

'I mean, it could be nothing, but it made me wonder if Charles might be hiding something. And if Jerry knew what it was . . . Well, might that be another reason Charles would want to shut him up?'

Pippa covered her eyes with her hand and bit her bottom lip.

'Oh God. Sorry,' said Asha. 'I shouldn't have said anything. I could be wrong. Don't listen to me. Overactive imagination that's all.'

'Oh darling, you don't know the half of it. It's one of the reasons I asked you to bring us here today.'

'You knew?'

'Sort of. I know about the non-existent squash matches and I believe he's been coming here when he tells me he's playing squash.' She motioned towards the flats she'd been staring at since they'd arrived at the park. 'Lately, I thought I was losing my mind. Alzheimer's, brain tumour, that sort of thing. A few months ago, I had to give up my job. It's why I've been making mistake after mistake. There was an oversight at work – completely my fault and cost my firm a lot of money – and I blamed it on a junior colleague. She almost lost her job over it but then it came to light that, not only had I messed up, but I'd made someone else a scapegoat.

That's not me, Asha. I've dedicated my life to helping people, not bringing them down.'

Asha said nothing, because all she could say was 'sorry' and that didn't seem like enough. She waited for Pippa to continue.

'That flat over there . . .' Pippa pointed. 'It's Charles's little love nest. Can't help but think my darling husband is having an affair on Sunday evenings when he's been telling me he's out with Jerry. It's all so sleazy, isn't it?'

Pippa pulled her oversized bag across her chest and hugged it to her.

Asha wasn't surprised – it was what she'd suspected – but being right brought her no pleasure. 'You seem remarkably calm about it,' she said. 'I'd be going ballistic.'

Pippa shrugged. 'I'm a little numb, I suppose, but that might be the painkillers. I do hate the fact that he's been playing me for a fool. When I asked him where all our money had gone, he blamed it on me losing my job, but I found out yesterday that he'd paid for twelve months' rent up front on this flat, so I didn't notice a monthly payment coming out of our joint bank account. He hadn't expected our income to drop so suddenly. Neither of us thought I'd be out of a job. His salary had always paid for the household bills and mine paid for the school. It was only when we couldn't pay the fees that it came to my attention, otherwise I might never have known.'

'Wow. I'm not sure what to say.'

'Anyway, I'm sick of being in the dark. I'm sick of everything and I want to know the truth no matter how terrible it is. I don't want to put you in a tricky situation, darling, but I don't suppose you're up for a spot of breaking and entering, are you?'

There were so many questions spinning around Asha's head. There was so much to say, but instead she stood up and said, 'Which apartment is his?'

Chapter 32

The day of the cricket match

Katy got in her car. Then got straight back out again. Something wasn't right. She should have felt the satisfaction of the day. But she didn't. She should be on her way home by now, but she wasn't. As far as Aberfal school was concerned, today had been a great day. As far as she, personally, was concerned, the day had been adequate.

She walked around the car. Her tyres were fine. The car was fine. But, for some reason, she didn't want to start her engine. There was the overwhelming feeling that she'd forgotten something. It was the same feeling she got when leaving home in the morning and having to dash back inside to check she'd turned off her hair straighteners.

Katy often felt unsettled being at the school when everyone else had gone home. Schools weren't meant to be quiet. She liked the silence of the school before the day got started. Full of potential and pent-up excitement for what the day would hold. And then, with a ring of the bell, laughter and shouts barrelled in on the backs of boys who bounced off walls and each other, from lesson to lesson. Even when the boys were busy, listening hard, there was a density in the air of a collective pulling together. By the end of the day the school had been wrung out. There were maybe a few students left behind for after-school clubs, and cleaners emptying the bins, but it became a shell.

She watched a car drive up the lane. It turned in front of the school, letting two women out, hardly pausing before speeding away and hitting the speedbumps hard. They must be cleaners arriving to make everything spit-spot and put the school to bed. It was, Katy thought, as if the school had two lives.

It was going to be a lovely hot weekend, though she had a fair number of English essays to mark. Charles thought he'd be able to stay longer at the flat on Sunday, make a full evening of it. She longed for the days when they wouldn't have to sneak around, when they could spend the whole night together. She missed being able to wake up with someone. Such a simple thing that she never knew she longed for until she didn't have it anymore. She didn't mind living alone, she liked her own company, but there was something comforting about falling asleep knowing that the person by your side would be the first face you saw in the morning.

She looked at the back seat of her car. Pristine, like everything else in her life. Her boot had a neat box of files, a first aid kit, an umbrella. Her glovebox had pens, hand lotion, a notebook and the number for the AA. Everything was as it should be. Everything in order. But something was irritating her.

Without knowing why, she locked the car and walked towards the school. Searching the windows for a sign of life, something to remind her what she was missing.

When she became a teacher, she'd assumed that she'd work in schools much like the one she'd attended.

Somewhere a little rough around the edges, shabby, with kids who swore at you. But when she saw the job at Aberfal advertised, she applied because it was in Cornwall and she'd always wanted to live near the sea.

She'd made the mistake of assuming that private schools would be swimming in money. That each child would get a new laptop every year, that the books would be pristine, but the budget restrictions were much the same here as they had been at her last place. Although, as she passed Jerry Newhall's shiny new car, she thought, 'Not everyone is struggling.'

She knew that Jerry's wife, Gemma, was away for the weekend. He'd stay here all evening if she didn't give him a nudge to go home. Perhaps that's what was niggling her, the fact that Jerry was still here when everyone else had been in such a rush to get away and start the weekend. And now she came to think of it, she hadn't seen Jerry all afternoon. She wondered whether he'd had another argument with his wife.

She keyed the code into the silver and black box by the door and pushed. Somewhere, in the belly of the school, a vacuum cleaner droned. Katy had been quite harsh on Jerry recently – especially about the bullying issue – but she didn't want to make an enemy of him.

She stopped outside his door and listened, but there was no sound. She knocked and went in. The sun was starting to slip through the sky, blasting gold around the room and causing her to squint. At first, she thought that Jerry wasn't there. But then she saw him on the floor by the desk.

The door closed behind her with a *clunk* and Katy jumped. And then, as she got closer to him, she saw that Jerry's eyes were open and his mouth was slack. She could hear the drone of a fly.

'Jerry?' she whispered.

She started reaching out to him, to shake him, or to check his pulse, but she withdrew her hand. It was no use kidding herself. His eyes, open and unfocused, the pallor, the slackness of his skin. She'd never seen a dead body before but there was no mistaking that's what this was.

'Oh God. Ohgodohgodohgod.'

An ambulance? The police? She should call someone. Do something. She closed her eyes a moment to calm her breathing, but when she opened them again the scene appeared worse than before because now she could see a cricket bat lying on the floor behind him and could guess what had happened.

She turned away from him for the moment and faced the open window. Couldn't concentrate with him looking at her like that.

'Think,' she told herself. 'Think.'

But the thoughts that came to mind weren't the thoughts that she'd wanted. She thought of Jerry saying the only way he was leaving this school was feet first. And then she thought of Charles, of the fact that he had argued with Jerry. Remembered Charles miming hitting Jerry with that bat. Oh God.

She thought she might faint. For the first time in her adult life, Katy Lane didn't know what to do. She looked around the room, almost as if she was expecting someone else to be in there with her. She clenched her toes inside her summer shoes and made a decision. She needed to buy

298

some extra time to . . . to make sense of it. To hear Charles's side of the story because there's no way he would . . . no. No way at all. She wasn't thinking straight.

She put her hand over her mouth and walked closer to Jerry. She stepped behind him, holding her breath and tiptoeing, trying to keep as far away from him as possible. She hesitated before she picked up the bat. She pulled the arm of her cardigan down over her hand and grabbed the handle, keeping it away from her body like she was holding a dead rat by its tail. She crossed to the open window with it and dropped it into the bushes below.

She wasn't concealing evidence. Not really. She knew exactly where it was and would be sure to tell the police as soon as she'd worked out what she wanted to tell them. She looked at the phone on Jerry's desk. She wanted to call Charles, but she couldn't let the phone records show that she called him first.

With no other options available to her and the story not yet straight in her head, Katy Lane walked calmly to Mandy's desk, called 999 and burst into tears.

Chapter 33

Four days before the summer ball

Asha hovered by the doorway of Charles's secret flat, wondering what she would say if someone found them here.

'What if he comes home in the middle of the day?'

'He won't. He's at Jerry's funeral.'

'Christ, is that today?'

It wasn't until they were inside the apartment that Pippa told Asha that she hadn't known whether the keys on Charles's desk were for the flat. If they hadn't fit, she was hoping Asha had some hidden lock-picking skills. In truth, Asha had been shut out of her house on more than one occasion and the old 'slide the credit card' trick worked quite well. She'd shimmied up drainpipes and squeezed through bathroom windows, too. She liked to think of it as ingenious rather than shady.

The apartment was fully furnished, but more like a holiday let than a home. The biscuit-coloured sofa was only one shade removed from the carpet in the lounge. The way that Pippa was dressed today left her camouflaged. Everywhere Asha looked it was beige and white. She hesitated, not wanting to step inside the oatmeal cocoon where she would stand out like a red wine spill on white shagpile.

'Should I take off my shoes?' Asha asked.

'Do you honestly care about his carpets?'

'No. But I do care about getting caught.'

'If only Charles had felt the same. What kind of a man rents a secret flat, lies about his whereabouts and then leaves the paperwork and the keys in plain sight?'

'Plain sight?'

'Well, hidden under some papers but plain enough. Honestly, darling, it took me less than five minutes of snooping to find everything I needed to know. If he valued our marriage he'd have lied better.'

'It doesn't look like he's here much,' Asha said.

There were no dirty plates in the sink nor discarded shoes stepping under the table.

'No, I suppose it's not as easy to get away now his alibi is dead.'

'Do you think Gemma knows?' Asha asked. 'Wasn't Charles worried that Gemma would mention how they didn't play squash anymore?'

'Oh, Charles has made sure that Gemma and I never speak. We fell out a while back over something Charles did. I supported him instead of her and somehow my crime was worse than Charles's. I suppose she expected bad behaviour from him. From me, she'd expected better. You know, we talk a lot about heartbreak when romantic relationships break down, but the breakdown of a friendship is just as hard. Harder in many ways. No one talks about that, do they?'

Asha ran her fingers over the sofa. 'You're right. I had a friend growing up who . . . I don't know, stopped being my

301

friend, I guess. To this day, I don't know what I did wrong. We'd arranged for her to come and stay with us at our last place in Gloucester. She was going to drop me a line when she got back from holiday and never did. I waited a couple of weeks, called, sent a few text messages. Even called her mum to check she hadn't had an accident or something. And she's ghosted me ever since. I think about her more than I think about my ex. A loss of a best friend isn't something you get over.'

Asha had spent many months trying to work out whether she'd said something to offend Esme. But, even if she had, it was a cruel way to punish her. For someone like Asha, who'd had lots of friends but not let many get close to her, it confirmed her greatest fear that she was unlovable. To her mum, her dad and her friends, she was expendable.

'I am sorry, darling. Women can be cruel sometimes. I can't say Gemma was my best friend, but I do miss having her in my life. Perhaps I should have told her that before now.'

The living room was separated from the kitchen by white kitchen units. Two doors were off to the right. A bedroom and bathroom, Asha guessed. There were no photographs, no personal touches. The apartment was cold.

Pippa walked into the kitchen and opened the fridge. There was an unopened pint of full-fat milk, assorted cheeses, four cans of Coke and a bottle of champagne.

'Of course,' Pippa said. 'Priorities.' She lifted a can of Coke out of the fridge, shook it vigorously and then placed it back again.

Asha crossed to the windows and looked out at the park and the small rectangle of balcony which had a round table and two chairs on it.

'What exactly are we looking for?' Asha asked.

Pippa was opening and closing the kitchen drawers. Cutlery, tea towels, plates.

'Anything I can beat him with,' she said.

She opened the bin and peered inside. She wrinkled her nose. 'I'd like to know who the woman is. At least, I think I do. And if he's hiding something, he's hiding it in this flat. There was a small part of me that was hoping I'd got it all wrong and all of this could be explained away. An office. A surprise. But no, this is his little love nest, isn't it?'

'Not necessarily,' said Asha. 'Maybe he needed a quiet space away from the family from time to t—' The look on Pippa's face stopped Asha's words. 'Yeah, okay. You're right. The bastard has been bringing his girlfriend here.'

Asha moved cushions then replaced them. She looked around the room but there was nothing to see. Looking over at the two closed doors she felt her heart sink. She could only hope that the remaining rooms were just as unremarkable.

The first door was a windowless bathroom. Asha turned on the light. Towels – both used and fresh. Shower gel and shampoo were on the corner shelf. A woman's deodorant was on the side of the sink. Pippa walked past Asha, picked it up and sniffed it. She put it down and leaned on the sink, both hands clinging to the edge of the bowl.

Pippa looked at herself in the mirror, swallowed hard and nodded to herself. 'Pull yourself together, woman,' she

303

muttered. She left the bathroom, switching off the light as she did so, and went to stand in front of the last door.

'No one will think badly of you,' said Asha. 'Everyone is going to hate Charles for this betrayal and you're going to find out exactly how many friends you've got.'

Pippa put her hand on Asha's shoulder. 'Darling, that is so true, but not in the way you think. They'll all desert me in case a failed marriage is contagious.'

'You're wrong,' said Asha. 'And if you're right, who cares? They're a bunch of arseholes anyway. Did you know, Rose kicked me out of the WhatsApp group?'

'Ha! I shouldn't laugh. Let me guess, you disagreed with her? She's a lovely woman but her insecurities make her a little prickly.'

'Insecurities? Are we talking about the same person?'

'You must make allowances for her. She's incredibly vulnerable and her life isn't all it appears to be.'

'I don't buy it.'

'Not long after Ollie was born, Rose found out that *she* was the other woman. The dirty little secret. She's never recovered from that. And who can blame her? Right, shall we check out the bedroom?'

'Whoa. Back up. What?'

'Mick has another family. A partner and three children over in Plymouth. His work takes him all over the world and so neither woman questioned his lengthy absences, but Ollie was born early, had some time in hospital and Mick rushed to be by Rose's side. As you'd expect. But it left his carefully planned schedule in tatters and his first partner found out.'

304

'But Rose stayed with him?'

'Yes. And so did the other woman.'

'Are you kidding me?'

'Mick plays them off against each other.'

'And Rose is okay with that?'

'She adores Mick and will do anything to keep him, but the betrayal hurt her. This will stay between us, won't it, darling? I don't want to cause Rose any more upset.'

'I won't say a word.'

'I suppose I should be grateful that Charles only has a mistress and not an entire family. Though, if this room's a nursery ...' Pippa's smile slipped from her face and, for a moment she looked on the edge of tears. She cleared her throat and, putting her hand on the bedroom door, said, 'Shall we?'

Neither woman moved.

'Why is this the worst betrayal?' Pippa asked. 'The very thought of him sitting on that balcony watching the sunset with whoever-she-is, is bad enough. The fact that she's probably heard him singing those old Dean Martin songs in the shower ... In many ways that's just as private, but this ... God, if it's a sex dungeon in there I'm going to kill him.'

'If ever a man has struck me as a strictly missionary guy, it's Charles.'

Pippa nodded. 'It's the beige socks, isn't it?'

Asha shrugged. 'Among other things. Doesn't seem to be a man who likes to get dirty. Fastidious people rarely make good lovers.'

'I wish I could tell you that you were wrong,' Pippa said.

She pushed open the door and they both bent their heads to peer inside. The curtains were still drawn.

'Okay,' Asha said. 'You check the wardrobe and I'll check the drawers. I don't think that Charles is stupid enough to leave anything lying around.'

'Really?' asked Pippa.

She wrinkled her nose and looked to the floor, kicking a pair of black lace knickers with her toe.

'Oh.'

'Oh, indeed.'

'I suppose it's too much to hope that Charles has a penchant for cross-dressing?'

Pippa stared at Asha for a second and then burst out laughing. Before Asha could return the smile, Pippa sat on the bed. Her hands went to her face as her laughs became sobs. Her whole body was shuddering with the pain. Tears were falling behind her cupped hands, dripping onto her shirt.

'I don't know how this happened,' she said. 'I know I've not been easy to live with recently but . . .'

Asha sat down next to her and put her arm around her shoulder. 'Don't you dare blame yourself for this. Don't you dare. His decision to have an affair is all about him, not you.'

'But we've been together for so long.'

'You don't hold on to a mistake just because you've spent so long making it.'

Pippa took her hands away from her face. Her eyes were already puffy and pink and, where she'd covered her bruises, her makeup was coming off. Wiping her nose on the sleeve of her shirt she shook her head. 'I alternate between wanting to walk away with my dignity intact and really, *really* wanting to make him suffer.'

'I'm sure you can guess which option I'd take.'

They sat with arms round each other, Pippa staring at the wall in front of them while Asha stroked her hair.

'Come on,' Asha said. 'Let's get out of here. I don't want to find any more of that skank's undies. I'm going to get you a glass of water and then we need to discuss our next move. Okay?'

Asha left Pippa in the bedroom and went into the kitchen. It felt like a breakthrough of sorts. Now that Pippa knew for certain that Charles was cheating on her, Asha hoped that she'd be able to tell the police about the issues between Jerry and her husband. Asha opened and closed several cupboards before she found the one with glasses in. She ran the tap until the water stung her hands.

'Are you okay in there?' she called to Pippa.

'Not yet,' Pippa replied. 'But I'm sure I will be.'

As she lifted a glass out of the cupboard, Pippa came up behind her. 'Can we ... Can we leave? I don't want to be here for a second longer than I must.'

'Sure.' Asha put the glass back and turned to see Pippa touch the apples in the fruit bowl on the counter. She chose one, tossed it from hand to hand then took a bite. Her face twisted in disgust and she swallowed with difficulty.

'Huh,' she said. 'You never can tell which one's the bad apple, can you?'

She slid open the doors to the balcony and threw the apple into the river below, coming back wiping her hands on her trousers. 'I'm so stupid, aren't I? All this going on under my nose.'

'Not stupid. No. But Charles is quite clever.'

'He is, isn't he? Cleverer than me at any rate. And I'll never come out on top because he'll always be one step ahead of me.' Though she was looking out of the window she wasn't focused on anything. 'He's going to get away with it and I'm going to be all alone, waving goodbye to my children every other weekend.'

Asha put her elbows on the kitchen work surface and cradled her chin. 'Unless the police arrest Charles for Jerry's murder.'

Pippa looked at Asha. 'Just because he's humiliating me in the worst way, doesn't mean he's a killer.'

'Have you never thought that he might be responsible?'

Pippa squirmed and turned away. 'He's the father of my children.'

'Good for him, but that doesn't answer my question.'

'I mean, yes, I know that Charles was angry with Jerry for not being more accommodating when we were having money problems. And yes, that problem seems to have gone away now Miss Lane is in charge. But even if I went to the police with my suspicions, why would anyone believe a woman like me – one who throws cakes and walks out in front of cars. Why would they believe a single word I say?'

'I believe you.'

'I lied in my last job and they couldn't wait to get rid of me. Then I made a very public display of humiliating Jerry at the open day. And let's not forget that I'm a jealous wife who has recently discovered her husband's infidelity. They'd be right to think I have ulterior motives.'

Asha straightened up. 'Okay. How about we hold off going to the police until after the ball. We can get him to incriminate himself somehow.'

'Why wait for the ball?'

'Because I haven't been to a good party in ages.'

'You never go to school functions,' said Pippa.

'No. This will be my first and last school event so let's make it a good one.'

'You're not leaving us are you, darling?'

'Yeah. Cass's dad. He didn't know that I was even pregnant. But now he knows that Cass exists, I'm worried he's going to come looking for us. It's a messy story for another day. Do you mind if I don't get into it now?'

'You can't run for ever. One day you'll have to stand and fight.'

'I know. But Cass and I don't fit in here.'

'Ah,' said Pippa. 'That's your first mistake.' She took a deep breath. 'See, none of us fit in. We're all misfits, darling. Just trying to do our best to hang in there and hope that no one works out that we've been faking it all along.'

WITNESS NINE

Asha Demetriou.
Mother of Cassius.

To hear them speak, you'd think that their sons were perfect. I mean, honestly . . . They talk about the high pass rates as proof that the teachers are the best, that the kids are the best, but it's self-selecting, isn't it? These kids pass exams to get in, so they're coming to the school at a certain level already, right? And the backgrounds most of them come from . . . I mean, privileged doesn't even come close. Aberfal High . . . it's a different level. It has a helipad. A helipad!

Sorry, that's not what you asked, is it? I'm . . . you know . . . I suppose the main reason I sent Cassius here was that I thought it would protect him from the nasty things in the world for a bit longer. I wanted to keep him safe. That's all any parent wants, right?

The day that Mr Newhall died I was at the school watching the cricket match. I don't usually go. I mean, I try and support Cass as much as I can, but I work. And I'm on my own, both in terms of parenting and working, so . . . But yeah, I was there from about two and left at four. I'd hoped to bump into Mr Newhall to talk to him about Cass being bullied but he didn't come out of his office all afternoon. I got the impression he might have been hiding from me. I'd been a bit confrontational at our last meeting. A bit emotional.

And before you ask, no, I didn't go inside to find him either. Once I was there, well, Cass was so pleased to see me and it was such a lovely day that I started enjoying myself and I ended up . . . I don't know, chatting, laughing. It was the perfect afternoon. I don't mean what happened to Mr Newhall. God, no. I only mean that, you

310

know, it was the most relaxed I'd felt at that school. There was no indication that anything bad was going to happen.

It's a good school – if only they could get a handle on the bullying. Mr Newhall's death has made me think a lot about the situation. I've said all along that they needed changes at the top. The boys have learned this kind of behaviour somewhere and the fact that the school haven't clamped down on it before now speaks volumes about how they – Mr Newhall in particular – didn't think that bullying was such a bad thing. So, if I were you, I'd be wondering who Mr Newhall was bullying. Who'd had enough of being treated badly by him?

Sorry, yes, back to that afternoon. Um, it was busy. Even Jerry's wife and their dog were there. I don't know if anything was different about that match because I'd never been to one before. What surprised me was how social the event was. Lots of coming and going and chatting rather than watching the kids. People were forever disappearing, going to get drinks. Charles Yardley even went and changed his shirt at one point.

I'd love to know what the other parents are saying about me. I get the impression they don't trust me. I'm from a different background to most of them. We're here on a scholarship, the uniform is second-hand, but if they try and suggest that I had anything to do with this . . . I mean, sure, I didn't like the guy. No, that's not true. I didn't like that my son was being bullied and, in many ways, I held Mr Newhall responsible for that. But he was all right to me. He was the one who persuaded me to send Cass to Aberfal High. He was the one that made me realise how much potential Cass has. And you know what, I'm grateful for that. Mr Newhall didn't deserve this and I hope you catch the bastard who killed him.

311

Chapter 34

Four days before the summer ball

Cass answered his phone after one ring. 'Late again?'

'God, Cass. I'm so sorry. Coming up the driveway now. Two minutes to park the van. That's all.'

'No rush,' he said.

Given their tentative truce, Asha wasn't sure he meant that.

'How was school?' she asked.

Though Cass was talking to her again, it was polite, not friendly. He'd promised to ignore any further messages from Mark and Asha had promised that she would tell Cass everything. But not today. He'd told her not to leave it too long or he'd go searching for those answers himself.

'Guess what?' Cass said. 'Benny got a detention for fighting.'

'Who with?'

'I know what you're thinking, but it wasn't me. Ollie said something about Benny's mum and Mr Newhall. They were laughing at first but, next thing, they were on the floor and fighting.'

'What did Ollie say about Pippa?'

'I don't know. I wasn't paying much attention until Benny flew over the desk in front of me.'

Asha could only imagine the rumours that were being spread by the parents. And, though kids couldn't hear you when you shouted at them to clean their rooms, they could pick up a whispered secret through locked doors and thick walls.

'Be honest,' said Asha. 'You liked Benny getting a taste of his own medicine, didn't you?'

'Liked it? I cheered.'

Asha was half-smiling as she parked and slipped out of the van while cradling the phone between cheek and shoulder. 'He's going through a tough time at home though. So don't be too hard on him.'

Hers wasn't the only car in the car park and there were still students milling around but Asha felt strangely vulnerable. She turned on the spot, half-expecting to see someone watching her, or move quickly out of view, but there was nothing.

'Anyway, I'm here now,' she said to Cass. 'Can you meet me out the front of the school?' She suddenly wanted to get back in the van and lock all the doors.

'Can't. Otis needs to talk to you about something.'

'Can it wait?'

Cass was silent on the other end of the phone. Asha looked up at the school and saw a figure in the window. She couldn't tell who it was, or even if they were facing her, but their stance projected anger through the glass.

'Fine,' Asha said. 'I'll, um, see you in a minute.'

She threw one last look around her before darting for the path. She still had her car keys in her hand so rearranged them until one sharp key was protruding between her clenched fingers.

Five minutes ago she'd been exhausted, only wanting to be able to lie down and sleep for a week, but now Asha was alert and looking for signs that someone was following her. Charles couldn't know that she and Pippa had been at the flat. Cass's dad couldn't have tracked down Cass's school. Yet, why was she so on edge?

It was all catching up with her now. Charles, Jerry, prescription drugs, affairs. And poor Pippa stuck in the middle of it all. Asha wasn't sure how she'd got drawn into the drama, but she was going to have to see it through to the end now. Couldn't leave Pippa to deal with this mess on her own.

Pippa had agreed to wait until after the ball to go to the police. Asha wanted to be certain of all the facts and there was still one more thing they needed to put in place. And when she did, Charles wouldn't know what had hit him. And then, the day after the ball, Asha and Cass would be leaving Cornwall. Cass didn't know it yet, but he wouldn't be seeing the end of the term at Aberfal High and, this time, she wouldn't tell her mum where they were going. She couldn't risk Mark tracking them down. Wouldn't risk losing Cass.

Asha moved swiftly through the garden and down to the lake. She was out of breath by the time she approached the shed.

Cass looked up at her and said, 'Look what I found.' He held his cricket bat aloft.

'Oh God. I mean . . . oh good. Where was it?' Asha's heart was pounding and her eyes were scanning the bat.

'The lake,' said Cass. 'Benny hid it on top of the lockers. But then the teachers said the police wanted to see our cricket bats and Benny thought you'd called the police because he'd stolen it, so he took it and chucked it in the lake. Otis went in and got it for me.'

'And Benny just told you? Volunteered the information out of the goodness of his heart?'

Cass smiled. 'The less you know, Mother . . .'

Otis got to his feet and put his hands in the back pockets of his shorts. 'You'd be amazed what I find in that lake.'

'I can imagine. Cass said you wanted a word?' And to Cass she said, 'Finish up what you're doing, buddy, and get your stuff together.'

Asha walked back into the comfort of the warm afternoon. A late summer afternoon was usually her favourite time of day. The promise of a long evening ahead, after all the work had been done. It signified the start of time to relax. Or would have done if her day with Pippa hadn't given her the worst headache.

'You okay? Otis asked.

'One of those days.'

Before Otis could say anything, Asha said, 'Listen, I feel uncomfortable about what I said, about, you know, thinking Cass could do better than being a gardener. What I meant was—'

'It's no bother. It's me who should apologise to you.'

315

'Me?'

'I overreacted. I have my reasons for wanting to be here and you weren't to know that. And your lad here reminds me a bit of my younger brother, so I was enjoying spending time with him. I realise that it might look strange, a grown man hanging out with a twelve-year-old boy, so I wanted to explain.'

It was on the tip of her tongue to say, 'Don't worry about it'. What did it matter? A few more days and Otis Blake would no longer be a problem.

'I must admit,' she said, 'I've not been that comfortable with it.'

'I know.'

'Did Cass say something?'

'No. Your face did. Quite expressive at times.'

Asha slipped her car keys into her pocket and tried to look relaxed and non-judgemental. 'Sorry.'

'It's okay. I get it. I'd like to tell you something that only Newhall knew about me,' Otis said. 'As far as I know he never told anyone else, so, when he died, well . . . if I don't tell anyone else, no one will know.'

'You don't have to tell me anything.'

'I attended Aberfal High.'

'Oh.'

He nodded. 'Me and my brother. It was . . . good. I have no complaints about my school years. Truly the happiest years of my life.'

'You liked it so much you came back?'

He scratched his chin and glanced towards the shed. 'Not quite.'

Asha sensed he was building up to something so gave him time to compose his thoughts. She watched a dragonfly hover in front of her then dart away across the lake.

'My brother,' he began. 'He was three years younger than me. I was the studious one and he was the fun one. They say that parents don't have favourites, but Arlo was everyone's favourite and I was okay with that. I'd finished my degree at Cambridge and was working in a bar in Mallorca before starting an internship with a tech startup. Arlo was finishing his A-levels and was going to fly out to join me. On the last day of his exams, he and some friends went and had a few drinks. Usual boys' stuff. Time passed, beer was drunk and someone realised they'd forgotten to jump in the lake and, it being tradition, they came back. It was before we had the gates at the end of the drive and they walked straight in. There were no lights. No one around.'

Otis paused and Asha found herself tensing up, afraid she'd already guessed what he was going to say.

'They all jumped in, splashed about and no one noticed that Arlo was missing. By the time they found his body and pulled him out, it was too late.'

Asha put her hand over her mouth. 'That's . . .' She thought about the day that Cass had gone in that lake. Her fear. Otis's anger. 'God. I'm so, so sorry.'

She'd heard the rumours about boys drowning in the lake but had dismissed them all as stories the pupils told to scare each other.

'When I saw Cass in the water,' Otis said, 'it was like seeing Arlo; those dark curls. And when I dragged him out

317

it felt, for a second, like I was saving Arlo too. I cared a lot more than I should have done. I know he isn't my kid brother; I've not lost my mind. But when he started coming by here after school, I admit, I encouraged him.' He frowned and said, 'Anyway, I thought I should explain. I'm not sure that makes it sound any less weird but at least you have the full story.'

He looked at his feet, scratched the back of his head as if what he'd said wasn't that big of a deal.

'I don't understand why you'd want to come back,' said Asha. 'Doesn't it upset you to think of what happened here?'

Otis shook his head. 'It started off as a cross between therapy and punishment. I sold my company and found a love for gardening. It helped a lot. I'd been working around the clock and not left much time to deal with the grief. It caught up with me. When I saw the job advertised here, I called up Jerry Newhall. He wasn't head when the accident happened, but he'd heard about it and I suppose he felt sorry for me and gave me a job without me having any tangible experience. I wanted to come back here because I had to face what had happened and you have to do that if it's staring you in the face, don't you?'

Asha took her time to answer. 'You don't do things by half, do you? It's amazing that you can bear to be here at all.'

He tilted his head to one side as if considering that. 'It means that I can keep an eye on any kids getting into trouble in the water and keep it clear of anything that could obstruct them. It's not much, but it's something. I'm happy for them to believe the story about ghosts if it keeps

318

them out of the water. And you might have noticed that I live here because I don't want anyone going in the lake at night.'

Asha wanted to reach out and touch him. Instead, she put her hands in her pockets and tightened her hand around her car keys until the metal bit her palm.

'I'm sorry,' she said. 'For misjudging you. I think the worst of people. It's what I do.'

'No problem. It happens a lot.'

'After the day I've had, it's nice to hear that there are some decent people in the world.'

He smiled and she felt the tension loosen in her shoulders.

'Who let you down today?' he asked.

'Well, it's not me, really. I shouldn't say anything, but I'm so angry and I don't owe him anything, so . . . You know Pippa Yardley, yeah? Well, her husband, Charles, has been having an affair.'

There was an almost imperceptible twitch of Otis's eyebrow as he looked away over the lake.

'You don't seem shocked,' Asha said.

'I've seen some behaviour from him that . . . let's just say he's not fooling everyone with his *upstanding member of the community* act.'

'You see everything that goes on here, don't you?'

Otis nodded. 'To most of the people here I'm a nobody. Part of the scenery. They aren't so bothered about checking themselves when they're around me.'

A thought suddenly occurred to her. 'Some people want to believe that Pippa had something to do with Mr Newhall's murder because of her accident, but I've got a hunch it was her husband and if I could help her prove it ... I don't suppose you know anything about the day Newhall was killed, do you? '

A small smile played at the edges of Otis Blake's lips.

'Well, now. It's funny you should ask.'

Rose Oliversmum: I HAVE GOSSIP! Ollie had a fight at school (more when I see you) and I had a meeting with Katy Lane to discuss. When I got there she was arguing with Mandy – something to do with an email?? Shut up when they saw me and then KL said she couldn't meet with me anymore because she HAD TO GO TO THE POLICE STATION TO SEE DC MULLINS.

Sarah Teddysmum: OMG! Wonder what that's all about? Do you think she knows who killed JN?

Rose Oliversmum: Got to be. Or she's discovered some new evidence.

Becky Rupertsmum: The ball is going to be juicy!! Do U think it'll B like Death in Paradise where they get everyone together in one room and then reveal the killer????

Clare Withoutani: You watch too much TV Bex! I hope they arrest someone soon though. I'm nervous about going to the school knowing there's a killer on the loose. Is it just me??

Rose Oliversmum: Safety in numbers Clare! What are our plans for tomorrow night BTW? Maybe a couple of pre-ball cocktails here first before taxis?

Becky Rupertsmum: Me and Russ R already sharing a lift with Holly and Beth. See U there?

Rose Oliversmum: Clare? Do you want to come here for about six and then we can have a couple of drinkies before we go.

Clare Withoutani: Sorry Rose. We're driving in with Asha. Cass is having a sleepover here with Freddy. I thought I'd already mentioned it.

Rose Oliversmum: Just me and you then @Sarah Teddysmum.

Sarah Teddysmum: Sorry, didn't I say? Had a better offer. Off to Tresco Island for the weekend on a pal's boat. Bit worried about forecast though.

Becky Rupertsmum: Bet U R wishing U hadn't kicked everyone out of the group now Rose 😒 #NoMates #MeanGirl

Rose Oliversmum: Very mature, Becky.

Becky Rupertsmum: 🤪

Chapter 35

The day before the summer ball

They were on the road fifteen minutes after Asha's alarm had sounded. The sun was doing what it did best and painting pinks across the sky in broad brushstrokes as they crossed the Tamar River. Only stopping at a drive-through for breakfast, they'd made good time and were sitting outside 53a Stanley Road while the curtains were still drawn.

It was a weekday. A school day. The email to Miss Lane about Cass's mystery illness would be the only lie Asha would tell today.

'Pinky promise,' she said.

'Really?'

'Cass, pinky promises are unbreakable. You know that.'

'Then I can ask anything?' Cass asked.

'Yes, but with a caveat.'

'Here it comes,' he said unbuckling his seatbelt. 'Should've known.'

'Hey! I mean what I say, I'm going to be one hundred per cent honest with you. All I'm saying is, before you ask your questions, have a think about whether you really want to know the answer because once you know something, there's no going back.'

'Got it.'

'Shall we?'

They got out the van, but Asha was slow to approach the pebble-dashed house. The small square of grass had been recently mown. The front door painted. From the street, it looked like a normal family could have lived here. The sort of family who got together over a roast on Sundays, with extra chairs brought in from the shed at Christmas. Paper hats. Laughter. Asha found herself nostalgic for a family life she'd never had.

Asha felt Cass's hand in hers. 'You're shaking,' he said.

'I know. Stupid, huh?'

'Do you want us to . . .' Cass nodded towards the van.

Asha shook her head and walked up the path, her finger already reaching towards the doorbell before she could change her mind. She saw curtains flicker above them and squeezed Cass's hand tighter.

She had to ring the bell twice more before she heard footsteps on the stairs. As the door opened, she saw that the woman was already dressed in a grey jumper and black jeans. Her bare feet were crowned by black-painted toenails. It didn't seem that long ago that she would answer the door in only a towel.

'Morning, Tessa,' said Asha. 'Don't suppose there's any chance of a cup of tea for your daughter and grandson, is there?'

'Ed'll be downstairs in a minute,' Tessa said. 'He's proper excited to meet you.'

The three of them sat at the edges of seats balancing mugs on their knees.

324

'I should get to the point of why we're here,' Asha said.

Though her mum had been full of hugs and exclamations and cries of 'Look at you!', she hadn't asked why Asha was here so early on a Friday morning.

Tessa threaded her fingers around her mug and looked at the carpet. Asha thought her mum knew exactly why she was here. You don't tell a man that he has a secret son and then forget what you've done. From the hallway there was the sound of the letterbox rattling. Tessa sprang to her feet. 'I'll just get the post.'

'Tessa, sit down.'

Tessa sat.

'I've got to say this now or . . . or I'll chicken out. About a month ago, Mark Dalgleish got in touch with Cass over Instagram.'

Tessa remained silent but her eyes darted to the closed door as if she was planning her escape route. 'What's that got to do with me?' she asked, tucking hair behind her ear.

'That's what I'd like to know.'

Asha placed her untouched tea on the carpet by her feet and pushed her hands between her knees to stop them from trembling. She glanced at Cass who was watching his grandmother with an eagerness that caused Asha's breath to catch.

'Okay, look,' Tessa said throwing up her hands. 'What was I meant to do? Mark asked me how you were and what you were up to.'

It took every ounce of her strength for Asha to keep her voice measured. 'You could have said I was fine and gone about your day.'

Cass moved position in his seat and Asha took a deep breath. 'But, having said that,' she continued, 'it was wrong of me to expect you to keep that secret for me when you came face-to-face with him. I wish you hadn't said anything. Like, *really* wish you hadn't, but I'm not here to argue.'

'Makes a change.'

'I knew that I'd have to address this sooner or later, but I'd hoped Cass would've been older. The reason we're here . . . well, there's a couple of things, but let's start with how much you told Mark.' Asha put her arm around Cass. 'Cass wants the truth and he doesn't trust me to give him an unbiased account. To be honest, I'm not sure if my recollection is all it should be either. I've told myself a lot of different things over the years to justify what I did. I don't regret it but, you know, if Cass hears it from both of us, he'll get a more rounded, um, picture. I want you to tell him what you remember about me and Mark and then he'll see that I was only ever trying to do my best for us both.'

Tessa was shaking her head as if she couldn't believe her ears. Before she could say anything, the door opened and an older man appeared. He was hairless and skinny like a whippet walking on hind-legs. He was tucking in his already tucked-in T-shirt and smiling a small-toothed smile.

'You must be Asha,' he said. 'Bloody hell, don't you look a lot like your mum?'

Though Asha was more like her mum than she wanted to admit, physically they were nothing alike. Asha got her looks and colouring from her Greek dad and she'd passed that down to Cass. Everyone said that she and Cass looked the same. But, as she looked at her mum, she saw Cass's high cheekbones in her mother's face. His long lashes framing Tessa's eyes. Perhaps there was something in what Ed said.

'And you must be Ed,' Asha said. 'Nice to meet you.' She put her hand on Cass's leg. 'And this is—'

'You don't need to tell me who this is. Hello there, Cassius Cornelius.' Asha threw a look at her mother and frowned.

'All right lad?' Ed said. 'Your gran talks about you all the time. Got a folder on her phone with all your pictures in it. Though you're a bit younger in them.'

'Hi,' said Cass. He was beaming. It must be nice to know that someone thought of you often. Asha shuddered.

Tessa got to her feet and slipped her arm around Ed's waist. 'Be a doll,' she said. 'Couldn't pop out and get some milk, could you? Wasn't expecting visitors.'

'Course I can.' He turned to Cass and said, 'Can I get you something, Cassius Cornelius? What's your poison? Sweets? Crisps?'

'No, thank you.'

'Biscuits then. I'll get biscuits. Everyone likes a Hobnob, don't they? Back in a jiffy.'

Tessa saw him to the door, pecked his cheek and waited until he'd gone.

'Cassius Cornelius?' Asha said to her mum as the front door slammed shut.

'Ed's taken a fancy to the name. Says it sounds like a Roman emperor.'

Asha didn't like her son's name in the mouth of a stranger. 'He seems nice.'

'You sound surprised.' Tessa sat back down and patted the sofa next to her. 'Come sit next to your gran, Cassius.'

He went to her and Asha had to sit on her hands to stop herself from pulling him back.

'How much do you know?' Tessa asked him.

'Nothing much. Mum said she didn't know anything about my dad but then this guy called Mark messaged. He said you'd told him he had a son and, yeah, that's about it really. He said he wants to get to know me better, but Mum says the guy's a waster and she doesn't want me to have anything to do with him. So, yeah, that's about all I know.'

'Your mum's right about him being a waster. But, knowing your mum, she used a stronger word than that.'

Cass smiled and Asha tutted.

'I never thought he was good enough for her. Could charm the stars out of the sky though. But, your mum being your mum, she wouldn't listen to me when I told her he was no good.'

'You never once warned me about him,' Asha said.

'Who's telling this story, you or me?'

Asha folded her arms.

'Anyway,' Tessa said. 'He was always flashing his cash around but never said where he'd got it from. Fancy watches, new trainers. You know the sort. He promised her the world and if there's one thing your mum has always wanted, it's to have a different life to the one she was given.'

Out of habit Asha almost disagreed, but it was true, she'd always felt like everything would be so much better if she could leave her life behind.

'To be fair to her,' Tessa said, 'life wasn't all that great for your mum growing up. We never had much money. Of course, her dad left us on her fourth birthday.'

'I was seven,' said Asha. 'And it wasn't my birthday, it was Boxing Day.'

'As she got older, she had to look after me and Georgie cos I wasn't up to it, see. I was ill a lot of the time.'

Asha snorted.

Tessa glared at Asha and then turned her whole body to face Cass. 'Whatever your mum might tell you, addiction is an illness. I'll have it my whole life, but some days are better than others. And it's better when Ed's around. He's good to me. Your mum thought she knew everything, of course. Hated me, she did. And along comes whatshisface and she couldn't get out of here fast enough. I think . . . and you watch, this'll get me one of those looks of hers, but I think she got pregnant on purpose because she saw a way out of here. If she had a baby to look after she couldn't be expected to look after me and Georgie anymore, see?' Tessa cupped her eyes. 'I'm scared to look. She's glaring at me, isn't she? Is it the death stare?'

Cass nodded and laughed. Tessa reached out and stroked his cheek. 'You're a good lad.'

Asha said nothing but made sure her sigh was loud enough to carry to Tessa's ears.

'Your mum and dad weren't together that long. Five or six months maybe, but to your mum it was a big deal.'

'It was over a year, Mum.'

Tessa lowered her voice and leaned towards Cass. 'It wasn't. Then one day the police showed up to talk to Mark for stealing money off old folk. He was . . .' She looked over to Asha. 'What were he doing, Kitten? Was it investments or something?'

Asha nodded. 'He said he was a financial advisor, but he was taking money off retired people. Mostly widows. He invested some of it, lost some of it, spent the rest on himself.'

'And you.'

Asha looked down at her hands. 'He told me that it was all a big misunderstanding and he'd not done anything illegal. He admitted he'd lost some money but said that was the thing with investments – no guarantee. He said they all knew that, when they gave him the money to invest, but then I heard the other side of it and I left him the next day. He went to prison and I never visited him or wrote. I don't think he expected me to, to be honest. As far as I know, he never tried to contact me or explain what happened, so I didn't feel the need to let him know about you, Cass. He wasn't even that bad to me or anything, but I knew he'd be out after three years and I loved you so much that the thought of sharing you at weekends, or having you spend Christmas with a liar who didn't deserve you, was unimaginable. That's why I kept us moving.'

'In the getaway van,' Cass said.

Asha shrugged. 'It's one of those jokes that isn't really a joke. I'd always keep the engine running if I could.'

'Is that it?' Cass asked.

'What do you mean, love?' asked Tessa.

'I thought he was, like, a serial killer or something, or a gangster. I thought you were hiding a lot worse than that.'

Asha almost laughed. 'There's nothing worse than the thought of losing you, Cass. Nothing. I thought he'd be angry with me for keeping you from him. But if he has parental rights then what world am I letting you into? I would move heaven and earth to keep you safe, buddy. You know that. I'm never letting him get his hands on you.'

'Don't I get a say in that?' Cass asked.

'No, you don't. I told you I'd be honest with you, but I'm still the one calling the shots. He's not your dad, Cass. He's a stranger.'

Cass wrinkled his nose. 'Okay.'

'Okay?' repeated Asha. 'What do you mean, "Okay"?'

'If you think this is the right thing for me then—'

'Is this a double bluff? Because if it is . . .'

'You're forgetting something,' said Tessa.

Both Asha and Cass looked at her.

'If Mark knows about Cassius and wants to see him, there's nowhere you can hide. Like it or not, he'll find you eventually.'

'Did you tell him we're in Cornwall?' asked Asha.

'Yes, but I didn't give him your address or anything.' Looking away, Tessa muttered, 'Since you won't even let me have it.'

'For Christ's sake, Tessa,' said Asha. 'Why did you tell him?'

'I didn't have a choice,' Tessa said.

'What did he do? Twist your arm? Get you drunk? Explain to me how he left you with no choice.'

'Not him,' said Tessa. 'You. It was you that left me with no choice. As long as you were keeping Cassius a secret you'd never come home and I would never get to make up for what I put you through.'

'You did this on purpose?'

'I didn't know I'd bump into him, did I? But when he started asking after you, I thought it might be a way to stop you running off again. I saw a way to make us a proper family.'

'Christ, I shouldn't be surprised that you were thinking of yourself again but honestly? This is low.'

'Now listen here,' said Tessa sitting forwards on the sofa. 'I love you, Ash. You're my daughter. Cassius is my grandson and I barely see him. I know first-hand what it's like to bring your children up on your own and, yes, before you say it, I did a terrible job of it. I regret cutting your dad out of your life because one thing I've learned over the years is that life is better when you're surrounded by people who love you. You've always been so defensive. Letting no one in. Why won't you let anyone help? Why won't you let anyone love you?'

Asha was about to get to her feet, drag Cass from the room but the look on Cass's face stopped her. Asha realised long ago that there was something about her that couldn't be loved.

'Too many people have let me down. Why would I put myself through that again? If you were allergic to something you wouldn't keep eating it, would you?'

The sound of keys in the door stopped Asha from continuing. She took a deep breath and sat back in her seat.

'Only me!' called Ed from the hallway. 'No Hobnobs. Can you believe it? I got Custard Creams instead.'

Tessa took hold of Cass's hand but was watching Asha with a smile on her face when she said, 'I swear, only your mum could compare love to a nut allergy.'

Chapter 36

The Summer Ball
7.18 p.m.

Just like Jerry Newhall had said it would be, the summer ball was the jewel in Aberfal High's social calendar. Asha had never seen anything quite like it. If it hadn't been for Pippa, she wouldn't have come but, now that she stood at the edge of the lawn gripping her glass of champagne, she thought she wouldn't have missed this spectacle for the world.

She was aware of people staring and, for once, she didn't mind. She didn't need to prove anything to them anymore because this was the last event she'd be attending at Aberfal High. They could gossip about her for weeks to come, if they liked, because she wouldn't be around to hear it. Though the other women were wearing pretty dresses, Asha had decided to go for something she felt comfortable in.

Her high-waisted pin-striped trousers were an absolute steal from the vintage shop, though she'd owned the braces since her teens. The cap-sleeved sheer white shirt and a pre-tied black bow tie were new though and her long gloves a cheap find in the fancy-dress shop. Her hair was in a low chignon, her lipstick a dangerous shade of red.

When she'd heard there'd be a fair, she'd pictured hook-a-duck, stuffed toys hanging at the backs of booths promising every one's a winner, the smell of fried onions in the air but, as she looked from the dodgems to the carousel, she thought she'd never seen colours so bright. The red and white striped helter-skelter towered above them all and Asha smiled as she watched Pam tumble from the bottom in a heap of sequins. As a child, Asha used to love streaming down the slide on rough hessian sacks and running straight back up the steps to go again and again.

Music cut through the laughter and shrieks, transporting Asha back a century, to when organs piped fairground melodies. Squeals of delight dashed the air as Waltzers spun this way and that, at speeds to make stomachs churn and visions blur. Everything had been slower when she was younger. Even the summers were languid, each day and week stretching for an eternity. Love affairs that had only lasted for three weeks had felt like she'd never get over them.

The nine months that Cass had been at Aberfal High felt like they stretched over years. They'd given it their all. Asha had even tried to make friends, at Cass's request. Cass might fit in here one day, but Asha never would. For one thing, she had to move before Cass's dad tracked them down. Her visit to her mother's had been surprisingly pleasant, once they'd finished exchanging insults and she thought that maybe she might let Tessa back into their lives. Occasionally.

Of course, Rose still wasn't talking to Asha. She was grateful to Clare for asking if she'd like to share a taxi tonight and if Cass would like a sleepover with Freddy. It meant she hadn't had to walk in here on her own.

Katy Lane wanted tonight to be an event people were talking about for years to come. Asha knew that Katy's wish would come true, but not in the way she envisaged. The day had been glorious, the evening still warm, but there was no mistaking the slate of cloud on the horizon. Tree branches were starting to wave and the usually calm surface of the lake was rippling like ridges of a thumbprint. Instead of bringing respite from the stuffy heat, the threat of storm made the air thicker. Men were already fingering their shirt collars, itching to take off their jackets and roll up their sleeves. The women, resplendent in tassels and sequins, had no need of shawls tonight. With their long gloves and feathered headbands, it looked like *The Great Gatsby* was being filmed at Aberfal tonight.

Asha had intended to cover up her tattoos with foundation, but at the last minute decided she didn't want to hide them anymore. Each one of them was inked at a time when she was celebrating something wonderful or coming to terms with something soul-destroying. They were trophies for surviving what life had thrown at her, reminding her of her own strength. She looked at the lighthouse on her forearm. She'd got it when Cass was born. His arrival had reminded her to steer them away from the rocks.

She became aware of a photographer pointing his lens in her direction and, instead of turning away, she looked straight down the lens. *Click, click, click.*

Hearing someone call her name, Asha turned to see Clare standing by the merry-go-round and waving her over. 'Come on!'

Asha smiled as she placed her glass on a tray and walked across the lawn. Standing around wasn't helping her nerves. If she could keep herself busy, she wouldn't keep thinking of all the things that could go wrong tonight.

'I've not been on one of these for years,' Asha said as she stepped up to the painted horses.

'I know. It's mad, isn't it?'

Asha noticed Otis standing with Hinch and Mandy. Or rather, she noticed other people noticing him. No one had expected the gardener to own a tux, never mind look so good in one. As the ride began, Asha told herself that the fear that gripped her stomach was the excitement of a childhood relived. As her horse leapt, Clare's fell and when Clare's took the lead Asha's dropped back. At first, she held tightly to the golden spiral of a pole in front of her but, as she got used to the rhythmic movement, she let her hands loosen and began to look around her.

People pooled in groups of four or six, faces split with smiles. Drinks lifted up and down and up, up, up and were then replaced. Though their partying might be less frequent now, it was still in the same vein. Most of these people were heavily involved with the school in the hope that they could recapture the past. This is where their people were. The untouchables. The protected.

The turmoil inside Asha's head threatened to split her in two. She was uncomfortable with the excess before her, resented the privilege and the entitlement, and yet she'd desperately wanted to be part of this world and for her son to make it his. She'd wanted an easy life and had mistakenly thought that money and status would bring

337

all she desired. Her battle hadn't been against people with money, it had been against herself and against the scars her childhood had left on her. For the most part, none of these people cared whether she had money in the bank, nor if she was descended from the Hapsburgs. They only cared that she committed to the school. But she'd been so closed and full of mistrust that she'd become over-defensive.

Not many teachers were here tonight – or not many that Asha recognised – but there were enough to make a full table. She wondered whether they worried about looking unprofessional with a drink in their hand. Did they, too, feel like they were lesser by the side of the Right Honourables and the descendants of those who'd had roads named after them and school blocks? Or was it because they didn't want to be accosted by an inebriated parent saying, 'Now, about Jacob's history assignment . . .'

Katy Lane was there, of course. It had been only days since Jerry's funeral and the ball was the school's way of honouring him. Mandy looked beautiful in red and Hinch was trailing her around like a puppy. Was it guilt that drove them all to dust off their fine clothes? Guilt because they'd complained about Jerry when he was alive. Fear that, if they didn't at least look sorry, then they'd be accused of his murder. There was something comical, rash even, that they could be sipping champagne alongside a killer.

Sudden screams grabbed Asha's attention, but she had to wait for the merry-go-round to rotate before she could see what was going on, by which time the screams had turned to laughter and her heart rate slowed again. As the lake came into view, Asha saw people splashing in the water. That's what happens when hard-working parents let off a bit too much steam. Heads bobbed up and down in the lake. It was another rotation of the merry-go-round before Asha saw Otis striding towards the water, his dress shoes slipping on the grass. He'd predicted that this would happen. In fact, it had been part of their plan.

'I love your outfit,' shouted Clare. 'You're so brave.'

'Thanks.'

At each rotation of the merry-go-round Otis was closer and closer to the water.

'Have you spoken to Pippa? I've been meaning to call her.'

Asha had heard a lot of 'I've been meaning to' recently.

'She's doing okay,' Asha said. 'The accident was a shock, but there's no lasting damage and, yeah, she seems to be doing well.'

Asha wanted to tell Clare that Charles had killed Jerry. She wanted to explain what she knew about the divorce, the affair and the drugs, but Pippa wanted to keep it a secret for now. She had her own thoughts about how she wanted the news to come out and it made Asha feel sick with trepidation.

'Such a shame that she won't be here tonight,' said Clare. 'But, if I was her, I wouldn't be showing my face for a while. Do you know what I mean? Obviously, *we* know there's no truth to the rumours that she had something to do with poor Jerry, but I'd just die if everyone was whispering behind my back and hiding the steak knives.'

Clare's words died in her mouth because, even above the fairground music, there was a sense of something happening. A shift in the atmosphere.

Asha bit her lip to hide her smile because, at the top of the steps leading down to the lawn, there was no mistaking the impressive figures of Charles and Pippa Yardley.

Chapter 37

**The Summer Ball
7.30 p.m.**

Katy stood in the school bathroom and took three deep breaths. She looked in the mirror as the water ran over her hands and told herself to hold it together. This was her chance to show everyone that she could lead this school, but pressure was threatening to reduce her to tears before the canapés had been passed around.

She'd been to the police station to give another statement but it had done little to calm her nerves. She'd received another one of those bloody emails and decided she'd had enough. She was sick of them. Sick of everything. And so, she'd finally come clean, like the email had told her to. Like her conscience had been begging her to for the past three weeks. God, had it only been that long? It felt like years since she'd managed a full night's sleep.

Katy had expected to feel better for getting it off her chest, but all she'd felt was dread snatching her breath away and the terror of wondering what would come next. There had to be consequences. There always were. The detective had said as much.

There was still talk of Gemma Newhall coming tonight. A place had been set at Katy's table, just in case. Though, seeing as it was only a matter of days since she'd buried her husband and a matter of hours since Katy told the police her suspicions about Gemma being behind the emails and the slashed tyre, Katy couldn't see that happening. And if it did . . . God help them all.

It was the conversation with Charles in the car that set Katy thinking about Gemma's involvement. It was possible and the more she thought about it the more likely it appeared. But when another email arrived, telling her she must come clean before the ball, Katy realised that she couldn't vouch for Gemma's state of mind or what she would do today unless stopped.

Katy had spoken to that detective who'd given her his card and then, with a lukewarm cup of tea in her hand, she'd told Detective Mullins and his colleague everything. The emails. The slashed tyres. The affair. But they'd been most interested in her admission that she'd thrown the murder weapon out of the window. The reason the bushes had been trampled down was because someone had pushed their way between the rhododendrons and taken the bat. And no, she didn't know where and she didn't know who. She could only guess that the murderer had seen what she'd done and disposed of it themselves.

Mullins said that, though it had been made to look like someone had climbed out of the window, forensics hadn't supported that theory. They'd been scratching their heads about the minute traces of blood and the broken branches, too. He didn't thank Katy for putting them straight. In fact,

342

he looked frustrated with her for taking so long to tell them. She explained her reasoning, in detail, but there was no sympathy.

It confirmed something though: that the murderer came and left through the door and Mandy's statement had some glaring holes in it.

'Yes. Sorry about that,' Katy had said. 'I encouraged her to say that she was at her desk all afternoon and that only Gemma Newhall went in. I was worried that Charles – yes, the man I was having a relationship with – I was worried that if Mandy admitted it could have happened at any time that you would suspect Charles because of . . . all sorts of reasons. Because he was having money problems, because he had access to Jerry, because . . . because Jerry suspected we were seeing each other and you might think Charles didn't want that coming out, but he didn't kill Jerry, I swear. And I don't have to back him up anymore because we're no longer a couple. Not that we ever were . . .'

The end of their relationship upset her more than she'd expected it to. It broke her heart in a thousand different ways. She mourned the time she'd wasted and the times she'd never have. Yet there was a part of her still hoping Charles would realise he couldn't live without her and beg her to take him back.

Katy had spent two hours at the hairdressers getting the soft wave of a Charleston bob, an hour getting her makeup done and, because her false eyelashes kept catching on her glasses, had spent another thirty minutes putting contact lenses in. Parents walked straight past without recognising her, but for the first time in a long time she felt beautiful.

She shook her hands, spraying water across the mirror and moved to the pitiful hand-dryer that did little more than breathe on her like an overfamiliar drunk at an office party. The door swung open and Helen-Louise dragged music and chatter in her wake.

'Oh, hi,' she said. 'Wow. Look at you. You look divine! Who knew you had such lovely legs?'

'Thank you. You too. Gorgeous dress.'

Helen-Louise went into one of the stalls and locked the door behind her. Katy let her hands slip from the dryer and the whirring stopped.

'So, we sold all the tickets in the end,' she called. 'The last two only went yesterday. The caterers were great about it. I hear the band are amazing. Have you heard them play before?'

Katy hesitated. 'No. I watched a video on YouTube and they seemed professional enough.'

'Professional?' squeaked Helen-Louise. 'I was hoping for something a bit wilder. Have you ever seen the film *Hocus Pocus* where they cast a spell to make everyone dance all night long? That's what I want. If I don't have blisters on my feet come morning, I'll consider this night an almighty failure.'

Katy heard the toilet flush. 'I'd better get back out there,' Katy said as Helen-Louise appeared beside her, pulling at the hem of her dress.

'Did you see who's turned up?' Helen-Louise's voice was woven through with excitement and mischief. 'Pippa Yardley!'

Katy felt her stomach drop. 'But Charles said ... Mr Yardley thought she wouldn't be well enough.'

As Helen-Louise readjusted her headband over her bobbed hair she said, 'I know. She looks great but a little bit vacant if you know what I mean. She completely blanked me when I tried to say hello to her.'

Helen-Louise turned on the tap and jumped backwards as it splashed her dress. Katy pulled open the bathroom door and walked out, leaving Helen-Louise to reapply her pink lipstick. The hall was almost empty. They wouldn't need to take their seats for another half an hour. Most of the guests were outside, either on the rides or watching those who were on them. Katy picked up a glass of sparkling wine from by the door. At past events they'd always served Bollinger. A complimentary drink of the highest standard, like most things at this school. But Katy didn't believe they could tell the difference between Bolly and the supermarket's award-winning fizz. No one was going to admit to not liking something they assumed was fine champagne.

Katy had promised herself that she wouldn't drink tonight, but now, knowing that Pippa was here with Charles, she needed some courage. Walking out into the warm evening, she could almost forget that this was a ball to commemorate the life of a murdered man. And she could almost forget that the man she loved was here with his wife.

Katy looked across the lawn, across the laughing faces and thought, 'I did this. This is mine.' In the past, Aberfal hadn't been known for its inclusion, but she was head of the school now and things were going to change. There was so much potential here. She could help so many children and give them the foundation needed to lead fulfilled and relevant lives.

It took Katy a while to find Pippa in the crowds, but once she'd spotted her, Katy couldn't believe she'd ever missed her. Her turquoise dress shone as if covered in a million crystals. The jewellery on her wrists, fingers and at her throat rivalled the sun for brightness, and Charles was by her side laughing at something somebody else had said. As Katy watched, he slipped his arm around Pippa's waist and Katy wondered whether Charles had ever planned to leave his wife.

Pippa and Charles looked so handsome. So good together. Was Katy kidding herself that someone like Charles Yardley could love her and want to build a future with her? Charles Yardley with his boarding school education, his Oxbridge credentials. Charles Yardley, the chair of governors, the man who ran marathons.

'Hello, Miss Lane. It looks like a good turnout.'

Katy tightened her grip on her glass to stop it falling from her hand. 'Gemma,' she said. 'I'm so glad you made it.'

Chapter 38

The Summer Ball
8.03 p.m.

At a table that should have sat eight, Asha was the odd number making them a lucky number seven. An empty place was set between her and Becky who sat to her left. Becky's husband, Russ, was telling stories and anecdotes, making everyone laugh. On the other side of Asha were Clare and her husband. Asha didn't quite catch his name when she met him a few months ago and, when he repeated it, she was none the wiser. It was too late to ask now. Opposite Asha were Pippa and Charles. A masterclass in keeping up appearances.

Pippa looked like a film star and Charles was her leading man. They rarely looked each other in the eye, but they were shoulder-to-shoulder. United. Asha noticed that Pippa wasn't drinking. Her water glass was the only one getting topped up by the attentive waiters. Charles had a pint of beer on the table in front of him, though Asha knew he'd given up drinking after that incident when they'd holi-dayed with Jerry and Gemma Newhall.

Someone slid into the chair next to her and made Asha jump. 'Sorry I'm late. What have I missed?'

'Rose?' Asha said. 'Where's . . .'

'Mick? Oh. Last minute change of plans. He's not well, so I asked to sit at your table. Looks like you're my date for the night, Asha. Cheers!'

As everyone raised their glasses and told Rose how beautiful she looked, Asha watched her closely. Her smile was too wide, her eyes too heavily made up. Sensing her scrutiny, Rose looked at Asha and, for a second, her smile slipped and the sadness shone through.

'Friends?' Rose asked.

'Friends.'

The food came and was mostly eaten, but the knots in Asha's stomach made it impossible to finish the plate in front of her. She placed her hand over the top of her wine glass each time the wine waiter appeared. She'd had enough to take the edge off, but not enough for her to forget what awaited them tonight. She hadn't expected Gemma Newhall to be here. None of them had. It had thrown a muffler on the evening. No one wanting to laugh in her earshot.

As the dinner plates were cleared away, Hinch got to his feet and asked for everyone's attention.

'The last few minutes for the silent auction ladies and gents. Get your bids in now. Don't forget that there's the two-week stay in Henry's villa in Malta. You'll have to pay for your own flights. He's too stingy to pay for those.'

Laughter.

'And my personal favourite, a day in an Aston Martin as donated by Elsmore's garage, largely thanks to the inordinate amount of money Cliff Travis has spent there over the last few years. Am I right, Cliff?'

More laughter.

'And after dessert,' Hinch was saying, 'we'll have the St Stephen Swingers – steady on there, Anton, they're not those kinds of swingers.' He pointed a finger at a man seated on the next table who didn't seem to find it as funny as the rest of the room. 'Now, joking aside, this is as good a time as any to thank the committee for organising tonight's ball.'

There was enthusiastic applause. Helen-Louise pretended to look abashed.

'And,' said Hinch, 'thank you to everyone who's bid on the lots, spent money at the bar and, well, bought tickets and turned up tonight. As you know, this evening is extra special because we're celebrating the life of an extraordinary man.' He paused a moment and looked at Gemma. There was a smattering of applause. A few cheers. 'And Miss Lane's speech at the beginning of the evening summed it up well. He was a great man, sorely missed and it's our duty to carry on and make him proud. Could you raise your glasses, please?'

Chairs scraped across the floor as people got to their feet.

Hinch held his glass aloft. 'To Jerry Newhall.'

'To Jerry Newhall,' they all echoed.

Gemma Newhall put her glass to her mouth and didn't look up when her husband's name was mentioned. The wine barely touched her lips and the pain in her eyes was evident to all who cared to look, but most preferred to look away. It was easier that way.

Asha took the opportunity to look for Otis but there was still a space at the table where he should have sat. At the back of the room there were three other empty chairs and she assumed they were the seats of the men who'd jumped into the lake earlier.

Asha noticed heads turning in her direction and felt heat rush to her cheeks before she realised that they were looking straight past her, to the woman seated opposite. Asha looked too and saw that Pippa had remained seated during the toast, not looking the slightest bit embarrassed.

Through a fixed smile, Charles hissed at Pippa, 'Get to your feet.' He put his hand under her elbow, but she shook him off.

Pippa remained seated and answered, 'Why, Charles? Why should I?'

People weren't even pretending to be discreet anymore. They were openly staring.

'Because it's a sign of respect for our dear friend,' he said, pretending to laugh, though his hard eyes showed he didn't find any of this funny. 'I know you're not feeling quite yourself, but . . .'

'I'm feeling perfectly fine thank you, Charles. I tell you what I'm not, though. I'm not a hypocrite.'

Slowly, Pippa stood up and addressed the room. 'Why don't we play a game,' she said.

Her voice cut through the silence. The waiting staff stood mute around the perimeter of the room, eyes sliding to each other, hands clasped behind their backs.

The light outside had changed to a peculiar yellowish grey. Darker than it should have been for this time on an early summer evening. A storm was coming in more ways than one.

Pippa lifted her glass. 'Let's play Last One Standing.'

'Sit. Down,' hissed Charles.

Asha saw Katy Lane reach for her drink with a shaking hand.

'Stand up. Sit down,' said Pippa with an exasperated sigh. 'Do make up your mind, darling. I think we're all in the mood for a bit of fun, aren't we?'

Everyone except Gemma was already on their feet, but they were exchanging glances and shifting uncomfortably. They wanted to know what was behind the game. Too intrigued to bow out now.

'Okay. So, this is how we play it,' Pippa said. 'I ask a question and if your answer is "no" you sit down and if your answer is "yes", you keep standing until we have a winner.' She beamed at everyone around the room.

'Is that clear enough?' asked Pippa. 'Sit down for "no", stay standing for "yes". Right then, we'll start with a simple question. Are you enjoying yourself this evening?'

There was a collective sigh as tension was released. Perhaps Pippa Yardley wasn't going to cause a scene. Everyone remained standing, there was a buzz of chatter, a lone attempt at a round of applause. Outside, the wind was starting to get stronger. A door rattled and a moan came through one of the closed windows as the glass pane vibrated in its frame.

'Lovely. It is a marvellous spectacle, isn't it? I must say you all scrub up rather well. Second question. Are you either a teacher, or do you have children currently studying at Aberfal? Remember, sit down if the answer is no.'

A few people – four of five at most – sat down. They were the trustees, the old boys. Associated with the school, but

351

not financially bound by it. Most people had relaxed into the game now, but Katy Lane was standing rigid.

'Good. Right then, next question. Do you truly – and I mean, be honest now—' Pippa wagged her finger and a few people laughed nervously. 'Keep standing if . . .' she looked around the room, making sure everyone was paying attention. 'Keep standing if you're happy' – she swallowed – 'that Jerry Newhall is dead.'

There was a gasp. People sat, either from refusing to play this game anymore, or from wanting to show they were not at all happy that their beloved headmaster was gone. They looked to Gemma who was still looking at her glass.

Charles pulled on Pippa's arm. 'Pippa, this isn't the time nor the place.'

'Oh, come on now,' Pippa said, ignoring her husband and addressing the room. 'Of course, I know that every untimely death is sad, but who's going to be brave enough to admit that life is that little bit better now that's he's gone? Mr Hinchwood, isn't it true that Jerry told you that, unless the boys won the southwest cup, he was going to fire you? Weren't you expecting this to be your last term at Aberfal? His death makes your job a little more secure, doesn't it?'

Hinch, who'd taken his seat again, looked at the white-topped table but didn't deny it. Mandy moved her chair closer to him and placed her hand on his.

'And Helen-Louise, where are you? Oh, there you are. Darling, you look lovely tonight by the way. Now Helen-Louise, am I right or am I wrong? Mr Newhall used to harass you, yes? Inappropriately?'

Helen-Louise looked outraged, but she blushed and put her hands to her cheeks.

'I know, dear,' said Pippa. 'It was grubby, wasn't it? The pats on the bottom. The way his elbow would casually graze your breast. And the little jokes about spanking and massaging the stiffness in his groin. Don't you wish, just once, that you'd slapped his smug little face? I saw you when I threw a cake at Jerry for grabbing at Rose. It wasn't shock, was it, darling? It was admiration. Now I know you wouldn't wish him dead, heaven forbid, but let's be honest, isn't it a relief? You no longer have to put up with the innuendos. You don't have to be afraid of being left alone with him.'

Rose laughed and then pinched her lips together to stop any more sounds from escaping. She caught Asha's eye and mouthed, 'Oh my God!'

Charles took Pippa by the elbow. 'Pippa, it's time for you to leave.'

She shook him off.

'Look, I don't want to upset Gemma but none of this is news to her. She knew what he was like, yet she loved him anyway. She seems to be the only person not pretending that her husband was perfect. She knows that he had his faults and that they got him killed. I'm sure she'd like to know who did it? Aren't I right, Gemma?'

Gemma looked up then, but still didn't speak.

'And Asha, my dear friend.'

Asha jumped at the mention of her name.

'Do you know,' Pippa said addressing the room, 'that Asha saved my life? I bet she didn't tell you that, did she? After my accident, she kept my heart beating until the ambulance arrived. I am only here today because of this woman.'

Rose nudged Asha and mouthed, 'Wow.'

Asha felt herself blushing. She sat down, trying to become smaller.

'Asha darling, I'm sorry to talk of delicate matters, but I hope you won't mind me telling our assembled friends that your son has been so badly bullied at Aberfal by the sons of the people assembled here, that he risked his life on a dare.'

Asha shrugged.

'And yet,' Pippa continued. 'Jerry's response was "boys will be boys".'

Asha glanced nervously over her shoulder.

'That's enough!' snarled Charles.

'Oh, behave yourself, Charles. Our son is one of the bullies, if not the main one. Asha knows but has been too kind to bring it to my attention. And where do you think he gets that from, Charles? How badly did Jerry bully you when you were at school together? Huh? And yet you don't realise that you are as bad as he is. Sorry, I mean *was*.'

She lifted her chin to address the hall once more. 'How can we stand here and talk about carrying on Jerry's legacy when it's a legacy of bullying and sexual harassment?'

There was silence all around them.

'And so,' Pippa said, 'let's try this again. Please stand if Jerry Newhall's death makes your life that little bit easier.' Charles was still on his feet beside her, so he sat down swiftly, not wanting anyone to doubt his loyalty to Jerry. He didn't care if people doubted his loyalty to his wife. Charles

Yardley might be charming, he might be handsome, but he was spineless.

The room was silent. The resolve and passion in Pippa's eyes were beginning to dim. Asha put both hands on the table in front of her and pushed herself up to standing. Pippa locked eyes with her and nodded, but Charles put his head in his hands.

It seemed like the longest ten seconds Asha had ever known but, eventually, all around the room, chairs creaked and scraped as people started to get to their feet.

Chapter 39

The Summer Ball
8.45 p.m.

Pippa waited for people to stand up. She felt no panic, no palpitations. It was as if she was exactly where she needed to be, doing exactly what she needed to do. Looking around the great hall, she was careful not to focus on anyone and make them feel uncomfortable. Instead, she looked at the shocked or smirking faces of the waiting staff. And she watched the candles pulsing in the middle of each table, as if she had nowhere better to be and could wait all night if she had to. It was a gamble, she knew, but there had to be others who felt the same as she did. She couldn't be the only one relieved that Jerry was dead, but she was the only one bold enough to speak the truth. She also knew that this was the best way to goad Charles into making a mistake.

Her patience paid off as, one by one, people around the room got to their feet. Cautiously at first, like the first snow-drops breaking through frosted ground. But as soon as she spotted one, she spotted another and another. Their faces were solemn, a little bashful, but they stood tall. To her right, Clare reached for Pippa's hand. She took it, gladly, gave it a squeeze and let go again. Pippa saw Mandy get to

356

her feet with defiance written all over her face. Hinch followed suit without taking his eyes off her. It was touching how loyal he was. It was a softer side to him that Pippa hadn't taken the time to notice before. Mandy turned to look at Hinch and took his hand in hers. Pippa smiled. She'd had her suspicions about their blossoming relationship. It was nice that it was out in the open now. They deserved happiness.

At most tables, at least one person was on their feet. With a sigh loud enough to make sure that everyone turned to her, Helen-Louise got unsteadily to her feet. Her husband had a fixed, confused smile on his face. Though she was drunk, she knew exactly what she was doing.

When it seemed like no one else was going to get to their feet, Pippa took a deep breath.

'Thank you,' Pippa said. 'I appreciate your honesty. And perhaps now we can move forwards, together, as a school. Because Jerry Newhall was not a perfect man by any stretch of the imagination. Not one of us is. So, let's not insult his memory by pretending that he was something he wasn't. He was a bully, a letch and a blackmailer. And that's just from my family's perspective. I can't speak for what he has done to any of you but it's not that difficult to understand why someone in this room murdered him.'

A gasp travelled through the room like a breeze over dry leaves. Not at the shock of it, because everyone knew by now that Jerry didn't die of natural causes. It must have been the shock of someone saying the words out loud. But now they were out of the box, they were words that needed to be dealt with.

'And, contrary to the rumours,' Pippa continued, 'I wasn't having an affair with Jerry. I didn't step out in front of a moving car because I felt guilty or because I was nursing a broken heart.' She looked around the room; every pair of eyes were upon her. 'In fact, even though he was a little handsy sometimes, I don't believe Jerry was having an affair with anyone.' She turned to look at Gemma. 'He loved you, Gemma. Only you. I hope you know that.'

Gemma nodded curtly and looked away.

'Back me up, Charles,' Pippa said. 'It wasn't *him* having the affair, was it?'

'What? I . . .'

Pippa turned back to the room.

'And I know that none of you standing tall with me this evening is responsible for his death either or, at least, not directly. I know this because you're the brave ones. The ones who dare to say that Jerry was running our school into the ground. At some point in the last year, many of us have had cause to disagree with Jerry and we've done it to his face, haven't we? So, let us take a moment to look at the liars among us.'

Pippa stopped, took a sip of water to steady herself and then she looked down at Charles who was sitting like a naughty schoolboy with his hands clasped between his knees. He jerked backwards as if to get out from under her gaze.

'Now hold on a minute,' he said and began to get to his feet.

Pippa put her hand on his shoulder and shoved him back into his seat. 'Too late, darling.'

Pippa turned away from Charles in disgust, blinked and continued. 'I know most of you weren't expecting to see me here tonight. And I know some of you were pinning your hopes on my absence.' She looked at Katy now who narrowed her eyes but didn't drop her gaze. Pippa smiled to herself. There was something wildly satisfying in pissing off the right people. That's how you knew you were doing something right.

'But here I am,' she said addressing the room again. Her voice was loud and clear. 'So, to the killer I say, enjoy your evening. Because your time's up.'

Pippa lifted her glass, held it aloft and said, 'To freedom.'

Charles valued his freedom too much to stand by and say nothing. She would make him show his hand, even if it was the last thing she did.

Chapter 40

The Summer Ball
9.49 p.m.

Katy walked through the empty school corridors, with no destination in mind. She wanted to be away from the main hall, putting space between her and the fallout from Pippa Yardley's little stunt. The night was nearly over, the term was nearly over and Katy was beginning to think that her time at Aberfal was over, too.

The band was playing an old Sinatra classic but even they knew it was the equivalent of playing while the *Titanic* sank. No one was dancing. Instead, they huddled and stared and whispered. Some were crying, some were angry but, either way, the alcohol buzz had worn off and no one could remember why they ever thought that coming to the school's summer ball was a good idea.

Katy pulled off her false eyelashes and dropped them in the bin next to the drinking fountain. Blinking hard, she hadn't realised how heavy the lashes were until she was free of them. Her eyes were stinging now, she wasn't used to the contact lenses but couldn't take them out until she was at home where her glasses were. She rubbed her eyes then looked at her fingers that were now grey with eyeshadow and mascara.

She bent over the water fountain, drinking in deep gulps and when she stood up her head swam. She started walking again, trailing her hand over the cool wall. She'd mostly managed to avoid talking to Gemma Newhall, despite sitting opposite her during dinner. The police would have spoken to her by now. Did she know that it was Katy who'd told them about the emails? Why else would she be here tonight? She couldn't be in the mood for a party so soon after her husband's death – no one was. Perhaps she was hoping to corner Katy and give her a piece of her mind. Or worse. At least Gemma would know that Katy had come clean, so whatever stunt she'd planned to humiliate her with tonight was no longer warranted. Katy had left her with nowhere to go.

And if that wasn't enough to worry about, Pippa Yardley managed to make the evening all about her. That ridiculous woman. Why did she have to ruin everything? It wasn't as if Katy asked for much. The open day had been her chance to show how capable she was and Pippa had thrown a cake in Jerry's face so it was all anyone could talk about. Then, tonight, the ball was Katy's chance to shine at her first event since becoming acting head, but Pippa managed to accuse half the guests of murder and sully Jerry's reputation all in one. Perfect. It was obvious what everyone would be talking about at the school gates on Monday and it wouldn't be the band or the fairground rides or the sumptuous food.

Katy tried not to take it personally but, despite Charles thinking that Pippa didn't know about them, it was obvious to Katy that he was wrong. Pippa was undermining her at every turn.

And then, of course, there was Charles. Katy hadn't realised how difficult it would be to see him tonight. She was used to seeing him at events and not being able to hold his hand or laugh loudly at his jokes, but this was agonising. Though he acted as if she didn't exist, Katy couldn't stop thinking about him. She wouldn't be able to work alongside him knowing they were never meant to be.

She thought she heard a door close and glanced over her shoulder, but there was no one there. She'd hoped that Charles might slip out after her, to steal a moment, but he'd looked straight through her as if she wasn't there. He might have turned off his feelings, but she didn't know how. If anything, she wanted him more than before.

Outside the DT lab she stopped walking, leaned on the door frame and tried to prise the shoes from her feet. Too much standing, in weather that was too warm, meant that her feet had swollen. As she freed them from their confines, she saw the beginning of a blister on the side of her little toe and raw skin on her heel. She didn't care how good they looked; high heels were never worth the pain. Same could be said for men.

The floor was cool under her feet. She wriggled her toes. She couldn't wait to get home and scrub the makeup from her face. She'd take a long hot shower and put on the softest pyjamas she owned. Right now, she'd kill for a cup of tea, but her taxi wouldn't be here for another hour and she really should stay until the excruciating end. She'd find somewhere quiet while she waited.

Again, Katy thought she heard a noise behind her. She twisted so quickly she almost lost her balance, but the corridor behind her was still empty. She waited for the noise to come again but all she heard was the thud of the beat coming from the main hall. None of the laughter and chatter that she usually heard at school events. Her head was swimming from too much cheap fizz.

With her shoes dangling from her fingers, Katy starting walking again, mounting the stairs towards the head's office. It didn't feel like her office and never would. Jerry had been right when he'd said this wasn't the job for her. She didn't know what she'd been thinking. Her? A headteacher? What an absurd notion. She'd tried so hard to keep the school running as if nothing bad had happened, but it was all coming apart now. She should have stood up to the governors and told them that she wasn't reopening the school until they'd had a suitable period of mourning and made some significant changes. They should have waited until the murderer had been caught and she shouldn't have moved straight into an office where a man had died, because she couldn't be in that room without picturing Jerry on the floor, a cricket bat by his head. The image was woven into every dream and the waking moments where she allowed her mind to drift.

Pretending not to be affected by Jerry's death had taken all her mental energy and Katy couldn't do it anymore. What would happen if she didn't show up to school on Monday morning? The school would keep going, that was for sure. Some people would be delighted. She needed some time to work out her next steps away from Aberfal High.

She slowed as she got to the top of the stairs, her heavier breathing making it clear that she'd neglected exercise for too long. In the morning she'd pull on her trainers and go for a long run. She pushed open the heavy wooden door but didn't switch on the light. The fairground lights illuminated the room and Katy padded silently to the window, dropping her shoes onto the sofa as she passed.

She'd made it clear that, once the guests went in for dinner, the rides were to be closed. She didn't want to be responsible for drunks being sick on the merry-go-round. Some of the rides were in darkness, already locked up until they could be attached to trucks and pulled out of there to the next event. Others illuminated the grounds, the sky, and lit up the office like a wonderland. Katy pushed at the window. Still closed. Katy couldn't work out why the window had been open on the day Jerry died. At the time, she'd been grateful because it had made it easier for her to dispose of the bat, but it still didn't make sense.

Katy rubbed her temples and looked across the grounds and down to the lake. She stepped closer to the glass, put her hands against the window, rested her forehead against it. Were there people by the lake? Hadn't she made it clear that no one was to go down there? She hoped that Otis was there to manage them and to send them back up to the school. Where'd he been this evening, anyway? Katy had seen him at the beginning of the night, but he hadn't come in to eat with them.

Katy noticed headlights as a car drove slowly across the grounds, passing behind the rides.

'What the hell?'

It had the unmistakable markings of a police car.

She spun round and groped in the dark for her shoes. She'd have to go and find out what was happening. It seemed she wasn't done with this school yet. Or, at least, it wasn't done with her.

She yanked open the door, to rush through it, only to find that her way was blocked.

'I don't suppose I could have a word could I, darling?'

Chapter 41

The Summer Ball
9.57 p.m.

Pippa pushed Katy aside and sank down on to the sofa. 'What a night.'

'What do you want?'

'Aren't you going to sit?'

'I'd rather stand.'

'Here,' said Pippa. 'I've got something for you.'

She opened her fringed bag and pulled out a handkerchief. She opened it carefully, one layer after another. 'This is yours, I believe?'

Instead of stepping closer, Katy moved away towards the desk. She turned on the desk lamp and blinked against the sudden light.

'I won't bite,' said Pippa. 'Come on.' She extended her hand, an opal ring clearly on her palm. 'It is yours, isn't it?'

'Where did you find it?'

'Where do you think? In the flat where you've been carrying on your affair with my husband. Right there on the side of the bathroom sink. Careless of you, darling. But I suppose you thought you were safe?'

Katy's eyes were on the ring, but she didn't take it. 'How long have you known?'

'I've known about the affair for a little while, but only found out that it was you when I saw the ring.' Pippa slid it onto her finger. It only got as far as her knuckle before getting stuck. 'Haven't you got dainty fingers? Does he comment on that? Does he tell you that you have beautiful slender hands?'

'What do you want from me? An apology?'

Pippa looked up and frowned. 'Why? *Are* you sorry?'

'Not really.'

'Then what would be the point?' Pippa sat forward on the sofa and tossed the ring onto the desk next to Katy. It spun then juddered to a halt. 'Even if you did mean it, it wouldn't change anything, would it? No. Keep your apology.'

Katy took another two steps away from Pippa, putting the desk between them.

Pippa smiled. 'Do I make you feel uncomfortable?'

'What do you want, Pippa? Charles and I are over. We split up when you were in hospital. He said he couldn't leave you. You've won. I'm the pathetic mistress, you're the victorious wife. What else do you want?'

'Do you love him?'

'I told you, it's over.'

Pippa smiled. 'But sometimes the love stays, doesn't it? I should know. Even after he asked for a divorce, I still tried to hold on to our marriage. Though that's the key word, isn't it? Marriage. It wasn't Charles that I wanted, as such. I simply didn't want to break up our little unit.'

'Just tell me what you want, Pippa.'

'I'm here to apologise.' Pippa got to her feet and Katy slipped further away from her.

'What for?'

'The emails,' Pippa said.

'That was you?'

'No. Not me. But still, they were because of me and I feel responsible.'

'I don't follow.'

Pippa sighed. 'I've asked Charles to move out. He's moved into that flat of his. Did he tell you?'

Katy shook her head.

'We're keeping things civil. Keeping up appearances, you know, while we decide on what to do next. We agreed that a bit of space might help us see clearly. But as far as the rest of the world know, we're still together. Sort of.'

'What's this got to do with the emails?'

'I sat the boys down and told them that Charles had moved out. And I told them why. All about you and their father. I thought about keeping it from them, but it's bound to come out, isn't it? And here's the thing: only one of my sons was shocked and upset. The other one had known about it for months. Poor Benny, I should've known there was something going on. He desperately wanted me to know about your affair, but he didn't want to be the one to tell me in case I shot the messenger. He had hoped you might tell me yourself if encouraged.'

Katy rounded the desk and sat down, deflating before Pippa's eyes. 'It was Benny? I never wanted the boys to find out. Not like this. I thought that Gemma . . .'

'He told me he'd emailed you telling you to come clean. That's right, isn't it? Come clean. And then when you didn't do anything he added in a timescale. Gosh, he's angry. Angry enough to throw paint over Charles's car and wreck your car tyres I gather. Kids, eh? I haven't told Charles yet. I'll leave it to you to decide whether to tell him. I'll only use it as a stick to beat him with. You might find a better way to let him know that his son hates him.'

Pippa walked over to the window. 'And it's only going to get worse for Charles. And you too, probably.'

'How can it get any worse?'

Pippa folded her arms. 'The police are here now. As luck would have it, those people splashing in the lake earlier uncovered a cricket bat. The same bat that killed Jerry Newhall. The same bat that you threw out of the window.'

'What? How do you know that I—'

'Otis Blake saw you. Do you want to know something interesting? Even when an object has been in water, the police can still lift fingerprints from it. I imagine your prints will be all over it.'

'I didn't hurt Jerry. I swear to you. I came in here, saw that bat and panicked. I threw it out of the window because . . .'

'Yes, do tell. Why hide it if you weren't guilty?'

'I told you I panicked. Wasn't thinking straight.'

Pippa smiled. 'Might I hazard a guess? By the way, I believe you when you say you didn't hurt Jerry. Which means the only reason you would tamper with evidence is to protect someone you love.'

Katy groaned, shook her head.

'We both know who that is, don't we, darling?'

'I've already been to talk to the police and told them everything. But I'll tell you what I told them. There's no way Charles would hurt Jerry.'

'It's sweet that you think so. He'll be touched that you did this for him. But you've got to ask yourself, Miss Lane, would Charles do the same for you?'

Chapter 42

The Summer Ball
10.06 p.m.

Asha stood in the twilight, beneath the bobbing branches of the lime tree, watching bats as they flitted overhead. Pippa's speech had been intended to flush out the killer. To cause someone – Charles, she hoped – to show their hand. Asha thought it was too risky, but Pippa was sure Charles wouldn't hurt her. She was gambling on the fact that, deep down, he still loved her. Asha was pretty sure he only loved himself. Though she didn't know where Pippa had gone, she was keeping a close eye on Charles.

Now the evening was coming to an end, Asha had taken off her gloves and left them on the table. It was too dark for people to notice the oil stains on her hands now. And even if they did, they wouldn't care. The waiting staff had set down thin wedges of lemon tart with raspberry coulis and then, ten minutes later, took them away again untouched. The night was over. The atmosphere in the room had spiralled from revelry to shock in minutes. People were on their mobiles entreating taxi companies to bring forward their bookings.

The fairground rides were silent now. No laughter, no music. They'd be taken away in the morning, leaving dents and divots on Otis's pristine lawn.

Charles burst from the building and, once out in the night, threw back his head and sucked in the purple air. Asha almost felt sorry for him. His night hadn't gone according to plan and it was about to get so much worse.

'Charles?'

He glanced in her direction but then looked over his shoulder as if wondering which was the lesser of two evils. Eventually, he walked over to where she stood and past her so he could lean against the tree trunk.

'I'd ask you if you were having a nice night but ...' Charles had his hands stuffed deep into his pockets but even through the fabric, Asha could see they were balled up into tight fists. He noticed something happening at the lake and strained to see past the fairground rides. Then he shrugged and looked at the ground, past caring.

The remaining lights from the fair made half his face red, while the other half remained in darkness.

'If I'd known all of Aberfal's parties were like this, I would've come to one sooner,' Asha said.

'This one has been particularly special,' Charles said. 'One to remember. I hear you're leaving us.'

'See?' said Asha. 'It's not all bad news tonight.'

'I've never wanted you and Cassius out of the school.'

'You've never made us feel welcome.'

'Pippa did enough of that for both of us.'

'A perfect partnership, huh?'

'Used to be.'

They stood in silence. He seemed so broken in the darkness. He'd lost his swagger.

'Have you seen we've got company?' she asked.

'Yes, what is going on down there? Is that a police car?'

'Otis called them. There were some parents in the lake earlier.'

'I saw. They didn't . . . They're not hurt, are they?' He pushed himself off the tree, about to head in that direction, a doctor first and foremost.

Asha put out an arm to stop him. 'No. They're fine. But the police think they've found the murder weapon in the lake.'

Charles straightened up, staggered backwards a step. 'Christ. Sometimes I almost forget . . . Not forget that Jerry's dead, but that we're still in the middle of all this mess. It never gets easier, does it? One thing after another. Relentless. I . . . God, I need to go home.'

'Aren't you curious to see what they've found?'

'I don't even have the energy to keep my head on top of my shoulders.' He rubbed his forehead and blinked hard. 'If you see Pippa tell her I had to go. After her performance tonight I'm in no mood to wait for her. See she gets home safely, will you?'

'I will.'

Asha watched him disappear beneath the archway by the chapel as Katy came out of the school with Pippa by her side. Katy's eyes were on the lake. When she saw Asha she said, 'Is it true? Have they found something?'

'Looks that way.'

'I'd better . . .' she started to jog barefoot through the lights of the fair. Pippa came over to Asha and threaded her arm through hers.

'Are you all right?' Asha asked. 'You look pale. This is too much for you, isn't it? I told you it would be.'

Pippa nodded. 'You were right.'

'Charles left, by the way. Said to tell you that he was in no mood to wait for you.'

'He won't get far though, will he?'

Asha glanced down at her oil-stained hands. 'Nope.'

'Have you seen Gemma?' Pippa asked.

'She's down by the lake with Otis.'

'Poor woman. And they definitely think it's the weapon they used to . . . you know.'

'I don't suppose they'll know for certain until they've done some tests, but it looks that way.'

'Okay.' Pippa took a deep breath. 'I'd better go after Charles. Give me five minutes then come and find me?'

'Don't worry. I know what to do.'

WITNESS TEN

Otis Blake.
Groundskeeper.

I thought you'd ask to speak to me sooner than this. Better late than never, though.

I see pretty much everything that happens at the school. There's this building, like a barn, where I keep all the equipment. And it's big. I've got a hammock in there. Sometimes I like to bring it outside and string it between two trees. I shower in the cricket pavilion and I have a heater for when it's colder. There's a stove. There's running water. I mean, what else would I need? I like to live off-grid. You know? It's refreshing after the pace of my previous career. It's nice to sit by the lake and watch the herons and kingfishers. My kid brother died here and I feel closer to him at Aberfal. Jerry knew all about it. It wasn't as if I was doing anything wrong.

The day of the cricket match, I was waiting for everyone to go home. I was going to have a couple of beers, sleep under the stars. I checked the car park but there were still two cars there. Katy Lane's and Jerry Newhall's. Anyway, I heard something in the bushes beneath Newhall's window. There'd been a cat hanging around the grounds and I wasn't keen on the idea of it digging holes in my borders. I rushed into the bushes, but all I saw was a cricket bat in the dirt. I poked around, but no cat so I headed back towards the lake with the bat in hand. Didn't think much of it because the boys often hide each other's bats. I've found a few in the lake or thrown up into the trees. I don't know why. Kids, huh?

It wasn't until I was clear of the foliage that I looked to see if the bat was named. At first, I thought the boys had written on it and then I realised that they weren't words, they were signatures. I thought it might be worth something, so I put it in the shed with the games equipment, thought I'd hand it in when everyone was back after the weekend. Then, before you know it, there are police and sirens and Jerry Newhall's dead, so I didn't think any more of it. Everyone was saying heart attack, so it didn't occur to me to even mention anything about the bat.

But then it all came out that he was murdered and I remembered that cricket bat. I got a bit jumpy when you guys got the wrong end of the stick and thought someone had climbed out of Jerry's window with the murder weapon. When I looked at it again, I thought that maybe there was blood on it, but it might have been dirt and I didn't know for sure that you were looking for a bat. My fingerprints were all over it by then and rather than tell you about it, I cleaned it off and threw it in the lake. To be honest, I expected you to find it when you searched the lake, but you did such a half-hearted job of it and I couldn't point it out without dropping myself in it. Someone like me of no fixed abode, well, I thought I'd make the perfect scapegoat and you didn't have any other leads.

I knew that someone would jump in the lake at the ball. There's always at least one idiot. I said I'd spotted something and got the guy to dive down for it. I'm sorry I went about it the wrong way and God knows this might have been sorted sooner if I'd handed the bat over, but weren't the signs there all along? Wasn't it obvious who'd killed Jerry?

Chapter 43

The Summer Ball
10.10 p.m.

The car park was almost empty. Most people had chosen to come by taxi – the invites had stated *Carriages at Midnight*. Of those who'd driven, half would abandon their cars in favour of a good time, to collect them tomorrow once their headaches faded. Pippa had noticed Charles drinking tonight but didn't stop him. She wondered what Gemma Newhall made of it; after all, he'd promised her that he'd never drink again after he'd *accidentally* given her that black eye.

Charles said he preferred being sober. He didn't miss the thick head and the money spent on taxis. He preferred to drive anyway. He liked to be in control of when he arrived and when he left. He didn't like it when things didn't go his way.

As Pippa approached the car, she saw Charles leaning against the car door, keys in hand.

'What's the problem, darling?'

Charles snorted. 'Take your pick.'

'Car not starting?'

He narrowed his eyes. 'Is this something to do with you?'

'Asha told me you'd left, but you're still here. I'm making the obvious assumption.'

'Do piss off.'

'Now, darling, that's not nice.'

'What were you playing at tonight? They're all in there laughing at you, you know. At least you can blame it on the accident. Maybe they'll forgive you if they believe you have a brain injury.'

'This is nothing to do with the accident, Charles. I know exactly what I'm saying.'

'In that case I really am worried about you.'

She stepped close to him and touched his bow tie. Straightened it. Then leaned in, resting her weight against him and whispered in his ear, 'The game's up, you despicable piece of shit.'

Charles shoved her away. Pippa could have kept her balance, but she didn't even try. She fell backwards, calling out as she hit the gravel, feeling the stones embed in the heels of her hand.

'Charles! Stop!'

Pippa knew that there were still people inside the hall and that they would have rushed to the windows, peered around corners, at the commotion. It was such an un-Yardley-like spectacle that none of them would care that it was rude to stare. Under the lights Pippa and Charles were illuminated as if by a spotlight. It was the show that the critics were here to see.

Pippa didn't try to get up, she wanted everyone to witness what had happened.

'Get up!' Charles said.

She didn't think she could stand, even if she'd wanted to. Time was doing that trick of slowing down again and she felt like she could close her eyes and drift away.

'For God's sake.' Charles moved towards her with his hand outstretched.

The wind had picked up now and the overhead lights were flickering. Pippa heard Hinch bellow before he was even out of the door.

'Oi!'

Charles looked up. 'She fell over.'

'Get away from her!'

Charles put his hands up and backed away. 'It's not what it looks like.'

'Really? Looks to me like you pushed her.'

'Well, yes, but it was only a little shove.' He mimicked a gentle push, but Hinch wasn't convinced. He was inches from Charles's face.

Pippa was still on the floor, her arms shielding her face. She flinched when she felt hands on her arms, pulling at them. 'Mandy?'

'Let's get you up.'

'I'm all right. I don't want to cause a fuss.'

More people had come outside now. Women with folded arms and shaking heads. Men looking at Charles like they'd been waiting years for a chance to take him down. Pippa struggled to stand. Her weakened ankle had twisted again. Rose appeared at her other side and helped get Pippa up again.

Charles was standing tall now, reaching up to try and see Pippa over the heads of the people in front of him. 'You've got some nerve,' he said. 'Tell them I barely touched you.'

Gemma Newhall's voice rose above the muttering. 'In the same way that you barely touched me, Charles?'

'Hardly the same thing,' said Charles. 'I was drunk. You got in my way.'

There was an audible gasp from the crowd that was gathering. 'Oh, come on,' said Charles. 'It sounds worse than it was. Pippa, tell them.'

Rose stepped forwards and poked Charles in the chest. 'You owe Pippa an apology.'

Charles laughed. 'Apology? What for? She should be apologising to me for tonight's little show.'

Pippa put her hand to her throat. 'I thought it was time we all stopped deluding ourselves, that's all. Aren't you tired of it all, Charles? Tired of all the lies?'

Charles shook his head and smiled. 'What d'you think you'll achieve with this . . . with this little display?'

'You treated me like I was stupid. You called me your beautiful little fool.'

'You *are* a fool. You're out of your mind. All your insinuations and hints that I had something to do with Jerry's death. No one's falling for it, you know. Look at them. They all know you're out of your tiny mind.'

Pippa felt Mandy grasp her arm and she took a deep breath before raising her chin and saying, 'I've had enough of lying for you, Charles.'

'Lying for me? Lying for – for God's sake, woman.' Even though he was speaking to Pippa he seemed to be addressing the crowd.

'Well, for one thing, darling,' Pippa said, 'I know about your affair.'

His eyes widened for a second and then closed as he smiled. He looked at her then with something like appreciation for a move well made. 'Ah. So that's what this is about.'

'I know you've rented a little love nest. Paid twelve months in advance instead of paying for the school fees,' Pippa said. 'And I can't quite work out whether Jerry was blackmailing you, or if you were prescribing him those drugs illegally out of choice.'

Behind Charles, Detective Mullins reached the car park. Asha wasn't far behind.

'Honestly, Pippa,' said Charles. 'No one's taking any notice of what you're saying. It's the accident.' He moved closer to Pippa. 'Brain injuries are notoriously—'

'Careful,' Hinch said, blocking his path.

Pippa pulled herself up as tall as she could. 'You're not denying it, are you, darling? I think that would be unwise in the circumstances.'

Mullins asked, 'What's going on?'

Charles gave a tight smile. 'Ah, Detective Mullins, how fortuitous that you turn up right at this precise moment.' He looked at Asha and sneered. 'I'm afraid my wife is making all sorts of baseless accusations. Too much wine, that's all.'

'I haven't had a drink all night, Charles, but do carry on. We're all ears. Which bit is baseless?'

Asha went to Pippa and took her hand. Rose stepped to Pippa's other side.

'For a start you're trying to make people think I killed Jerry,' Charles said.

'Am I? I don't think I . . .' Pippa shook her head slowly. 'I don't remember saying that. Though now you come to mention it . . .'

'Okay,' Mullins said. 'Let's take this elsewhere, shall we?'

'No need,' said Charles. 'My wife's a crazy woman with a grudge. There's nothing to concern you here. Yes, I made a mistake. One tiny mistake. She's angry with me and trying to put the blame on me for everything that's ever gone wrong. And now she's trying to make it look like I killed Jerry. You can see through this, right? The woman is obviously unstable.'

'What were you running from?' asked Asha, looking at Charles's car. 'As soon as I told you the police were here, you couldn't get out of here quick enough.'

'I wasn't running. The night was over, thanks to my wife. Everyone was getting ready to leave. But then my car wouldn't start and—'

'But you saw the police cars, right? I would've thought you'd have been curious to know why they're here,' said Asha. 'As chair of governors, don't you have a responsibility to find out?'

On cue, Katy started making her way towards them. Small, cautious steps.

'It was you, was it?' Charles said to Asha. 'You tampered with my car. I see my wife has got to you with her fanciful stories, but I don't have to explain myself to someone like you.'

'Someone like her?' said Rose.

Everyone was silent. The music inside the hall had stopped. When Pippa spoke, her voice was croaky. 'Will you at least admit that you're having an affair with Katy Lane?'

382

'Let's not make more of this than we need to,' Charles said, as those who'd come to watch shuffled closer, spoke behind cupped hands. 'You've known for months that we've run our course. It happens. The affair was more to do with the state of our marriage than Katy. It could've been anyone. Anyone at all.'

He patted down his hair and stood up straight as if suddenly remembering himself. He turned to Detective Mullins and put his hand on his heart. 'I'm so sorry you've had to hear all that. This should have remained a private matter.'

'No, no,' Mullins said. 'Not at all. I'd love to hear more about why your wife thinks you had something to do with Jerry Newhall's murder. Especially seeing as we've gone and found the murder weapon in the lake.'

There was a rush of whispers through the crowd, caught up by the wind and magnified.

'Isn't it obvious what's happening?' Charles said. 'She's set this whole thing up. Given her recent behaviour, I wouldn't be surprised if my wife was responsible for the whole thing. I don't know anything about a murder weapon. Wouldn't know anything about Jerry's death.'

'Jerry knew enough to destroy you, didn't he?' said Pippa.

'What?'

'You were scared that Jerry was going to report you to the GMC for prescribing those tablets you'd got him addicted to and you'd lose your job,' she said.

'That would've made it difficult to fund your secret life,' Asha said.

'This is bloody ludicrous!'

383

'Yes,' Rose said. 'Yes. And the day of the cricket match you disappeared for half an hour and came back wearing a different shirt. What happened, Charles?'

'Pippa spilled her drink on me. You know that.'

'Do I?'

'Besides, that whole time I was absent from the match I was with Miss Lane. She can vouch for me.'

'No,' said Katy stepping forwards. 'I don't recall seeing you until after the match had ended.'

He snapped his head around to look at her, his eyes showing genuine surprise. 'I didn't realise you were there.' Charles coughed. 'This is ridiculous. Jerry and I had some issues, of course. But he was alive last time I saw him and that's the truth. For one thing, if I was going to kill him, I wouldn't have hit him round the head with a cricket bat, would I? I would have drugged him, done something far more subtle than overpowering him with brute force. Not really my style. Now, if you'll excuse me, I'm not going to stand here and listen to this rubbish.'

Mullins shook his head and held out a hand to stop him going anywhere. 'Now, sir, I don't believe that the murder weapon has ever been made public, so do you mind telling me why you think Mr Newhall was killed with a cricket bat?'

Charles looked confused, then alarmed. 'I heard it somewhere. Everyone knows it. It's all around the school.' He looked to the faces of the assembled parents who shook their heads. Shrugged. No one was admitting that they knew anything. 'Rose. You knew about the cricket bat, right?'

'Nope. Last I'd heard he was strangled with a school tie.'

Charles looked between Pippa and Katy. 'Oh, come on now. You can't be serious. Can't you see what's happening here? They've set me up. They're in it together.'

Rose cleared her throat and said, 'As someone whose husband is currently on holiday with his other woman – not ill, as I told everyone – I can tell you that no one could convince a wife and a mistress to work together, Charles. You've pissed off two women who have no reason to support each other. You're fucked.'

'Pippa,' Charles said. 'Say something. Back me up here.'

'I loved you, Charles. I loved you so much. And, more than anything else, you were my best friend. No one knows me better than you do. We used to laugh about things that other people wouldn't find funny. Jokes, meant just for us. We're the only two people in the world who know how it feels to love our boys, to hear their first words and how they look when they're asleep. Our . . .'

Pippa's voice cracked but she felt Asha squeeze her hand and she continued. 'Our family is the most precious thing in the world to me and I wouldn't have changed it for the world. I always, *always,* thought that – no matter what happened – at least we'd have each other. But you changed all that. So, no Charles, I can't say something to back you up. And it's not because I'm angry about the affair, or because I'm trying to prove you killed Jerry. It's because I have nothing to fight for anymore. But remember this, darling, you gave up on me long before I gave up on you.'

Charles ran at Pippa then, arms flailing. Mullins reached for him, but his fingers did nothing more than glance his jacket. Hinch was a moment too slow and, by the time he'd turned to chase Charles down, Charles was only a few yards from Pippa. The lights were flickering and with every pulse Charles was closer.

Asha dropped Pippa's hand and pushed her out of the way. She stepped towards Charles, her fist clenched, elbow bent. Charles's momentum did the rest.

Chapter 44

The Truth

'Here,' Asha said to Cass. 'Put your hat on.'

'I'm fine.'

'Did I ask if you were fine? Hat. Now.'

The summer holidays were almost at an end, but the sunshine was still hard and strong. They'd all headed to the beach: Cass and Asha, Ollie and Rose, Rupert and Becky, even Benny and Pippa. Asha had brought the body-boards, chairs and barbecue in the back of the van. The others brought food and drink. Though they'd arrived before the beach filled up, they were still there as it began to empty. Their skin was tight with sunshine and salt, their hair brittle from the seawater. Hearts as full as their cool box was empty.

The boys ran back into the sea, to catch the faintest of waves, cheering with delight. With the arrest of his father, Benny had gone from being king of the school, to being ridiculed and ostracised, but Cass stood by him. In his words, 'With a dad like that, no wonder Benny was being a dick.'

At first Pippa had retreated into herself. Always feeling under the weather, busy or double-booked whenever she was invited out, or if Asha dropped by. Her husband's arrest and the realisation that Charles was a killer, would have been enough to make anyone crawl under a stone. By anyone's standards, it was a lot for Pippa to wrap her head around.

A new headteacher had been appointed to Aberfal High. She'd held meetings over the holidays and vowed to make Aberfal the school it had always pretended to be. There was a buzz about the place again which made them all proud to be part of the Aberfal family, despite what had happened there. They'd lost fewer students than they'd expected due to the loyalty of the current pupils and their families and they were all determined to make Aberfal shine again. Asha knew, better than most, how satisfying it was to fly in the face of other people's expectations.

Unsurprisingly, Charles had been charged with Jerry Newhall's murder. The prescriptions, the affair, the secret flat, everything was out in the open now. The post-mortem had surprised them all. The blow to the side of the head with a cricket bat hadn't killed Jerry, only knocked him unconscious, but with the cocktail of drugs in Jerry's system, it had been fatal. Codeine for the pain, Pregabalin to take the edge off. It had caused respiratory suppression and Jerry had simply stopped breathing.

Without the drugs in his system, Jerry could have survived the blow. Charles had admitted to prescribing Jerry those tablets but he was still denying that he'd hit him. He blamed Katy Lane. The woman he thought he'd loved. The woman with a grudge.

Katy Lane was no longer teaching at Aberfal. She wasn't going far: there was the small matter of a court case and her part in disposing of evidence and perverting the course of justice. Katy had been incredibly helpful once she started talking. Charles made a terrible mistake announcing to those people assembled at the ball that the woman he was having an affair with could have been anyone. And Katy had a lot to say.

Charles was accusing her of setting him up. A woman scorned. His entire defence appeared to depend on proving it was Katy who hit Jerry with that bat, not him. But seeing as she had an alibi – having been teaching English at the time of Jerry's death – Charles's legal team would have a hard time shifting the focus away from their client.

So many people had something to hide. For a start, Katy Lane had not been the first person to find Jerry Newhall's body. That honour went to his PA, Mandy. She'd left her desk to meet with Hinch, allowing the killer to get in and out unnoticed. Katy Lane had told her that if she left her desk again and something went wrong, she would lose her job. And so when Mandy *did* leave her desk and everything *had* gone wrong, she panicked.

Which explained the open window.

Upon finding the headmaster's body, Mandy opened the window to make it look like the killer had come in and out that way and not past her vacant desk. She couldn't apologise enough for putting her own welfare over that of Jerry, but she reasoned that he was already dead and there was nothing she could have done to help him anyway.

When the police searched Charles's flat, they found his shirt on top of the wardrobe. And it had traces of Jerry Newhall's blood on it. He had denied he'd been wearing that shirt that day and said while, yes, he had changed his shirt during the match, it was because Pippa had spilled her drink on him. That, at least, was true and there was evidence of blackcurrant cordial on it too.

Pippa explained that she was about to tell the police her suspicions when she was hit by a car and then she'd doubted her own recollection of events. The feeling that she was losing her mind had diminished once she got treatment for her hormone imbalance. She'd been prescribed HRT and testosterone by a *darling* private doctor and she felt like a new woman. It had enabled her to start working again. And instead of having less time for her children, she found she had more because, now, each moment mattered.

Asha had made some changes too. She got in touch with Cass's dad, Mark, who came down to Cornwall and spent two days getting to know Cass and trying to convince Asha he was a changed man. He gave her enough money to pay for a year's school fees. Said he owed it for all the years he wasn't there for Cass. He didn't say where he'd got the money from and hadn't contacted his son since.

Cass had hoped he and Mark would have had a natural bond but, with so little in common, it had been exhausting to try and connect. Just yesterday, Cass had said to Asha, 'You know, Otis is nice. I mean, I have a better relationship with him than some guy who's meant to be my dad, you know?'

Asha had resisted the urge to say, 'I told you so.'

'I can talk to him about stuff. And he makes me laugh and he makes me feel good about myself, which is really all

I wanted a dad for. So, if you wanted to, I don't know, like go on a date with him or something . . .'

'Cass . . .'

'Don't you want me to have a father figure to look up to?'

'Let's agree to keep out of each other's love life, huh?'

'Well, I would, but I kind of already invited him to go for pizza on Friday.'

Flustered, the first thing Asha thought of to say was, 'But your grandmother and Ed are coming to stay this weekend.'

'Yep. And they've already agreed to babysit. No need to thank me.'

Asha had thought about cancelling the . . . whatever it was. She didn't want to call it a *date*. It was just pizza and a beer with a friend. And people had to eat, didn't they? Seeing as she had no intention of leaving Cornwall, or Aberfal High, any time soon, she needed all the friends she could get.

Chapter 45

The Whole Truth
The day of the cricket match

Pippa pushed open Jerry's office door tentatively, ready to back away if he was busy, but he was alone, standing at the massive window which took up most of the far wall. He didn't immediately turn as she walked in, but as the door clicked closed behind her, he glanced over his shoulder. There was the slightest of pauses between his annoyance at being disturbed and his face moving to a smile.

'Pippa, what a nice surprise.'

He stepped away from the window and slid in behind his desk, motioning towards the chair in front of him.

'How can I help?' he asked.

Pippa didn't sit. The sounds from the cricket match rang through the closed windows. Though the walls were thick, the windows were not.

'It's about the school fees, Jerry. I know you said I should stay out of it, but—'

'Does Charles know you're here?'

'No.' She shook her head and glanced towards the window. Charles would be angry if he knew she was talking to Jerry behind his back. 'Look, Jerry darling, I need to know the full story. Every sordid little thing. Let's put our cards on the table, shall we?' Pippa walked to the phone, lifted his handset, listened to the dialling tone and placed it back in its cradle. 'You know, I always thought this was for decorative purposes only,' she said. 'Isn't it quaint?'

'What do you want from me?'

'Okay,' she said. 'Here's the thing. I know you're threatening to report Charles to the GMC. And I know all about the prescriptions. That's a nasty little habit you've got there.'

'I don't know what you're talking about, Pippa.'

'Oh, come now, Jerry. Let's not lie to each other. What I haven't yet worked out is why Charles can't pay the school fees. Is he paying money to keep you quiet? Or is there something else that you have over him? Where has all our money gone, Jerry?'

Jerry licked his lips and rubbed his hands together, like he was appraising a fine meal. 'You're barking up the wrong tree there,' he said. 'I haven't taken a penny off him. Whatever he's done with his money it's nothing to do with me. Or rather, it wasn't until he started asking me for more and more time to pay the fees. I don't see why the school should suffer because he made some . . . ah, questionable choices.'

'You threatened to report him. You refused to give us extra time to pay the school fees—'

'I've already given him extra time, but he wanted more.'

'You and Charles used to be so close. Goodness, you even forgave him for hitting your wife. What's he done this time that is so unforgivable?'

'That's what you want to know?'

'Yes, that's what I want to know.'

Pippa walked around the back of Jerry's desk and he spun his chair round so that he could keep his eyes on her. 'Where has Charles been hiding you?' he laughed. 'I've underestimated you.'

He reached out and plucked at the hem of her denim skirt. Pippa stepped backwards and knocked over a cricket bat that had been propped against the wall. 'I'd appreciate it if you didn't paw at me,' she said.

'You know,' said Jerry, 'perhaps we could work something out between us.' He looked her up and down, his eyes lingering where her shirt stretched across her chest causing the material to gape a little.

'Do you ever hear yourself?' she said.

'Oh, come on. Lighten up, Pip. I'm just having some fun. Remember fun?'

'What is wrong with you?' Pippa asked. 'Charles is your friend. He's a good man. A good husband.'

Jerry threw his head back and laughed. Pippa folded her arms and watched him. She couldn't think what was so funny.

'So, you don't know *everything*, then?' He was still chuckling to himself as he turned away from her, swivelling his chair back to his desk.

Confused, Pippa bent down to pick up the cricket bat she'd knocked over. It was still in her hands when Jerry said, 'I know too many of his secrets. That's one of the reasons he'll do anything to keep me quiet. That's why Charles will keep prescribing me my pills, no matter what he says. He'll crack before I do. He doesn't want you to get wind of his indiscretions when there's still the matter of the divorce settlement to work out.'

'Indiscretions?' Pippa felt her skin begin to prickle. There was no air in the room.

'Seems like I know a lot more than you do, doesn't it? Your loyalty, though commendable, is entirely misplaced. No wonder Charles has been looking elsewhere for comfort.'

And then Pippa had another one of those episodes like she'd had at the open day. She could see herself and Jerry and a cricket bat, but she was viewing the scene from above. It crossed her mind that it was just like the incident with the cake and that had been so satisfying.

As she watched herself swing the cricket bat, cheers erupted from outside, like everyone was applauding her. Though she wasn't sure she'd really done anything except throw a cake in his face, only this time it had been shaped like a cricket bat to the side of his head.

And then Pippa was back in her body, the bat was on the floor and the smile had disappeared from Jerry's face. She looked at the phone. Looked at the window. Looked at Jerry lying there with his eyes half open.

'Get up, Jerry,' she said.

He made no sound. Didn't move.

'I'm not messing around.' She crouched over him. His face was flushed. 'I said get up! This isn't funny.'

Jerry groaned. Pippa staggered upright. Thought she might be sick. She swallowed it down. Whimpered. She was going to be in so much trouble. Charles would be furious with her when he found out what she'd done.

She rushed to the window, waved, shouted and hit her hands on the glass to get someone's attention, but everyone was focusing on a dog running across the pitch. No one was looking in her direction. She backed away from the light. It was her word against Jerry's. If she denied ever being here . . . No. That was ridiculous. Someone must have seen her come in. She'd never get away with it.

She backed up to the door, yanked it open, about to tell Mandy to call an ambulance but she still wasn't at her desk. Pippa left the door open, but she heard it close behind her as she ran down the stairs. She told herself that if she saw someone, she'd raise the alarm but, if she didn't . . . And the corridors were surprisingly empty, all doors closed. She slipped out through the kitchen, through the open doors and into the sunshine. She felt faint. Too hot. Pippa took the cordial from her bag and swigged it. It was no good, she still felt an all-consuming thirst that wouldn't go away.

Her next thought was to tell Charles what had happened, but when she ran to him and tried to talk to him, he shouted at her and walked away. So, she waited. Expected the news to break at any moment that Jerry was hurt. But then she'd seen someone in Jerry Newhall's office window and panicked. She'd dashed from the school, not slowing for the speedbumps. Didn't want the children humiliated in front of the whole school. At least let the ramifications come in private.

When Katy had called to say that she'd found Jerry dead in his office, Pippa felt the strength in her legs leave her. Charles went to the school while Pippa stayed home and waited for the police. But the call never came and the

396

doorbell never rang. When Charles came home, he told her that they didn't know for sure how Jerry had died, that they still hadn't found the murder weapon. He told her that Mandy hadn't left her desk all afternoon. The suspect had most probably escaped through the window.

Pippa began to think that maybe it wasn't her. That someone had come in after her. After all, she was the woman who put orange juice in her tea, perhaps she was wrong about killing Jerry. And would anything be gained by saying otherwise?

Chapter 46

And Nothing But The Truth

In Charles's flat, his love nest, Asha had said, 'Come on, Pippa. Let's get out of here. I don't want to find any more of that skank's undies. I'm going to go and get you a glass of water and then we need to discuss what we're going to do next. Okay?'

The confirmation that Charles was having an affair wasn't the shock it should have been. Jerry had hinted at it; the lease agreement had sealed it. If anything, it was a relief to know that she'd been right. Pippa sat on the bed that Charles had been lying in with his lover. Katy Lane. Pippa had recognised her ring on the side of the bathroom sink. She managed to conceal it before Asha saw. She needed time to think about what this meant.

With Asha out of the room getting a glass of water, Pippa reached into her handbag and pulled out a supermarket carrier bag. She peered inside it and saw the neatly folded blue shirt she'd been wearing on the day of Jerry's murder. It was one of Charles's old shirts. She'd taken to wearing them more and more, hoping it made her look cool and casual rather than too fat to fit into her old clothes.

She reached up and shook out the bag onto the top of the wardrobe. She hated having to do it, especially as she and Charles used to have such a glorious life together but needs must. He shouldn't have treated her this way. It could have all been so different. Seeing Katy's ring had helped her make up her mind.

'Are you okay in there?' Asha called from the kitchen.

'No,' muttered Pippa to herself, as she smoothed down the bedsheets. She cleared her throat and called, 'Not yet. But I'm sure I will be.'

She left the room, making sure nothing looked out of place and joined Asha in the kitchen.

'Can we . . . Can we leave? I don't want to be here for a second longer than I must.'

'Sure.'

Pippa looked at the apples in the fruit bowl. Her fingers danced over the polished domes as she chose the shiniest one, the one that looked the juiciest. She tossed it from hand to hand, before taking a bite and immediately grimaced at the bitterness.

She swallowed hard and looked at the fruit, almost impressed by how it had hidden its true nature behind a perfect exterior.

'Huh,' she said. 'You really never can tell which one's the bad apple, can you?'

Pippa Bennysmum: Happy back-to-school day my darlings xx

Rose Oliversmum: Here's to a better term than the last one LOL!!

Becky Rupertsmum: Can't B any worse 😄

Clare Withoutani: Talk about tempting fate!!

Becky Rupertsmum: 💀

Asha: Saw lots of new kids at drop-off this morning.

Rose Oliversmum: Yes! Did you meet the gay dads? We should invite them to the next girls night. I bet they're a scream!

Asha: Stereotyping much??! 🤦‍♀️

Clare Withoutani: My nemesis Tash Saunders has her two starting in year seven today. I KNEW we should have asked to vet new parents.

Pippa Bennysmum: Oh, that must have been Tash that I was talking to this morning. Gorgeous curly-haired twins? xx

Clare Withoutani: Don't be fooled Pippa. Those curls are hiding their devil horns. Don't you dare make friends with her or I'll get Rose to kick you out of the WhatsApp group again 😬

Pippa Bennysmum: I must say I'm impressed by the new head. Mrs Thompson has big plans for this year xx

Sarah Teddysmum: Have you seen the new English teacher?

Rose Oliversmum: Seen him??? It was all I could do not to LICK him.

Becky Rupertsmum: Already looking 4ward 2 parents evening!! 🤭 🤭 🤭

Pam Geoffreysmum: I can't believe I have to say this but I'm sure he's been employed for his teaching ability, not his looks. Please do not objectify our boys' teachers.

Rose Oliversmum: Yay! Pam's back. I missed you Pammy. No one to keep me on the straight and narrow over the summer hols. I've gone FERAL. What's the news?

Pam Geoffreysmum: If you must know, we're looking at new schools for Geoffrey. We're on a waiting list for Truro school.

Asha: Oh no! That's a shame, Pam. I know Cass will be sad to see Geoffrey go.

Rose Oliversmum: No way! Why???

Pam Geoffreysmum: I can't talk about it other than to say I am familiar with "Mrs Thompson" and the upshot is – either she goes, or I do.

Rose Oliversmum: FFS Pam. What a way to pique my interest. Do you want us to take her down for you? Cos, if so, we're in!!

Acknowledgements

Thank you to everyone who has supported me to write this book. I'm always nervous to let anyone read early drafts of my books, so it's testament to the loveliness of Emily Koch and Kayte Genders that I felt able to ask them to cast their eyes over *One Bad Apple* before it was ready. Thank you both for being so generous with your time and feedback. Thanks also to Jake Hard for the medical advice around Jerry Newhall's death. And of course to Imogen Pelham, my agent, who gave such invaluable insight through the MANY drafts.

The whole team at Constable have been a dream to work with. Thanks, in particular, to Krystyna Green and Amanda Keats. Thank you to Liane Payne for the map in the front of the book (I've always wanted a map!). There are so many other people involved that it's impossible to list them all. I'm grateful to everyone who has played a part in getting this book into the hands of readers.

Credit must go to crime writing superstars The Ladykillers who do their best to keep me sane, amused and (sometimes) drunk. The support of CS, and all the wonderful writer friends I've met along the way, is much appreciated. A special mention to Roz Watkins who has been an excellent sounding board over many coffees on the beach. It's often said, but those who write the darkest storylines are the nicest people.

The WhatsApp sections of *One Bad Apple* were the easiest to write because I've been in several 'Mums WhatsApp' groups over the years. I must stress that they are nothing like the group in this book – though they have been equally amusing at times. Parent groups were a lifeline for me after my boys were born. I must thank the NCT mums for early days advice and cake, the Markeaton Mums who still let me gatecrash their holidays, even though I now live hundreds of miles away, and the DGS mums whose friendship I miss now we've moved schools. I hope this book shows how important these connections can be.

I have dedicated this book, as with my others, to my ever-supportive family but maybe I should have dedicated it to teachers everywhere. I know it's not an easy job, especially with pupils like me. I recently came across an old school report of mine which said, 'Joanne needs to apply herself and stop daydreaming'.

They're not wrong but I fear it's too late for me now.

Thank you James, Alex, and Danny for always being my cheerleaders and putting up with my absent-mindedness when I'm deep in creative mode. I love you more than I can put into words.

The final word of appreciation must go to readers who have picked up and enjoyed my books. I will always be grateful for your support. If you want to keep up to date with new releases, news and giveaways, please do sign up to my newsletter on my website. Though, I must warn you, I don't send them out regularly because that teacher was right. I really do need to apply myself and stop daydreaming.

www.jojakeman.com

Book Club Questions for *One Bad Apple*

1. At the beginning of *One Bad Apple*, Asha doesn't think Aberfal High is the right school for her son. Why does she change her mind? Does she make the right choice?

2. When Asha tells Pippa that she and Cass are leaving the school because they don't fit in, Pippa says, 'None of us fit in. We're all misfits, darling. Just trying to do our best to hang in there and hope that no one works out that we've been faking it all along.' How are the other parents 'faking it'?

3. Who did you initially believe was the killer? How did this change as the book progressed? Were you surprised by who dealt the final blow to Jerry Newhall? At what point did you begin to piece together what happened?

4. Is Aberfal High anything like the school you attended? What are the similarities and differences?

5. The inciting incident in *One Bad Apple* is the murder of Jerry Newhall. Were you surprised that the author didn't focus on Detective Mullins and the murder investigation? Why do you think she chose to tell the story from the point of view of the parents and teachers instead?

6. Katy Lane received threatening emails telling her to 'come clean' about what she'd done. Did she do the right thing by ignoring them for so long? Would you

have done anything differently? Was she wrong to embark on an affair?

7. How does Asha's relationship with her mother, Tessa, affect her relationship with Cass? How different will these relationships be going forward?

8. In the first chapter of *One Bad Apple* Cass bats Asha away 'as if her mothering was smothering'. Do the parents have too much involvement in their sons' lives and education? If so, in what way, and why do you think they do it?

9. Charles Yardley doesn't appear to care strongly about anyone but himself. How does this backfire on him at the summer ball? Does he deserve what happened to him?

10. How have the characters changed by the end of *One Bad Apple?* Who was your favourite?